Stitches in Time

Leba Wine

MANY NAMES PRESS
CAPITOLA, CALIFORNIA

First Edition
ISBN 978-0-9773070-2-9
Produced & Distributed by Ingram Content Group

Many Names Press
P.O. Box 1038 Capitola, CA 95010 USA
Kate Hitt, Publisher 831-427-8805
khitt@manynamespress.com
ManyNamesPress.com/books

Reiter Family Album Quilt by Katie Friedman Reiter (1873-1942) & Liebe Friedman-Gross (life dates unknown), Mckeesport, Allegheny County, Pennsylvania, c. 1891-1892, re-assembled 1976.
Cotton and wool, 101" x 101", Collection American Folk Art Museum, #2000.2.1, Photo by John Parnell, New York, N.Y.
Gift of Katherine Amelia Wine in honor of her grandmother Theresa Reiter Gross and the makers of the quilt, her great-grandmother Katie Friedman Reiter and her great-great-grandmother Liebe Gross Fried-man, and on behalf of a generation of cousins: Sydney Howard Reiter, Penelope Breyer Tarplin, Jonnie Breyer Stahl, Susan Reiter Blinn, Benjamin Joseph Gross, and Leba Gross Wine.

Library of Congress Cataloging-in-Publication Data

Wine, Leba 1932-
  Stitches in time / Leba Wine. -- 1st ed.
      p. cm.
   ISBN-13: 978-0-9773070-2-9 (pbk. : alk. paper)
  1. Wine, Leba 1932---Fiction. 2. Jews--Pennsylvania--Bohemia--Fiction. 3. Immigrants--Pennsylvania--Bohemia--Fiction. 4. Bohemia (Pa.)--Fiction. 5. Domestic fiction. I. Title.
PS3623.I625S75 2006
813'.54--dc22
                      2006029833

To my children
Deborah, Howard, Katie, and Abigail

CHAPTER ONE

THIS MEMORY IS ALMOST SIXTY YEARS OLD but, even when I am sitting in the sunny window-seat of my oceanside house in Northern California, it raises ever-lurking feelings of being controlled by others, of pain and terror and betrayal. That this kind of experience can end in beauty and knowledge is a lesson I must learn again and again. Why do we constantly polish that dark nacre and seldom force ourselves to search for the already gleaming moment it envelops?

On a visit to my grandmother, I was four years old and happily tucked between Uncle Adolph and my mother on the front seat of the car instead of my accustomed place in the back where I was usually wretched with carsickness. I wriggled in anticipation of the unexpected outing, trying to guess if we were going to Kennywood Park or to lunch at a diner—my favorite—or even for milkshakes at Isaly's, where there were seats with armrests like desks at school except they were painted in pink enamel. I noticed the glances above my head but ignored the portent of them until we pulled up at a tall building in downtown Pittsburgh.

That was when they told me I was about to get my tonsils out. I knew what tonsils were. They had certainly plagued me enough in my short life. It was the "out" that had me screaming up three flights of stairs and into the doctor's office. I clutched at doorjambs and chairs but all too soon was strapped on a table, wrapped tightly in a blanket with my hands underneath me. The black cone of ether descending on my face has reappeared over and over in my dreams. My shrieks accompanied me into a terrible maelstrom in which I spun for what seemed an eternity. The trip back to my grandmother's house in McKeesport, probably less than two hours later, is gone from my memory. But I do remember being carried into the front parlour, which had been prepared for my recuperation. Tipsy from the anesthetic, I remember the room bursting on my senses as a fantastical garden, alight with pink birds and golden elephants and great orbs of pineapples. There was an apple tree laden with scarlet globes. Peacocks and small dogs with amethyst eyes glimmered in the sunlight. Jeweled hands beckoned me to the huge bed which had been carried down the steps and placed by the window. I sank, stunned by pain and magic, into its depth and dreamed away the night.

The next morning, the pain was still there, but so was the magic. The room was full of refracting color, moving and shifting in the sunlight. I slowly gathered the rainbow shards by squinting through my eyelashes and awoke like a princess under the glorious quilt my grandmother had made a half-century earlier. My grandmother's quilt — ah, what a garden of earthly delights. There, of course, were the apple tree and the peacocks, hands with rings on the fingers, dogs and hippos and elephants, pineapples and snakes, all trapuntoed and appliquéd in pulsating color onto an expanse of white. And in its center, unnoticed by me the night before — and what dreams it might have evoked —was a black chevalier on a black horse. Such darkness in the midst of all that opulence. I shivered and tried to look away, but he was too fascinating to ignore.

He was proud and erect, his hands lightly on the pommel. The horse was elegant, mane and tail in repose but ready to fly in the wind at a slight movement or whisper from the rider. Unlike the rest of the images, the horseman was conceived of heavy black wool embroidered in gold thread. Who was he? Why did he make me so sad? I spent hours communing with this fierce dark figure, realizing his mystery but too young to form the proper questions.

I extended my convalescence as long as possible, but it was still not long enough to divine every figure on the quilt. I knew it would soon have to be folded into its protective sheet and returned to whatever grotto it had been taken from to give me pleasure. Parents, grandparents, aunts, and uncles anxiously spooned ice cream into my mouth, and I soon could not avoid being set on my feet and ordered to stop complaining. The bed was hoisted back upstairs, the parlour became a parlour once again, the magic quilt receded into my unconscious, not to be resurrected until another terrible betrayal brought it back into my life.

My family lived ninety miles away from McKeesport, but we visited my grandmother often. She was always busy in the kitchen, where she loved — and probably hated, too — to tell stories of her life. I was her youngest granddaughter, but none of my cousins know any of the stories and none of them remembers ever having seen the quilt.

Now I am the age that she was when I was a child, and I am remembering my grandmother's life and unraveling the mysteries of the magic quilt.

My grandparents lived in a huge — or so I thought, then — brick house of no particular architectural style, on a corner in the green and leafy part of McKeesport, Pennsylvania, a mill town outside of Pittsburgh. My mother was the youngest of their seven children. I loved visiting them and loved the house, so much bigger and less familiar than the plain square double house my family lived in.

One entered a large hall with a heavy stairway at the rear. To the left was the front parlour. On the mantle was a clock that my grandfather wound ceremonially once a week. Only he and I knew where the key was hidden. I recently learned that each of my cousins were part of the same secret. It must have been quite a sturdy clock to have taken so many windings.

Between the parlour and the dining room behind it, were heavy wooden sliding doors that parted in the middle and could be pushed into the walls. They had a special mechanism in each door that could be pressed to lock them open or closed. Last year I was at a party in a Victorian house in San Francisco, where the caterers were unable to close the doors between living room and dining room. I walked to the archway and, retrieving an ancient memory, touched the familiar buttons and slid the doors shut.

The staircase to the second floor, rising out of the front hall, turned in the middle, and in that bend was a stained glass window depicting Sir Galahad holding the Holy Grail. It fascinated me, another mystery, because nobody would tell my little Jewish self why that man was dressed so funny or why he was gazing so raptly at a cup.

Under that window was a seat, the perfect place to play paper dolls, and without the cushions, jacks. The bedrooms were large, with fireplaces and armchairs, and the beds were all so high they had wooden steps up to them. When I visited, I got to have breakfast with my grandfather in his bed, where we sat like royalty drinking creamy coffee out of big cups. His was a special cup with a little curved shelf inside to keep his moustache dry.

All the beds were covered with quilts, sewn by the same meticulous hands that had sewn the magic one, each tiny stitch the same as the thousands of other tiny stitches—but these were calmer, repeated appliqués of flower pots and plants that matched the colors of the bedroom walls. These were happy quilts, reminiscent of that other, but there were no dark figures at the center, no shadows. There were many of these quilts, not only in my grandmother's house but also in the bedrooms of her two married daughters, who heedlessly washed them with the sheets and hung them out to dry—and fade— in the sunlight.

The back-stairs was my favorite part of the house. Behind the parlour and the dark, gothic dining room were a bright kitchen and sunroom, the pantry, and the narrow, enclosed steps leading either to the basement or upstairs, and then up again to the attic. Though she had a *shiksa*—a maid—my grandmother did all the baking herself, and I loved to listen to her talk while she kneaded dough and folded eggs and plumped raisins. *Shiksa* actually means a non-Jewish woman, but in the Yiddish vernacular it meant any Gentile who cleaned houses.

My grandmother was small and beautiful, her brown eyes always looking as though they were about to fill with tears. She dressed only in black, high-necked dresses that fell to her ankles. In the kitchen, she was brightened by the colorful aprons she wore, aprons brought in by the *shiksas*. Her curly hair, streaked with gray, was always in a bun, softened by the locks that escaped when she bent over the wooden table where she worked. Surrounded by the good smells and concentrated on her cooking, she told me the stories of her life. I could tell that she was reliving each moment in her mind, and I was, too, listening with my chin in my hand and my legs swinging back and forth over the polished slate floor. We were transported by her stories into a faraway place that smelled like vanilla. The long-ago past became tangible to me and she, as a little girl named Katie, was as real as my friends at home.

But Katie is not the beginning of this story. Katie's mother, my great-grandmother, was named Liebe, and that is my name. I know so much about these women—Katie and her mother Liebe—and I am aware of them in my life, not only through the magic quilt, which is now mine, but also in my attitudes and emotions, my posture and my stride, in the very mystery of my consciousness.

CHAPTER TWO
1870

HOW DO I PORTRAY REAL LIVES THAT WERE LIVED IN TINY STITCHES, when all I know are the bold flashes of color that have been told to me? It is an impossible task—history is fiction, after all, and the past an endless cloth unreeling. I can merely name the names, identify the patterns, and illuminate the designs that my grandmother pointed out to me.

I see Katie's mother, Liebe, sitting quietly outside a low stone house, her hands automatically shelling peas but her thoughts flying across the autumn-colored countryside to her new love. She was just fourteen years old, but in the Bohemia of the 1860's she was a woman, and knew much of life and death.

The object of her reverie was the beloved youngest son, Adolph, from the next farm who had, for the first time, accompanied his many brothers to bring in the harvest for her father. This yearly event usually held no interest for Liebe, meaning merely that the kitchen work was even harder as she and her mother served two great meals a day. The men of the farms traveled as a group through the country-side, lending their arms and shoulders to their neighbors in exchange for the same favor on their own land. Growing up, she was little aware of what went on in the fields and, at harvest time, experienced that inexorable Earth-turning as a week of endless cooking that she helped plan, serve, and clean up after, only to have to start again the next morning.

The dirt-floored kitchen was crowded. It was the main room in the house except for the loft above and a larder, through a narrow door in the back. Baskets of corn and flour and salt were usually stored in the larder, but today they lined the walls of the kitchen. Iron pots were all in use, steaming on the table and benches. Navigation was hazardous for Liebe and her mother. The kitchen was smoky, the huge fireplace making it a flame-lit cave. They worked silently in the gloom, their figures illuminated now and then as they passed through the shafts of light from windows set in the thick walls.

"Liebchen, what would I do without you?" her mother murmured as their heavy skirts brushed in passing.

When she felt she could endure the heat no longer, Liebe filled her arms with pitchers of beer and carried them out of the house to the long table under the trees where the harvesters would soon gather to eat. The late summer air cooled her face, the beauty of the Bohemian countryside, sloping golden to the horizon, refreshed her soul. She went to the table already laden with crockery, when she felt her petticoats grasped from behind and lifted from the ground. She whirled, dropping pitchers and plates as her arm met the shoulder of the boy behind her. He shook his wet head and opened his water-starred eyes as he realized what he had done.

"Oh, no!" he stammered. "I was bending down for the towel by the wash-basin." He pointed to the basin on a low bench. "I must have gotten your skirt instead. I'm so sorry—so sorry. Please forgive me. I didn't mean. . . . "

He stopped in confusion, remembering his dripping hair, his dusty shirt, and the broken dishes around his feet. Liebe ventured a giggle, he made a manly sound deep in his chest and then guffawed. And they laughed together, her peals twirling her through the flower garden, his bringing him at last to the wash bench where it had all started. He sat down, holding his side, gazing into her flushed face.

Liebe's mother, brought to the kitchen door by the unexpected sounds, noted the look. It made her catch her breath. From the shadow of her kitchen, she peered at her little girl and saw the woman she had become, unnoticed and unremarked. Why, Liebe was the same age she had been when she married. She shook her head, sighed for her broken dishes, and turned back to her work. This Adolph, this boy now picking glass and crockery from her kitchen garden, was from the next farm, the most successful farm in the district, although that didn't mean much the way things were. Still, maybe it was time to think of such things. Tonight, she resolved, as she ladled the thick soup into bowls. Tonight she would speak to her husband.

The men gathered quickly for their lunch, grateful for the respite from their labors and quiet in their enjoyment of the peace under the trees. This garden, like their own beyond their kitchen doors, had yielded the beets and onions and cabbages that fed them so well. The foamy beer and young wine were made in this very valley.

Bohemia was an emerald set in the highlands between the Danube to the south and the mountains of the German Republic to the north. Its peacefulness was deceptive. It had been swept for centuries by the Turks, the Poles, the various Germanic tribes, all dragging their war wagons across its fertile fields on their way to greater spoils beyond its border. Napoleon had led his armies west, Russians had brought hordes from the east, the Ottomans had plundered here on their way north. Fields had been ravaged, families separated as they sought refuge, young men dragged off to serve armies whose goals and languages were unknown. The French were the last to cross its vastness, but that was in 1848, and since then wars and rumors of wars had disturbed the farmers very little.

Instead, it was the small details that enlivened their existence, and the men gathered at the harvest table that morning noted with interest the glances and smiles exchanged by Liebe and Adolph. There was a certain shyness among these people, isolated on their farms as they were most of the year, but they were not bashful. Liebe was frankly admiring the handsome young man, totally absorbed by his blue eyes. He, in turn, was enchanted by the deftness and grace with which she moved about the table, filling the beer mugs, keeping her eyes lowered except when she came to him.

By the end of the week, an understanding had been reached between Liebe's father and Adolph's. These families had lived in close cooperation for generations, farming and raising small herds of goats. They possessed very little. The valley was populated almost entirely by Jews, and Jews were not permitted to own land. Instead, they farmed for the aristocracy, who lived in Vienna or Prague. They supported life styles and philosophies neither imagined nor wondered about. A betrothal here was accompanied not by dowry but by fervent hopes for good harvests, many children, and long life.

L'chaim echoed around the table as the men ate their last meal before moving on to the next farm. Liebe and Adolph parted awkwardly, the first hesitation of their week together. Did he actually dig his booted toe into the dirt of the kitchen yard? Probably, for he was only a country boy besotted by love.

"It will be more than two months before we see each other again," he said, standing straight and tall under the gaze of the other men slowly moving past, their tools on their shoulders. Liebe could hardly bear the thought. The days, which had before been crowded with the busy routine of country life, would now be empty because he would not be there. Her eyes filled with tears, but she managed a smile as she offered her cheek for his kiss.

"And it will be a year before we marry," she whispered to the face close to hers, "but after that we will always be together." She had a moment of panic. "Don't forget me."

He touched her hand and walked down the dusty road after the other men. She watched him until he disappeared into the haze at the top of the hill.

Now, barely a month later, she turned her head again to the hill, and her fingers ceased their work among the peapods. A small figure was visible at the crest, quickly growing larger in its haste.

She rose in alarm, for casual visitors were unheard of among the Bohemian farms. It could not be the Inspector, who came unannounced but always on horseback, nor the tax collector. He arrived hard on the heels of the harvest workers, and that had been almost three weeks ago. She was poised to run for her father when she recognized Adolph's blond hair and, with a shout, swung open the gate and ran to meet him. He, too, began to run, and they met in a swirl of butterflies and dust.

Her joy died in her throat when she looked at his face.

"What's the matter? What happened?" she demanded, as she clutched his arm.

Adolph was breathing hard. "Come," he gasped. "I must speak to your father." He took her hand, and they hurried along the road.

Liebe's father, called from the field, sat them down with a pitcher of beer and calmed Adolph with talk of goats and lambs until the boy caught his breath.

"Now! You must tell us why you have come all this way. What is the matter?" Liebe was unable to contain her dread any longer. Adolph gave her a long look, then turned his gaze to her father and mother.

"I left home before the sun was up this morning," he said, "because I want you to know what has happened. While we were harvesting, the soldiers came to our farm. The Hapsburgs are at war again and need more men to fight. They knew from the census that we are five brothers at our farm, and they told my mother that my oldest brother, Jacob, must report to the army in Prague by the end of this week."

He looked around the table. Liebe's father's face was dark with hatred of the Hapsburgs and their endless battles. He had seen some of these battles with a musket in his hand. Her mother was rigid with the fright of sending sons off to war. But Liebe was suffused with relief. She hardly knew Jacob, after all.

"But my father has a plan," Adolph continued with an uncertain smile. "He and I are going to Prague, just the two of us. He will tell the authorities that I am Jacob, and that his household is proud to have a son in the service of the Emperor, and that he is proud to send me to war even though I am only sixteen. He says this is a civilized government even though it's always at war, and they will never take a sixteen year old boy."

There was silence in the kitchen. The autumn sun slanted through the deep windows, stirring a stray bee to buzzing. All eyes were bent to the dark scarred table as they contemplated the bold plan. A log snapped in the fireplace, and Adolph looked up with a grin.

"And so I shall be back here in less than a week. Father is following me, but I just had to hurry to tell you the news. We will walk on together to Prague and see the authorities. That will take another three days, and a day in the city. Then we will be back here on our way home to tell you how we have fooled the Hapsburgs!"

Liebe's father looked sharply at Adolph. "Is it that you are out of favor with your father?"

"Oh, no!" Adolph was confused by the question. Then he smiled, understanding. "Father knows the Hapsburgs want only men. They would never take me instead of Jacob. This is how he is going to save us both."

"Fool the Hapsburgs! It is your father that is the fool! Do you think the Hapsburgs care whether a soldier has fuzz on his cheeks?" A glance from his wife and a shake of her head silenced him. *Lochinkopf,* a hole in the head, he muttered, as he waved the two children away from the table.

Liebe shared her father's doubt, but she could never say the words that were loud in her head. It would show disrespect for Adolph's father that she had no faith in his plan. And Adolph seemed so sure that it would work. How could she disagree with him, make him disloyal to his father? She pushed the doubts away, rose, and pulled her shawl around her shoulders. Adolph rose, too, and they walked out into the orchard. The afternoon was golden around them, the trees burnished by autumn, the ground pungent with fallen leaves. Their kisses were sweet, and it took several shouts from the road before they were aware of Adolph's father calling them.

"We must keep going!" he cried. "Only a few hours of daylight left, and we've got a long way to travel."

Adolph shouldered the pack he had left at the gate. Liebe clung to his hand, imploring him with her eyes not to go. Adolph hesitated, then hurried to his father.

"We'll be back in about a week!" Adolph shouted from the road.

"Don't forget me," Liebe whispered.

She followed them in her mind as they threaded their way along the track, but soon they passed beyond the boundary of her small travels away from home. The golds and reds faded in the twilight, the brown fields turned ashy, the sky purpled, and soon her imagination had frozen the two tiny figures in a dark and lonely landscape.

The pea basket over her arm, Liebe walked slowly back to the cottage, confused, sad and exhilarated at the same time. She had always imagined she would marry some day but had not thought much about how such a state would be brought about. Now her wild longing for this real person who would become her husband surprised her. She had never considered her parents as anything but two people who happened to live under the same roof, but maybe they had had these kinds of feelings, too. Maybe they still felt them. She began to think about her parents in a different way and wonder what really occurred between them. Did they kiss and hold each other? She had never seen them do that. She decided to ask a few questions.

Liebe also began to plan the week that lay ahead so that it would not seem an eternity before she saw Adolph again. The first three days she would work diligently and try to keep her mind on her tasks. The middle day, the day they would fool the Hapsburgs, she would ask her father to tell her about Prague. And the last three days, she would spend as much time as possible with her mother, asking the almost formless questions that had begun to trouble her.

The schedule went well. Her industry so engrossed her that thoughts of Adolph's journey merely nibbled at the edges of her consciousness. The fourth day she trailed after her father while he made repairs to the hoes and plows he would need in the spring. They were both bundled in wool sweaters and scarves against the numbing November cold. Liebe's breath hung on the frosty air as she questioned him about Prague. But his answers were short and incomprehensible to her provincial imagination. She could not visualize three story buildings of carved stone, nor wide boulevards, nor fancy carriages drawn by horses with feathers in their manes. Her father's descriptions, delivered with ill-concealed hatred from his memory as a returning soldier, arrived at her ears in the guise of fairy tales.

Preparing for bed that night, Liebe congratulated herself on her management of the past four days. Her wait for Adolph was more than half over. She snuggled under the huge feather comforter and drew herself into a ball against the cold. Maybe the next three days would be only two if he wanted to see her as much as she wanted to see him, she thought, but she thrust the idea away guiltily. No, she decided, she was prepared for three more days and she would conquer them. She slept.

She spent the fifth day making *dachanas*, feather quilts, with her mother. Feathers plucked from the geese and ducks eaten throughout the year were stored in bags in the winter cellar. When there were enough bags, they would be brought to the glowing kitchen. Liebe separated the downy breast feathers from the others, and her mother sewed into huge squares the material bought earlier from an itinerant peddler. Careful as she was, Liebe could not prevent the snowy feathers from floating in the rosy air. She and her mother giggled as the tiny plumes soared about them, settling in their hair and brushing their noses. Liebe loved the soft *dachanas*, loved sleeping wrapped in something her mother had made. It meant "home" to her.

"Mother," Liebe said shyly. "What is it like to be married?"

"Well, Liebchen." Her mother considered carefully. "The most important thing is to be frugal. There isn't the tiniest scrap of anything that can't be used for something else." She motioned with her chin to the pot steaming on the wood stove, awaiting her husband's arrival for the noon meal. "There isn't anything in there your father hasn't seen on the table the past three days, but he'll never know it."

"But, Mother, what else do married people do besides cook and clean and work the fields and feed the animals? There must be something that makes people want to get married. Otherwise why would they do it?"

Liebe saw a familiar stubborn look fleetingly cross her mother's face. If she wanted a conversation about love that afternoon, she knew then that she wasn't going to get it.

"Ah, yes. There are many other reasons to get married. Children, for instance. Where would I be if I didn't have you?" She reached over to pat Liebe's hand, then got up quickly as her daughter opened her mouth for another question. "Where is your father? He should be here by now. Liebchen, put the plates on the table."

So another day passed, and it was the Sabbath. The kitchen had been unburdened of its feathery drifts and the new *dachanas* stored with the others under the eaves. There was a bustle about the farm to be ready for the early twilight. The two brass *shabbus* candlesticks were polished to a high luster by Liebe. She made a last trip to the chicken coop to be sure the noisy hens were bedded safely for the night, then she allowed herself a forbidden glance at the darkening hills to the south. A figure was just beginning to descend the slope. She looked quickly away and then allowed her eyes to focus slowly again in the gathering dusk. Her prayers were not usually answered so quickly.

There was someone coming up the road. Shouting over her shoulder to her parents, she gathered her skirts in her fists and ran through the gate. Surprised that the traveler was not Adolph but his father, she gave him an impulsive hug and danced from his arms to peer farther up the hill. But there was no one else. The road was empty to the horizon. Her mouth formed a question as she turned back to the old man, but she was too stunned to utter a word. He was exhausted and leaned on her arm. Together they walked to the cottage. The clouds behind them were spangled by the setting sun. The dome of the sky glistened with winter constellations. Mars gleamed redly on the horizon.

CHAPTER THREE
1870

THE SHABBUS CANDLES WERE FORGOTTEN THAT NIGHT. The family sat at the table listening to the old man, exhausted and highly agitated, telling his story over and over. Each telling was slightly different, a new angle explored, a word varied, but each ending was the same — Adolph, now known as Jacob by the Hapsburgs, was led away by the soldiers, through a carved door at the end of an ornate room, his face turned over his shoulder, amazed, beseeching. Here the father smacked his head with his fist. "*Oy Gott.*"

Finally, the four of them dragged their fatigue to bed. The old man stretched out by the fire. All night they heard the slap of his hand against his forehead. He left early in the morning, bent against the wind and his misery.

The routine of the small cottage swallowed Liebe. There were animals to be fed, meals to be cooked, wood to be chopped, clothes to be mended. She fought silently with her feelings, mostly unrecognizable scalding gusts across her very soul. She was leaden now, where only yesterday she had been buoyant and gay. She drew Adolph's laughing face into her mind's eye, then watched in horror as it darkened and twisted in fear. She quickly closed an imaginary door on the vision and summoned it no more.

She longed to talk to her mother but again could not find the words. *Mother, may I cry? I want to scream and beat my fists against something, anything. But you smile at me with questions in your eyes that I can't understand. What does it mean to be in the army? You know, because Father was in the army. Do we not speak of it because it is unspeakable? Do you know that Adolph will not return? Hold me, hold me, so that I may quiet my fears.* But no one held her, and she turned a stoic little face to her world.

Soon it was spring, and Liebe watched the soggy road. The first travelers were the peddlers. These peddlers came year after year, the same ones, bringing manufactured goods and news to the scattered farms. They had tidings of battles being fought farther and farther away.

"And this war has a name," one of them said with a chuckle. "They name their wars like they name their babies. This one is the Franco-Prussian War." Then his face darkened. "But the Prussians are in this one. They are ruthless. Ruthless and cruel." He shook his head as he said this, unwrapping his huge bundle on the stones by the kitchen door. They were mostly cheerless men, these peddlers, hardened by the lonely and difficult lives they led, exposed to the elements, sleeping in haystacks, often attacked by bandits. They were the main link between the isolated peasants and the world beyond their horizons, for each had a scrap of news to pass on.

Adolph's father came often to see Liebe's family that first year, dragging his guilt across the hills to worry it again and again at their hearthstone. The first time he arrived, Liebe flew to him, seeking his recognition of their mutual grief, but he thrust her from him angrily. Perhaps his was so heavy he could not bear to share hers. She, rebuffed, crept to the fireside to hug her knees. She watched him smack his head, pace up and down. His visits stopped after the second winter.

"Maybe the old man died," said Liebe's mother, her look seeking denial.

"Maybe," said her father, and the old man was not spoken of again.

The weeks and months and dim hours slipped and shuffled into seasons and years. Five times the harvesters came, but Adolph's family was no longer among them. Liebe looked solemnly at the young men, but she knew her love for Adolph was meant for her whole life and she would keep it so. They, in turn, sensed something unyielding in her and treated her as a friend and neighbor, nothing more.

She matured into womanhood, losing her youth along with the joy of it. The routine of the farm soothed her spirit and gave her some comfort. She felt she could endure forever in the kind of peace the farm offered, and she hoped that nothing would ever occur to raise her expectations and passions again.

Liebe realized, watching her parents, that her childish vision of being married to Adolph was like playing a game. As she participated more and more in the life of adults, she became aware of the aching labor and worry that her parents endured. They were at the mercy of nature, and had to be concerned not only for themselves but also for the absent owners in Prague. Horsemen came regularly for the taxes and cared nothing for the storms and droughts that occupied the minds of the peasants.

The summer of 1875 was a glorious one for central Europe. The spring rains and the summer sun produced the best crops in years. Fat goats and white geese punctuated the green fields behind the cottage. Every peddler who stopped at their gate brought news of the end of the war and the return of the soldiers. Liebe, so long a stranger to hope, allowed herself to look again at the sun-splashed lane. Her parents, who silently cherished the thought that Adolph's fate could somehow be learned in the capital, began to talk of a trip to Prague. Liebe, at the age of twenty, deserved to see the beauty and elegance of that great city. No one mentioned that they all deserved to know, if it was possible to find out, what had happened to Adolph.

Victoria was on the throne of England, Tsar Nicholas ruled Russia, Ulysses Grant was President of the United States. Railroads were just beginning to knit together the great cities of the world. A trip of a hundred miles was no light undertaking for a poor peasant in Bohemia. First, there was the week of harvesting. Two members of the harvesting team were persuaded to return to care for the farm while they were gone. As Liebe and her mother prepared food for their journey, her father went to make arrangements to hire a horse and wagon.

The trip to Prague took on a festive air for the family. It was Liebe's very first journey from home, and she was roused from her usual feelings of unreality by her imaginings of the wonders she would see. Her mother had not been far from home since her marriage, and she, too, anticipated with pleasure the change in routine. Her father, even with his dark memories of the city's military aspect, was determined that the time spent on this venture would make worthwhile the trouble of preparing for it.

They traveled in a hired wagon pulled by an old and gentle horse. Liebe's parents sat on the seat, Liebe in the well among many bundles. In addition to the food they carried to eat and to offer as gifts, there were three *dachanas* to keep them warm. Sleeping under the wagon was what they prepared for, curling up by a friendly hearth in the home of a rabbi was their hope.

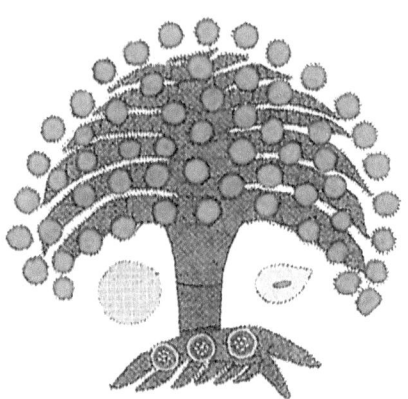

CHAPTER FOUR
1875

LIEBE HAD NO KNOWLEDGE OF PAVED AVENUES, tall buildings, opulent stores, huge mansions, symphony halls. Her father, earlier determined to pay no homage to the Hapsburgs and their excesses, felt his heart soften at the sight of Liebe's wide eyes. He carefully counted the meager cash in his pocket and then led them to a coffee house, where he plied his dazed wife and daughter with coffee *mit schlag,* amused by the twin moustaches that appeared on their lips. Emboldened by this success, and perhaps by the unaccustomed infusion of caffeine, he took his little family to the heart of Prague to watch the aristocracy arrive at the opera house. They stood at the curb, incredulous, gasping at the gilded carriages, the liveried attendants, the tiaras and furs, satins and velvets, snowy shirtfronts and gleaming top hats.

Holding tightly to her mother's hand, Liebe whispered, "I didn't know such things existed." Her mother nodded, bereft of speech.

But such was merely preamble to the real significance of this journey. On the last day but one in Prague, Liebe's father announced that they would go to Government Square and look through the lists of war dead. This had been his plan all along, though he had kept to himself the grim purpose of the trip. He had had enough of Liebe's aimlessness and his wife's secret tears. He wanted to settle at last Adolph's existence in this world and his daughter's chance for marriage. He led his wife and daughter to the marble vastness of the government building and to the room with The Lists. He had been here before, looking in vain for the name of a brother who had never returned from France in 1848. Liebe and her mother were speechless. Never had they seen such an enormous space, and every inch of wall from their ankles to a foot above their heads was covered with paper, each sheet black with written names.

"I didn't know that so many people lived in the world!" Liebe marveled.

And yet, that inconceivable number was young, male, and dead.

Hours, later, they emerged into the sunshine like divers bursting from the sea. Liebe was ecstatic. Adolph's name—Jacob's name—was not on the list! He was alive! Her mother and father were not quite so optimistic. What did the name of a dead Jew mean to the Hapsburgs? They were back where they began. They did not know.

As they passed down the marble steps, huddled together in the strangeness of their new experiences, they saw crowds gathered along the wide avenue. People were shouting excitedly and pointing to the long lines of soldiers marching toward them. There was much jostling; music shimmered in the far distance. Caught up in the commotion, Liebe and her family were drawn to the spectacle. Soon they were in the street as the soldiers marched past. Dizzied by the long lines sweeping across her vision, Liebe began searching the faces. Maybe Adolph was here. Her eyes darted quickly down the rows. So many faces. They began to blur. Her heart beat faster. A roaring began in her ears and grew louder. She felt sick and began to turn away, when she realized that the wall of sound was the approach of the Hussars, the mounted cavalry.

The thunder of a thousand hoofs was almost overwhelming as the elite troops approached Liebe's vantage point. She could see the feathers atop their fur *shakos* against the blue sky. Gold buttons and epaulets caught the sun, making her blink against the glare. The crowd behind her was silent for one single moment, then raised a mighty roar at the sight of these young men in all their aristocratic glory. Liebe's eyes swept upwards, and she saw the captain, tall and strong on his black horse. He was dressed all in black, a huge moustache giving his face a fierceness belied by the astonishing blue eyes above it. Those blue eyes turned to her and widened in disbelief. He shouted something to the horsemen behind him and swung toward her. Rooted to the ground, Liebe could only stare, dumbstruck, as the horse pranced to her place at the curb. In a moment, the handsome hussar was on the ground and she was crushed in his dark embrace. He picked her up and swung her around, then held her away and looked into her face.

"Liebe! It's me! It's Adolph!" he shouted joyfully. And then Liebe fainted.

CHAPTER FIVE

A SOLDIER RETURNS from the war. A cliche in literature, but the central event in the lives of those who wait for him and pray for him and think of him every moment he is away. They picture in their minds the moment of his return, the indescribable joy of the occasion. What stories he will have to tell, and they, too, of the events in their lives, the struggle to keep things going without him, this funny thing and that near tragedy. The celebration could go on for days, weeks, possibly forever, in gratitude for the safe return of the warrior.

Such unmitigated joy doesn't often happen as we, who have experienced so many wars, know all too well. It is a stranger who dismounts from a train or limps off a ship or is greeted at an airport, a stranger who has lived through much that we simply do not want to hear or even think about. Adolph must have realized this as he looked at the firelit faces in Liebe's kitchen a week after his return. He had, after all, left this very room a trusting sixteen-year old and returned to it a mature man of twenty-one. The transition, for him, had been long and painful, but none of the pain or glory did he wish to share.

"I was very lucky," he said to them, Liebe's hand cradled in his own. "The commandant of our unit was Count Barkoczy, a great soldier. For some reason, he liked me and, when there was a promotion to be made, he chose me. He carried his library with him all through the war. It was beautiful, hundreds of books packed into special mahogany cases that opened up to look like bookshelves. It occupied a whole wagon, and two soldiers did nothing but pack and unpack it as we moved." Adolph paused to let his rapt audience marvel at the odd habits of the rich. "His library was mostly books about chemistry, because he owns distilleries all over the country."

Liebe's father nodded. Water throughout Europe was undrinkable, the cause of many diseases, and was not thought of as a beverage. Young and old alike drank beer, wine, and whiskey. To own a distillery license was a privilege granted only to the aristocracy and a guarantee of great wealth.

"Count Barkoczy put me at the head of all his troops. I never knew if he was trying to get me killed or trying to educate me." Adolph's face darkened, but he shook off the memories. "Just before we were mustered out, he made me Captain of his Hussars."

"A Jew, a Jew made Captain of the Hussars," Liebe's mother breathed. Such a thing was unheard of. She wouldn't have believed it had she not seen Adolph atop a horse with her own eyes. But he shrugged off the appearance of awe in her eyes.

"Barkoczy was young and seemed very lonely. I think I was the only person within a hundred miles who could read and write. He started off by having me copy his orders and read them to the troops. Then, when we were stuck in some godforsaken place for a long time, he needed someone to pick up the books that he had strewn all over his tent and put them back in their proper places. He needed someone who could read to get them sorted out. He was lazy at everything but fighting." Adolph laughed. "Well, not everything. He seemed determined to turn me into a chemist. And by the time the war was over, he seemed pretty satisfied with what he had taught me. He thinks that I could earn a living working for a distillery."

Adolph squeezed Liebe's hand.

"I should say working for a distillery of his," said Adolph, his voice full of pride. "He offered me a job after the war. And when we parted, I reminded him of his promise. And he actually remembered what he had said. After our marriage, we leave for the Sazava River and the Count's holding there. I am his new steward."

Liebe and her family were stunned by the announcement. Her father was filled with new respect for this young man whom he had previously considered a callow youth. Liebe would be marrying well. She and her husband would not be peasants but have a chance for a better life. He leaned back in his chair, took another pull at his pipe, and crossed his hands comfortably over his stomach.

Liebe's mother fought back the tears. Her only child moving so far away, more than a week's journey. It was something she had never contemplated. She had thought maybe a small house at the far end of their farm or, at worst, something on Adolph's father's land. But how could she oppose this opportunity for an easier existence for her daughter? She couldn't. She stood quickly to put the teapot closer to the fire, dabbing at her eyes with her apron.

"*Ach*, but this is wonderful," she said, steadying her voice. "Yes, quite wonderful. We must have some *schnapps*."

Liebe looked from her mother to her father, her emotions mirroring theirs, excitement at the thought of something different and unexpected, dread at the thought of leaving the protection of her parents' love. She didn't know this new Adolph. He was confident and assured. He didn't ask her what she wanted, as his sixteen-year old self would have done. A frisson of fear shook her hands as she poured the whiskey into the small glasses. Is this what she wanted? To move far away from the home she had always known to be with a strange man in a strange place? She clenched her teeth. Things had moved too far along for her to change her mind now. Events would have to take their course.

The wedding was in the garden behind Liebe's house, the same garden where the harvesters had eaten and Liebe had surprised Adolph at his ablutions. Liebe wore the beige dress, removed from its protective sheet, that her mother had worn at her own wedding. Adolph was tall and fierce in his black uniform of the Hussars. They and their families stood under the *choopah*, the wedding canopy, rejoicing in the happy ending to the five year "joke" on the Hapsburgs. Missing from the feast were the two victims of the joke, Adolph's father, who had indeed died, and his oldest brother, Jacob, the real Jacob, who had been quickly dispatched to America when Adolph was taken by the army.

The festive party gathered around the wagon to say goodbye and shed tears as the new husband and wife gathered their belongings for their long journey. Liebe, her eyes brimming, could think only of the past and the familiar routine she was leaving behind. Her experiences had not taught her confidence. The future, from the first turn of the wagon's wheels, was a mystery.

Almost a week was spent negotiating the seemingly aimless dirt roads that wound through the lush valleys of Bohemia, linking farm to farm. The dray horses were slow, and Adolph's black stallion, tied behind the wagon and unhappy with his inferior position, was difficult to control. The first day was passed almost in silence as the two young people grew accustomed to their new status. Secret glances, tremulous smiles, questions about comfort or hunger. Adolph began to dread the night ahead, until the wagon hit a particularly deep hole and Liebe went head over heels into the back of the wagon. Her skirts in disarray, her hair loose and flowing in the breeze, she looked at her husband in amazement. How had all this happened so fast? She began to laugh, and Adolph, relieved, relaxed into his familiar guffaw. They remembered how they had met—they could see it in each other's eyes—and recognized that laughter was the bedrock of their love. Each laugh brought Adolph farther into the back of the wagon and Liebe to her knees until they were in each other's arms and the horses munching comfortably by the side of the road.

They reached the Sazava, flowing heavy and brown through the flat plains of the valley. Liebe was awed by its breadth and strength, its immutable luster under the blue sky, reflecting sparkles from horizon to horizon. They followed it east, comparing with Adolph's knowledge of Count Barkoczy's estate each land-holding they passed. Here the estates were tremendous acreages, sweeping back from the river in well-kept fields, fenced paddocks and numerous outbuildings. Grand mansions dazzled their eyes. At last, they found the landmarks they were looking for and passed between stone pillars into the Barkoczy estate.

Adolph pulled the horses to a stop. He took Liebe's hand and pressed into her palm a small box.

"My wedding present to you," he said. "I want to give it to you on the threshold of our new life."

Inside the box was a pair of earrings, hand-worked gold with garnets and seed pearls, beveled to catch and reflect the light. Liebe put them in her ears and shook her head, watching the light shards dance on Adolph's face. Then she put her hand under his chin and kissed him, a long, deep kiss, a wife's kiss.

A shake of the reins got the horses started again and they soon arrived at a long low cottage, shaded by a great elm and centered in a smooth lawn. French windows were open to the breeze, soft shadows played on the white-washed walls, and bright geraniums clustered along the curving walk and beneath the tree. Adolph turned the wagon into the cinder drive and headed toward an open building in the rear.

At the clatter of the wagon, the back door of the cottage opened and a large woman hurried out, wiping her hands on her apron and smiling broadly.

"Greetings, greetings!" she called as she beckoned toward a man working in the barn. "Greetings, greetings!" he echoed, watching their faces to see if they understood his German. He reached for the bridles and halted the horses.

Adolph jumped from the box and readied himself to meet his first employees, and this he did by smartly clicking his heels together and bowing from the waist. As he told them his name and they fluttered around him, assuring him of his welcome and that they knew who he was, Liebe watched with a mixture of awe and amusement, determined to follow his lead as a person deserving of respect.

She allowed herself to be lifted to the ground but followed slowly the bustling couple as they herded Adolph toward the front of the house. "Yes, this is your house! Walk in, do! Indeed, it is your house!" Liebe tucked her chin into the ruching on her collar, tilting her hat and throwing her face into shadow. She did not want these new employees to see her shining eyes as she surveyed her new home. It was beyond all imagining, this serenity, this richness, this order. The lawn was emerald velvet, buttoned by the red and white geraniums. The elm sighed softly as it cast its shadow over the house and tempered the arctic whiteness of its bulk. The house contained the promise of air and coolness, of privacy, of contentment.

She passed through the carved wooden doorway and barely restrained a gasp of delight at the beauty of the interior. To her left was a parlour, low-ceilinged and beamed, with a deep couch and two large chairs flanking the fireplace. On the plank floor was a dark crimson rug, on the walls actual oil paintings. In the corner was a spinet piano. Liebe pushed her rough hands deep into the folds of her dress.

Opposite was an office, its casements open to the lawn, the leafy elm, and the river. Here, under the window, was an elegant desk. Bookcases lined the wall, full of ledgers and reference books. Liebe followed voices to the back of the house, past an enclosed staircase, into the bright kitchen. Adolph was maintaining his military decorum, his hands clasped behind his back, his head inclined first toward the voluble woman, then toward the old man, as he listened to their reports. He glanced at Liebe, allowed a twinkle to escape his blue eyes, then again bent his gaze on the two servants.

Finally Adolph had heard enough. He straightened his back and quietly delivered his orders as Liebe marveled at his authority. He introduced her. She smiled timidly. Then he took her arm and led her out of the—*his*—office. Closing the door to the parlour behind them, they fell into each other's arms, whispering and giggling like school children.

CHAPTER SIX
1892

THE DAYS PASSED slowly and the years quickly at the cottage on the Sazava. Count Barkoczy's distillery prospered under Adolph's stewardship. The men who worked for him respected his knowledge and liked his management. He was out every day but Saturday on his black stallion, inspecting the hops and grains flourishing in the fields. He was meticulous about the fermenting and bottling, earning praise from the monthly inspectors and enabling the Count to fetch a fine price for the beers and whiskeys he sent to the cities.

Liebe, though proud beyond measure to have a servant, Grete of the ample bosom, did not abandon her peasant beginnings. She kept geese and goats and tended a large kitchen garden which provided vegetables for her table and for the root cellar. She had milking privileges of a few of the cows kept on the large estate, so butter, cheese, and cream were in abundant supply.

"This cupboard is for dishes on which we serve meals that contain meat," she instructed the astonished Grete. "And this one is for dairy meals. And the flat-ware for the table must be kept separated, too, and all the pots and all the kitchen towels. And never, never serve milk with meat, although we can have it with chicken or fish." Liebe had thought that everybody kept a kosher home and didn't realize until she had to instruct Grete in its intricacies how complicated it was. Liebe was well launched into an explanation of the Biblical reasons for keeping kosher when Adolph, passing through the kitchen, silenced her with a dark look.

"So. . . different parts of Bohemia have different customs," he finished for her, unwilling to disclose their Jewishness to the hired help.

To Grete and her husband, Jews were a rarity in this part of Austria and totally beyond their narrow experience. Adolph knew that the less he was thought of as a Jew the better it would be for him.

His employees valued their jobs and feared Count Barkoczy. Any objections they had they should keep to themselves.

Every Friday evening, Liebe lit the *shabbus* tapers in Adolph's office as the sun disappeared behind the peaceful hills. She covered her head with a snowy napkin and recited the prayers she had so often heard her mother whisper over the candles. Her mother had wept as she passed her hands through the golden light, and Liebe now felt her own throat constrict and her eyelids burn. She thought of family so far away, of happiness present in the darkening room. Tears were flowing down her cheeks as she turned for Adolph's *shabbus* kiss.

Before two years had passed, Amelia was born, eased into the world by the faithful Grete. And shortly after Amelia had taken her first tentative steps, little Katie arrived. The babies were apple-cheeked and robust, tanned by the sun, and the pets of all who worked on the estate. They passed uneventfully through infancy and soon were sturdy little girls participating in the busy lives of their household. They stood on chairs by the kitchen table, wrapped in aprons, to sort the nuts and apples for strudel. They rode in front of their father on his horse to inspect the crops. They teased the mules at the water pump, canned fruit for the larder, and sewed and knitted. Their little fingers quickly became adept at tiny stitches and French knots. By the time they were seven and five, they were tending the geese and chickens that inhabited the back garden.

One fine summer day, they were flapping their pinafores to herd the geese to their dinner. Adolph rode through the gate, his face long, his shoulders sagging. Katie and Amelia hurried their charges into a pen, then raced across the lawn to the kitchen door.

"I don't know what went wrong," they heard Adolph say to their mother. "Every vat we tap is bad. The beer can't even be swallowed, and it smells unlike anything I've ever smelled. We've checked everything—checked twice!—and I can't find the answer. We've got to hold this batch back while I analyze every vat." He was muttering aloud as he strode into the study to pore over his books.

Liebe shook her head and touched her finger to her lips so the little girls would be quiet. Their worried frowns mirrored their father's, although they had no idea what he was talking about. They returned slowly to the more predictable geese and were once again interrupted by a scowling man, this one a worker from the distillery.

"Where is your father? Hurry, now. Hurry!" And he took a little hand into each of his as he rushed them along. They wriggled from his grip at the study door.

"Sir! The inspectors are on their way! They'll be here before the day is over. They're just down the road." Every estate sent a warning up the line on the days of the inspector's surprise visits.

Adolph did not allow the consternation he felt to show on his face. He sent the man back to the barns and went to his horse, tied to the elm by the study window. This was serious business. Expensive, too. The inspectors were unpredictable and could decide not to certify any of his output if they found his beer to be bad. This would be an enormous financial loss and might even tarnish the reputation of Count Barkoczy as a distiller. He patted the horse absently as he cast about for a solution. Confess an error and throw himself on the inspector's mercy? Foolish. Admit to being late and having no beer ready for inspection? Unbelievable. Get rid of the beer? But how? By the time he reached the distillery, he had a risky but workable plan.

Every man on the estate was summoned to the vats. By incredible effort, a sluice was built from each vat to the river, and within the hour thirty vats were spewing their unpalatable contents into the smoothly flowing Sazava. By the time the inspectors arrived, there were men in the vats scrubbing away as though they had been in there for hours.

Adolph stood silently as the inspectors entered the huge barn. He chose not to explain why his men were scrubbing vats that should, at this time of year, be full of fermenting hops. He waited nervously for the inspector to begin the conversation.

"Well, Herr Friedman." The inspector clapped Adolph on the back and smiled. "You must have a very efficient source of information. I see you have already heard about the fungus and have cleaned out your vats."

Adolph admitted modestly that he was alert and efficient and listened with interest to the report that his neighbors to the east had been plagued by a mysterious fungus that changed the taste of their beer. He gravely accepted the compliments on his foresight and cleanliness, shared a stirrup-cup of brandy, and accompanied his visitors to the gate. Then he sagged in the saddle, unable to believe his narrow escape. It was late at night that he rode home, weary to his bones but buoyed by the thought that he had, by his own wit and expertise, avoided a calamity. He had lost some of his employer's money, true, but he had saved even more.

Adolph slept deeply and late. Liebe had long since been in the sunny kitchen with the little girls, exchanging morning gossip and beginning preparations once again for the Sabbath. They were old enough now to help with the baking and loved to braid their own special loaves of Sabbath *challah*, which Grete was happy to accept as Viennese bread, braided for extra beauty. These were put to rise behind the warm oven before Amelia and Katie went out to drive the geese to the river's edge.

Amelia unlatched the gate to the pen, and, running about like a pair of puppies, they chased the unruly birds to their morning bath. At the river's edge, they pulled up with a shriek at the sight that greeted them. From one bend of the river to the next was a sheet of silver, the undersides of thousands of fish, with an occasional lazy plop here and there as a fish parted itself from the molten accumulation to leap twisting into the air. The mass moved sluggishly, constantly reflecting dullness then shine as various configurations changed from belly to back. The whole group was at the same time wheeling itself about like a galaxy turning in the heavens.

Katie and Amelia faced each other, wide-eyed, mouths open in pink amazement. Without a word, they galloped back to the house, pigtails flying, skirts above their knees. Their unintelligible description delivered at the top of their lungs woke their father, who was dragged, wiping the sleep from his eyes, across the lawn, past the elm, down the slope. Liebe followed slowly.

Adolph was stunned by the sight. He pushed a few unresisting fish into the general melee and watched as those in the space he had cleared turned somersaults in the water. Kneeling on the verge, he looked up at his chattering children and incredulous wife.

"They're drunk!" he cried. "Every last one of them is drunk!" He threw his head back and laughed aloud to the sky. "They're drunk on Count Barkoczy's beer."

CHAPTER SEVEN
1881

ADOLPH DANDLED HIS THREE-YEAR OLD SON EPHRAIM on his knee as Liebe adjusted the sashes on her daughters' dresses. Ephraim was a cherubic vision in a cream linen suit, his chubby knees sticking out from his short pants, his little feet laced into white shoes with leather spats. Behind his angelic smile he was plotting to remove the sailor hat from his blond curly head. At last, the three children were arranged to Liebe's satisfaction, and they progressed serenely to the wagon where Dieter, Grete's husband, awaited them.

In this spring of 1881, the family presented a Victorian portrait. Liebe was dressed in pearl gray cotton, long sleeved, high necked, embroidered with tiny gray flowers, a huge skirt belling from her waist and brushing the clover in the lawn, stirring the bees to desultory buzzing. Her wedding earrings flashed at her ears. Amelia, at ten, was increasingly annoyed at her short skirts and unconsciously imitated her mother's walk as she imagined the swish of her own blue petticoats on the grass. Katie, all in white, harbored no such thoughts of grown-up things and suffered the lisle stockings, cotton vests, ruffles and furbelows as necessary coverings. Her favorite possession, a white eyelet parasol that Amelia had embroidered, was tucked under her arm. She shot it open as she passed the black stallion tied to the elm tree, causing him to jump and paw the air. Her father gave her a severe glance. He, not being a part of this exciting excursion, wore his riding boots, fawn gabardine pants, and a soft shirt open at the throat. He released Ephraim with a noisy kiss under the ear. The boy scampered toward the wagon, hat bouncing at the end of its ribbons.

Every week, Dieter made the long trip to Aperius to purchase household and tack supplies and to get the mail. They all laughingly called Aperius *Lesta Posta*, because it was the postman's last stop. Chakow, where Count Barkoczy's estate was, was far too small and unimportant to merit any postal deliveries. When her daughters became old enough, they and Liebe began accompanying Dieter a few times each year so that Liebe could give her children glimpses of a life more sophisticated than that on the estate. They wandered the curving streets of the small town, looking into shop windows and admiring the town folk, much more elegant than the Friedmans, even at their finest.

This was Ephraim's first trip to Aperius. The two girls delighted in showing their brother their favorite places. He was impatient to leave the windows full of hats and jewelry but gazed longingly at the clocks, ticking and clacking in intricate motion behind a thick pane of glass. He wet his fat little hands at the fountain in the square, and only the sternest restraint kept him from wetting his feet as well.

Katie and Amelia particularly liked to climb the cobble-stoned residential streets to look at doors and fanlights and knockers. They showed Ephraim the lion heads, the ostrich feathers, the hands, all cast in brass and hung on doors of red, green, and blue. The fanlights over these doors were of great intricacy, often made of lace or embroidered linen, sometimes of stained glass or wrought iron. They visited the choicest of these with their little brother, quite proprietary about their discoveries.

The excursion ended with a treat at the sweet shop. There they sat on bent-wood chairs, primly spooning colored ices into their mouths. Liebe sighed with contentment that the trip had gone so well, even with Ephraim in tow. They strolled slowly back to the wagon, not so comfortable now that it was filled with Dieter's purchases. They disposed themselves among the lumpy packages of salt and harrows and leather hides and soon were on the dusty road back to Count Barkoczy's estate.

When his family drove off, Adolph hurried immediately to his study, eager to begin a few hours of uninterrupted work. Flies buzzed at the open windows, and the air was soft. He was intent on the papers on his desk when his attention was diverted by noises and movements from the lawn. He looked up to see his black horse plunging about the elm tree, winding himself tighter and tighter in the rope that fastened him. Adolph flung down his pen and rushed outdoors. The stallion's eyes were rolling wildly as he heaved and pulled to free himself. Adolph reached up a soothing hand as he sought to grab the rope and begin to unwind the animal from the tree. With great effort, he pushed and cajoled the animal into a position where he could free its head. The horse bucked and stamped in panic. The last kick caught Adolph squarely under the jaw. It broke his neck.

Dieter pulled the wagon into the cinder driveway and was met by Grete, crying incoherently and pointing at the still figure under the tree. The stallion stood nearby, trembling but calm. In the instant it took Liebe to raise her hand to her mouth, the entire scene took place in her head. She saw Adolph running to unloose his beloved charger, saw the plunging beast and heroic man struggling together, felt the blow and ensuing nothingness. The heavy air wafted her from the wagon and across the lawn. She knelt above Adolph, studying his face intently, and knew that he was dead. The voices about her, Dieter's, Grete's, the wailing of her children, were murmurous in her ears. Someone—she?—sent Dieter to fetch the men from the distillery, sent Grete with the children into the house. She continued to float above her husband's body, her ears ringing, until he was carried away. Liebe could barely lift herself from the grass. She had no sensation of touching the ground yet felt impossibly sluggish. She swam through the sullen air to the kitchen and her sobbing children.

They clutched at her, shouting questions. She held them to her, wondering at the warmth of their little bodies. When they were somewhat calmed, she looked at their faces and they looked beseechingly at her. She could hear their thoughts.

"It is true, my darlings. Our dear father is dead." More wails. "But we will go on. This isn't the end of us. We have each other, and we will go on. Don't be frightened. We're going to be very sad, but we will go on."

They held each other for a long time with silent tears, noisy tears. Grete and Dieter hovered at the edge of the miserable little group, offering tea, offering cookies, wringing their hands.

Late in the night. the children allowed themselves to be put to bed. Liebe hugged each of them before she tucked them into the three trundles under the eaves. She could, by the candle light, see their swollen eyes. "Remember, we've got each other. We're going to be all right." She heard their shuddering sighs as they settled to sleep.

Liebe crept down the stairs and into the parlor. It had never seemed so large. The corners sloped into the darkness, yet the ceiling hung oppressively low. She stirred the fire. The sudden new flames brought her neither light nor warmth. "What am I going to do?" she whispered to herself. "What will become of us?" She leaned her forehead against the cold mantlepiece and wept.

CHAPTER EIGHT

THE ROUTINE OF THE ESTATE did not vary. Each morning, Katie and Amelia rode off in the wagon with Dieter to the little schoolhouse, and Liebe blessed the name of Empress Maria Theresa for providing her daughters with an education as well as a distraction. She had found a history of the Hapsburgs on a shelf in the office and read with fascination the life of this woman, alive until a decade ago, who had been the only woman to lead the Holy Roman Empire. Among the many kindnesses of her rule was the encouragement of free education for women and, in fact, the establishment of free and private schools for girls. Her little girls must remember how fortunate they are to be educated and respected. "Remember Maria Theresa!" she would call as they left the cinder driveway, and "We will, Mama!" they shouted back as they always did. The two little girls, though they hardly realized it, spoke several languages because treaties were constantly transferring control of their lives from one tyrant to another. They knew of the changes in their political fortunes only when the books and the language changed at school. They could read and speak German and Slovene and Turkish and Hebrew. Slovene was spoken on the estate, German in their house.

Six months had passed since Adolph had been killed, but Count Barkoczy had not been told. Though there was no spoken agreement among them, none of the peasants who worked on the estate wanted to cause the eviction of the widow and her children. After eleven years of Adolph's management, the distillery functioned well. Liebe sat night after night at his desk and painstakingly taught herself the bookkeeping of which she had earlier been blissfully unaware. During the day she tended her garden and kitchen, always making certain she was cheerful when her little ones were nearby.

On a gray morning when the little girls were at school and Ephraim at his favorite pastime of tormenting the donkeys at the well, she wearily dragged herself up the steep staircase to her cold bedroom at the top. Leaning against the closed door, she surveyed the room with tired eyes. The large bed was rumpled on one side, only one pillow held the impression of a head. The cheval mirror sent her reflection back to her, a round-shouldered woman with a colorless bun sliding from the back of her hair, wrinkled dress, expressionless. They stared at each other for a long time. Then Liebe walked to the mirror and put her hand on the other face, leaving a smudge on the glass.

With a sigh, small, inaudible, she turned to the trunk that had accompanied her on her bridal trip and lifted its heavy top. Slowly, she began to empty it of Adolph's clothes. The fine linen shirts and whipcord breeches she folded on the floor. What use would she ever have for them? The boots, too, she put on this pile. Finally, from the dark recess at the bottom, she pulled the black hussar's uniform, its epaulets still stiff, the buttons still shining. The tears she had held back for so long would not be denied, and she sobbed and sobbed into its mustiness. There was no relief in the crying. The well, hot and deep inside her, was emptied by not even a drop.

Exhausted, she sat back on her heels. She could not bear to give away the uniform, so she wrapped it in a linen bed sheet and laid it again at the bottom of the trunk. With a ragged sigh she closed the lid and turned to the pile of clothes and boots. Her first thought was to deliver them to the distillery for the men to divide and use, but her spirit quailed at the thought of seeing Adolph's image across the lawn or in the fields. Frugality lost the short battle, and she hesitated only a moment before tossing the heavy bundle through the casement and onto the driveway beneath.

She hurried to the kitchen, grasped the startled Grete above the elbow and led her outdoors. Wordlessly, the two women carried the last material vestiges of Adolph's existence behind the stable and, with Dieter's help, set the clothes afire. The smoke was now black, now clear. The heat shimmered the fields and hills behind it. The fire crackled. After a time, there was nothing but ashes, a few bone buttons. Dieter swept them into a pile, put it into a box, and carried the box away.

Liebe spent the rest of the day seated at the desk in the study, her chin in her hands. She gazed unseeingly across the frozen brown lawn and the almost leafless elm. She knew she would have to formulate a plan for her future very soon. The estate had survived her efforts at management, but soon the operation of turning the fields and preparing the brewery for spring must start again. She had been equal to finishing the year's work, to completing the process begun by Adolph. But the effort of beginning was beyond her knowledge and her will. Count Barkoczy, mysterious and distant in Prague, must be told so he could install another manager by winter's end. Maybe he would ask her to stay, find someone to teach her how to run the estate, show her how grateful. . . .

That would never happen.

She gazed at the river, now brown and swift as it swept past the meadow. Her lips tightened as she focused on the elm, writhing in the winter gusts that blew down from the hills behind the estate. Far up the road she could see a lone horseman bent against the wind. Lost in reverie, she did not register his existence until he turned into the driveway.

"Why, he is coming here!" Her voice in the quiet room startled Liebe into awareness. Immediately, there was a heavy knock on the door and Grete's footsteps in the hall. Grete had been watching the horseman's progress also. When she appeared in the study to announce the presence of a Herr Gross, her face was a collection of contrasting emotions. Curiosity, apprehension, and disapproval were all there, had Liebe been able to pay attention.

Visiting among the estates was not common. They were large, often thousands of acres and like little villages themselves, containing the huts and tenant farms of the peasants as well as the rolling fields and barns and businesses of the owners. The peasants, men and women, did backbreaking labor for their masters from dawn to dusk every day and withdrew wearily to their own hovels at night, often to continue working on their own leaseholds. The other managers and resident owners did not include Adolph's family in their infrequent social gatherings. Jews were beneath contempt, not to be considered and rejected but rather never to be considered at all. Though Adolph had never talked of his religion to anyone in his new life as estate manager, he was sure that there was speculation. And if there were a possibility that someone was a Jew, he was treated as though the possibility were the absolute truth.

This is not to say, however, that the existence of Liebe and her family was unnoticed. Market day was rich with gossip among the peasants. It was known for many miles up and down the river that the manager of Count Barkoczy's estate had been killed and that his widow awaited eviction. Herr Gross, himself a widower, had been contemplating this knowledge for several months. He was a merchant in a village more than a day's ride from Chakow, lonely, shrewd, and ambitious. He had a strong instinct for improving his lot in life and, after turning the matter over and over in his head, had decided that he could manage an estate and brewery as well as a new wife.

Liebe searched in panic through her memories for a similar situation on which to model her behavior. She had no idea how to welcome a visitor into her home and certainly not a lone man. The few men who had visited Adolph had met with him in the study behind a closed door. She had no idea of their errands or their conversations. Was this man perhaps an agent of Count Barkoczy? She was filled with alarm but stood resolutely. She did not want a stranger in her parlour, *that* she knew. Her hand flat on the desk—Adolph's desk—she said quietly to Grete, "Please bring him in here."

Liebe was silent as Herr Gross appeared in her doorway, bulky in his greatcoat and heavy boots. She motioned to the other chair and sank anew into hers. He rose again, causing her to shrink back, then to rise and return to the door and close it. There was a long pause in which Liebe looked inquiringly at him and he looked appraisingly at her. Her steady eyes and soft mouth drooping with sorrow convinced him to come straight to the point of his visit.

"Madame," he said. "I am Marcus Gross, a Jew of the village of Dobrany. There I am a dealer in small things—jewelry, china, clocks, and many things second-hand." He paused, seeing she was having difficulty following his Slovene.

"Shall I speak to you in German?" She nodded wordlessly, mesmerized by his huge and enigmatic presence in her study. He continued, telling her of the death of his wife four years ago, of his lonely life and difficulty in caring for his children. She shuddered. Four years! It seemed an impossible amount of time to be without the person one loved and needed most in the world.

"I have a desire to marry again," he said. He told her that he would be able to manage an estate and distillery with the help of records and books and that he considered himself capable of making decisions and guiding peasant workers. He spoke at length about his business acumen and his experiences in the wider world of cities and towns.

Liebe stared at him, uncomprehending. Why was this strange man sitting in her husband's study talking to her in reasonable tones about things in which she had no interest? Was this all one of the curious dreams that befell widows and against which she had no defenses? She felt a thrill of fear and leaned forward, hoping the apparition would disappear if she moved.

Herr Gross, perhaps mistaking her movement for curiosity, hardened his voice as he came to the stark truths of her existence. "When Count Barkoczy learns of your husband's death"—Liebe marveled at how much this man knew—"he will want you away as soon as possible. Have you thought of where you will go, what you will do? Can your family take you in? Can they feed four more mouths?" So he knew of her children. He was echoing the very fears that beset her only hours before. The corners of her mouth trembled, and she struggled to control herself.

"Madame," he said. "I am proposing that we marry. I have brought many letters of introduction for you to read so that you may know that I am decent and hardworking. I can manage this estate successfully through its first harvest and bottling, and then we can inform the Count that you have remarried a man who can continue your husband's work." He stopped again, realizing how difficult the subject must be for her. More gently, he said, "You would have nothing to fear from me, Madame. I am a kind man, and strong and healthy. I'm a *landsman*. We would learn to respect each other. I cannot live alone any longer because I need the comfort and warmth of a real home. You cannot live alone here for other reasons. You will never be able to face the spring and the work it brings. And,"— here he looked again into her face to speak the hard truth—"you will probably not be allowed to stay until spring."

There was a long silence, which Liebe could not break. Her emotions were in a turmoil, her thoughts spinning and tangling in her head. Only Adolph can help me with a decision like this, she thought. Surely the past six months have been only a bad dream and he will be here to help me as soon as he is finished with his work.

She jumped when Herr Gross stood up and removed his coat, looking down at her solicitously. He realized the tension in the room had become almost unbearable. "Madame, if I could share your supper and spend the night in your barn, I would be most grateful."

Liebe rose from the chair, found she could make her way across the room, and put her shaking hand on the door. There she turned to meet his eyes, then walked slowly to the kitchen to ask Grete to set another place at the table. Her voice was hoarse. She had not spoken a word since Herr Gross had appeared in her house.

CHAPTER NINE

GRETE, LIPS PURSED, USHERED HERR GROSS into the kitchen. He had shed his coat, his fur hat, and his leather gloves, but he still seemed enormous to Liebe. She backed up against the wall. Why had she allowed him into her kitchen? This was the center of her home, the place where she and Adolph and her children had actually lived. And, to make matters worse, Grete had set the extra place at the very head of the table, the place where Adolph sat, the father's place. What was she thinking?

"What am I thinking?" Liebe said aloud. She blushed and covered her exclamation by introducing her children. They stared, round-eyed and silent, at the massive stranger. Liebe went to the head of the table to remove the dishes, but Herr Gross interpreted her gesture as an invitation to sit down. And there he was, in Adolph's chair smiling at Adolph's children, lifting Adolph's spoon. Liebe looked down at her plate, sick with despair. How could they, any of them, eat with this stranger in their midst? She had made a terrible mistake. How could she undo it?

She was startled by a giggle, then two, then laughter in which Grete and Dieter joined. Herr Gross had pulled from Amelia's curls a golden coin, which he dropped into her hand. Then he found another one behind Ephraim's ear. And a third under Katie's glass.

"How did you do that?"

"Where did it come from?"

Herr Gross's beard parted in a conspiratorial grin. He teased them with wild explanations of his magical prowess as they ate Grete's excellent dinner. He told stories of fairies and ogres, he drew from his pockets little trinkets to please them, he spun spoons through the air that landed noisily but without splashes in their coffee cups. Blessed laughter again. How Liebe reveled in it. Her shoulders relaxed, her fists unclenched. She smiled at Herr Gross.

"Oh, my dears!" Liebe looked at the watch pinned to the front of her dress as Herr Gross accepted a last cup of coffee. "It is much too late. You must go to bed now. Say goodnight to our guest." Herr Gross bent gravely over two little hands and shook the third and stickiest one. As the children turned reluctantly toward the stairs, he touched Liebe's elbow.

"Madam, I shall return in a month for your answer, and, if you accept, we will put our agreement into effect immediately." He took her hand and touched his lips to the back of it, then turned it over and kissed the palm. He hurried from the room in search of his coat as she led the children up the staircase to their beds. When she returned, he was gone. And when she awoke next morning to a leaden sky and bursts of rain, he was already many miles away.

"Who was that man, Mama?" Amelia asked as she bent over her steaming porridge.

"Just a man, my darling. Nothing important. He had some business to discuss. About the beer." Katie and Amelia exchanged confused glances. It had seemed like much more than business to them, but they did not know more of what.

Ephraim banged his spoon on his glass. "I liked him," he said.

Liebe laughed. Another laugh, she marveled. And, oh, it felt so good. "He certainly knew a lot of tricks," she said. Tricks. Maybe that explained his visit. Maybe it was all a trick to deprive her of something. She had no idea what her position was with Count Barkoczy, what belonged to her, what belonged to him. Perhaps Herr Gross knew something she didn't know. She shrugged off the panic as she hustled the little girls out the door to school.

"Maria Theresa!" they all chorused together, then laughed again. Katie and Amelia rushed back from the wagon to give their mother another hug, mystified by her mood but elated by her smile.

Liebe's emotions during the day alternated between euphoria and despair. She knew nothing of this man yet was considering entrusting her future and that of her beloved children to him. This argument decided her definitely against the marriage, and she drew a strong breath of relief at the peace it brought her. But what will I do without him? she asked herself. She fled to her room, where she paced and muttered and cried out for someone to help her. It was too much for her to think about. She needed Adolph to tell her what to do. This brought a dismal smile to her lips. If he were here to help her, there would be no problem in the first place.

Liebe took the plain gold hoops from her ears, the carved hoops that Adolph had once brought her from Chakow, and fastened Adolph's wedding earrings instead. Perhaps Adolph would whisper to her through them. They hung sparkling by her cheeks, lighting up her face, silent. She sighed and returned to the library to pore over the books. The mathematics were there, Adolph's orderly figures, and the daily tasks to be done, but not the fine hand for managing the peasants, not the talent for predicting the weather, not the educated palate for assessing the flavor of the beer. Certainly the peasants would never allow her, a woman, to direct their labors. And Count Barkoczy? He was always the final conundrum.

"Hush, Ephraim. Your noise is bothering Mother." Katie drew down her mouth in imitation of Liebe's expression, the signal that she and Amelia and Ephraim should take their after-school games outside. Their breath frosty in the winter air, they speculated on the reasons for their mother's distress.

"She's got a headache," said Ephraim, satisfied with the explanation.

"Yes, yes. But why? She was never like this before Father. . . before he. . . I know it must be different for her. But we're still here, and that must make her happy. We've been so good, and Grete and Dieter are a big help. Maybe she has a secret."

"But what can it be?" Amelia could not accept this explanation. They were a close family, and there had seemingly been no secrets before.

The days passed, winged when Liebe was desperate for more time, achingly slow when she had made yet another irrevocable decision and wanted to act on it and be done. She did not even know which day would be the day that Herr Gross would arrive and was breathless as the month neared its close. She was constantly at the windows, straining her eyes through scudding rain. On better days, she paced the lawn, muddying her skirts and fine boots as she scanned the rutted road.

"She's thinking about that man, that Herr Gross," Grete muttered to Dieter as they carried the provisions from the wagon to the barn. "He proposed marriage to her, I know he did."

Dieter was astonished. "How do you know this?"

Grete crossed her arms across her bosom and faced him squarely. "Of course he did. Why do you think he came here? If it hadn't been him it would have been someone else. She is in great trouble and yet she is the key to great opportunity. He realized it first, that's all. And she will marry him, mark my words. What else can she do? Too bad she doesn't know it. It would save her much grief." Grete was a prosaic woman, and life was a matter of necessities.

Dieter shook his head. He handed a sack to his wife and gave her a push. "If what you say is true, there will be changes." He pulled another sack from the wagon. "Keep working."

Precisely at the end of thirty days, Herr Gross turned his horse into the driveway. Liebe felt a flood of relief. She had to marry this man. There was no alternative. If he had not reappeared, she would have been desperate. She needed his protection. It was as simple as that. She drew him into the parlour this time, searching his face for a sign that he had changed his mind. But his look of hopefulness was as great as hers.

Liebe motioned him to a chair, then went to the kitchen to ask Grete for tea. When she returned, she ventured her first good look at him. He was of medium height and pleasing to look at, though not handsome. He was probably in his forties, his eyes were brown and clear, his hair lavish both on his head and on his face. That beard! It was abundant and lustrous, curling over his mouth and cheeks and covering his chin into his greatcoat.

She reached for the coat and he caught her hand.

"I can't wait any longer for your answer, Frau Friedman. What have you decided? Are we to join our lives?"

Liebe took a deep breath.

"My answer is yes, Herr Gross." She dropped her eyes. Why, I don't even know his first name, she thought. But her foot was on the path, and she stepped firmly. "You do me and my family great honor. Please tell me what you have planned."

Herr Gross suggested that he and Liebe return to Dobrany the next day to be married by the rabbi. Herr Gross' three sons—Liebe pressed this disquieting information into a deep place to be examined later—would pack his wagons, and Herr Gross, his three sons, and the new Frau Gross would return within the week.

Amelia, Katie, and Ephraim were overjoyed to see the big stranger again. He made their mother laugh, and that was enough to endear him to them. Their dinner together lasted well into the evening, and they were once again reluctant to say goodnight. Alone with her children in their bedroom, Liebe was at a loss how to tell them of the enormous change in their lives that was going to occur the very next day. She regretted deeply not having prepared them for her announcement, but there was nothing for it but to tell them now, as quickly as possible.

"My darlings, I am so glad that you like Herr Gross," she said. "I like him, too. In fact, I like him well enough to accept his offer of marriage, and in two days he and I will be married." Liebe didn't look at them as she hurried on. "That means I will be his wife, but it doesn't have to mean that he will be your father. You must always remember your own dear father. Nothing will change that. Herr Gross will be our protector, and he will run the farm. I haven't been doing a very good job of that, and I will be happy to have him make the decisions that have been so hard for me." This time she did look at them, right into their eyes. They must understand how necessary this marriage was for her, and for them, too, even though she could not put that thought into words.

So absorbed was she in her own momentous plans that she accepted their stunned silence as acquiescence and was soon gone from them to ready herself for her journey. She did not realize until she had closed their door behind her that she had not mentioned Herr Gross' three sons. She hesitated, her hand on the doorknob. Tomorrow would be soon enough, she reasoned. She would remember tomorrow.

The next morning was frantic. The forlorn little ones huddled together in this corner and that as preparations whirled around them. Liebe, bundled against the cold and rain, took her place in the wagon next to Herr Gross. As they turned into the road, she twisted in the seat to wave goodbye. The children had disappeared into the house. The last sight she saw as the wagon drew away was Herr Gross' brown gelding tied to the leafless elm.

CHAPTER TEN

ONCE AGAIN, GREAT-GRANDMOTHER, you are off on a wedding trip. But you are no longer an innocent girl, full of chatter and playfulness. The man next to you is not young and handsome, someone you have known and loved for many years. You have actually never seen his face, covered as it is with his rough beard. You are apprehensive, unsure. Nevertheless, the decision has been made, and you are more relaxed and comfortable than you have been since your real husband, your only beloved husband, died more than six months ago. This new marriage had to happen, it was necessary. But why could you not tell your children what you had to do, both for yourself and for them? Did you not remember the secrets your mother kept from you and the anger you felt when you realised they need not have been secrets? You, who value knowledge so much that Empress Maria Theresa is your kitchen goddess, kept important information from those you loved the most. As you return home from your second wedding, you are understandably apprehensive. Nevertheless, you look to the future with a brave face.

At the end of the week, the wagon returned as promised, piled high with Herr Gross's belongings, his valued "little things," his new wife, and three large noisy boys, the sons of Herr Gross. Liebe rushed to her children, clasping them in her arms and whispering quickly into their ears. "Don't gape, my darlings. These are your new brothers, and you will soon grow to like them, I know. They are full of games and songs, you'll see. You can show them around the estate when you're ready, and they will show you all the wonderful things they have brought with them from their old home. Please come along and say hello politely." She gave them a little push.

Grete and Dieter were no less astonished by the presence of Herr Gross' sons. "What are we going to do with all these extra people?" Grete muttered. "Those hooligans will have to sleep in the barn, that's what. And they look as though they belong there, too. I wonder if she knew what she was getting into. Dieter, *schnell, schnell!* Get the boys' boxes right into the barn before they settle themselves in the cottage." She began separating the excited little crowd just the way she separated the sheep before shearing.

Where before there were four sitting down to supper, now there were eight in the little cottage kitchen. Herr Gross, at the head of the table, beamed at the six children and his wife sitting opposite. He was as determined to manage this large family with strength and authority as he was to manage the distillery. The promises made to Liebe a year earlier were not empty ones. He was kind. He was attentive to her children. He earned the respect of the servants and the peasants. Life for Liebe was no longer an unbearable burden, and there were moments when she actually hummed a little song.

But there was a price to pay and it was paid by Katie. The three sons of Herr Gross, teen-aged and boisterous, found in her a challenge they could not ignore. Amelia, at twelve ready to be sent off to Prague to the Gymnasium to continue her education courtesy of Empress Maria Theresa, was self-possessed and self-absorbed. Ephraim had been smitten immediately by hero worship and was dandled and coddled by his stepbrothers like an animate toy. But Katie did not fare so well. Her deep and inarticulate longing for her father changed her high spirits to sullenness. She was quick to take offense, her tongue was scathing, her temper fiery.

She noticed these changes in herself and despaired of them. What is happening to me? she would ask herself in the night. Why does nothing please me anymore? Why can I not be a puppy like Ephraim or away like Amelia? The trees don't look green anymore. The sky isn't blue. Oh, why can it not be as it was?

Tears ran down her cheeks as she wept silently into her pillow. She hotly resented her mother's quick marriage to Herr Gross. How could she have been so happy with Father and now so easily content with this bearded stranger? She hated Amelia's ready acceptance of those rowdy boys. Even Ephraim was a traitor, sitting on Herr Gross's knee as happily as on Father's and trotting after those boys like a little lamb. She tossed and turned as noisily as possible, but Ephraim did not awaken, her mother did not come in to comfort her, and Amelia's bed was folded away in the storage room until her return from Prague.

Katie had no one in which to confide her misery. She spent her days in silence and her hours in screaming fights with anyone who crossed her. So delightful a target was hard for her stepbrothers to resist. They tormented her endlessly, jumping at her from the bushes, pulling her braids, salting her puddings. Even Ephraim joined in, bribed by a sweet to hide her shoes so cleverly that she often did not find them until Dieter's wagon had left for school with the other children.

"Don't forget Maria Theresa!" called her mother, eyes clouded with worry. But Katie, in her pain and frustration, chose even to forget the revered Empress. She walked the long miles, seething with anger.

Liebe was not ignorant of her daughter's torment, but she was paralyzed with indecision. She was profoundly grateful to Herr Gross for saving her from poverty and ignominy. Even after a year of marriage to him, she addressed him as Herr Gross. He and his children would forever be strangers in her life, but respected strangers and necessary ones. She was ever cheerful in their midst, fearful to displease and risk abandonment. Her timidity prevented her from speaking of her misgivings about Katie. This was her home no longer. It was Herr Gross's. His labor, his talent made it his. He could order her out as soon as she failed to please him. She had no doubts where his choice would lie in a conflict between her children and his. His sons were useful in the brewery. Her children were mere babes and, she faced it squarely, merely charming.

For more than a year she watched in silent agony as Katie grew thinner and more rebellious. She herself was in a constant state of tension as she smoothed the whirlpools and eddies in a house of six children. She awaited with trepidation the tide she would not be able to tame, and it finally arrived.

Liebe awoke on a spring morning. So glorious was the day, she found herself singing as she pinned up her hair. Breakfast was peaceful and prolonged, and she marked Katie's absence with guilty contentment. Herr Gross arrived famished from the fields, accompanied by Ephraim who had ridden happily on the saddle in front of him. The three boys came in soon after, jostling each other and seeming to share a great joke, filling the sunny room with deep laughter. Liebe and Grete served a special Passover breakfast they had planned for days.

After a prolonged washing up, Liebe went to her garden. The sun, hot on her back, the murmurous insects, the sweet smell of earth and blossoms lulled her senses. Whether she heard the cries first and then remembered Katie or the other way around, she suddenly was aware that her daughter was calling her from far away. She turned this way and that, seeking the source of the sound. Gathering her skirts, she ran to the top of the hill behind the stables, and the sight that greeted her stopped her breath. Her daughter, her beloved Katie, lashed to the water wheel, was being hauled and dragged round and round the well by the uncaring donkeys. With a cry of horror, Liebe raced down the slope.

"Help! Help! Oh my God, help!" she screamed to the empty landscape. She pulled and tugged at the cruel ropes as she, too, joined the relentless circling. The three donkeys could not be stopped but kept walking, forcing the heavy wooden wheel on and on.

"I can't do it," she panted. "Oh, my darling, I can't release you. I must get help. Be brave, don't fight it. You can last two more minutes. I know you can." Liebe began to run, carried up the grade again by sheer terror.

As she swept down the other side of the hill, she saw Dieter in the stable yard. Not slowing her flight, she swept around him and started back up the hill.

"Bring a knife, a big one! Now! Now!"

Her strength flagging, she blessed his obedience as he passed her on the rise. And she sensed his quick comprehension as he crested the hill and disappeared down the other side. By the time Liebe reached her, Katie had been freed from the wheel and was sobbing in Dieter's arms. Liebe put a trembling hand on her daughter's forehead and was reassured by the moistness and heat. She inspected the wounds on Katie's hands and gasped at the shredded shoes and stockings. As she felt for broken bones, she motioned to Dieter to carry Katie back to the cottage.

"I can't move," she breathed. "Go on without me. I'll be right there." She faltered on the hill and finally sank, holding her side, into the tall grass. She allowed herself to sit there, wailing, until she was calm.

A minute? An hour? She didn't know. But Grete had bathed the little girl, dressed her blisters and scratches with *smetna*—sour cream—and green leaves, and tucked her into the coolness of her bed under the eaves. Katie's face was stony when Liebe burst into the room. Then her lower lip trembled, her eyes filled with tears, and she reached out her bandaged hands to her mother. They rocked together, sobbing quietly.

At last they drew apart and gazed into each other's eyes. "Mother," Katie shuddered with exhaustion. "I want to go away. I cannot live with those boys. They try to do terrible things to me. I'm afraid to be here." She shook her head to dispel memories Liebe did not want to imagine. "Can't I go to Gymnasium with Amelia? Or maybe into service. I can cook and clean and...." Liebe laid a finger on Katie's mouth. The Friedmans hired servants now, they didn't provide them.

The childish voice going on and on with fantastic plans for her escape made Liebe too agitated to think. She stood up, her hands in front of her as though to ward off a blow. "Go to sleep, Liebchen. We'll talk of this later. Everything will be all right. You'll see." She dragged herself to her room and fell onto the bed. Her mind was reeling and she had a terrible pain in her back. In spite of herself, she went to sleep. She dreamed of Adolph. He was laughing. She ran to him, but he was ever out of reach. She woke with her cheeks wet and the bed full of blood.

Liebe looked dully at the red sheets. The thought that she was pregnant had crept into her mind recently only as another obstacle to overcome, another rock in the road of her survival. If the blood and the pain meant that she had lost the baby, she would not be any more miserable. She had lost control of her life. Nothing that happened from now on would be a surprise.

In the frantic activity caused by her mother's miscarriage, Katie was left to heal alone. Grete, while tending to Liebe, was sternly warned to say nothing to Herr Gross, and she in turn instructed Dieter. "Say only that the little girl had some silly accident," she told him. "And that Frau Friedman...no, Frau Gross," hissing, "injured herself helping her daughter." Herr Gross's sons, in the household's disarray, escaped punishment for their deed.

Katie now was seldom seen by the family. She ate her meals with Grete and Dieter, who fussed lovingly over her. She spent her time sitting in her mother's room silently tending to her needs, feverishly plotting an escape. Katie's seeming serenity was a comfort to her mother.

CHAPTER ELEVEN

Two years earlier, when Amelia was sent off to Prague to attend Gymnasium, it became Katie's lonely responsibility to tend the geese. Every morning before school she fed them an apronful of grains and table scraps, then herded them, hissing and crowding, to the river's edge. She gladly abandoned them there—they were mean little beasts, she thought—and hurried back to the run to collect their eggs. These she carried to the peasants' cottages, thrown together into a little village at the edge of the estate, where she sold them, receiving coins and shy smiles in equal measure. Because she no longer had to share the egg money with her sister, Katie's store of coins fattened quite satisfactorily the chamois bag she kept them in during the two years of Amelia's absence.

After quiet afternoons in her mother's darkened room, Katie limped to the river and her dreaded but lucrative chore. Liebe had kept to her bed for more than a week after her miscarriage, but Katie had judged herself well enough to leave her own room after only two days. Though her feet were cruelly cut by the cinders at the well, they were healing. She hated driving the geese back to their pen in the evening. They nipped her ankles and flew screaming at her face. Sometimes they bit the edges of her apron, which she kept flapping to keep them ahead of her, forestalling lateral attacks. The reward for this daily battle was a visit to her little fortune, for which she now had a plan.

"Mother," she said, when she came to Liebe's room the next afternoon. "I have decided that I should go to America." She walked to the dresser and stroked the cold silver backs of her mother's hairbrushes. Herr Gross's brushes were there, too. Katie opened the top drawer and pushed them in, watching her mother in the mirror. "I can't stay here any longer. I have money now, surely enough. I will go to America and have a fine house, and I will send for you and Ephraim and Amelia and we can live together in America without those hateful Grosses." She waited an agonizing minute for her mother to protest, to promise to ask Herr Gross and his sons to leave immediately, to choose her. To choose her!

No sound came from the bed. Her mother, propped against a mound of creamy pillows, had not moved. Katie turned around but her mother did not meet her eyes. Then Liebe sighed. "Please leave me, Katie dear. I'm so tired. I'm going to rest. We'll talk of this later." Later, later, her mother was too full of later.

Katie crept from the room with a heavy heart. But at last she knew what she was going to do. Going to America was not so hard. This person and that had made the wondrous trip. She had heard stories from Adolph about going to America since she had been old enough to sit at the dinner table. Her Uncle Jacob was in America, sent away because of some mysterious misunderstanding about names, and he now lived in Castle Gardens, New Jersey. What a place it must be, with minarets and towers and quiet brooks, and somebody else to take care of the geese. She would look for him when she got there. Letters from him had arrived early on, telling of the marvels he had seen, and with money, too, to share with those left behind. They hadn't heard from Uncle Jacob in a very long time, but it was assumed that his life had become so fortunate that he forgot his humble beginnings.

Katie sleepwalked through the days as she dreamed of the trip by carriage to a great seaport, then the magnificent ship crossing the ocean. Her imagination balked at picturing America, but she knew it was a place where a mannerly little girl could stay with kind families until she could manage a fine house by herself. By the time her mother was strong enough to resume her household duties, Katie was determined to be away to the promised land. She caught Liebe at every solitary moment, begging and pleading. She was not above protracting her pathetic limp or insisting that Grete rebandage her little hands, even though they were quite healed.

At first Liebe refused to listen. "Not now, Liebchen. This is foolishness. Things will get better. You'll see."

Katie shouted at her retreating back. "Then make Herr Gross go!"

Life was a torment for them both. Katie could hear her mother and Herr Gross talking at night in their room, her voice plaintive, his deep and commanding. His sons, sensing the unrest, resumed their teasing. Katie's ribbons were missing, there was a frog in her bed, her lovely feather pillows teemed with ants. By the end of the summer,

Katie decided to take matters into her own hands. "If you don't help me, Mother, I'm going to kill myself!" She held her mother by the elbows, looking up at her with a face so determined that Liebe was frightened.

"Katie, little one. Be sensible. I can't let you go off on a long trip and never see you again. This plan of yours is foolishness, it cannot be. We'll find a solution to the problem soon. Just be patient."

Katie's patience was in small supply. That night she crept from her room with her comforter, some books, and, after a stop in the kitchen, as much food as she could remove without drawing attention to the loss. She had chased so many geese into secret places about the estate that she was able to go immediately to a hidden copse where she would be invisible, yet able to observe the consternation her absence would cause. She would show them what was possible if she didn't get her way. She would show them that she could kill herself if she made up her mind, and how sorry they would be when she was gone.

The first day, she watched avidly the excitement around the white cottage as her name was called and shouted. She relished the sight of her mother crying and, at dusk, being supported into the house by Herr Gross. The next day, Katie fought down the shame as she convinced herself that this was a necessary part of her plan, that her mother had forced her into it, that it was the only way. Her heart quailed as she watched, on the third day, the distillery workers draining the well, her mother drooping and silent on the hill with her back to the activity. At dinner, Katie burst through the kitchen door, trailing the leaf-strewn quilt.

"Now you know how you'll feel if I really am dead!" she shouted to the astonished group. The candle-flames swooped and shuddered as she swept around the table and up the stairs. She heard the angry scrape of a chair, probably Herr Gross ready to whip her within an inch of her life. She reached out a hand to the bannister to steady herself as she imagined her mother's hand reaching to hold Herr Gross's sleeve. No one had ever spanked a child of Adolph Friedman. Katie breathed a small sigh of relief as the door below her remained closed. Herr Gross would not punish her. Excited talking followed her into her room, where she closed the door and sank onto her small white bed. The evening breeze stirred the curtains at the window, filled the room with the smell of honeysuckle, lifted the damp hair on her forehead.

Would her mother fly up the stairs to see her, hold her in her arms sobbing in relief that her daughter was still alive? Katie hunched over the grimy comforter, picturing the scene below. As the room grew darker, the frogs in the river began to sing. She watched her image in the cheval mirror darken and become indistinct, shadows gather in the corners, night arrive. Aching, she lay down on the bed and stretched her arms behind her head. Herr Gross had probably persuaded her mother to finish her dinner. She would be up as soon as the dishes were washed. Katie heard the noisy end of dinner, the muted washing-up, the growing silence as the boys slouched off to the barn, finally the quiet as her mother and Herr Gross closed the door of their room. Had her mother forgotten her?

The next morning, Liebe drew Katie into her room. Liebe sat on the bed, Katie on the window-seat, her feet swinging above the polished wooden floor.

"I have discussed it with Herr Gross," she said. Katie made a face. "You may go to America." Katie was stunned. So she was to go and Herr Gross to stay. She felt ice flow from her heart to her toes, but she set her jaw and stared silently at her mother. "You can leave from Linz next week, before summer is over and it is too cold to make that long trip. You will find Uncle Jacob, and he will take care of you."

Liebe smiled wearily. Trapped between her need for security for her family and Katie's relentless demands, she was too overcome by grief, by illness, by the dislocation of her life to withstand any further assaults on her aching soul. It was all too much. She took Katie's cold hand in hers and gazed deeply into her face. Once or twice she opened her mouth as if to speak, but she said nothing. Katie did not return the pressure on her hand, letting it lie in her mother's as she slowly withdrew her spirit from this woman, this room, this home. At last, with a sigh, Liebe released her. Katie went slowly to her own room.

She pulled her father's old cardboard suitcase from beneath the bed and began filling it with clothes. The white dimity dress she loved went in first, carefully folded. It reminded her of Aperius and the excursions there, excursions from which she had returned into her father's arms. Her eyes were hot, but she did not let a tear escape. Then, of course, the blue serge. It probably got cold in America. Then the fluffy petticoats, some white gloves, her white parasol, two pair of kid boots—white and black—the reticule her mother had given her. By now the valise was overflowing. She would need another. But who would carry them from here to America?

"Well, I guess Amelia will have some new clothes in her wardrobe," she thought. Katie took everything out of the bag and hung it all carefully away in the chiffonier. She stood the parasol in the corner. Then she stuffed tightly into the suitcase her practical linen dresses, gray and brown, none needing petticoats, her sensible school shoes, sweaters, jackets, knitted caps, lisle stockings, all the while entertaining the new and uncomfortable thought that America might be foggy or rainy. On the very top, she put the chamois bag full of coins and closed the suitcase. It shut with a satisfying snap.

Katie sat back on her heels. She was frightened. One week. How would she get through it without losing her nerve? But she reminded herself of her mother's uncaring dismissal, of Herr Gross's suffocating presence, of those terrible boys, and she felt her courage returning. She would go! She would! Nothing could stop her!

The day before her departure, Katie discovered her money was gone. The slight indentation in her clothes at the top of the suitcase indicated the bag had been there, but it was missing now. "Those boys stole it, I know they did! Make them give me back my money!" she roared through the cottage. She was in a state of utter dread, knowing that she would never leave if she did not leave tomorrow. Liebe helped Katie search every cranny of her room. Herr Gross sternly questioned his sons, but they denied any knowledge, smirking at Katie all the while. She went to bed with a heavy heart, staring for hours at the ceiling with her fists clenched at her sides.

Then, in the darkness, her mother crept into the room, careful not to wake Ephraim. She took Katie's hand and pressed into it a thick wad of bills.

"Herr Gross loves you and thinks you will be happier in America. He wants you to have this money," she whispered. And then she laid a sheet of paper on the suitcase. "Here are the names of people we know who have gone to America. You will find them and they will help you." In her mind, Katie conjured up a picture of Aperius, only bigger and with cleaner streets. She knew she could find someone there quite easily. She hugged her mother, at first gratefully, then fiercely. They parted, and Katie turned over and went to sleep.

The next morning, early, Katie was on the wagon seat, both hands clutching the iron arm rest, staring straight ahead between the horse's ears. She had had too much of farewells—the absolute farewell to her father, to her mother when she hurried off to marry Herr Gross, to Milly every time she left tearfully for Prague. She had a pain across her shoulders, in her stomach. She felt she could not bear a moment more. She needed to be gone and to forget everything behind her. She thought of the many miles to travel and of this scene getting smaller and smaller until it disappeared behind the horizon of her mind.

Liebe was mechanically giving her last minute instructions as she supervised the placing of the suitcase in the wagon box, but Katie had ceased listening. Her mother had been no farther than Dobrany, what did she know of the great world? Katie was embarking on a journey across Germany, an ocean voyage, a new country. She did not want to hear about keeping a kosher diet, or hiding her money in her petticoat, or even how to find a hospitable rabbi in a strange village. She just wanted to leave.

The moment arrived. One last embrace from her mother, a kiss on Ephraim's solemn face, a despairing thought for Amelia still away at school. Herr Gross bent apologetically over her hand, and then Katie was rattling down the drive and onto the lane. Suddenly, she ordered Dieter to stop. She leaped down, raced across the lawn and into the house. Moments later, she emerged with the white parasol. She opened it, settled it on her shoulder, and skipped back to her seat in the wagon. Its twirling whiteness hid her from view as the wagon turned the last bend in the road. She was twelve years old.

CHAPTER TWELVE

YOUR PARASOL, GRANDMOTHER, HAS RESTED these many years in a pillowslip at the bottom of a garment bag in my closet. I take it out every once in a while to gaze at it and reflect on how it has gotten to San Francisco, California. It is still snowy white, its mechanism works, it is here with me and you are not. It has been a mute observer of your history, and it is now mute in its relationship to your life. I certainly can read nothing in its folds and lace, so I have been unable to imagine your trip across Europe to Germany and the sea. I know it was long and hard, but you shared only a few of those memories with me. We will hurry through those days and deliver your small self to the pier and the entrance to your future.

Katie looked up at the ship towering above the canopied gangplank. It was not a shimmering mansion floating in sky blue water but a rusting factory creaking in a greasy sea. The heavy rain was punctuating the water, and Katie was cold and damp and anxious. She had done two of her labors—she had made it from her cottage to Linz and then by train from Linz to Bremen. If she could just get on this ship, she would have done another. Then remained only America—and what? She did not let herself think so far ahead. She tightened her jaw and looked carefully around the concourse that separated the cobbled street from the pier.

The marble floor was wet from the many boots tracking across it, and travelers were having difficulty with their footing. Little boys in heavy suits and lace-up shoes were running and sliding on the slickness until caught and shaken into decorum. Shouts rose to the rafters and echoed there among the mist and cobwebs. Porters hurried through the crowd, causing jumps and glares from the groups they disturbed with their ponderous carts. There were hours before the ship was to leave, but Katie was unsure of the boarding arrangements. She wandered slowly through the gloom, trying to find some clues to what she must do next. A mother and father and little girl seemed about to board, so she followed them at a distance.

The little girl slipped and would have fallen if her father had not been holding her hand. He swung her to his shoulders, and she laughed and pulled at his moustache. She gathered some fur from his collar into her fist and rode above the crowd. Katie sighed and moved closer. The man took a blue envelope from his pocket and handed it to the little girl. At the foot of the gangplank, she leaned down and showed it to the attendant. He bowed, pointing upward, and the three ascended higher and higher and out of Katie's sight. She looked at her envelope. It was yellow.

The suitcase was heavy and pulled hard on her arm. Katie wanted to put it down, but she made herself walk to the next gangplank before she permitted herself some relief. The press of the crowd was greater here, and Katie watched tearful goodbyes and eager leave-takings as travelers separated themselves from those who had come to say farewell. They mounted the gangway, waving to those below. She looked for their envelopes, but there were so many people she could not see what color they were showing the attendant. Needing desperately to sit down, Katie decided that at the next break in the boarders, she would proffer her ticket at the gangplank. At last, a space opened for her. She stood very straight, smiled at the man, and showed him her envelope. He immediately frowned.

"Back there," he growled, jerking his thumb over his shoulder. "That's where you get on." And he stepped in front of her to greet a laughing young couple holding green tickets. Katie struggled with her valise to get out of the way when she felt a heavy hand on her back. She looked up again into the face of the attendant.

"Wait a minute," he said. "Are you traveling by yourself? We don't let children on this ship alone. You must be running away from home, right? Well, you won't do it on this ship. You won't be able to get on, see. You better go home or you're going to be in trouble." He raised his hand menacingly, but, whatever his intention, he was interrupted by another group ready to board the ship. His face quickly arranged itself into a smile as he turned away.

Katie ran, slipping and sliding across the floor, her suitcase bumping against her leg. Her heart was pounding by the time she found a quiet corner in which to assess this new information. It was a terrible blow. She had traveled alone by train all the way across Germany, sitting up all night on a hard wooden seat. She had eaten sparingly of the kosher food her mother had packed, trying to make it last all the way to Frankfurt. She had found her way alone across that big, ugly city, frightened by its size and noise, buoyed only by her determination. She would not be stopped here, so close to her goal.

She crept closer to the last gangway. This one was merely thick boards bridging the gulf between the pier and the hatchway almost level with it on the ship. Crossing it were women in babushkas, carrying babies. The men, shuffling and bent under heavy bundles, were holding children by the hand. The families were being stopped by the attendant, who took their yellow envelopes and motioned them aboard. There was shouting and much trepidation as the ship rose and fell in the dark water.

Katie took the scarf from around her neck and tied it over her head. She approached the attendant with her ticket in her hand. "Papa, Papa!" she shouted into the empty space ahead. She switched from German to Slovene. "Wait for me!"

"Well, little girl," said the attendant in German. "Where is your father? You're much too little to be traveling alone on this big ship without anyone to take care of you. We'll wait here until your father comes back for you." He took her hand and gently pulled her to his side. She looked up at him, feigning incomprehension even as she suffered a pang at deceiving the first kind person she had met in a week. "Papa, Papa!" she shouted again, and a man far ahead actually turned around. She waved desperately.

"Please let me go." She spoke in Slovene. She sobbed. She loosed the tears of frustration and loneliness she had been holding back for so long. "Here is my yellow ticket, here is my suitcase, and here am I. I can go only forward and I will not let you stand in my way! You must let me get on this ship." She pointed with her free hand at the man disappearing into the shadows at the end of the gangplank, the father from whom she could not be separated. The attendant looked dumbfounded at the flood of words and tears. He reluctantly took Katie's ticket.

"I guess you know your father better than I do." He chuckled at the joke he thought the little girl couldn't understand. "Hurry up, now. Your family will be waiting for you right inside." He smiled, and she put her foot on the swaying boards.

The space she entered was enormous, lit by gas jets high up on the steel walls. It was absolutely empty of anything but the people crowding in. Noise resounded through the bleakness and rose to the balcony far above. Katie could see faces looking down, then lift away to be replaced by others. She hurried to a far corner, put her suitcase down, and sank to the cold floor. She was so tired she could not keep awake. She leaned back against the worn leather of the valise, cradled her parasol in her arms, and fell asleep.

The vibration, the intense noise of the engines slowly penetrated her consciousness, and Katie woke. For frightening moments, she had no idea where she was. The noise was overwhelming, and as she gathered her senses, she marveled that she could have slept so deeply. As her eyes became accustomed to the gloom, she noticed that the throng of people filling the huge space had separated into groups, each gathered around a cooking fire on the metal plates of the deck. Faces were illuminated in the garish glow. Mouths moved, but no separate sounds could be heard above the roar that penetrated her very bones. Grotesque shadows danced on the walls. Steam rose from cooking pots. Katie's stomach heaved, and she turned to the dripping wall. With tremendous effort, she took a deep breath and tightened her jaw.

She turned back and surveyed the scene as it dissolved from her worst imaginings of Hell into simple domesticity. Others, she realized, had arrived equipped with bedrolls, food, and kitchen utensils. She had nothing more practical than the parasol still clutched in her sweaty hands. The food her mother packed had lasted only until yesterday. She had not eaten for almost twenty-four hours. An unbearable longing for home engulfed her. She lifted her strong little chin and pushed away thoughts of the past. She was here and this was now. She had gotten herself on this ship through scheming and temper tantrums. Now her survival depended on knowledge and wits. She became very calm, rose from her place, and looked around.

At first she was confused by the huge crowd, seemingly aimless, random, swaying with the movement of the ship. She shook her head and mentally quartered the hold, then studied the small areas. She saw family groups, some eating, some cooking on braziers, all occupied with claiming a space for themselves in the featureless landscape. There were people of all ages, babes in arms, old babushkas, strong young men. Her eyes swept back and forth, seeking an opportunity, any opportunity to become attached to someone in this mass of humanity. Then she saw a child toddling toward her, fingers in mouth, feet unsteady on the pitching metal floor. Katie ran to her and lifted her up, smelling the sweet milkiness of Ephraim. She murmured in the little girl's ear as she looked around for a worried young mother.

"Ana!" The mother appeared, torn between relief and scolding. Katie looked up and smiled, clutching the baby more tightly.

"I'll take care of her," Katie said. "Please let me help you." She spoke all in a rush. There was too much noise to get involved in a long explanation. "I'll carry her. You must be so tired." Doubt and relief chased themselves across the woman's face. Now the final plea, Katie's brimming eyes attesting to her sincerity. "I have a younger brother that I miss so much." Katie felt a warm hand on her shoulder.

"Come along then. I could use some help." A family circle opened and Katie entered.

Katie sat with Ana and her two older brothers, telling them stories and making them laugh as she inspected their mother and father through her eyelashes. Definitely not Jewish. What were they cooking in the pot that smelled so appetizing? Nothing she could eat, she realized. She had never been in a house that was not kosher, never seen food that was *trafe*, never had even thought about the fact that people who were not Jewish ate differently from her. But she must think about it now. She had jumped too fast when she saw Ana wandering toward her. Now she would just have to die of starvation, causing no end of trouble for this kind family which had befriended her. She sighed, tightened her arms around Ana, closed her eyes.

A sharp hiss interrupted her morbid thoughts, and she looked up into a kind face. This was the sort of face she knew. A Jewish face. A black fur, broad-brimmed hat was square on his head, his graying *payess*—earlocks—swayed at the sides of his head. Four little children clung to the skirts of his long black coat. She struggled to her feet.

"Rebbe! What have I.... What do you...?"

"Little girl." He smiled sweetly. "I have been watching you. Even admiring you. You are going to grow up to be a fine woman. I know this. And I know your present problem. So let me tell you something. God wants you to land in New York fine and healthy. It is all right for you to eat food that is not kosher." He patted the four little heads. "I saw you sleeping in the corner and would have asked you to join our family, to eat with us. But you have taken care of yourself very well. Believe me. It is all right for you to eat the food these fine people are cooking. Eat it and be happy. But just one thing." His face became sad, but his eyes twinkled. "When you chew around the bones, don't take all the meat off. The meat closest to the bone is the most succulent, and God wants that you shouldn't enjoy it too much."

Katie reached for his hand, pressed it to her cheek. "Thank you, rebbe. Oh, thank you."

She watched him walk away until he was lost in the permanent dusk of the hold then turned to the clamoring children.

"Who was that funny man?" they demanded.

"An angel," said Katie. "An angel who has come to take care of us all."

CHAPTER THIRTEEN

THREE WEEKS LATER THE SHIP DOCKED at New York. The steerage passengers, crowded on the lowest deck, marveled at a huge scaffolding in the harbor. The graceful folds of a woman's skirts, gigantic, could be seen through the metal girders. They looked at each other in amazement. Katie heard the whispers.

"It is a statue from France."

"Yes, they call it the Statue of Liberty."

"Is that America?"

"No. It's New York!"

The immensity of it silenced even the most voluble. Katie, hugging Ana, gazed at the skyline coming ever closer, growing ever larger. She had no idea it would be like this. America was supposed to look like Bohemia. And this was only a tiny part of it. A city so big could only be part of a country that was unimaginable. She was aware that the ship railing came all the way to her chin, that she had to look up to see faces, that she was surrounded by elbows and bosoms, that she was small. She looked at Ana, and the little girl gazed solemnly back. "What have we gotten ourselves into?" she whispered into the pink ear. And had no answer.

Slowly, slowly, the city became separate shapes, the shapes revealed facades and windows, then all was swallowed by masts and sails and great billows of dark smoke. For hours, the great field of steerage passengers was winnowed by uniformed inspectors until they became as they were when they had boarded—frightened, separate, anonymous. They shuffled across the greasy water from ship to pier, some gazing back over their shoulders at the hold, as though they were once again leaving their countries, their homes.

Katie was smothered in kisses by Ana's mother, by the two older children, by the young father. She hugged Ana until the little girl squealed. They had no addresses to exchange, no promises to make. In the end, Katie watched them walk away, laden by their bundles, cross the gangplank, and disappear into the dark cavern of the pier.

She squared her shoulders once again and tucked the parasol under her arm. She was waved off the ship by an inspector and stood under the vast roof of the concourse. Her legs unsteady, she stood swaying as the crowd eddied around her. Here were more men pushing heavy carts laden with luggage, here were laughter and shouts as women in furs embraced travelers coming down the gangways, here were officials frowning at her indecision. She stood there a long time. The tumult slowly subsided, late-comers hurried their friends out to the taxis, here and there a shout from a porter, then only shadowy groups too far away to hear. The old ship loomed behind her. Far away was the door to America, lit by the sunlight reflecting from the cobblestones.

A figure detached itself from the dimness. He spoke in German. "Is there anything I can do to help you?"

Katie had noticed this man earlier. He had been watching her, moving when she moved. At first she was frightened, but as she watched him walk toward her, he became a more friendly figure. He had a nice face, and the mouth under the gray drooping moustache was smiling. He was old, older than her father would be, and his blue eyes were steady and kind. She let him carry her case to a bench where she sat down with a sigh.

"I often meet the boats," he said in German. "Maybe I'll find somebody from home, maybe I can help someone." He gestured at the groups still walking aimlessly about. "So many people with no place to rest or feed their children. I can usually find them somewhere to go until they know what they want."

Katie looked into his face. Something soothing and familiar looked back at her. She wanted to climb into his lap, put her head on his shoulder, and let him take care of her. She was tired and her stomach did lurch so.

"Most people don't know what it's like here." He had switched to Slovene, hoping her face would brighten with understanding. It didn't. She was beyond surprises. "They think it's going to be like the old country." Another smile. "I try to help them."

His voice trailed off, and they sat in silence.

Finally he said, "Do you have a place to go?" Katie shook her head miserably. Another silence.

"Tell me about yourself. Where have you come from and why are you here all alone and so little?"

Katie's mind was so awhirl with new impressions, decisions, disappointment, and hope that she had a hard time speaking. Her German and Slovene mixed up together, spluttered, stopped. She looked into the blue eyes and began again, more slowly.

She told him everything, encouraged by his grave look. She told him about the brewery and the geese, the parasol and Ephraim, about the piano in the parlor, about the black horse and her father. Her lips trembled, but she forged on. Now Herr Gross and the sons. Now Amelia and her mother and Grete. Then all in a rush across the ocean. And now, here she sat, with her fists in her lap and no place to go.

The man sat fingering his long moustache and looking at her. Bars of sunshine lay long across the pier. Sounds reached them slowly through the late afternoon silence. He seemed overcome by great emotion and searched through his pockets for a large white handkerchief, with which he wiped his eyes. Then he took Katie by the elbows and stood her up before him.

"I am your Uncle Jacob. Yes, it is I. I was called to the war when your father and his father—my father...." He paused. "My father wanted to play a trick on the Hapsburgs." He smiled wryly at the joke. "It would not have been good to have two Jacobs in the family, so I was packed off to America. Adolph, your dear father, became Jacob in the army and I am Jacob here in America. Ach, it's probably too much for you to understand. But do you understand? Come. Look at me. What do you see?"

Katie gazed at him in wonder. She knew the story of her father's war. She had loved hearing the adventures told and retold. She had admired his black uniform, now in her mother's trunk, had fingered its bright buttons. Here was her father's face grown older, the blue eyes, the curly blond hair now grayed. She flung her arms around Jacob's neck and he lifted her in his arms, twirling her round and round.

"I come here to find people from the old village," he exulted. "But now I have found someone from the old family!" He laughed aloud and held her off to look at her. "You will come home with me now. I have a store and a good wife. You will be happy with your new family, you'll see. We'll take good care of you." He gathered up her trunk and parasol and held his free hand out to her.

Katie hesitated, trying to foresee what might befall her if she trusted this man. In a breath's time she imagined death, dishonor, and betrayal. But that was what she had fled, and she knew that none of that awaited her in this big country of America. She put her hand in his, and her Uncle Jacob took her to Castle Gardens, New Jersey.

CHAPTER FOURTEEN

My grandmother, Katie Reiter, told me that story just as I wrote it for you. Do you believe it? I do. Every word. Great journeys always have about them some element of magic, else how could they be accomplished? Think of Lewis and Clark finding Sacajawea. Think of Stanley finding Livingston. Think of Phineas Fogg finding Passepartout. All of these travelers required a miracle, and Katie, also, could not have continued if Uncle Jacob had not materialized. Not only in the right place, but at the right time. So Katie stepped farther into her future, with her little hand in her uncle's calloused one.

Katie pushed her heavy dark hair into a bun at the back of her head as she peered into the mirror. Her face gazed back at her in smudges and dislocations from the grayed old glass, but she could see that she was thin and haggard. Castle Gardens was not the paradise of her imagination. It was dirty and gray and noisy, full of Jews just off the boat like herself. She was the only help besides his wife that Uncle Jacob had in his little store, and Katie was awake every night until past eleven o'clock because Uncle Jacob insisted that the streets be empty of any potential customer before she locked up and turned out the lights. Every night for five years she slept on a cold and rigid pallet behind the counter.

She was up before dawn to sweep the store and arrange the boxes and cans on the shelves. She was in the store all day, to wait on customers or await their arrival. The store was a small grocery on a dingy street in Castle Gardens, not the great emporium she had imagined when she met her uncle on the New York dock. Aunt Reiter was uncle's wife, and who knew what her given name was. Reiter was her last name and, in the custom of the time, it became her first name when she married. Aunt Reiter and Uncle Jacob lived in the back room, ate there, slept there. Their life was the store, and they expected it to be Katie's life, too, for they paid her nothing in return for her hard work. Aunt Reiter had grumbled and cast beseeching looks heavenward when Jacob appeared with his young niece, but she had appreciated quickly the work that could be gotten out of the girl. *The girl.* Aunt Reiter called her nothing else. Aunt's complaining had not ceased, but it had been reduced to more subtle indications that Katie was in her home on sufferance and could be told to leave at a moment's notice. "Another mouth to feed," was her welcome.

Katie accepted this situation with unaccustomed meekness. She appreciated her good fortune in finding her uncle. What would have happened to her had he not met the immigrant ships in the harbor? She listened and learned in the store, quickly understanding the Yiddish that most of the customers spoke, though she pretended not to. It was close to the German she brought with her from Bohemia, where Yiddish was considered undignified and sloppy. Katie did not wish to lose her dignity.

The money was a little more difficult, but she was proud that she had never made even a penny's mistake. Aunt Reiter counted the money each hour and let it be known that any discrepancy would be deducted from the amount of food Katie got at her stingy table. If the little bell over the door in the store rang while they were at supper, it was Katie who went to see what was wanted. When she returned, the table was usually cleared and Aunt Reiter washing up with a grim, triumphant look on her face.

For the first year, Katie's world had been what she could see through the fly-specked window and what she saw up and down the street before she closed the store at night. Her presence enabled Aunt Reiter and Uncle Jacob to be away from the store occasionally, but Katie was never invited to join them. She was just as glad, for during the hours of their absences she would stand outside in the sunshine and revel in being in America with her future ahead of her. Outwardly, she was docile and accommodating; inside she was once again scheming.

"The first thing is to go to school." She smiled as she remembered Empress Maria Theresa. That great woman had not ever imagined that one of her beneficiaries would be thinking of her on the streets of the New World. Katie sought information as she chatted casually with customers. On these occasions, she was not too proud to speak Yiddish.

"Oh, Frau Gerstien, what a darling little girl. Does she go to school?" Of course. And there is a school on the next block. "Pauli!

You are such a bright little boy. Here is an apple for you to take to your teacher." Aunt Reiter would have a fit! "Tell me, what do you learn in school?" Why, English, of course, and other things like adding and history and music. "Herr Klinkov, you must be so proud of your son. But, tell me, how will it be when he can speak English and you cannot?" Don't be silly. I learn English, too, but I go at night from work. "Mrs. Pavel, you have so many children! Surely it is expensive to send them all to school." My dear, here in America school is free.

Free! School is free! English is free! What a wonderful country!

Katie bided her time as she gauged her aunt's attitude toward her. When, after another year, she had coaxed a grudging smile from the dour woman, Katie began her campaign. If only someone in the store could speak English, she pleaded, their clientele could expand beyond the Jewish immigrants. If only someone in the store could read English, the bargains in the trade papers would be available to them. If only someone in the store could write English, negotiations with the jobbers would be so much easier. Katie sighed. Soon Aunt Reiter and Uncle Jacob were sighing with her. The next year Katie was in night school.

Aunt Reiter allowed Katie five minutes to run the two blocks to the school and five minutes after school was finished to run back to the store. Uncle Jacob was waiting for her, watch in hand, when she flew home late each night. But a rich experience was encapsulated in her few hours of freedom. She was avid for information, hungry for words and meanings, impatient with those unable to match her speed. Though it was forbidden, old Professor Horowitz allowed her to take books home at night. And, though it was forbidden, she kept the gas light on in the store until the early hours of the morning while she studied. The occasional customer who wandered in for a bottle of milk or a physic was dazzled by her smile of gratitude, for it allowed Katie to show her aunt an extra coin in the morning they would not have had except for the solitary beacon glimmering through the night in the squalid New Jersey street.

In three years, Katie was fluent in English and adept at all her other subjects. Her pronunciation was almost perfect, with only the trace of an accent soft and sweet behind her speech. She shared her knowledge with Aunt Reiter and Uncle Jacob and stood proudly with them when they all became citizens on Katie's sixteenth birthday.

The new customers never materialized, goods became no cheaper, the wholesalers were just as difficult, but a change was wrought in the little grocery store and it arrived in the person of Herr Horowitz, Katie's teacher.

Flustered at seeing him in an unaccustomed setting, Katie was struck silent when he walked into the grocery store. He tipped his hat.

"I am so glad you are here, Katie," he said, as though she had ever been anywhere else. "I have brought you a few old books that you may keep for your own." He laid a large package on the counter. "I will leave you to sort through them if you will introduce me to your aunt." Astonished, Katie led him through the curtains into the dim back room. Her aunt was chopping vegetables for soup.

"Aunt Reiter!" Katie found her lost voice, but now it was too loud. German or English? or Yiddish? Katie realized she had never introduced anyone in her entire life. Deep breath.

"Aunt Reiter, I want you to meet Herr Professor Horowitz, my teacher from the gymnasium—from school." That sour penurious woman turned on Herr Horowitz a look of such graciousness and welcome that Katie felt for the first time a rush of affection for her aunt. She excused herself quickly and spent the next hour, elbows on the scarred counter, poring over her new books. Twice she was interrupted by shoppers announced by the bell over the door, but she served them quickly and returned to the beloved volumes that were about to be her only personal possessions. She even forgot to be curious about Herr Horowitz's visit.

Finally, Herr Horowitz opened the curtains, and Aunt Reiter followed him into the store. She was smiling, actually smiling, and they both looked at Katie. Aunt Reiter and the old teacher shook hands, and she accompanied him through the door and out to the sidewalk, bending her head attentively to his low voice. When she returned, she was rubbing her hands in satisfaction.

"A very nice man," she said. "No wonder you learned so quickly." Her smile faded as she noticed the books open on the counter. "Get to work." She disappeared through the curtains, and the sounds of chopping began again.

That night, as Katie tossed and wriggled on the hard pallet behind the counter trying to get comfortable, she heard the voices of Aunt Reiter and Uncle Jacob in unaccustomed conversation. Her voice was steady, but his rose and fell in surprise and anger. Finally he was soothed, and the talk trailed off into the darkness. Over their meager breakfast, Aunt Reiter told Katie that Herr Professor Horowitz had wanted to arrange a marriage for her. Katie gasped. She had never thought of this method of escaping the dreary Newark grocery. She looked expectantly at Jacob, but he stared down at his coffee, unable to meet Katie's eyes.

"But of course I told him no," Aunt Reiter said. "Why should you marry outside the family when I have seven nephews." She smiled proudly. "They are seven brothers. Can you imagine? One of them will do for you. And then you can live here. Jacob and I can move nearby. I will get in touch with my nephew Benjamin immediately. He can probably make arrangements because he's too young to be thinking of marriage himself. We'll see. I wonder I never thought of this. It will work out perfectly."

Within a week, Aunt Reiter had an announcement. "Benjamin Reiter will arrive tonight to talk over arrangements," Aunt Reiter said. "Which brother will do for you, your lack of dowry...." Here she shot a look of significance at her husband. She didn't want him doing something foolishly generous. "We will close the store when he comes." Close the store! This was a shock as great as the announcement of her impending marriage. Katie felt her temper heating and rose from her chair to declare her independence. She would no longer be treated as merchandise, nights on the floor, days pottering among shelves and barrels, and now being sold to a middleman at a private sale.

She banged the pots on the stove as she poured herself another cup of tea. Katie knew this would bring a frown to Aunt Reiter's face. Wait, a small voice inside her counseled. At least see this nephew. Maybe he would want to run away with her. Maybe he had a castle, or a house, or a farm, or maybe just a room on the other side of Castle Gardens. Anything would do. She was beginning to look forward to the evening. When she turned, cup in hand, her face was demure and grateful. She looked around the little room with satisfaction. There was no place to banish her from their presence. She would be here to see this man, this Benjamin Reiter, and listen to what he had to say.

CHAPTER FIFTEEN

THAT NIGHT BENJAMIN JOSEPH REITER CAME TO CALL. The store was closed at seven o'clock, an unprecedented hour. On the oilcloth-covered table were a candle, a teapot, lump sugar in a bowl, and sweet cakes that Aunt Reiter had made. Uncle Jacob had a tie under his stiff collar and was constantly pulling it away from his neck, popping out the collar buttons and getting annoyed looks from his wife. Katie peered once more into the cracked mirror and sighed over her pallor. Nothing more could be done with her thick hair, already escaping from its bun, but, with a guilty glance at her aunt, she pinched some color into her cheeks. There, that was the best she could do.

Her linen dress, lengthened and let out, was one she had brought with her from Bohemia. Her only shoes, new two years ago for some-one else, were a gift from her uncle, bought at a second-hand store last year. Thank goodness the nephew would not be able to see her petti-coats and stockings, darned and patched and threadbare. Katie turned at last from her reflection, dissatisfied but a-tingle with the excitement of this change in routine and the further changes it might bring.

Katie sat down at the table with her aunt and uncle. She folded her hands in her lap and stared down at them. All was silent in the little room except for the sputter of the candle and the creak of the chair as Aunt Reiter leaned forward every now and then to test the heat of the teapot.

At last the knock came at the door, and the bell rattled from its force. Jacob jumped, then rose and went through the locked and dark-ened store to admit the visitor. Katie allowed herself to look up through her eyelashes as Mr. Reiter was introduced to Jacob.

"My nephew, B.J. Reiter," Aunt Reiter said with pride in her voice. There was no mention of Katie's name, nor was her presence acknowledged. She listened to the talk of Henry Reiter, B.J.'s brother, whose future would be offered to Katie. Henry had excellent prospects, he was kind, he had a job in the steel mills, he desired to have a nice home.

Katie learned of her own lack of a dowry—Aunt Reiter had not invested any money in Katie's past and would certainly have none available for her future—but Katie's strength and willingness for hard work would make up for that deficiency. Aunt Reiter smiled reassuringly. Katie's thrift and knowledge of English were extolled. Her needlework was praised, her cooking eulogized. Aunt Reiter had never allowed her even to boil an egg. Katie was enjoying the charade immensely.

The interview came to an end, and the last cake was eaten. Benjamin Reiter turned to her, and she scrambled from her seat to make the curtsy Aunt Reiter had demanded from her. But Mr. Reiter had her hand and pulled her up from the foolish gesture.

"You are very pretty," he said as his moustache touched the back of her wrist. Katie's face flamed and she backed away, grateful for the scraping of chairs and the confusion as the three negotiators made their way back through the store.

Nobody had told her she was pretty since Adolph had died. Henry Reiter. Katie repeated the name as she dreamily cleared the table. Pretty, she murmured as she blew out the candle. She hoped the proffered Henry would look like his brother Benjamin—tall, straight, blond. And the drooping moustache. She felt it tingle again on her arm. Her misgivings fled. She would willingly marry, and she would be a good wife. Her quiet observations and harsh judgments of her Aunt Reiter had given her some idea of what a happy home could be. Not like this, never like this, but a place of light and laughter, of smiles and conversation, of children and plentiful food, and friends welcome to call.

She remembered her childhood, before her father had been killed. Her parents loved touching each other, their fingertips lingering on shoulders and hair. She had heard their laughter at night, after she had gone to bed. Though there were few visitors, the kitchen afforded food to the peasants who came to the door for their work orders, and it always smelled luxuriously sweet and rich. Katie drew in her breath.

Her imagination admitted Henry, looking very much like Benjamin Joseph, into a gas-lit parlor where a chubby baby cooed on the rug before the cheerful fire. She, in pearl gray embroidered with flowers, lifted her cheek to be kissed. A log snapped. A cup crashed at

Katie's feet. She bent to gather the pieces as Aunt Reiter berated her clumsiness.

But Aunt Reiter's heart was not in the reproach. Katie could see that she was relieved that the meeting had gone well. The nephew was presentable, even good-looking. He was well-dressed, well-spoken. The family of her cousins had some future, she said. Unlike Katie. They were ambitious, they were well recommended. Aunt Reiter wanted to strike a deal as soon as possible. Uncle Jacob sat silently at the table, listening to his wife go on and on with an animation he had not witnessed for more than thirty years. He hadn't realized the depth of her dislike for Katie, how anxious she was to have Katie out of her sight. And he was just beginning to realize how important Katie was to him, the only link to his own family, the only cheerful face he saw in his long days.

Aunt Reiter was now inventing attributes for the unknown Henry Reiter, painting a rosy future for any wife he would choose, but when she found herself extolling Katie's virtues as that possible wife, she stopped.

"Go to bed." She nodded curtly to her niece.

Katie rolled herself into the *dachana* behind the counter. Once again, the cold joined the voices in the other room to keep her awake. "But he's a Hungarian," she heard her uncle say, "don't do this to the girl." Her aunt's snort finished the conversation, and Katie slept.

The next day proceeded as though nothing of import had taken place. Katie was puzzled. Had she dreamed the appearance of Benjamin Joseph Reiter? Was she about to be married to his brother Henry? What if she desired the marriage and her aunt and uncle did not? Or what if she refused? She began to perceive that she herself had no choices. Where could she go if she defied her relatives? There was apparently to be no discussion with her. Aunt Reiter would make up her mind, Uncle Jacob would agree with some show of reluctance, and Katie would comply. She felt ill with the enormity of it all and with her helplessness to determine her own future. Staying in the grocery store was bleak beyond belief. She refused to imagine a life of standing behind this counter all day and sleeping behind it every night. But, for a girl like her, the future could be determined only by *mishpocheh*—relatives—marriage, or a miracle.

Katie smiled wanly at her little joke. Alliteration, she thought automatically, and then remembered Herr Professor Horowitz. Who was the young man he wanted her to marry? What would her future have been like with him? Life was very much a minute-by-minute business, she thought, and not the dramatic tableaux that made the novels she read so compelling. She was confused, torn between mute misery and elation that needed a voice. She longed for her mother, or even Amelia, to share this moment in her life when so much was about to happen.

A week passed during which her aunt seemed only very much the same and her uncle even more timorous. Katie was beginning to think that perhaps marriage offers were a more frequent occurrence in the lives of young girls than she had thought and that Aunt Reiter was awaiting another suitor. She was drowsing over her late dinner when the bell sounded in the grocery store. Aunt Reiter looked at her. Sighing, Katie pushed her chair from the table and entered the store, to encounter Benjamin Reiter.

He removed his hat and smiled at her. "Wait," he said. "I want to speak to you before we see your aunt and uncle." He pushed aside some cans and boxes and seated himself in the window, motioning her to follow him. Wonderingly, she did so.

His blue eyes were sparkling with excitement. "I know you were listening to me speak to your aunt and uncle, even though you were quiet as a little mouse in your corner."

He glanced at the curtained doorway. "Let us speak in English. And if they're listening, maybe they won't understand so quickly. What I want to say to you is this. My brother Henry is a fine fellow and all the things I said he was. He has good prospects and will be a success. But the truth is he stutters." Benjamin grinned apologetically. It was the only bad thing he could think of to say about his brother. He hurried on. "My prospects are as good as his. I'm a hard worker, I can support a wife. Marry ME, Katie."

He began to laugh. "I know this is not how things are done. But we have at least seen each other, and here in America we are free to choose. Say yes to me, and I will talk to your aunt." Katie, even in her confusion, noted the omission of her uncle.

Katie's mind raced. If she agreed with Benjamin to marry him, no one could stop her. She would be asking not for permission but for a blessing. No dowry was at stake, no exchange of money. The only sacrifice made by Aunt Reiter would be the control of Katie's life. This was an intoxicating thought. But how could she know if Benjamin would be able to take care of her? What would his future be like? How could she make this decision by herself? She gazed at him under her straight brows, then laughed at her thoughts. Aunt Reiter didn't know the answers to any of these questions either. Nor, for that matter, did Benjamin Joseph Reiter. His answering smile, his white teeth, his blue eyes and soft moustache dissolved all practical considerations. She had felt that soft moustache on her hand. She felt it tingle there again.

She put that remembering hand on his. "What my aunt said about me was not true," she said. "I'm not a good cook or housekeeper. I didn't get to practice those things here. But I know arithmetic and I can read and write three languages and I work hard. If we remember that we made this choice ourselves, and if we try to make each other happy we can have a good life together." Katie spoke slowly and quietly, mindful of the sullen pair behind the curtain, who were probably wondering where she was. Then she lifted her hand to her mouth to smother a giggle. "Now what do we do?"

Benjamin leaned toward her and kissed her softly on the cheek. "Leave the rest to me. I've been planning what to say to your aunt for a week. I know I can convince her to say yes." He shrugged. "And if I can't, you can leave with me tonight. My landlady will let you stay with her until we can be married."

Katie parted the curtains with her free hand, the other being tightly held by Benjamin. The look of shock on her aunt's face raised in her heart a song of triumph.

CHAPTER SIXTEEN

THE MARRIAGE TOOK PLACE three weeks later in the small *shul* around the corner from the grocery store. Katie and Benjamin sat on a hard bench awaiting their turn with other young couples, mostly immigrants like themselves. Aunt Reiter and Jacob sat with them, she with her mouth turned down, he gazing straight ahead with a gnarled hand on each knee. The room was silent, but the occupants were stealing furtive looks at each other, comparing what they had with what they saw. A hand would come up to a mouth, whispers would be exchanged, a blush appeared, there was a quick laugh.

Katie was content with the young man by her side. Benjamin Reiter—BJ he liked to be called—was by far the handsomest man in the room. His hair was bright and curled over his collar, his eyes were blue and full of fun, and his skin was smooth. She had shyly touched his face once or twice and was thrilled.

But much as she tried to concentrate on the moment, on BJ, on the enormity of the occasion, Katie was filled with longing for her mother. Though she was surrounded by evidence to the contrary, she felt that marriages were not meant to be celebrated in dingy anterooms of ugly buildings in squalid cities.

She had seldom let herself think of her life in the old country—*the old country*, what a perfect phrase. She wanted to banish those memories as not serving any purpose, as *being* old and therefore disposable. But, unbidden, they formed in her mind like clouds taking shape in a summer sky. The green lawn of the estate near Aperius spread across her consciousness, speckled with clover, and she, grown up, walked across it on the arm of her father, youthful and handsome as he was on the last day of his life. She could almost feel his rough sleeve under her arm, and the warmth of his nearness caused her mouth to tremble. She could see her mother, slim and young, waiting for her, arms opened wide, under the old tree. Katie's skin prickled with anticipation of the embrace, and she leaned forward on the hard bench.

"Not yet," BJ said, "we still have to wait." He patted the pocket that held the license and looked into her face, still radiant from her thoughts. "There are two more ahead of us."

The ceremony, swift, impersonal, the rabbi smelling of garlic and neglect, took only a few minutes and they were out in the watery sunshine again, no different from before yet unalterably changed. Set up on the sidewalk was a camera on a tripod. A plaid-coated man accosted the couples as they descended the steps.

"Hey! D'ya wanna pitchur of the lucky day?"

"Oh, BJ! A picture! Please let's have a picture to send to my mother."

BJ stopped, embarrassed. He had exactly enough money for the license, the rabbi, a small dinner for the four of them, and a hansom cab back to his boarding house. He was loathe to give up the hansom. It was the only aspect of the day that would satisfy his sense of elegance, that would mark this day as special and different.

"I'm so sorry, Katie. I never thought about a picture. And I don't have—I didn't bring—there isn't—" He looked expectantly at Aunt Reiter and Uncle Jacob. She was stonily inspecting the horizon. Uncle Jacob shrugged and gazed over BJ's shoulder.

"Never mind," Katie said. "It's all right. We can do it later and pretend it was the same day. My mother won't have to know she's seeing an old married couple instead of newly-weds." She smiled up at him, tucked her arm in his for the first time, and moved him toward her uncle and aunt. "Let's have our wedding feast and go home." She tasted the last word in her mouth. It was the first time she had used it in five years.

Katie thought often of the wedding picture for her mother in the following months, happy months for the most part. They lived in BJ's boarding house, his tidy room overwhelming her with its light, space, and privacy. Oh, the ineffable joy of having a door to close on the world, a chair to read in, a lamp that she alone controlled, a soft warm bed to share with love.

They ate at a long table with the other boarders in the dining room of the large house. She was bashful for many weeks, responding only with a warm smile to the gentle teasing, content to listen to the animated conversation around her. Silent meals in the windowless back room of the grocery store had buried the memory of the lively kitchen in Bohemia. There, her childish enthusiasms had been accorded attention and respect, at least while her father was alive. Now, as she glanced from one boarder to another, she realized that she comprehended the heavy matters being discussed with many accents. Her early education had given her a critical nature. —Thank you, Maria Theresa—and Herr Professor Horowitz had provided her with books and a curiosity about the world. She read the American papers every day, and, though she participated only in her head, she followed the heated political arguments at dinner with great interest.

Though she had really nothing to do, her days were full. She woke to watch BJ dressing every morning. She loved inspecting him as he washed and shaved and put on his clothes. There was no place in the little room to hide. He had from their first night together appeared naked in front of her in so unabashed a manner that she was able to watch him with frank appreciation. He was lean and strong from his physical work in the Newark mills and, returning begrimed and greasy late at night, seemed to her like a work of art in the sputtering gaslight.

Katie was not quite so bold as her new husband. She dressed and undressed in the closet and stayed under the quilt until he left her for work each morning with a kiss on her mouth and a whistle from below the window. She then bathed—a real bathtub down the hall—tidied their room, and set herself to improving his neglected wardrobe with buttons, darns, and mendings.

She spent time with the other women in the boarding house, her spirit expanding like a bud under their warmth and interest. And once every afternoon, Katie flung herself on the bed in the silence of her very own room and gazed happily at the ceiling. She lay spread out like a starfish on the counterpane, sighing deeply and watching the sunshine dancing above her head. Every minute away from the grocery, away from Aunt Reiter and Uncle Jacob, increased her contentment.

She roused herself from these quiet moments and, arms outstretched, revolved in slow circles around the room, touching BJ's hairbrush, clattering her fingernails on the window-glass, making faces at herself in the clear mirror as it moved across her orbit. At seventeen, Katie felt her life was complete. Except for the wedding picture, she had everything she wanted.

The wedding picture was taken a year later, when Katie was four months pregnant. She no longer fit into the dress she was married in. Instead, she wore the first dress bought just for her since she had arrived in America. It was brown silk, with black braid trimming and a frogged panel down the front that covered what should have been her small waist. She didn't write to her mother that she was expecting a baby. It was enough to announce her marriage. The other news could wait for the next letter.

In fact, there was a great deal of other news. Katie and BJ were about to move from Newark to McKeesport, Pennsylvania. A man with six brothers gets to hear of many opportunities, and BJ had learned through this network that there was property in McKeesport, Pennsylvania, to be had cheap. His brothers suggested that BJ move there, buy a downtown lot with money they would find for him, and build a commercial building with an apartment in it for himself. It was a chance to step up, to become an owner of land, a landlord. BJ couldn't resist the idea and hurried them through the packing.

"We must seize the opportunity," he whispered in Katie's ear each night to quell their apprehension. "I don't want to work in a steel mill all my life. This will be the right thing, you'll see. We'll pretend we're going to Jerusalem. A trip to Jerusalem. And only good things happen there."

They took the train to Pittsburgh, then a trolley to nearby McKeesport. BJ left Katie in the gritty trolley shed while he searched for a rooming house. She sat drowsing among their belongings in the spring warmth of the station, her hands folded across her stomach. When BJ returned he laughed at her.

"You look like a little chimney-sweep," he said. "Your face is dirty. In fact, you're dusty all over, as if I had left you on the shelf for months."

Katie stood and brushed herself off, although it wasn't dust but actual grime that stained her clothes and his, too. "Let's get out of this dirty place," she said.

They trudged the few blocks to the boarding house he had found, he with a box on his shoulders and one in his hand. Katie carried her father's suitcase and the white parasol. Even it was suddenly dirty. She frowned. Her heaviness made it difficult to walk very fast. She wished she were in the bathtub in Newark.

They settled quickly into the furnished room and ate dinner at a cheap restaurant around the corner. Weary to the bone, they fell into bed. But there was little sleep for them that night, their real introduction to McKeesport, the Steel City. Alarmed by the reddish light crossing the ceiling, they rushed to the window to see if there were a fire nearby. The sight that greeted them was a view from Hell. Across the Monongahela River, huge smokestacks were belching black smoke and flames, great clouds against the red sky. Flames leaped at regular intervals as trainloads of waste were dumped on ever-growing mountains of slag. The sky heaved with flashes of orange reflecting from the smoke and clouds. The hills around them brightened like day for a moment, then slid back into darkness. They noticed for the first time an odor in the air that offended their nostrils and throats. *Loki!* Katie thought, remembering the Teutonic legends. This is a scene from the Underworld.

The noise they had attributed to a busy city during the day was even more intense at night as the monstrous furnaces moaned and grumbled. Soft soot was falling on their faces, their bare arms, on the windowsill. They looked at each other, appalled.

"How can anyone live here? It's horrible. Can anything stay clean? Can anyone sleep?"

Another spurt of fire illuminated them clearly. BJ's eyes were wide. "No wonder land is so cheap here. Who would want it?" They looked at each other questioningly. "Let's try to sleep. Tomorrow I'll see about the property and find out about getting a job in the mill until the building is ready. If I don't get good answers, we'll go back to Newark."

Katie smiled wearily. "I guess it wouldn't be right to pray for bad luck," she said.

CHAPTER SEVENTEEN

KATIE RAISED THE BOTTOM HALF OF THE WINDOW next to her chair. The soot had arranged itself in rivulets after the recent rain. Even the windowsill had splashes of soot. She washed her hands and picked up her embroidery. She was making a jacket for the baby, a gray jacket. She knew she could never manage anything white in grimy McKeesport. She had bought cheap odds and ends from the draper. The richness would be in her perfect stitches, the love with which she worked. She sighed often in contentment, happy in the warmth of the sun, the comfort of the chair, the intimacy of her own room.

BJ was seldom there. He left before midnight to work his ten-hour shift at the Carnegie Steel Mill, ten hours of back-breaking work, dangerous, dark. He labored, bare to the waist, in the intense heat of the blast furnaces. The mill was lit only by the glare of the furnaces, huge monsters requiring constant feeding by the stokers. He was one of a line of men with shovels of coal who moved toward the blazing maw. They tossed in their shovels-full, unable to bear for more than a minute the searing heat. Then they went back for more coal. The line was endless. As the shifts changed, exhausted men dropped out and fresh ones moved in, faceless, nameless to all but themselves.

When a hoarse shout was heard, the line dissolved, each man searching in panic for the snakes of white steel that could sizzle across the floor, escaped from the extruder that shaped them into wires and coils. The wires snapped about from the sudden cooling, able to take off a leg in an instant, to burn the skin, to flick out an eye. When this happened, the foreman would rush in to remove the injured man, fire him, and send him home on a makeshift stretcher. The friends who bore him bleeding to his stricken family were docked their pay for the time they spent away from the insatiable furnaces.

BJ had his place in this line seven days a week, ten hours a day. He came back to the boarding house, weary, before noon, to begin the real work of his day, putting a building on the lot on Market Street.

After a bath and a meal, he took the streetcar to "The Place" and joined the crew that would provide his escape from the mill.

The plan was to build a three-floor structure on the narrow lot. The lowest level would be a store with living quarters in the back. Katie could not repress a shudder as she pictured her Uncle Jacob's dark establishment and the even darker rooms behind. The second floor would be their new home. Katie's imagination flooded this area with light and laughter from the beautiful children with which she and BJ would produce. The top floor would be another apartment, into which Katie mentally moved a handsome young couple just like themselves.

The building was already framed. BJ, less interested in lawns and gardens than rentals, decided to put a long, low building at the back to house unmarried mill workers in small, unconnected rooms. These were called "cribs" in the construction business, he explained to Katie. Each crib would have its own door to the outside, and a washroom would be at the end, together with three privies for the tenants of the larger building.

The crib building, although cheap to build and promising more income, threw into disarray BJ's careful financial planning. He and his brothers had figured to the penny the amount of money it would take to pay for the land, to employ the workers, and to provide material, while still having enough left to maintain BJ and Katie in the boarding house. BJ knew the wisdom of the quarters at the back of the lot but, even with his job at the mill, was falling farther and farther behind in the payments he was obliged to make to Mr. Kraus, the mortgage holder.

Without Katie's knowledge, he had looked for a cheaper boarding house but had found nothing that would justify a longer and more expensive journey on the streetcar. He considered using cheaper materials in his buildings but discarded the idea as false economy. Cheaper material would result in expensive repairs later. Hiring fewer workmen would merely delay completion.

Reluctantly, he concluded that the money to build the men's dormitory would have to come out of the payments he was making on the land. Each month he had subtracted a small amount from those payments, and now he was more than a month behind.

The gaslight over the little table was turned low, so that Katie could sleep as BJ pored over the entries in his payment book. He had only recently returned from his work at The Place and would have only a few hours of sleep before it was midnight and he had to go to the mill. He supported his heavy head on one hand as he added and subtracted figures, unable to make them come out differently. A letter from Mr. Kraus lay before him, warning that the property would be repossessed if a second payment were missed. BJ could imagine the little man's glee in taking back a property with two almost finished buildings. His head ached.

"Please come to bed, BJ," Katie whispered. "You need to get some rest."

He looked over his shoulder, barely able to make out her form on the bed. His plan for keeping Mr. Kraus at bay involved her, and he was consumed by shame and guilt. He had no idea how to broach the subject. He had put it off too long, had not shared with Katie any of his difficulties, and tomorrow was the day he must put his plan into effect. As he rehearsed this approach and that, his guilt changed to resentment, resentment at the mill owners who worked him so hard for so little money, resentment at Mr. Kraus who recognized his trust-worthiness but was unwilling to extend credit, resentment finally at his wife and unborn baby who had changed him from a carefree young man to an exhausted debtor.

Unable to resist the heat of his unreasoning anger, BJ strode to the bed and stood over Katie, his fists clenched.

"It's about time you helped me with some of this." His voice was low and hoarse. They were always aware of others sleeping behind the thin walls. "I'm going to lose the land if I don't do something."

He hurried on, avoiding her bewildered look. "Getting this building up is the most important thing now. Whatever we have to do must be done. It doesn't matter what we think or feel about it. You're the only one who can help me."

Katie eased her body into a sitting position. BJ had never talked to her about the land. She had actually seen it only once, her pregnancy having forced her close to home in consideration of the delicate feelings of others. BJ had been so hard-pressed with his labor at the mill and his work at The Place, he had been with her only to eat and sleep. Her few thoughts about The Place had been fervent wishes that it be finished so that he would be once again the engaging companion of the early months of their marriage.

"What can I do, I have nothing." Katie felt tears rising. "Oh, BJ, you're angry now that I didn't have a dowry. But it's too late to go back. Uncle Jacob doesn't have anything either."

"No, no. It's nothing like that," BJ said impatiently. He had forgotten that he never told her of his finances or the complicated arrangements he had made to pay off the property and erect the building. "Listen to me. We're in trouble with the payments on the land. That land is important to us, to you and me. It's the only thing that will get me out of the mill. Listen to me! Do you know what it means that possession is nine-tenth of the law?" Katie looked at him in astonishment. Was BJ losing his mind with all the work and worry?

"We've got to take possession of the building, be there, live there. Without the expense here, we can pay Mr. Kraus a little bit each month, enough to hold him off for a while until we finish. Then, when we rent the store, we'll pay him everything we owe." Katie noticed the new use of "we" and BJ's avoidance of her eyes. There was more to come and it will be worse, she thought.

"If you sit in The Place every day—you can sew and read and— if you're there every day, he can't possibly put us out in the street, not the way you...." BJ reached out his hand to hers, but she drew away in horror.

"You mean you want me to sit in an unfinished store—like this?" Katie's voice quavered. "You want us to live there and have everyone looking at me and argue with the police and be alone all day and be nice to this Mr... Mr...." She could not go on. The idea was monstrous.

"No, Katie." BJ was calm now. "I don't mean I want you to. I mean you must. There's no other way. It won't be for more than two months. We'll move out of here tomorrow."

He fell into bed beside her, his strength used up. In three hours he would be feeding the angry furnaces at the mill. Katie stared into the darkness, tears running down her cheeks, careful not to disturb his rest.

CHAPTER EIGHTEEN

BJ SUPERVISED THE LOADING OF THEIR FEW POSSESSIONS INTO THE RENTED WAGON, begrudging the few coins it cost to hire the conveyance. He was strong and could have made several trips carrying the rocking chair, the books, and their clothes on his shoulders. Katie, however, could not walk the distance to Market Street, so he had bowed to necessity. He handed her up to the seat, clucked to the horses, and guided them into the uneven brick street.

Katie sat stonily beside him. Her throat was thick with dread, and her eyes burned with unshed tears. She had stood silently as he packed their belongings, not offering to help. She fumbled down the stairs and into the wagon without a backward glance, without a farewell to her fellow boarders, without a word. She tried unsuccessfully to avoid BJ's assisting hands but could not mount the wagon steps alone. When the bouncing wagon jostled them together, she inched quickly away.

BJ had built a small shelter for them at the back of the ground floor of the building, with scraps of lumber to shield them from the street. He hung their clothes, newly removed from the furnished room's armoire, on nails driven into the plasterless, windowless walls. The four-poster bed at the boarding house had yielded its heavy blankets and pillows, and BJ arranged these in a corner. The rocking-chair, a huge extravagance purchased impulsively and out of pity from a newly-minted "Bessemer widow", he placed at the front of the building between unfinished joists and behind a framed-in window.

"Now you sit there," he said grimly to Katie, "and rock and sew. Don't say anything to anybody. When you're hungry, I'll bring us food." He was humiliated, but he met her forbidding silence with a fierceness of his own. He could see the future and prayed she would also in good time. This was a bad period to be gotten through, and they would get through it because he was strong.

Katie could not see the future.

"I hate him," she muttered to her inner self. "I hate him! How could he make me do this? I'm so ashamed." She stabbed the sharp ivory hook into the crocheted cockleshells, tears running down her cheeks. Every time she heard footsteps, she gritted her teeth, imagining the sniggers of the workmen and the embarrassed glances of the passers-by. She kept her flaming cheeks low over her work "I shall never forgive him for this."

For a month she existed in a cocoon of silence, never speaking a word to BJ though he was solicitous of her every need. He dragged himself to the mill in unutterable weariness, returned to Market Street at noon with coffee and bread and cheese, sitting at her feet while they ate. Then he worked feverishly on the building, exhorting the carpenters to ever greater feats of speed.

He thought his efforts super-human. Katie thought about him not at all, feeling the days dragging by in agonizing slowness punctuated only by moments of deeper degradation. She had a month's worth of little jackets, hats, and receiving blankets, more than any baby could ever need.

Twice in the month, Mr. Kraus came to see his property. The first time, in the morning before BJ returned from the mill, he was so dumbfounded by Katie's presence amidst the squalor of the unfinished building that he actually raised his hat to her. She saw only his shoes. He immediately grasped the situation and was unable to repress a smile. One shrewd businessman could recognize another. These damned Hunkies, he grumbled. Most of them can't write their own names but they can all say *Possession is Nine-Tenths of the Law*, loud and clear and in English, yet.

The next week Mr. Kraus came in the afternoon and confronted BJ. They shouted in German and English, mostly about money, sometimes about honor. Out of the corner of her eye, Katie could see them pointing at her and knew that each of them had different reasons for doing so. Finally Mr. Kraus stomped away, and BJ had a new agreement with him, deferring all payments for another month. As he sat on the floor that night, eating the meager meal he had brought, he murmured something about having rented the first and third floors. She paid no attention.

The next week the building was finished, and they moved into their new home. The move consisted of carrying their bedding to a second floor corner, hanging a rope from one wall to another for their clothes, and placing Katie's rocker behind a real glass window. She looked around the large clean space, aware that she should be feeling joyous at having a home of her very own, at being the mistress of an entire building, at the first taste of success in America. But it was all ashes. She felt a bitterness so deep, so enduring, that it would never stop festering. She managed a smile when BJ looked at her with an appealing mixture of apprehension and pride. But the attentions to her comfort, the tiny bouquet of flowers he whisked from behind his back, left her unmoved.

That night, a Friday, Katie put her *shabbus* candlesticks on the floor and covered her head with a clean scarf. The flames sent shadows dancing around the darkening room and reflected back from the windows. Standing as close to the candles as her long skirts permitted, she looked down at them over her swollen stomach, clasped her hands in front of her, and repeated the ancient words *Boruch Atou Adonai* sighing deeply. Her fortunes had multiplied—a parlor, a kitchen, two bedrooms—but she had lost something elemental, something precious. She couldn't quite define it—was it innocence she had lost? Was it trust, trust in the future, trust in BJ? She felt she had been forced to do something without having the right to object, without participating in the decision. Is this the way life would treat her from now on, *happening* to her without her volition or control? She dried her *shabbus* tears and turned to give BJ a perfunctory *shabbus* kiss on his *kepelah*, drawing his head down so she could reach his forehead, not his lips.

CHAPTER NINETEEN

M. KIRSHBAUM, GROCERY had been carefully painted on the window of the store downstairs. The muted tinkle of the bell coming through her open windows let Katie know that business was brisk from the moment Michael Kirshbaum opened his doors in the newly finished building. He had asked for permission to make soap in the backyard and had already put out his kettles and molds. The tenant had moved in upstairs, also. Katie had watched the fancy furniture being carried past her back windows and up the steps to the third floor. She wished some of it had stopped in her parlour, which still held only the rocking chair. But she was grateful for a kitchen with a table and chairs so that at last she could cook and serve meals like a true *hausfrau*.

BJ was haggard from the terrible schedule he had subjected himself to, as well as the almost inedible dinners he had coaxed from the kosher butcher's wife down the street for what seemed an outrageous sum. Now Katie was trying to put some weight on him. It satisfied her wifely instincts to cook and allayed the nagging guilt she felt when she ignored his warmth and enthusiasms. Home from his shift at the mill, BJ would come bounding up the stairs and burst into the room, his arms wide. Katie did not enter his embrace willingly.

"We have found Jerusalem!" he cried, capering around her. If he noticed her chilliness, he said nothing. "Now this is ours. We have a roof over our heads and we have the rent paid to *us* every month. What could be better?"

Better? Better would be if he apologized to her, apologized for the pain and humiliation heaped on her every day that he had caused by putting her in the window, imprisoning her, pregnant, for all the world to see that they had... that he and she... like animals they had.... Instead he exclaimed happily over Katie's cooking, ran errands for her, and rubbed her back at night. The future was all that mattered to him. She had tried to shake off her resentment. One word from him could have changed everything, but he went cheerfully on, never looking back. Freedom from building the place, the reality of the place itself, had brought back his engaging good humor and optimism, but not hers. They gazed in wonder at the first month's rent spread on the kitchen table, green bills from the lady upstairs, stacks of coins from Michael Kirshbaum and the men in the rooms at the back. BJ's blue eyes were clear and happy as he looked at Katie. Her brown ones were narrowed and cold as she gazed back at him.

He dropped his eyes and looked away quickly. "I won't be at the mill much longer," he said. "With all this money from the rent, as soon as I pay Kraus I'll be trying something else. I've been thinking about insurance, selling insurance. "Sheeny Mike,"—everybody called the grocer Sheeny Mike—Katie hated it, "Sheeny Mike should have insurance, the men at the back need insurance. They're all supporting families in the Old Country or trying to get enough money to bring them to America, all the people around here. Insurance is important, and I'll bet they never even heard about it. For just pennies, these people could be safe, and their families could be safe."

He started pacing the small kitchen, getting in Katie's way as she scrubbed the pine floor on her hands and knees. She slowly backed him out the door, making soapy half-moons around herself.

Katie stopped listening. Won't he ever be satisfied? Her thoughts were a counterpoint to his voice. We haven't been here a month and he's wanting things to change again. Insurance! I never heard of....

A nagging pain was beginning in her back. She waited a moment, but it went away. Then it came again. She sat back on her heels, surprised by the intensity.

"BJ!" He looked at her blankly, caught in mid-sentence. "I think—" She didn't know how to express the thought. "I think my time has come." The groan that escaped her clenched lips brought BJ to her side.

"No! My God! It's too early! I don't know, what shall we do? Here." He grasped her under the arms and lifted her to her feet. "Come and lie down."

He guided her to the bedroom and the clean bedding in the corner, lowering her to a sitting position. "You just stay here and be calm. I'll be back in a minute."

Katie tried to loosen her apron but could not. The pain was

almost constant, and her ears were ringing. She felt as though she were in a box that was getting smaller and smaller. No, she was swelling, swelling into a room that could no longer hold her. She wanted to cry out but remembered the men in the back and Sheeny Mike downstairs. Sheeny Mike, what an awful name. Why does BJ call him that? So humiliating. I don't want him to hear me screaming. But somebody is screaming. It must be that woman bending over me. But who is she?

Katie looked up into a face, felt fingers at her clothes. No, no! Don't touch me! I don't know you! What are you doing here? Oh, I'm so afraid. Why didn't I think more about this baby? I don't know what to do. I want my mother. Mother, I'm so afraid.

"Okay, honey." The woman was saying something. "You're in good hands. I've done this often, so don't worry." Done *what* often? What was happening? "I'm going to take off your clothes, but we've got all the time in the world. Yell as much as you want, don't hold back."

Katie was nauseated by perfume. She struggled against the fingers at her buttons and ribbons. "Who are you? How did you get here?"

A deep throaty laugh floated around the room so infectious that Katie almost smiled. "I live upstairs. I don't get much chance to make social calls, and I guess it was too hard for you to climb another flight of steps. BJ came up to get me when your pains started."

She continued in a conversational tone as she undid snaps and hooks. "My God, you wear a lot of stuff. No wonder you can hardly breathe." Another chuckle. "Right. I live upstairs. We'll get acquainted as soon as we have this baby." Her brow furrowed. "Don't hold back. If you gotta push, push."

Katie was mortified. She felt cold air on many parts of her body and reached for a covering. But everything was dark, and the woman's presence was everywhere. The pain was unbearable.

"The name's Blossom," said the woman. "Just go with the pain. When it hurts, just go with it. And don't worry about how you look or who's watching. I've seen plenty of women without their bloomers."

Katie was drenched in sweat and something else, hot and unpleasant. A cold cloth settled on her forehead, dry towels were put beneath her body. Where did they come from? Katie could still see her own two towels hanging on the back of the bedroom door. They undulated closer and closer.

Faces floated through the darkness of the box. Sheeny Mike, eyes wider and wider until the whiteness exploded in a scream. Red flowers, blossoms, blood red. Noise came and went, voices, shouts.

The box resounded and magnified and echoed and then got smaller and smaller and smaller until everything disappeared.

Katie could tell by the way the winter sun was coming through the window that it was morning. She was consumed by an unutterable tiredness, a weariness so deep she could feel every inch of herself touched by the blankets and sheets. They were so clean and warm and smooth that she floated off on them into... voices. Soft and low. BJ's. A woman's. An unfamiliar face. Bearded? Yes, bearded. He was talking to her, but his voice was too low to be heard. She couldn't make the effort even to look interested, although she heard the voices sliding around her.

"I don't think she's listening to you, Doctor." This was the throaty voice. Blossom? What a name.

"Yes. Well. I'm very busy." This voice came through the beard. Katie could see the man's eyes inspect the bare room, then move to BJ and rest on BJ's hand. "I'm afraid I must go. You have a fine son, but you should have come to me much earlier, before the baby was born. You immigrants... well, I must go." The doctor straightened his shoulders. "Why don't you pay me now, Mr... um, Ryder. Save me from sending you a bill, don't you know."

BJ walked out of the room with the doctor, fumbling in his leather purse for money. Katie could feel Blossom looking at her and tried to pull herself from the delicious lethargy. Blossom was holding her hand and talking softly. Katie focused on the wide, heavily painted mouth. She tried to sit up, and her hand crept to her stomach, small and flat, and she heard the roaring in her ears begin again.

"Mrs. Reiter... Katie," Blossom began. "The baby came last night. You were in labor." From the frown on Katie's face Blossom could tell that she had never heard that word before. "It was very difficult, but the baby is fine." She tightened her hold on Katie's hand. "You had a hard time, though. BJ was so frightened he brought the doctor." Her lip curled. Who needed a doctor just to birth a baby?

Blossom left the room to get some whiskey for Katie. She found BJ marveling at the sleeping baby, wrapped in a pillowslip, he held in his lap. He looked up, anxiety replacing the awe on his face.

"She'll be okay. Don't worry. I'll pour some of this into her and she'll sleep," Blossom said. She put a hand on BJ's shoulder. "Why don't you go upstairs and get some rest on my bed. Nobody's there yet. I'll take care of the baby. I want to get my hands on him anyway. He looks like you, you know. And I'll fix you and Katie a meal before you go to work."

"I'll never be able to thank you enough for this, Blossom," BJ said. "I don't know what I would have done without you" He passed a hand wearily over his face. "I still don't know what to do. Will Katie be able to feed him? Where will we put him? It all happened so fast. We weren't ready."

"Listen, I'm glad I was here to help," Blossom said. "I've done this a lot, you know. Not very many as bad as that, though. And we'll get things fixed up. Don't worry. Enjoy." She thumped his shoulder again. "Listen, she'll get better pretty quick, especially when she sees this little one. She's young—how old did you say? Nineteen? She'll be up and around and ready for more babies."

BJ shrugged. "I don't think she's going to want to go through this again, any of it. I'll take the *schnapps* to her." He put the baby into Blossom's arms and went into the dark room.

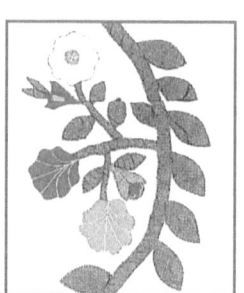

CHAPTER TWENTY

THE WORLD FELL SLOWLY, slowly back into place. Katie lay for days on the pile of bedclothes in the corner of the empty bedroom. She roused herself at intervals to accept the baby that Blossom, cooing and clucking, placed in her arms, barely aware of the sensation of nursing, lost in the thoughts that churned inside her. Blossom spooned soup and then soft puddings into her mouth.

Blossom spoke to Katie endlessly, and Katie registered every word though she raised not an eyebrow. Blossom, quickly running out of small talk, explained that she ran a bawdy house, broth-ell she called it with an ironic French accent. Blossom and BJ had a strictly financial arrangement—this said with emphasis and a hard look at Katie—BJ had space to let, Blossom needed a place to conduct her business. Katie should have been grateful for this information, but she was indifferent. In truth, she had no idea what a broth-ell was and, at this particular moment, had no desire to ask. Blossom ventured a few risqué stories for Katie's amusement, laughing at them herself in her infectious chortle, but Katie lay impassive under her gaze.

BJ brought her supper every evening. He brought her the baby when it was feeding time. She responded not at all to his touch, merely opening her mouth obediently for the approaching spoon, opening her nightgown for the baby. But, as her strength returned, she looked at him curiously through her eyelashes. How could he be so calm? she wondered. What was going through his mind? Did he realize it was his fault she almost died? It was God's punishment for his treatment of her. BJ hadn't asked her to sit in the unfinished store, he hadn't consulted her, he had *made* her do it. How could he go about his life knowing he had caused her so much pain and misery?

She watched him in the darkened room. He was haggard, his hair lank, his mouth turned down under the drooping moustache. He looked so sad. Why didn't he say something, apologize? Or at least make much of her for producing a fine, healthy baby even after being so badly used? He should be the first to speak, not she. She would wait him out. She had felt so close to him, but now he seemed very far away. What had happened to their promise to be as one? Now they were strangers. BJ, say something! And a smaller voice—*Katie, say something*. Katie put that thought away immediately as she watched her husband leave the room. She soon heard the creaking of the rocking chair and the soft hiccuping of the baby. She hated that rocking chair. It symbolized the bad things that brought her to a pile of cloth in an empty room.

The baby! She felt the hot rush of milk to her breasts. BJ was taking care of the baby! The poor little thing didn't even have a name! She couldn't remember what he looked like. BJ was taking care of her baby, *their* baby, and she was lying in a corner like a beaten dog, drowning in spite and anger. Tears spilled down her pale cheeks.

"BJ." Her voice, hoarse from disuse, was inaudible even to her. "BJ," she croaked a little louder, and he suddenly appeared, the tiny boy over his shoulder, a bowl of soup in his hand.

"No more soup," she mumbled. "I'm drowning." She held out her arms, whether for BJ or the baby she did not know. But BJ knelt by her side, put the baby in her arms, and gathered them both in his own strong arms whose warmth seemed to melt the iron around her heart.

"Let's call him Adolph," she said into BJ's shoulder. "After my father."

"Yes," said BJ. "That will be a very good name."

The next afternoon a great banging and scraping on the stairs was preceded by BJ's entrance into the bedroom.

"I've bought us a bed, and it's on its way right now!" he whispered. Very slowly, waiting for her protest, he raised the blind on the window. No objection from Katie. He looked down at her, curled in the corner, and gently pulled the threadbare blanket up to her chin. "We'll be the foremen on this job."

Laboriously, the delivery men assembled the enormous bed. A dark mahogany headboard, reaching almost to the ceiling, was leaned against the wall. It was deeply carved with roses and acanthus, twining together in great profusion. The only slightly less massive footboard was laid on the floor. The heavy sidepieces were pushed into the metal brackets, and the slats laid. The sweating workmen made one more trip to the street and came back bearing the spring and mattress, flopping above their heads like a great fish. BJ paid them off with cash from his leather purse and turned to meet Katie's look of wonderment.

Encouraged, he cried, "There's more!" and returned to the living room to get a huge package of sheets and pillows. "Now I'll show you what a good housewife I am."

He spread on the heavy pad, then smoothed over it a creamy linen sheet, needing to climb the small steps to reach the middle of the huge expanse. Hospital corners, marveled Katie. Finally, he unwrapped a yellow wool blanket and sent it sailing over the bed with one flip of his wrists, folding it at the bottom in a series of pleats that she could easily pull up. He picked Katie up and deposited her on the bed, watching her as she slowly relaxed against the billows he had created and stretched her legs down the satiny sheet. After making a bundle of the bedclothes from the corner, he dumped them out the window.

"No more muslin," he said and ventured a smile.

BJ watched Katie, regal in the big bed, as she unwrapped the baby and inspected him for the first time. Blue blue eyes. "Like yours, BJ," she whispered. And a round head covered with apricot fuzz. "He'll be a blond." She put a finger in the waving fist, touched the tiny toes, lowered her head to smell the milky fragrance.

"Isn't he a sweet baby. You've done a good job taking care of him. A whole week. That was hard for you, I know. Now, as much as I would like to stay in this lovely bed, I'm going to get up and be a mother and a wife. Thank you, BJ, for letting me have this time to...to get well."

BJ gave a great grin.

Before Katie's very eyes his hair curled, his face regained its ruddy glow, his shoulders straightened. He stood up and stretched his arms to the ceiling.

CHAPTER TWENTY-ONE

Two years later, Katie was standing in her living room, again in her wrapper. The heavy summer air was swelling the white curtains at the windows. The sun picked up the ruby colors of the oriental carpet and gave the horsehair sofa a satisfying shine. The prisms on the chandelier shimmered the walls. Through the door, she could look into the bedroom and see the mahogany bedstead, the harbinger of this wonderful richness, with its matching vanity. An ivory set—comb, brush, nail file and buffer, hair receptacle—was arranged carefully on an ecru doily she had made. Benjamin Joseph Reiter was doing well as an insurance salesman for Metropolitan Life. Feeling content and slightly lazy, Katie had a dustrag in her hand. The place was impossible to keep clean—no, almost impossible, she amended. She was determined to prevail over McKeesport's dirt. Market Street below the window, dusty in summer, mired in mud spring and autumn, icy in winter, was always filled with pushcarts, stirring things up, depositing a thin film of powder in her living room. This, mixed with the ever-present soot from the mills, drove her crazy. But not today. Today was too beautiful to spend on dirt. She gave a last flick of the cloth to the lampshade, sending the fringes dancing, and turned her attention to her husband and son.

The little boy sat astride BJ's shoulders, ducking his curly head every time BJ said Jee-RUS-alem, chortling each time they skimmed a door jamb, swooping over Katie.

"BJ, stop! You'll give him a stomach ache." But she couldn't help laughing, so pleased was she at the sight of her two handsome men.

"So tell your mother where we're going today, little one," said BJ, straining his neck to look up at his son.

"Jee-RUS-salem!" shouted Adolph.

"Right! We're going to the fair, Mama. Lots of balloons and rides and horses and donkeys and monkeys...." BJ swung Adolph from his perch and nuzzled his neck. "You're the monkey!" The little boy shouted with glee.

Katie frowned. The fair. It would be so crowded, so dusty, so noisy.

"Why do you want to go there? He's too little, BJ. Too much excitement." She watched the little boy's mouth turn down. How could he understand what she was saying? Only two years old and already so smart. She smiled at him, but his eyes filled with tears. "Oh, all right. Go then. But be back soon. He has to be fed, you know."

Katie was proud that she had nursed Adolph until he was almost two years old. According to Blossom, nursing could postpone a new pregnancy as long as possible. She sighed as she looked down at her stomach. But if the new baby was as much a delight as Adolph, she was willing to go through the terror again. There was no helping it, in any case.

"And none of that *trafe*, you hear? He shouldn't get a tooth for that food. Promise me, BJ, promise me."

BJ held her chin in his hand. "I promise," he said. "I promise he'll still be Jewish when we come back."

Katie couldn't let them go. She fussed about the jacket, or should it be a sweater? Summer storms came up so suddenly. And maybe the lighter-colored boots. The black ones showed the dust. And all that scuffling in the dirt.

"BJ, you'll carry him. He shouldn't get too tired."

"Yes, yes. We're going. Wave goodbye, Adolph. No more hand-kerchiefs, no more hats. Goodbye, goodbye." The door slammed.

Katie sighed. She knew the little boy needed to be out of the house, needed to be alone with his father, needed experiences she couldn't share, but it was hard to let him go. She stifled the desire to watch them through the window, to watch until they got to the end of Market Street. She hated the sight of their figures growing smaller, their not turning back to wave at her, forgetting her as soon as they went down the stairs. She lived every moment of their lives away from her, although her imaginings were fraught with much more danger than they ever told her about when they got home. She timed this walk, that errand, meetings and meals and possible delays, and if she didn't hear footsteps on the stairs within a half-hour of her mentally finishing BJ's workday or Adolph's adventure with him, she was at the window, biting her lips.

Finally, finally, their footsteps on the stairs. No. One set of foot-steps. Heavy. BJ must be carrying the little boy. And the door opening. How happy they looked, BJ's fair skin ruddy from the sun, Adolph flushed and sticky. Katie's hand went automatically to his *kepelah*—forehead—and she drew it back with a cry.

"Why, he's so hot! Is it the sun? What's the matter, little one? Here, let Mama hold you. Does something hurt? Tell me how you feel."

"Katie, stop fussing. He's excited, that's all. We had a good time, didn't we?" BJ tickled Adolph under his chin while peering worriedly into the little boy's eyes. "We saw an elephant, didn't we? And men on stilts, tall, tall men, didn't we? And the watermelon! Iced watermelon! Delicious!"

Katie frowned at the pink blotches on Adolph's white shirt. She hoped they would come out. The shirt cost almost a dollar, too much for a boy's shirt. But he looked such a little man she couldn't resist.

"Ice!" Katie thought of the cost of the iceman bringing his wares to her own icebox in the kitchen. It was exorbitant, but since he deliv-ered to Sheeny Mike downstairs and to Blossom on the top floor, he was willing to give them all a special price for the three deliveries. And it was a relief to know that the food was fresh and healthy.

"Ice!" she said again. "That does sound delicious. Maybe he just has a stomach ache from the coldness. Do you, my darling? Do you just have a little stomach ache? Let's put him to bed, and then I'll give him some soup to warm him up." She felt the damp little forehead and frowned again. Even in this summer heat, compounded in the small apartment, he was really quite hot. Should she be giving him hot soup to counteract the ice or something cold to lower the fever? Adolph moaned as he was lowered into his crib and immediately turned on his side and pulled his knees up, hugging them and rocking back and forth.

"We must try to cool him off a little, BJ," Katie said. "Pump some water into the sink for me, and I'll soak sheets and wrap him up."

She heard the squeak of the pump and then the steady sound as BJ put his back into it. She carried the sheets into the kitchen and pushed them into the big sink, crushing the heavy bubbles of linen. BJ helped her squeeze them out in a long rope, then carried the heavy pail she put them in to the bedroom. He unhooked the side of the crib and folded it down.

The little boy protested the cold sheets, kicking and shouting as Katie tried to wrap him up. Finally, BJ held him at arm's length as she enfolded him in a cocoon. She struggled with the squirming bundle to the rocking chair and tried to soothe his screams and hiccuping. It was difficult to hold him comfortably against her protruding belly. BJ stood looking out the window, his hands behind his back, his shoulders bowed.

"BJ! BJ! What's happening? What's he doing?"

BJ whirled around. Adolph was rigid in Katie's arms. His eyes were wide and staring, his mouth open.

"Run and get the doctor! Oh, do hurry! I'm frightened. I don't know what to do!" She rocked faster, clutching the toddler, shaking him to get him to relax.

"He'll be all right! Get him out of those sheets and walk with him. I'll run as fast as I can. Don't worry. Don't worry." His voice trailed after him as he ran down the stairs.

It seemed a lifetime, but BJ was soon back with the doctor. Katie remembered him from her confinement, the same beard, the same disapproving look. But there was nothing to do but give up her little boy to his stern care. BJ put the now flailing child into the crib and held him down as the doctor pushed and prodded. She endured the screams as the doctor bent her baby back and forth, forced open his unyielding jaw, tapped his tiny chest. Then she wrapped Adolph again in his flannel blanket and held him close in her arms. He was limp with exhaustion.

BJ cleared his throat. "Well, doctor, what do you think?"

"These cases are always difficult." The doctor, too, coughed, a somehow more professional sound. "It's what we call the summer flux. It's a condition that happens in the summer, children and adults, too. Most often with two-year olds. We don't know what causes it, something in the air, something eaten too cold...."

Katie gasped. "The ice! Summer is a dangerous time." The doctor looked appraisingly at her bulging waist. "You're lucky the baby won't be born in the summer. We lose a lot of summer babies."

He picked up his bag and held his hand out for the two dollars. "I'll be back tomorrow. Keep him comfortable. We'll know more then."

Katie gave BJ a scathing glance as she put up the side of the crib. "Get out. I'll take care of him." Stricken, BJ left the room.

Katie pulled the rocker up to the side of the crib, reached between the bars to clasp Adolph's hot limp hand, and began to croon the lullabies he loved so much. Adolph was restless, grunting little sounds, pulling up his legs, twisting and turning but always reaching again for her touch.

She sat with him all through the night, cooling his face with a cloth, changing his diapers, holding him when he could bear to be held. BJ came in at dawn, indicating with a nod of his head that he would take over, and she trailed forlornly into their bedroom and was asleep as soon as her feet left the floor.

The sound of the doctor's voice wakened her a few hours later. "There's not much I can do," he was saying. "There is no cure, of course, but sometimes these little ones shake it off in two or three days. I'll be back tomorrow. And you, missus." Katie had appeared, tousled, at her bedroom door. "You take care of yourself. No sense having two sick ones in the same house." He chuckled sympathetically. "It's three dollars today, Mr... um, Ryder. It's Sunday."

Adolph was different now, lying inert with his eyes closed. She lifted him from the crib and held him close, walking slowly around the apartment and singing softly into his ear. She walked for hours, humming quietly, his soft hair whispering against her face. The heat increased during the day. She heard BJ fixing lunch but refused his offer to hold the little boy. The bells from the nearby church struck the hours, but still she walked.

At dusk, she put the baby back in his crib. How small, she thought. How small and—she searched for the word—unresponsive. Maybe he was feeling better. He wasn't pulling up his legs anymore. Maybe he was sleeping and gathering his strength. She crept into the kitchen and permitted BJ to make her a cup of tea.

"What about your collections?" she said. BJ went weekly to the homes of his clients to gather their insurance quarters. He looked so gray, so beaten, that she couldn't look at him without a stab of fear. She wanted to see his business face, his smile, his eagerness. "Shouldn't you be out with your clients?"

BJ pulled himself together. "Its all right. They'll be happy to wait. I want to be here with you and the boy. I'm sorry about the fair...the whole thing. You said not...."

Katie raised her hand. She didn't want to hear it. She bent over the table, wrapped her chilly fingers around the cup.

Minutes after she returned to Adolph's room, BJ heard the terrible shriek. He ran to her.

"He's dead!" She shook the little body. "He's dead!" She turned to BJ and beat her hands against his chest. "Look at him! He's not moving! He's dead!" She collapsed in the rocking chair.

BJ touched the little boy, raised his arms and dropped them, pinched his cheeks between his fingers, rubbed him and tickled him and finally slapped him. No reaction. He took Katie into his arms and wept into her shoulder. She clung to him, her arms strong around his chest, rocking against him, struggling to catch her breath.

Then she stiffened in his grasp.

"Watermelon!" she shouted. "He had to have watermelon! What were you thinking! My baby! My baby!" She ran from the room and slammed her bedroom door behind her. BJ heard the creak of the springs as she flung herself on the bed.

CHAPTER TWENTY-TWO

Blossom once again came into Katie's life, once again as a buffer between Katie and BJ. It was she who held Katie, racked with sobs. It was she who wrapped her strong arms about Katie as they stood in the little cemetery next to the *shul*. It was she who carried tea to the bedroom afterwards, who whispered the soothing words, who reminded Katie that another baby was about to come. "It won't be the same, I know," Blossom said. "But it will be a baby to take care of, a beautiful baby, to fill the hours and take your mind off your troubles. Another wonderful boy, you'll see." Blossom knew that Jewish women had boys first. It was what they wanted, and they had a secret way of doing it. She patted Katie's rounded belly.

Blossom visited the middle apartment every day, arriving after she heard the door slam behind BJ in the morning. She encouraged the tears, adding a few of her own as she remembered the little boy who sometimes toddled about her own establishment. She told Katie funny anecdotes about her clients, teasing out an occasional smile and realizing that Katie had no idea why her stories were always about men. She ignored the disarray of Katie's apartment until, one day, she decided Katie had mourned enough.

"BJ has certainly turned this place into a mess," she said. She knew the word mess would get Katie's attention. Katie blinked and looked around. There were cups on the end-tables, newspapers on the floor, the wastebasket was overflowing, dust was everywhere. Katie looked stricken.

"How did this happen? I must have been out of my mind." She gave a rueful laugh. She knew when she was being manipulated. "Where's the mop? Let's get to work."

Katie was like a woman possessed. By the end of the day, the apartment sparkled and three *kuchen* sat steaming on the kitchen counter.

"Please, Blossom, one of these is for you. You have been so kind to me. Have something good for your dinner for once, a good Jewish dessert." Katie wrapped the pastry in newspaper so it wouldn't burn Blossom's hands and ushered her out onto the landing. "When you return the dish, I'll make tea for you. And *kugel*. Thank you, thank you," she said to the ascending figure, watching the satin skirts brushing the stairs. She closed the door. There was something about Blossom that Katie mistrusted, good-hearted though Blossom was. Something mysterious. She couldn't put her finger on it. She shook her head. Maybe BJ would know. BJ. Her eyes filled with tears. They would have to put their lives back together before this new baby came.

As her waist expanded, Katie struggled to diminish her sadness. "So many deaths. Two Adolphs I've lost. But BJ," she put her hand on his. "I think that maybe there is only one death in a person's life. I felt my father's death so deeply. His was the death for me. I miss him now as much as I ever did. It prepared me for everything bad that is going to happen in my life. I can stand this loss. The new baby will come and will make us happy. Please forgive me." She took a deep breath. "Again."

BJ buried his face in Katie's hair, lifting her from the chair and into his arms.

She remembered the strength of his forgiveness as she gazed down on Market Street the next morning. Footsteps on the stairs and loud knocking at the door disturbed her reverie.

"Mrs. Reiter!" It was Sheeny Mike. "A letter has come for you. It looks important, so I thought I'd bring it up myself."

Katie opened the door, unable to conceal a frown of distaste as she looked at the grocer. The name that he allowed himself to be called precluded any good feelings that she might have about him. Besides, she knew he was a heavy gambler and suspected that sometimes when BJ said he was going out to collect the insurance money he was actually headed to the back room of the grocery to play cards. Mike caught her look and cheerfully refused her perfunctory invitation to come in. She turned the letter over and over as she closed the door. BJ received a few letters from the Metropolitan Insurance Company, but she never got mail. Except from her mother. She took a sharp breath and opened the envelope with shaking fingers.

My darling Katie. Herr Gross is dead! I can't stay here. Count Barcoczy will not allow a woman to take care of his distillery. I don't know what to do. I am coming to you. With Ephraim. We will be no trouble. We will help you with the baby. Katie shook her head angrily. The letter about Adolph's death hadn't reached her mother yet.

This letter must be old, too. She looked at the postmark. June. It was now August. She read on. Passage booked in June. Arriving August 29th. Will meet you at Uncle Jacob's. Liebchen, liebchen. Katie heard the familiar voice in her ears. Mother. Mother!

She sat at the kitchen table waiting impatiently for BJ. They would have to furnish the baby's bedroom for her mother and brother. Two iron bedsteads and a chiffonier, maybe a rug. And a lamp. The room had been closed since Adolph had died. Adolph. The familiar pain clutched at her heart.

Finally she heard BJ's step on the stairs. She still wasn't used to his job with the insurance company and was always slightly amazed at the way he looked when he came home at night. He was dressed in a dark gray suit with a watch chain across his waistcoat, a white shirt with a high celluloid collar and a dark cravat, a homburg on his head. This he doffed with a deep bow and a twirl of his blond moustache. She laughed. "You really are a dandy," she said. Then the laugh faded. "But come. Look at this letter from my mother. She's coming to stay with us and we need to make some plans." She watched him carefully for a sign of annoyance, but there was none. His good humor was dependable. He read through the letter, his brow furrowed over the German, easier for Katie to read than for him. He glanced at her with commiseration.

"Um. Maybe I should go to Newark next week and fetch her and the boy. We'll come back by train, and by then we can have furniture in the other room." Katie relaxed her tense shoulders. Sometimes he could read her mind.

"What about work?" she said. "Can you leave your work for three days?"

"I think I can arrange it," he said, squinting his eyes, thinking of all the doors he knocked on to collect the ten-cent-a-week insurance premiums. "Some people I'll have to miss for a week, but I'll make it clear that the next week I'll be collecting double. And the prospects. Well, I can just move them to another day." He took her hand in his. "It will work out fine. And I'll be pleased to meet your mother and your little brother." His young face clouded. "It's been fifteen years since I saw my mother. I'll probably never see her again." Then the slow grin that had so enchanted her in Uncle Jacob's shop. "It will be nice to have somebody's mother here."

BJ left for Newark within the week. On the third day of his absence, Katie haunted the window. Late in the afternoon she let the curtains fall back and was turning away with a sigh when she heard noisy wheels on the dirt street below.

They're here, she breathed. A pat to the hair, an adjustment to the skirt over her heavy stomach, and she was down the stairs and into her mother's arms.

Hustle and bustle, trunks to be carried up the steps, exclamations over the beauty of the parlour, the comfort of the bedroom.

"Let me look at you!" Liebe said. "Oh, I'm so glad you're here," Katie said at the same time. They both laughed delightedly. Katie turned to her brother.

"Ephraim, what a young man you've become. Do you remember...?"

Liebe glanced discretely at her daughter. Katie looked so worn out. BJ had told her about young Adolph's death, and she had wept on the train. Now, she had better not mention it, open up old wounds. Better to say nothing, wait and see.

Finally, they were settled at the dinner table, lit by the brilliant sunset of a summer night in McKeesport. The smoky air caught the dying rays and unfurled great flags of purple and orange and yellow across the sky. They all sighed in unison, then laughed.

"This is a great day," said BJ. "We are very happy to have you here with us."

He raised his glass of wine, and they all drank. BJ carved the chicken, and Katie proudly served the meal she had cooked so lovingly. For a few minutes there was silence.

"Mother," Katie said. "Would it upset you too much to tell us now how you decided to come here? Your letter told us practically nothing. But I want you to enjoy your dinner. If you'd rather wait until later, please say so." She glanced at Ephraim, who had laid down his fork.

"No, no, Liebchen," said Liebe. "Ephraim and I think of nothing else." She took her handkerchief from her sleeve. "I told BJ all about it on the train." She looked apologetically at BJ. "I hate to make him feel bad again, but it is always on my mind. It is so pleasant here, no danger, no hatred. It is good to be far away from such things." She took a deep breath. Katie could tell that she had told herself this story over and over.

"Herr Gross was a good husband," she said. Katie's mouth tightened. "And he managed the brewery well. Count Barkoczy was satisfied. And the men respected him. Not like Adolph, of course." Liebe's eyes filled with tears. Katie looked away.

"But everything went well. There was no trouble," Liebe continued. "His boys worked hard, too. They married. Nice Jewish girls from the town they came from. And they stayed on the estate to help their father. Ephraim worked, also. And went to school." Liebe squeezed Ephraim's hand and did not let go.

"It was Passover last year, in April. Passover was late last year. We all worked hard in the kitchen to make a good seder. Nine we were, sitting at the table every night, that night, too. I had my back to the window, the sons and their wives were along the sides, and Herr Gross was at the head of the table as he always was." Liebe's face was pale, her eyes wide, reliving the scene in her head.

"We heard hoof beats on the road, many hoof beats, and at that time of night. We looked at each other, wondering where they were going, who they were. What could it be? They turned into our road. One of the boys started to get up, to see what it was." She was talking faster and faster, on her face a look of disbelief.

"And then there was a loud noise—one loud crack. The glass in the window broke, and we all jumped." Liebe's shoulders jumped, too, and she took a deep breath.

"The broken glass seemed the most important thing, to sweep it up, to cover the window. The hoof beats went on down the driveway, and we couldn't hear them anymore. And when we stopped sweeping, stopped talking about what it was . . . we looked back at the table and Herr Gross was still sitting there. Dead. One bullet, right in the head!" Liebe shuddered, and Ephraim put his head on their intertwined hands.

"Oh, but it was terrible. A pogrom, they said. I had never heard the word. A pogrom? They have a word for it? They do it for sport. Killing Jews at Passover. Because they think we soak the matzos in the blood of Christian babies. Can you imagine such a story? We, who aren't allowed to eat the blood of anything, taking the blood of babies? And they do it—this pogrom—on one of their own holidays, too. All Hallows Evening, or something." Her words were now tumbling out as she folded and refolded the white napkin in her lap.

"Count Barkoczy himself came to the brewery." Ephraim continued the story, but his eyes lost their haunted look and began to shine. "Very splendid he was, too, Katie. Footmen on his coach, fur on his collar. He tried to be nice, but he said we had to leave. It was a mistake to hire Jews. Grete was very sorry to see us go. She cried. But we got to ride on a train and a boat. And here we are."

Katie got up from her chair to hug her brother. Through the patina of tragedy, she could still recognize the happy boy from her childhood.

He wriggled from her grasp. "Really, I like it here. I don't want to be a farmer. I think I could be a businessman, like BJ." Ephraim looked admiringly at BJ's vest and gold watch chain.

After dinner, Katie lit the lamp in the back bedroom and helped her mother unpack.

"We could bring so little," Liebe mourned as they shook out the clothes. "But look, I brought the my *shabbus* candlesticks. And a *dachana!*" Katie shouted with joy as she and her mother shook the crushed feather quilt into a great cloud. "One for your bed, Liebchen, one for mine."

"Oh, Mother, I'm so glad. I missed having a *dachana* so much. It reminds me of home." To hide her tears, she wrapped her arms around Liebe and kissed her on the cheek. "And what's this at the very bottom of the trunk?" Katie pulled out the heavy wool uniform. Brass buttons reflected the lamp light. Katie stiffened. "It's father's uniform," she breathed.

Katie and Liebe looked at each other, the pain in their eyes so naked they looked quickly away.

"Hush. It's all right," Liebe said. "We are together here at last in this wonderful country. Let's go back in the parlour and see what Ephraim and Benjamin are doing."

CHAPTER TWENTY-THREE
1893

LIEBE AND KATIE ENJOYED WATCHING EPHRAIM become an American. At first, unused to living in a city and too shy to seek friends, he stayed close to the Market Street apartment. With his many questions and loving nature, he filled some of the space in Katie's heart yearning for her lost baby. He made her laugh, his quick wit always ready for teasing and jokes. The long hours that BJ was away were now filled with stories of Ephraim's explorations into McKeesport, sometimes with his mother proudly on his arm.

"Let's go to Jerusalem," Ephraim would say in imitation of BJ, and he and Liebe would venture into the crowded, dirty streets to exclaim over window displays and sip sodas at an ice-cream store. Katie, who had spent her three years in McKeesport either pregnant or in mourning, had seen little of the town and awaited eagerly the stories of their adventures.

Now she was kept at home caring for the new baby. Sydney had arrived in September, quickly, easily, with his grandmother attending him on one side and Blossom on the other. He was named for BJ's father, Schmuel. Sweet, so sweet he was, blond hair whispering on his head, blue eyes groggily following every movement. Constantly being handed from one loving arm to another, he was warm and contented, nursing voraciously, sleeping fiercely, the center of attention.

At night, Katie and Liebe sewed and mended in the gas-lit parlour. Ephraim was in bed, Sydney in his cradle, BJ working.

"Why is Benjamin never at home?" Liebe asked her daughter.

"Mother, he works hard at the insurance office all day and then he collects from his prospects mostly at night. That's when his prospects are at home, after work." Prospects. Katie was pleased with her mastery of the language of insurance. "That's when he collects the weekly dimes. Really you shouldn't be so critical. This isn't the old country, where everyone quits at sunset and goes home." Katie looked at her sconces and handsome lamps. "We aren't peasants here. We're not dependent on sunshine."

Liebe continued sewing and compressed her lips. Her needle plied its tiny stitches, in and out, in and out. Every night she heard the footsteps on the stairs going past her bedroom wall. She had her suspicions of what was gong on in the third floor apartment, which the sight of Blossom, rouged and marcelled, did nothing to allay. But BJ was not a customer on the third floor, because his footsteps were always going down, down to Sheeny Mike's. She didn't have any doubts about *that*. Why didn't he tell Blossom to leave? She had tried to be hospitable when Blossom came to tea to meet her but had spent the hour grimly polite. Katie was mystified.

"Why were you so quiet, Mother?" she asked. "Blossom dresses so beautifully, and she knows so much about this country. And her stories are so funny. I know she talks a lot, but she's been so kind to me, and she's interesting . . . . " Katie's voice trailed off at her mother's lack of response.

"And Sheenymike?" Liebe said. It was always "And Sheenymike?" after a visit from Blossom. Katie was amazed at her mother's curiosity about the tenants above and below her apartment. She hadn't had as many questions about them in the two years she lived on Market Street as Liebe had in only two months. She had a strange aversion to telling what she knew, suddenly feeling that what she knew was completely inadequate. Most of all, Katie was reluctant to tell her mother what Sheeny meant. She didn't want her to know there were bad words for Jews even in America, but she had to suppress a wry smile when Liebe spoke the two words as one.

"What does Benjamin do down there in the grocery so late at night? I can hear them laughing and carrying on when I'm trying to sleep. Those Hungarians. They like to gamble and drink and God knows what else. Why do you put up with it?"

"Mother! BJ deserves some relaxation after he works so hard. They're just talking in the back of the store. Mike isn't married, and he needs company, too, after a hard day." Katie knew that Sheeny Mike had a serious pinochle game in his back room three or four nights a week and that BJ was a regular player. It worried her, but she didn't know whether to express her concern after BJ had been so good about welcoming her mother and brother into their small apartment.

The trust she had felt in him from their very first meeting had evaporated in the rocking chair in the unfinished window of this apartment house. She knew that she had lost her sense of humor, as well, and that her temper was quick and her tongue sharp. Did she have a right to insist that BJ come home and spend his evenings with her and her mother? What did they have to offer that could compete with the careless ease of Sheeny Mike's back room?

And, besides, her mother, too, had developed a very sharp edge, a way of talking that was censorious and fault-finding. Katie heard the word Hungarian dripping with disparagement. She had heard the very same tone from her Uncle Jacob and Aunt Sadie, whispering in the night.

Katie watched her mother return to her mending. Maybe now she'll ask me about Adolph, how it was, tell me how sad she is, Katie thought. And maybe we should speak about Father. I never had a chance to tell her how much I love him, how I miss him. And I don't know how she feels, either. Did Herr Gross replace him in her life? Does she think of Father first when she thinks about the old country? There was silence. Maybe this is something women don't talk about. Maybe it's a secret that women don't share because it's too enormous, too devastating. Maybe if we spoke of it, of childbirth and death, it would be too much to bear. I know it's too much to bear in silence, but maybe it's even worse if we give it voice. Katie punched the needle through the fine linen, making a hole in a thread. She grumbled under her breath.

"What? What did you say?" Liebe asked eagerly.

"Nothing. Let's go to bed. I'll leave a lamp lit for BJ."

They went to their separate bedrooms silently, each hungering for the goodnight kiss, neither willing to ask for it. The next morning, a tense silence pervaded the kitchen. Ephraim looked from one face to the other. "Um. I think I'll go out now. One of the boys has a rowboat, and he said he'd give me and some other fellows a ride. I'll be back by dinner."

He waited for an objection, but none came. "Well, I'm going now." He waved, but neither his sister nor his mother was looking.

It was the autumn of 1893, and during the past summer Ephraim had made friends of his schoolmates on Market Street. The little neighborhood, enclosed by the railroad tracks on one side and the

Monongahela River on the other, was mostly Jewish, Jews from Eastern Europe with the German language or Yiddish in common. The summer, always humid and gritty from the mills, had slipped into fall. The air was cleared by the crisp breezes. The trees were ablaze on the hills and escarpments above the river. Katie shivered as the afternoon grayed. She glanced out of the window as she passed on her way to the bedroom to see if the baby was warm enough and saw a group of boys running, shouting, down Market Street.

"Mrs. Reiter! Mrs. Reiter! Come quick! Something's happened! Come quick!"

Sheeny Mike hurried from the store as Katie dashed down the stairs.

"My goodness! Such a fuss. What's the matter?" She tried to make sense of the din. Then she followed Mike's gaze down the street. A group of men was struggling to carry a shutter, a dripping shutter.

"It wasn't our fault?" the boys shrilled at her. "We told him to be careful." They danced around her in a frenzy. Mike put his hand on her shoulder.

"You wait here. I'll see what happened," he said.

The shutter was lowered to the ground. Katie saw Mike bend over it, lift up an arm, turn the body over and shake it. She closed her eyes and leaned against the storefront.

Mike returned and grasped her by the elbows. He riveted her eyes with his strong gaze.

"Yes," he said. "It's him. He drowned. He must have fallen out of the boat. It's Ephraim. He's dead."

Liebe heard the last four words as she reached the sidewalk.

CHAPTER TWENTY-FOUR

BLACK. BLACK. Will we ever shake off this blackness, Katie wondered. The mirrors, turned to the wall, were draped in black. BJ, his face drawn, sat quietly in his armchair, black band on his sleeve, black tie. Liebe had worn only black for ten years, first for her husband Adolph, then for Herr Gross, now Ephriam. Katie shook her head hard, hoping to feel a pain, dizziness, any deviation from the numbness that enveloped her, heavier than the heavy silk of her dress, heavier than the heavy coil of her hair. Nothing changed. She felt suspended inside her body, an odd sensation of being smaller than her skin, insulated.

Three months had passed since Ephriam's funeral. He was buried beside little Adolph. BJ had bought a large area in the Jewish cemetery around the baby's grave after Ephriam's death. At the funeral, Katie had looked at the empty expanse and shuddered. Space for so many dead. Is this what life was about, a mere preparation for death? As the pine coffin was lowered into blackness, she clearly saw a line of figures, young, old, heads bent so she could not see their faces, each hesitating on the lip and then inexorably tumbling into the hole that would receive her darling brother. It took an effort of will to ban this image from her sight.

BJ rose heavily from his chair.

"I've got to go to work," he said. He looked at them helplessly, knowing he would find them in almost the same poses when he returned home that night.

"Can I get you anything? I'd be glad to leave a list with Sheeny Mike, he can deliver anything you need. Maybe I can come home for lunch. Maybe we can eat together."

"No, no, Benjamin," Liebe said. Her voice was hoarse. "Of course you must go to work. Katie and I will be just fine here." Tears, unremarked, slid down her cheeks "We'll see you tonight."

Katie walked down the steps with BJ.

"What are we going to do?" she said. "Nothing seems to change here. The days are endless, and we do nothing but take care of Sydney. We've got to do something, but we just sit and look at each other. We're both so listless. When I go back up the stairs, I'm going to have to think each time I lift my foot." Katie clutched BJ's sleeve but immediately loosened her grip and smoothed the material. "This isn't for you to worry about. You go to work, and Mother and I will...." What? She didn't know.

BJ kissed her cheek and hurried away.

That afternoon, as the first snow began to soften the dreary grayness of Market Street, Katie and Liebe folded away Ephriam's clothes. His shoes and store-bought suits and pants they put in a box to be sold to a pushcart vendor. The soft shirts they had both sewed so lovingly they wrapped in paper, tied the bundle with string, and put away at the bottom of the armoire.

Back in the parlour, small in the corner of the settee, Liebe looked down at her hands. "Now what are we going to do, Liebchen?" Katie's mother said. "Who shall we do for? Benjamin buys his shirts ready-made at the store, we cook more food than anyone can eat, it is impossible to keep ahead of this soot. Are we to be useless?"

"Mother, let's sew a quilt! Blossom has wonderful quilts on her beds." Katie blushed to admit she had been in Blossom's apartment.

"A quilt? What would we do with a quilt?" Liebe looked stricken. "Aren't the *dachanas* I brought good enough?" She had two dachanas with her in her trunk, their bulk crushed and squeezed into corners. Once shaken, aired, and on the beds, they had expanded into the huge featherbeds Katie remembered from Bohemia.

"Yes, they're wonderful for the winter, but quilts are better for the summers. You know how hot and humid it was here in the summer. And quilts are so beautiful. I want you to see them. We can buy some material and use the scraps we've saved from our sewing. And it will keep us busy instead of sitting here with our hands in our laps."

Katie set her mouth firmly. "I'm going upstairs to see Blossom, and I'll bring down the quilts for you to look at. I know you'll think its a wonderful idea." She had no such thought, but she was determined.

Katie returned with three quilts folded on her arms. When they were spread across the settee, the chair, and the rocker, Liebe looked at them with unconcealed delight.

"Ach, Liebchen," she said. "They are lovely. Look at this! Purple flowerpots and white flowers, daisies, I think. And this one! Just squares of blue, but it looks like the ocean. And this one! Like flowers opening." Liebe turned a corner over. "But look at these stitches. So uneven and so big. The wrong side should be just as beautiful as the right side. We can do much better then this." Katie hid a smile. "But how does one start? So much planning and thinking." Since Ephriam had died, Liebe seemed unable to make decisions or want to think ahead more than one or two days. It's too much, she would say. Who knows what will happen by then? She would shake her head.

Katie was at a loss, but it could be done, the proof was right before their eyes. "First, we'll go to the drapers and buy some material, lots of material. Beautiful colors. And threads and needles. Then...we'll come home. That will be enough for the first day. And let's go *now*."

Katie swept the baby up from the floor and began stuffing him into his snowsuit. "Sweet little Sydney. We're going to have an adventure. Just two more buttons, hold still. And, Mother, get your hat." Her voice grew stronger as she spoke. The last sentence was an order.

Katie put on her own hat and poked the pin in firmly. When she turned, she saw her mother standing uncertainly, hat poised above her head, before the black-draped mirror.

"And that's enough of *that*," Katie said. She pulled the crepe from the mirror and turned it so the glass was once again facing the light. Liebe looked silently at her reflection. "That's funny. I still look the same." She bent closer. "I thought I would look like a witch, a *dybbuk*, but it's the same face I had before...before...."

"*No!*" Katie almost shouted. The baby jumped and started to cry. Katie tucked him, none too gently, into his buggy. "Let's go."

They both gasped as the cold air hit them. They had hardly been out of the apartment for three months. Katie knew that if she hesitated they would both be back inside in a minute.

"Let's go this way," she said, pulling her heavy shawl closer and tucking her arm under her mother's. By the time they reached the draper's, many blocks away, their breaths were misty and their eyes sparkling. They welcomed the warmth of the large store but Liebe was overwhelmed by the seemingly endless bolts of material stacked on shelves from floor to ceiling. Katie had been here often before.

"We better just watch for awhile," Katie said.

Open-mouthed, Liebe and Sydney gazed at the black cylinders whizzing along wires close to the ceiling and carrying the money to a balcony at the back of the emporium. The click of scissors and the sound of ripping cloth filled their ears. Bright colors flashed before their eyes. Mesmerized, they watched the scene for many minutes before Liebe turned to Katie laughing.

"This will be fun," Katie said. "I think we're supposed to make our own choices and bring the material to the cutting table. Let's look by ourselves. I'll take Sydney this way and you go over there, and we'll each choose five bolts. Surprise me."

Back in the apartment, still tingling from the cold, they swooped around the parlour, flinging their purchases on the tables, chairs, and settee in the dusk-dark room. Then Katie lit the lamps.

"Oh!" they said in unison.

The bright cottons leaped to life—cobalt, scarlet, lemon, purest white, emerald green flowered, striped, dotted. They had each chosen the most vibrant hues, the clearest shades. They looked at each other in delight.

"Tomorrow we begin."

The next morning, Liebe and Katie hurried BJ out the door and settled Sydney under the kitchen table with wooden spoons and pots and biscuits. They laid out the shears and thread, their hearts quickening at the vibrant colors glowing in the morning sun.

Liebe raised her scissors. "Now! What do we do?"

Katie looked at her mother and burst out laughing. In a moment, Liebe joined her. They laughed and laughed, Sydney raising his arms to join in the fun.

"Oh! That felt so *good*, Mother! We haven't laughed in months." She raised her hands, palms up. "I don't *know* what to do. All this material, and no plan. If you'll take care of Sydney, I'll go back to the drapers and ask them. Maybe they can help us turn all this stuff into a quilt."

Katie was back within the hour, two books tucked under her arm. "These are called pattern books, the draper said. People use them for designs and ideas and even templates." She held up her hand to forestall the question. "That means we can cut out the picture and draw around it on the material to help us cut the material out. Let's look."

With Sydney on her lap, Katie opened the first book.

"Oh, my. What's that? A pineapple! What on earth is a pineapple? And here is an elephant. An elephant, Sydney! Think of that on a quilt. And a Tree of Life! Let's do that. It seems just right."

They paged through the books, agreeing, disagreeing, gradually selecting patterns that pleased them both. Appliqué and trapunto were now in their vocabularies. They couldn't wait until Sydney was ready for his nap.

"I'll start with the pineapples," Liebe said, still shaking her head over what exactly a pineapple was. Some kind of fruit, perhaps. "Whatever they are, they look easy. We can each make one and see what happens."

These two practiced seamstresses quickly cut the yellow and green material and sewed them as directed by the pattern book. They each had a pineapple with green leaves at the top and a green stem at the bottom. They embroidered the leaves with green thread to simulate the lines in the leaves and appliquéd the finished pineapple to a square of white cloth.

"But leave a little hole in the side, Mother, so we can stuff it."

"Stuff it! What do you mean by that?" Liebe was amazed.

"That's the trapunto part, Mother. That's what gives the quilt texture. We're going to push cotton under the pineapple to give it a shape."

With the pineapples—what were they, exactly?—finished to their smug satisfaction, they decided to do a Tree of Life. This was more complicated, involving the cutting of narrow branches and round red apples. The floor was littered with red and green before they were ready to sew. Only fingers accustomed to needlework since the age of five could manage the tiny stitches. When it was finished, they chortled with delight and appliquéd it quickly to the white square. The apples were stuffed with small pieces of cotton. Three squares finished, and Sydney was stirring in his bed, ready to get up and complicate the project.

Over the next month, the women put together two rococo vases with sprays of many-colored flowers, and several small hands with rings. Blossom descended from her apartment to fashion two peacocks, which Liebe embroidered with colored thread. Sitting at the kitchen table, the little boy crawling among the scraps at their feet,

Katie and Liebe eased their bruised hearts with talking and crying and sharing secret thoughts and stories of the six years they had spent apart. They looked forward to these hours together even more than finishing the quilt.

When the squares had been sewn together and the border painstakingly fitted, the really hard work of quilting began. At first, Liebe and Katie saved the quilting for the evening, sitting with the finished quilt cover on their laps. But it soon became apparent that there was not enough light from the gas lamps for them to outline the complex front designs on the back cover of the quilt. Mornings were designated for this work, and it went much more slowly because of the other chores which had to come first.

One spring morning, a year later, they declared themselves finished. They carried the heavy quilt into the bedroom and, four hands clasping the quilt, poised it high above the bed. Quick flicks of the wrists, and the quilt floated up and over the bed, settling with a soft sigh. Katie and Liebe gazed at it in wonder, hardly believing that the rolls of material they had brought home more than a year ago had been transformed by their hands into this fantastical entity. The little room had become a garden.

CHAPTER TWENTY-FIVE
1896

"AND WHAT'S THIS, MOTHER?" Three-year old Sydney never tired of lying on his stomach on Katie and BJ's bed, questioning her about the figures on the quilt. Right now his pudgy fingers were tracing a black rocking-horse on one of the squares.

"Ah, my darling," she began the expected story. "When we knew we were going to have a handsome baby come to live with us, we made him a big black horse to ride and sewed it *right here!*" Katie hugged the little boy and nuzzled his downy neck.

"Horsey, horsey!" Sydney wriggled from her grasp and pointed to the black centerpiece of the quilt. Appliquéd onto the white background was a black wool charger in perfect detail, hoofs embroidered of silver thread, mane flying, one leg raised as though in parade walk. Sitting stiffly on its back was a hussar in the same heavy black wool, a row of tiny buttons on his chest, epaulets with fringe on his shoulders, a hat with plumes set jauntily on his head.

Katie ran her fingers over the figure. It had taken her mother a full month to get it exactly right. Liebe had agonized over the decision to cut apart Adolph's Hapsburg uniform for use in the quilt. But once she had decided, she worked feverishly. She cut out and discarded a dozen horses, one of which became the rocking horse, before one pleased her. Somehow the first rider had been just right and had been immediately mounted on his steed.

"Yes," Liebe said. "That's how I remember him, riding toward me in Prague." She sighed.

Then came the painstaking appliqué and embroidery, blue French knots for the eyes, silver ones for the buttons and spurs, white feather stitch to outline the plumes, black running stitch for the moustache and fringes and the stripe down the trouser leg. Finally, Liebe had declared herself satisfied, and the square was sewn into the center of the rapidly growing quilt. Now, the quilt was finished and on Katie's bed, an endless source of questions for her children, Sydney and the new baby, one year-old Fred.

"And what's this?"

Katie looked into their eyes, one pair blue, one pair brown, and laughed.

"That's a pineapple! Yes, yes, it is!" she said to their dutiful expressions of disbelief. "Blossom bought a pineapple from Mike for *a-great-deal-of-money* " . . . this punctuated by soft pokes to their bellies . . . "and Bubby and I made a picture of it and sewed it on the quilt for you to see before we *ate it all up!*" A joyful chorus accompanied by a tickle.

"And here's the tree from Bubby's back yard in Bohemia," Sydney crowed as he was scooped from the bed and set on the floor.

"Yes. And now it's time for lunch. Let's find Bubby."

Liebe took the wriggling Fred from Katie's arms and hugged him. Fred, solemn and dark, was named after Ephraim. Fred was his American name, Ephraim his Hebrew name. Ephraim had been dead for three years. *Gott in himmel,* Liebe sighed. Children were such a joy and such an affliction. She settled the two little boys at the kitchen table.

The Market Street apartment, once seemingly palatial, was now cramped and confining. Sydney slept on a cot at the foot of his parent's bed, Fred in a trundle in his grandmother's room. The parlour was a daytime battlefield where the two boys had a fort under the davenport and a castle made from the lamp-table and the contents of the bookshelves. Liebe instructed them in the intricacies of Austrian royalty as they moved their clothespin soldiers about the furniture legs.

"This can be Franz Josef," she would say, picking up a wooden peg. "And this is his cousin, Prince Rudolph." Liebe knew she was mixing up the generations, but the little boys, German speakers both, loved the guttural R's. "And don't forget, they must go home every night to Empress Maria Theresa." And she would herd the army into the clothespin bag in preparation for BJ's arrival after work.

BJ no longer spent most of his evening walking the gas-lit streets to interview prospects and collect dimes from the impoverished Jews of Market Street. He worked at a desk in the Metropolitan Life Insurance Company in downtown McKeesport and had clients that he advised on their insurance needs. His shirts with the buttoned-on celluloid collars were long gone, replaced by those of fine linen with the collars attached. These were starched and ironed flawlessly by a self-effacing Chinese whose family had elected to stay in Pennsylvania after the railroad had been brought through McKeesport. Katie's long hours over the washboard and ironing board were much diminished.

BJ lit a cigar and spread house plans on the cleared table as Katie put the little boys to bed and Liebe washed the dishes. Through his careful management of the rents from Mike's store downstairs, Blossom's apartment on the third floor, and the rooms in the back—to say nothing of a salary that grew more astonishing each year—he had recently bought a corner lot on Carnegie Avenue. Carnegie Avenue, a boulevard of large houses, grassy fields, and old trees, was a far cry from crowded, push-cart clogged Market Street. Katie was happily anticipating more space. She was again pregnant and wondering where to put another crib in their four rooms. She was dubious about leaving the familiar Jewishness of Market Street but enticed by the news that Andrew Carnegie had endowed a library to be built just a block from the proposed new house. She envisioned happy walks with her children to this repository of learning or seeing them off to travel there alone, her admonishment to *Remember Empress Maria Theresa* ringing in their ears.

Now, in the quiet of a spring night in 1896, they pored over pictures of houses and floor plans obtained from the Sears-Roebuck Company. The Swiss Chalet and Spanish Villa immediately landed on the floor. An English Half-Timber merited more than a passing glance, but it, too, was discarded. "Pretentious," muttered Katie.

At last, there was one picture left. Of brick, three story, deep porch in front and sunroom on the side, four bedrooms and a bathroom upstairs, large attic, large basement.

"A bathroom," Katie breathed. "Is it possible we can afford such a house?"

"The house will cost about three thousand dollars," BJ said after checking the back of the picture. "The plans will be twenty dollars. I'll take out a mortgage with Metropolitan and save our cash for furniture. I think we can do it."

Mortgage was an English word that neither Katie nor Liebe had ever heard. BJ explained as simply as possible, skipping the parts about amortization and trust deeds as he saw their eyes grow wider and wider.

"What a country," murmured Liebe.

Finally all the necessary decisions had been made. Katie and Liebe brought out their sewing. BJ remained at the table, filling out the forms torn from the back of the Sears Catalog. Then he loosened his tie, checked his pockets, and went downstairs to join Sheeny Mike's pinochle game.

CHAPTER TWENTY-SIX
1897

THE NEW BABY WAS BORN before the house on Carnegie Avenue was finished. Fred now slept cozily next to his grandmother, Sydney was in a cot at the foot of her bed, and the new baby, named Howard, was in Fred's old crib moved into his parent's room. The apartment was cramped, the two women constantly at the scrubbing board and the clothesline that was down steep stairs into the Yard, capitalized in their imaginations because, full of one-room accommodations and a soap-making industry, it was a source of much money.

BJ's schedule reminded Katie of their early marriage. He worked all day at his office and spent the long summer evenings inspecting the workmen's accomplishments at the new house. Once again, as with the building on Market Street, Katie was not a part of the planning or decisions. She was too far into her pregnancy to make the mile-long trip by streetcar and then too busy with two small boys and a new baby.

Katie was anxious and irritable. The situation was heavy with the memories of their earlier house-building—she pregnant, BJ away making decisions that affected but did not include her. Would his exuberance humiliate her again? She relived the degrading experience in the unfinished store, this time under the puzzled glances of her mother, who sensed Katie's anger but kept silent. When Katie thought of her husband, her mind's eye saw no difference between the mill-stained young immigrant of five years ago and the confident business-man of today. He was impetuous, he was carefree, he was Hungarian.

BJ talked at dinner about furnaces, washing machines, flooring, and fireplaces.

"The house should be red brick, don't you think?" he said to nobody in particular. "The yellow would be cheerier, but it would get stained so quickly with the soot. Red brick is better. I told them so last month." He wiped his mouth with the linen napkin, ironed that morning by Katie, and was off, excited, energetic. They could hear his whistle all the way down Market Street until he disappeared around the corner.

BJ's new position at Metropolitan Life meant that he often had to visit homes on The Hill. He knew how things should be, Katie assured her mother, silently reserving the right to criticize.

When the babies were finally down and asleep, she and her mother pored over the Sears-Roebuck catalog, marking pages for BJ's consideration. Rugs, a dining-room table with sideboard, beds for four bedrooms, and armoires and dressing tables. Katie cast her feelings of isolation from BJ aside for the moment and had a wonderful time. It was like furnishing a doll's house, the tiny pictures from the catalog being transferred into a tiny house that existed only in her mind. BJ approved this, rejected that, made suggestions, then filled out the order blanks and wrote the bank drafts.

When BJ announced, one soft August evening, that the house was ready for her inspection, Katie was gripped by fear. It *had* become a game, this Carnegie Avenue house. She thought of it in terms of tomorrow, never today. She thought of it as BJ's house, not her own. She was used to the clutter in the small apartment, accustomed to Blossom's visits and Mike's grocery deliveries. She could send Sydney to play in the street and take Fred and Howard for walks in a carriage, and nod to a dozen people who greeted her by name. She had created her routine. She liked her routine.

"I can't go now, BJ," she complained, her hand at her bosom. "I've got to nurse the baby. Who knows when he will be hungry? I'll go when the baby is predictable. Wait a little."

But BJ was handing her her hat.

"We'll be back soon," he told Liebe. "We're going to Jerusalem!"

The streetcar brought them to the bottom of the hill, then a hansom to the heights of Carnegie Avenue. Here, the air was cleaner. The angry red of the sky, lit by the mills, was far away at the horizon. In the quiet, Katie could hear the leaves move in the breeze. BJ's hand on her arm turned her around.

"Well?"

Katie gasped. "*Mein Gott!* It's so big! I had no idea! Are you sure this is ours?" A pang of envy assailed her as she realized the joy he must have had in putting together this grand structure. "Of course

you're sure. It's just that it's so big. Let me look at it a little at a time."
She shook her shoulders and took three steps back so she could see the
whole house.

A porch, reached by three steps, covered the whole front of the
house and shaded four windows and the front door. There were five
windows across the front of the second floor. The steep slate roof had
two dormers. Katie looked up in awe.

"Let's go in," BJ said.

He unlocked the door with a flourish and pressed the switch just
inside. The hall sprang into light.

"Electric lights! I never dreamed . . . . " Katie stepped carefully into
the front hall. It was large, and at the back a staircase rose, turned,
and rose again to the second floor. Brown eyes round with wonder, she
was steered by BJ's hand on the shoulder through a curved doorway
on the left. BJ touched a switch, and a chandelier illuminated the
parlour. A fireplace with a mantle, a rug, heavy damask curtains
awaited the acceptable furniture from Market Street and the much
more appropriate shipments from Sears. A little push from BJ sent
Katie into the dining room through sliding double doors to the right.
Here the pictures from the Sears catalog came to life. The dining table,
chosen for the massive carvings that would hide the hard knocks visited upon it by growing children, was surrounded by eight baronial chairs.

Katie frowned. It looked so different in the stamp-sized picture.
She turned to the sideboard against the back wall. It was huge. So
much space to fill. She pictured her cracked dishes and jelly glasses on
display there and laughed. BJ laughed, too, and took her hand.

"Keep going. I want to see it all," she said as she checked the
watch pinned to the pleats of her blouse. "But remember, I've got to
get back to Sydney and Fred and Howard. Mother's arthritis is getting
too bad for her to take care of three children for very long."

Past the door to the backstairs and into the kitchen, where Katie
admired the six-burner gas stove. The water pump was right there in
the sink, practically a brass sculpture. No more pumping water in the
yard. A small barred door in the wall opened onto a large box, most
of which was outside the house so that the iceman could load it without coming into the kitchen. Her eyes glowed. A breakfast room, a
sun porch, then back through the bright rooms to the hall again. They
climbed the carpeted stairs, hand in hand.

"What in the world is *that?*" She was arrested in mid-step by the stained glass window at the landing, now dusky in the gathering dark of the evening.

The window, colors dulled by the evening light, pictured an armoured knight standing beside a white horse. Knight and horse were in a wooded glen, flowers at their feet, twisted branches behind them. In the knight's hand, held high above and the focus of his reverence and awe, was a jewel-studded cup.

"I think he's called Sir Galahad," said BJ, and he pulled at his moustache. "One of the carpenters found it in a building he was tearing down and offered to put it in here. I couldn't resist, it was so beautiful. It reminded me of the quilt you and your mother made. And it reminded me of our name. Reiter means rider in English, you know. He's a rider. It all seemed to fit." BJ looked doubtfully at the picture, towering above them. "I guess I didn't pay enough attention to the details. Do you like it?"

Katie was not sure if she liked it or not. It brought back memories of her father, although Adolph's horse was black, not white. But there was something about it that made her uncomfortable. She couldn't remember much about Sir Galahad. Something to do with King Arthur and a round table. She giggled. The dining room table and chairs could have served King Arthur. As soon as the Carnegie Library was built at the end of the street, she would look for information about Sir Galahad.

Katie's laugh made BJ playful. He covered Katie's eyes as they reached the second floor and walked her to the end of the hall.

"Now," he whispered. "Open."

They stood in a room of white, white tile on the floor and shoulder-high on the walls. A white tub stood on claw feet. The sink was a Greek column fluting into a seashell. Porcelain towel racks were on the walls. And in the corner, a . . . .

"What *is* that?" Katie said.

BJ coughed. "A water closet. A toilet."

Katie stood looking at this wonder. "And what's that?" she said, pointing to an oak box hanging above the bowl.

"Watch." BJ pulled the chain hanging down its side and, with a rush, the toilet emptied and then filled. They looked at each other, she in disbelief, he with a wide grin.

"It's miraculous!" she said. Then, in the quiet of the new house, BJ opened his arms and Katie moved close to him. BJ sighed. His mouth trembled. It had been so long since Katie had willingly suffered his touch. He tightened his arms, and she relaxed against him, her undeniable yearning spreading warmth through his body.

"Katie," he murmured in her ear. "Here's a chance for a new beginning. Let's leave the past in Market Street and start fresh in our new house. No old memories. Things will be easier and we can be happy with each other."

She pushed out of his arms. "Don't be silly. I don't know what you're talking about. Of course it will be wonderful here, who said it wouldn't? It will be a wonderful place for the children to grow up." She headed briskly down the stairs. "We better go back. The children will be ready for bed and Mother won't be able to take care of them."

BJ shook his head and locked the front door behind them.

CHAPTER TWENTY-SEVEN
1907

THE HOUSE ON CARNEGIE AVENUE FILLED QUICKLY. There was a piano in the front hall, a fine clock on the parlour mantle, handsome china displayed on the sideboard in the dining room, the cherished quilt on the bed in the master bedroom. And a maid—the *shiksa*—in the kitchen, homely Pauline, born of Polish mill workers, quiet, willing, and constantly criticized by Katie.

The house was filled with children, also. Sydney, the oldest, then Fred and Howard. Then Helen. And Adolph. Then Sylvia. And now in 1907, Katie gazed at the new baby at her breast.

"What shall we call this little *nebbish*, Mama?" she said, pinching the soft cheek to keep the baby awake and nursing.

Liebe bit off the thread close to the soft mauve cotton. She was making another quilt, this one of purple flower-pots side by side on a white background. She considered the baby-naming. It was important to her that long-gone family members be recalled by future generations, known if not by their American names then by the Hebrew name that is given to each Jewish child. Sydney, now fourteen years old, was named for BJ's father, Schmuel. Her beloved Ephraim had been remembered in the sturdy presence of Fred, twelve. Her husband Adolph, so long gone, twinkled behind the mischievous blue eyes of his namesake. Liebe was overjoyed when Katie named this baby Adolph, even though the first baby Adolph had died so tragically. She needed to pronounce the name. Adolph was six. She watched Adolph and Sylvia, on their stomachs in front of the fireplace in Katie's bedroom, trying to decipher a book under Helen's tutorial eye.

"That's an N, not an M," Helen said in her self-important voice. "You'll have to do better than that if you want to go to school." Katie eyed her wearily and tightened her lips. She thought that Helen was developing into an overbearing child. They fought often, and BJ was quick to take his daughter's side. She's her father's daughter, thought

Katie, the Hungarian side of the family.

Katie settled the baby more comfortably in her arms. This little one seemed to be sucking the strength out of her along with the milk. Then she realized Liebe was speaking to her.

"What would you think of calling her Maria Theresa, after the Empress?" said Liebe.

"Ummm. The Holy Roman Empress. The *Maria* sounds..." she couldn't put her finger on it. "...*holy*," she finished lamely. She suddenly thought of Sir Galahad presiding over her stairwell. I've got to get to the Library, she decided. "Theresa is a beautiful name, though. I remember when you sent us off to school telling us to remember Maria Theresa." She stopped. Her mother remembered, too, and her eyes were filling with tears.

"Don't cry, Mama," Katie said. "What good does it do?" She buttoned the front of her nightgown and handed the sleeping baby to her mother to settle in the cradle. "Theresa is a wonderful name. We'll tell BJ when he comes home."

Liebe carried the baby near to the fire. "Come, children. Come look at your sister." Three pairs of eyes turned dutifully to look. "Her name is going to be Theresa." Now there was a bit more interest. Liebe tucked her finger into the little fist. "Say goodnight to Theresa."

"Good night, little Tess," said Helen.

"Good night, *Nebbish*," giggled Adolph, who had heard the name —helpless one—his mother had called the baby.

"'Night, Tinkou," lisped Sylvia, trying to curl her tongue around the name.

"Now, where are Fred and Sydney and Howard? They should have been home from school long ago. It's getting so late. Where can they be?" Katie's perpetual anxiety was making her fretful.

Liebe straightened the pillows on the bed to make Katie more comfortable. Seven babies in eleven years. Eight babies, really. She mustn't forget the first Adolph, the sweet little boy she never met who died of the watermelon. It was too much. She knew Katie loved each child fiercely, unable to imagine a world without every one, but she knew the fatigue, the strain, the terror that grew as the family grew. How can a mother survive the waiting for them to come home safely? She shook her head and sighed. *Ach, mein Gott.* Liebe was always sighing. Nobody looked up.

"Helen," said Katie. "Go to the corner and look down the hill to see if they are coming, please, dear. And bundle up. It's snowing, and it's very cold. There's a good girl."

Helen made a face but got up to do as she was told. She was gone a long time. Katie was irritated. I'm so tired, she thought. Two weeks won't be a long enough rest for me this time. I could sleep for a month. Oh, to read a book. Just to sit and read. Or take a walk. Yes, a walk. She imagined a green lawn, scattered with daisies. She had a white parasol. And just walk. Up and down, up and down. No, I'm too tired to do even that. There is so much work, even with Mother and Pauline to help. And BJ. But he's so demanding. I wonder if I can tell BJ that I won't...that I can't.... Hungarians. Aunt Reiter was correct. But how could I have known? Perhaps all men are the same. Could I say no? Katie drifted into a troubled sleep.

There were heavy footsteps on the stairs, three children yelling and calling her name. Mama! Mama! Katie struggled upward through layers of heat and heaviness.

Howard, Fred, and Helen burst into the room. "Mama! Mama!" Their words tumbled over each other as Adolph stared open-mouthed and Sylvia put her hands over her ears. The baby woke screaming.

Liebe grasped the two boys by their shoulders and shook them. "Stop this! One at a time. What has happened? And oh, Howard! Your poor foot! Look, Liebchen." She sat him in the rocking chair by the fire and removed his torn shoe, holding it up as its tattered leather hung in strips. She rubbed the cold, bruised foot in its ragged sock.

Katie slid weakly from the bed and took Fred in her arms. "Tell me, tell me! What happened? Are you both all right?"

Fred held her tightly. "W-w-we w-w-were w-w-walking...oh I can't!" he said in despair, as his stutter overcame him.

Howard took a deep breath. "We were walking home from school, Fred and I." Howard looked at his grandmother's worried face and switched to German. "It was so cold. There's a storm coming up and it's snowing really hard already. And it's dark, you know." Helen was impatient at this announcement of the obvious. "Hurry up!" she yelled.

"We were crossing Prothro, 'way down at the bottom of the hill. It was icy and dark, and I slipped. My foot got caught in the streetcar track. The harder I twisted, the more it stuck, until it was in so tight

I couldn't get my foot out of the shoe. And then I could feel the street-car coming!"

Adolph's eyes widened. "How could you do that?" he asked.

"The track started to buzz in my foot. Honest, I could *feel* it coming. And sure enough, a minute later we saw the horse and car turn the corner, and we could see the light coming toward us. We were both yelling, let me tell you." *Let me tell you* was Howard's favorite phrase from third grade. He realized he had said it in English and smiled at his grandmother.

"All right, Bubby, German again. Fred was standing in front of me waving his arms and yelling Stop! Stop!"

"More like st-st-stop," muttered Helen. Katie gave her a black look.

"But they didn't see us. It was dark, and the horse hid us from the conductor. And the clacking was so loud we could barely hear ourselves. So Fred ran toward the streetcar. 'My brother's on the tracks!' he was yelling. And not stuttering either. Clear as a bell." Howard pounded Fred on the back. "He banged on the door, but the motorman must have thought he wanted to get on and kept pointing ahead to the regular stop. So Fred grabbed the horse's reins, Mother! The horse's reins! And pulled!"

Katie sank to her knees.

"Well, Fred didn't stop the horse. But the motorman was so mad, he stopped the horse himself. And he got out, ready to hit Fred with his whip. But Fred just stood right there, pointing at me! So when the motorman saw me, he was really surprised. 'You're a real hero,' he said to Fred. 'A real hero.'" Howard pulled at Fred's hand. "You *are* a real hero, Fred. You're a great brother."

The story had to be told again to Sydney when he came home from his afternoon job of delivering newspapers. And again when BJ came home from the office. Katie could hear the excited words drifting up from the dinner table.

How could she keep all these children from harm? Even walking home from school held terrors. She thought of Sydney, blond, handsome, responsible. Fred, brown eyes like hers, quiet and shy, compassionate, stuttering painfully like his Uncle Henry Reiter, the Reiter brother she was supposed to have married. Howard, his grandmother's golden boy, bright, serious. Helen, too much like me, Katie thought, wanting her own way, resentful, efficient, strong, too strong. Adolph and Sylvia were roly-poly babies, he a cherub, she a beauty. And now another baby, another life to worry about, another catch in the throat, another tug at the heart. No more babies. No more danger, no more fear.

She was falling asleep, down, down a dark icy slide toward a bright light growing larger and larger.

"Ummm. Must tell BJ the baby's name is Theresa."

CHAPTER TWENTY-EIGHT
1908

KATIE HELD THREE-YEAR OLD SYLVIA'S HAND snugly in her own as they threaded through the Christmas crowds in downtown McKeesport. Katie hated Christmas and usually never shopped in December. All this religious fuss, the silly bells and trees, the false cheerfulness. If they ever realized it was the birthday of a Jew they were celebrating, ah, then there really would be a fuss. Sydney's face rose in her mind. Jesus looked like Sydney, at least the statues of him looked like Sydney. Blond hair, blue eyes, a sweet sad face. But how could that be? A child of Nazareth would be dark, dark. Big dark eyes, black hair, brown skin. She was amazed by her three blond children, Sydney, Howard, and Sylvia, all little *goyim*. But they looked like her father. And their own father, too, of course. But he was Hungarian. Who knew where he got his blue eyes? Katie shrugged off thoughts of BJ.

Though she feigned indifference to the crowd, Katie was interested in the new fashions swirling about her. Skirts were narrower and shorter in 1908, men were wearing soft ties under their heavy chesterfields. No more whale-boned waists. She was aware of her too-long skirt, dragging over the slushy sidewalk.

The snow transformed the dirty city into something almost lovely. The electric lights were on in the gathering evening, and, masking the fine soot, snowflakes fell lazily through the golden light. The cold air held the sounds of jingling harnesses and laughter. Katie began to smile and return greetings. She couldn't quite bring herself to say Merry Christmas, but it was Hanukkah, too, after all, so she said Happy Holidays. The *goyim* didn't have to know which holiday she meant.

She and Sylvia looked into the bright store windows, exclaiming over the displayed bounty. Walsh's window full of dolls stopped Sylvia in mid-sentence. Her mouth formed a circle of wonder as she leaned on the glass to get a better look.

"The one with the little fur, Mama, look at that! And the baby all in lace. And that one there, with the crown."

They discussed the dolls, sitting ones and standing ones and babies and princesses, while snowflakes gathered on their eyelashes and shoulders. It took a few minutes before Katie was aware that Mr. Walsh was beckoning to her from behind the heavy brass rod that held up the curtain separating the store from the window.

She pointed to herself, her eyebrows raised. He nodded.

"Let's go in, Sylvia. I think Mr. Walsh wants to talk to me, although I can't imagine why," she said.

"Mrs. Reiter. How nice to see you," Mr. Walsh said. "May I wish you greetings of the season." Katie looked at him with respect. He had turned that phrase very nicely.

"And who is this young lady?" Mr. Walsh knelt down to take Sylvia's hand in his. "Sylvia, eh. What a beautiful name for a beautiful little girl. No, not a little girl. You are like a living doll. A real living doll. How old are you, Sylvia?"

Sylvia knew her manners. "I am three years old, sir," she said.

"And which of the dolls in the window does a real living doll like?" Mr. Walsh stood up and led Sylvia to the window. Parting the drapes, he lifted her into the Christmas wonderland. She stood, gravely looking around.

"I'm not sure," she said. "I haven't seen them all."

She took off her gloves, tucked them into her muff, and handed it to Mr. Walsh. With a rosy finger, she poked a baby in the stomach, jumping back as the baby wailed. Then she found a tiara awry and straightened it on a curly head. A bisque face caught her fancy, and she smoothed the short skirt for an ice-skater. Soon, Mr. Walsh was also holding her coat, and Sylvia was sitting in the window with her skirts spread around her, having a serious talk with a collection of princesses.

Katie was growing impatient. She had things to do at home, and it was getting dark. But Mr. Walsh was delighted. He had closed the curtain and was assessing the crowd gathering outside the store to watch the beautiful child playing with his inventory.

"Mrs. Reiter, I have an idea. Would you let Sylvia come every day and play with the dolls in the window?" His speech had just a touch of a German accent. Could he be from the old country? Katie wondered. "One of your boys could bring her here every day and stay with her. I would pay him a fifty-cent piece each day. And when the, ah, season is over, Sylvia will choose any doll she wants." Katie inclined her head. "...And for her sister, too. And I understand there is a new baby. A girl? She shall have a doll, also." Katie's eyes crinkled just a bit.

Mr. Walsh glanced at the women now crowding through his doors, suddenly finding a need to buy the doll that the "darling little girl in the window was playing with."

"And, if you would let me, I would make a generous contribution to your, ah, synagogue in your name and BJ's."

Katie permitted a smile. "Sylvia does seem to be enjoying herself. But of course I would have to speak to my husband. If he agrees, Sylvia and Howard will be here tomorrow." Katie rattled the brass rings holding the curtains. "Come along, Sylvia. Put the dolls away where they belong."

Sylvia dutifully put the dolls back on their perches and was lifted from the window, to murmurs of disappointment from the onlookers.

For the next two weeks, Sylvia played happily for a few hours each afternoon in Mr. Walsh's window. Her eyes shone as Howard took her hand and led her to this paradise. He sat behind the curtain and did his homework as she excitedly unwrapped the beautiful boxes and set the new dolls on their perches. She briefly mourned the absence of particular favorites when they were carried off by the saleswomen, but mainly she fed her little family, changed diapers on some babies, whispered about Prince Charming to various Cinderellas, shook an admonitory finger at miscreants, and immensely pleased the people who gathered each day to watch her. She was as oblivious of them as she was to Howard's good cheer and the jingle of coins in his pocket.

Mr. Walsh greeted Sylvia with courtliness each day in the window. He bowed and shook her hand before he helped her with her coat and boots, shaking off the snowflakes and inquiring about her family. He later appeared with a tray of little cakes and a small Victorian pitcher of milk, which she generously offered to the dolls before eating them herself. Dozens of these charming pitchers were sold by Mr. Walsh's store before the early Christmas Eve closing. That evening, about an hour before he locked his doors for the holiday, Mr. Walsh climbed into the window. He bent over the little girl, took her hand, and helped her choose a doll for Helen and one for baby Tinkou.

"Now, Sylvia, you may have any doll here that you want. Which one will you have for yourself?" he asked.

"Oh, Mr. Walsh," breathed Sylvia. She looked around the window anxiously. She didn't want to hurt anyone's feelings by showing favoritism. The babies really needed her, but the grown-up dolls were closer to her own age. And they were all so beautiful. She was in a rapture of indecision.

Mr. Walsh watched her.

"Sylvia," he said and knelt so that his eyes were level with hers. "I don't want to influence you, but I think this should be your doll." He took from a chair behind the curtain a box he had chosen himself and wrapped in red paper with a green velvet bow. Inside was a perfect vision with long golden curls, apricot cheeks, and violet eyes fringed by dark lashes. "I've called this doll Sylvia from the very first day you came to play in my window. You never saw it because I kept it in my office just for you." The crowd on the sidewalk applauded. Sylvia sighed. Of all the dolls she had played with, this was the one she would love the best. She put her hand into Howard's and left her little Christmas family, waving goodbye to them and Mr. Walsh over her shoulder until they turned the corner to walk up the hill. Helen insisted on her doll as soon as Howard and Sylvia arrived home, all the while protesting that she was much too old to play with toys.

"Really, I would rather have had something else," she said as she shook out of the box a lovely creature all in plaid with a tam o'shanter and patent leather shoes. Helen ran to her room, where her joy did not have to be so closely contained.

Sylvia decided that Tinkou's doll should be saved for her first birthday, soon to come in January. Meanwhile, it could have a home in her own room, where she could take care of it, feed it, diaper it, and perhaps even play with it just a little.

Theresa's first birthday was on a typical Pennsylvania winter day. The leafless trees were hung with gray icicles, the streets ridged with dark, frozen slush. The sky was low, the air full of soot and sleet. The older children arrived home from school in a blast of cold air that rattled the windows in the chilly sun porch. Although each child had a special wooden peg on the wall, there was much jostling and shoving to get into the warm kitchen first. Helen held her own in the fray, aiming a few good kicks at the knickered legs around her.

Fred was usually the peace-keeper. "S-s-stop that! If you w-w-would all line up to hang your coats, it w-w-wouldn't be so—ouch! That's enough!" No one listened to Fred.

Birthdays were celebrated by permitting the birthday child to choose the meal. Sydney's favorite was always stuffed peppers. Adolph concentrated on desserts and followed the advice of others, usually Helen, for the main course. Tess was too young—not pablum! they had all chorused—so BJ chose the menu. A Hungarian meal.

The first course was *intergeschluganah*, not the children's favorite food but their favorite word. It was a cold soup of green beans and beaten sour cream. BJ had two bowls. The main course was chicken with green peppers and tomatoes, accompanied by "worms," so named by Helen because they were little finger-sized cylinders of mashed potatoes, mixed with egg, rolled in sugar and cinnamon, and fried in deep butter. Tess could manage these, her little fist hooked into her round-handled silver spoon.

Katie observed her family from the end of the table. Her mother, seated next to her, was growing old. Arthritis had bent her hands and her back and had made her petulant. For years, the family had spoken only German at home because of Liebe. Sydney, Fred, and Howard had learned English for the first time at school. But now Liebe was old and distant and absorbed in her own thoughts, and the children preferred English. Adolph, Helen, Sylvia, and probably Tess would never even learn German, would probably start school speaking English as well as their classmates.

The boys were growing up nicely, handsome and strong. Sydney, Fred, and Howard were already taking music lessons, and Katie had noticed Adolph playing with Fred's clarinet and doodling on the piano in his spare moments. Maybe he was ready for lessons, too. Fred had taken it on himself to give piano lessons to Helen. And he often sat with Tess on his lap as she banged on the keys.

Eighteen years of marriage to BJ. He was even handsomer than when they had met. There was gray in the hair on his head, but his moustache was fierce and blond, his eyes clear blue. She sighed as she gathered the baby in her arms.

"Time for Tess to go to bed," she said. They all sang Happy Birthday again while Tess looked at them solemnly. "And Sylvia, do sit up. Take your elbows off the table. Good night, all. Do your homework. Come, Mother, I'll put you to bed, too."

CHAPTER TWENTY-NINE
1909

MARCH BLEW THROUGH MCKEESPORT with Arctic intensity. The billowy snows had turned to dirt-streaked icy drifts. Soot-laden flakes continued to fall in unending succession. Each morning BJ got up in the darkness, put on his dressing-gown, and descended to the basement to do battle with the huge furnace. He shook the night's cinders into the pan under the furnace, then shoveled load after load of coal into the open door, stuffing newspaper around it to catch fire from the burning embers. As the roar of the fire traveled upward through the registers, the children tumbled from their beds, complaining and coughing and sniffling, hoping to work up enough symptoms to be able to stay home in bed.

Katie was in despair of ever having her whole family free of the sicknesses that the older children brought home from school. First one, then another, sick in bed, wanting attention, wanting hot lemonade, wanting to be read to, watched enviously by the others. It was very nice indeed to be tucked up so cozily, able to dream and drowse, avoiding the frigid walk to school, reading story-books, having meals on a tray. Sydney was no sooner declared well than Fred complained of headaches, then Helen with a bad cough, then Howard with a runny nose. Howard, learning to play the trumpet, delighted in musical nose-blowings, and engendered a great competition of upper-respiratory noises. Everyone but his mother thought this hilarious.

She eyed them anxiously. She was in dread of the diseases they got, her hand constantly darting to a flushed cheek, her breath catching at a sneeze.

"Wear your scarf!" she shouted as they crowded out the door. "Buckle your galoshes!"

Howard and Fred exchanged shrugs. Boys with scarves were not highly respected at school. Galoshes were meant to be worn unbuckled. Necessary sartorial changes were made around the corner.

The best day to be allowed to stay home, all agreed, was the day of the coal delivery. This could be viewed comfortably from the sunroom window. The coal wagon pulled up at the back of the house, and the burly coal-heavers, their blackened faces streaked with sweat, leaped out. They opened the basement window into the coal room and pushed into it the long metal coal chute. Then, standing in the wagon, they shoveled what seemed a whole mine full of coal onto the chute. It clattered down with a great deal of noise. The children could hear it piling up far below them in the dark cellar.

The horse, his head wreathed in steam from his breath, waited patiently, first one huge hoof and then another gracefully tipped on the frozen lawn as he shifted his weight. His skin twitched in the freezing air, his eyes, brown and mournful, fixed somewhere past the horizon.

"I'm glad I'm not that horse," said Adolph, his nose pressed against the window. They all sighed in agreement, frosting the glass. Then began the face-makings, the letter tracings, a few forbidden words written by the boys, until the *shiksa* rushed in with a towel to remove the traces.

April finally brought some relief from the weather. As she walked to the *shul* for Saturday morning services, Katie felt the sun soft on her face. She sighed as she loosened her hold on BJ's arm.

"The ice is actually melting. Maybe I won't fall and break my neck," she said. Katie's one small vanity was her pride in her shapely feet and ankles. She loved shoes, buttoned, buckled, always polished, and refused to defile them by putting them inside rubber boots.

"What's that, BJ?" Katie pointed at a colored paper fluttering on the front door of the house on the next corner.

"That's a quarantine notice, measles I think, if it's pink. Whooping cough is green."

Katie shuddered. She was so absorbed in her own children, she had forgotten that others might be endangered, also. She glanced behind her at the straggling group of little Reiters.

"Thank God we got through..." She caught herself. It doesn't do to say these things aloud. *From my heart to God's ear,* she thought, amending the old Yiddish saying.

That night she regretted her lapse. Sylvia's cheeks were red, her eyes unnaturally bright.

"What a hot *kepelah!*" Her hand was on Sylvia's forehead.

"Hush, darling, don't cry. Mother will put you to bed and Daddy will fetch the doctor." Katie implored BJ with her eyes. Quickly. Quickly! She held the hot little hand in her own, offering sips of water, putting cool cloths on the burning forehead.

The doctor arrived in his snow-flecked overcoat. "Come out in the hall with me, " he said, when he had finished the examination. Katie motioned that BJ should accompany him. She did not want to leave Sylvia's bedside. Then she strained to hear the voices, but no sound except quick, shallow breathing assailed her ears.

She sat by the bed in the darkened room. The *shiksa* would have to manage the other children while she herself nursed Sylvia. BJ could do the marketing, her mother would cook. It shouldn't last too long. Sylvia would be better in a week at the most. Four sharp knocks on the front door stopped her mental race through the days ahead.

Where is everybody? Why doesn't somebody answer the door? She ran through the quiet hall and down the stairs to fling open the front door. A yellow paper was tacked there. Scarlet fever! A man was hurrying down the walk, but he did not stop at her shout. Katie shivered uncontrollably. The paper crackled in the wind. It was like a funeral wreath, hanging there. Scarlet fever? She had never heard of it.

Sylvia died on Wednesday, quietly sleeping away the sixth year of her life. Once again Katie, BJ and Liebe stood in the cemetery, staring incredulously into a small open grave. She had willed it not to be, but it was. Sodden April closed around Katie, and squeezed her and wrung her.

Three days later the other children returned from Sheeny Mike's on Market Street where BJ had taken them on the doctor's orders to remove them from the house. Words of admonishment rose to Katie's lips—Why did you take them *there?* Is that any atmosphere for children?—but what was the use. She herded the children immediately up the stairs.

"Each of you take a bath," she rasped. "Scrub, scrub, scrub. The big ones take care of the little ones. I'll take Tess." She left them in a huddled mass by the bathroom door, scrabbling at each other's buttons.

Theresa was seldom out of her mother's arms. Katie smoothed the soft cheek with her own, whispering endlessly into the pink ear.

"I can't stand it. I would die myself, but what would happen to these babies? Never have children, *Nebish*," she keened into the dark curls. "It isn't worth it." She confined her grief to this bewildered audience of one. With the other children she was brisk.

"Don't just sit there. Get busy. Is your homework done? Are your beds made? Move! Move! Move!" She found them in corners, caught them whispering together in their rooms, surprised them gazing out of windows. Theresa tried to wriggle from her arms, but Katie held on more tightly.

"No, my darling. Stay here with me." She nuzzled the warm neck. "My heart is too cold to let you go. You are my warmth. Tomorrow you can play with the others." Tomorrow. Tomorrow would be just like today. She would never be free of terror. How could she protect these children and her own aching heart from new blows?

Liebe sat quietly in the corner of the parlor, her gnarled fingers always busy with the mending. Though tears sometimes coursed unchecked down her wrinkled cheeks, she kept her lips shut tight against the torrent of grief that would pour out of her should she relax her guard. Occasionally, she caught Katie's eye, and they exchanged an agate gaze, neither flinching from the misery she read in the other.

CHAPTER THIRTY
1911

TESS WAS TWO the following January, then three, then four.

"Don't do that, darling, you'll hurt yourself," her mother said. And, "Don't touch that, Nebish, it has germs and you'll be sick." And, "We won't play with this one, that one, the other one. She's a dirty little girl and my Tinkou is clean."

Tess was a solemn child, grave, serious. Her brown eyes were deep with the pain and unshed tears of her mother. The other children protected her, sometimes unwillingly, and despaired of her caution and reserve. They were constantly daring her to venture into the unknown, to slide down the banister, to refuse to eat her vegetables, to say No! to her mother. Tess was not tempted, only coerced into sulks by her need to obey Katie and her desire to please her brothers and sister. She vented this ambivalence by screaming and crying until all activity around her stopped and everyone petted her and dried her tears and agreed she was perfect.

It was Fred, tall and gangly at fourteen, who finally took pity on her wretchedness. Tess moved from Katie's arms to Fred's lap.

Katie gazed at the two dark heads bent so often over the story books. What a good boy he is, she thought. He loves to read, she loves to listen. A good arrangement.

Fred did, indeed, love to read, especially to Tess. His halting speech was no impediment to her. His voice fell as sweetly on her ears as his dear earnest face pleased her eyes.

"*And n-now was acknowledged the presence of the Red D-Death,*" Fred intoned. "*He had come like a thief in the n-night. And one b-by one dropped the revelers in the b-blood-bedewed halls of their revel, and died each in the despairing posture of his fall. And the life of the ebony clock w-went out with that of the last of the day.*"

Fred shut Poe with a snap. He relished the horrific stories, relished the roll of the elegant language unimpaired by his stammer. That Poe was unsuitable for his four-year old sister did not occur to him. If he read to her, he would read good literature. Let her hear long words, let her imagine sweeping vistas and complicated relationships. If the *House of Usher* was not truly a picture of reality, neither was Rapunzel. Besides, Mother never asked him what he was reading.

Fred tipped Tess from his lap.

"N-Now it's time for bed," he said. He took her hand. Tess followed obediently, darting an anxious glance at the ebony clock on the mantle.

When she was five, Fred began teaching Tess to play the piano. He put her pudgy fingers on the ivory keys and, with gentle guidance, led her through a passable little tune. She was enchanted. Fred played the trumpet, not the piano, and had no technique to impart. But trumpet and piano intersect on a page of music, and music itself Fred understood very well.

"These little dots on the staff are just l-like words in a book," he told Tess. "When you can read them, you'll have the whole world of m-music at your fingertips." Fred, realizing he had made a figure of speech, warmed to his task.

"Now, the spaces here," he traced them on the staff. "They're called F and A and C and E." He saw Tess wrinkle her nose in confusion. "But we'll give them better names. F can b-be Fortunato. Remember him from *The Cask of Amontillado?*"

Tess did, all too well.

"And the A can b-be Amontillado, all right?' Tess preferred abyss. "R-right. Abyss it is. And for C, how about Camille?" Tess shuddered, remembering Camille hanging head down in a chimney in the Rue Morgue.

"I'll remember that for sure," she said.

"And E is Edgar, of c-course. Now for the l-lines." Another wrinkle of the little nose. "It'll be easy, you'll see. There are only five. The bottom one is E again. How about *El Dorado?*"

This pleased Tess. Poe's poems were Tess's favorite listening, and she had insisted so often on their repetition that she was able to put herself to sleep at night by reciting their soothing cadences.

"And then G, for Goodfellow, *duplicitous Goodfellow,*" he chanted and drew down his eyebrows. Tess giggled. "And next is B for Berenice of the Ghastly Teeth." He laughed as Tess rolled her eyes.

"Now here's a nice one. This line is D, for Dupin, the Great Friend. And last is F. What shall F be?"

"Fred, of course," said Tess promptly. And she named the lines and spaces back to him, stumbling only over Dupin, because they disagreed on the pronunciation.

"Now read to me," Tess demanded. She pulled Fred over to BJ's chair and settled in his lap. He picked up the book lying on the footstool and found their place.

"Okay, here we go. *Fool. M-might I not have known that into the pit was the object of the burning iron to urge me. Could I resist its glow? Or if even that, could I withstand its pressure? And now, flatter and flatter grew the lozenge, with a rapidity....*"

Katie, passing back and forth behind the dining room door as she set the table for supper, watched them fondly. She herself had instilled the love of books in her children, and Liebe had marched them up to the Carnegie Library on the corner at least once a week since they were able to walk. But why was she puzzled by the names that were being whispered between Fred and Tess at the piano. Camille? Berenice? What were these? Had Fred gotten out the German copy of *Grimm's Fairy Tales* she kept in her bedroom? Surely not. She had warned him against reading that book to the younger children. It was too wild, too frightening. She wanted them to sleep peacefully at night.

But of course he would not disobey her. Fred was a good boy. She crossed her arms over her apron and smiled a little smile of satisfaction. She never even imagined Poe!

CHAPTER THIRTY-ONE
1916

THE GREAT WAR HAD BEEN FOUGHT IN THE REITER'S BREAKFAST ROOM since 1914. BJ read the newspapers aloud every morning, banging his fist on the table, rattling the eggs in their fragile cups.

"The Hapsburgs will have us in their quarrels again!" he shouted at his children. "Ferdinand was a nobody, a nothing, a *nudnik!* He's shot by a madman, and it's an excuse for slaughter! Katie! Katie!" He shouted to her in the kitchen. "Come here. Listen to this!"

Katie sat down and poured the last of the coffee. She listened to BJ's insistent voice as he read off the battles. I'm glad Mother didn't live to see this war, she thought. She sighed for her mother, *Ach, Gott,* dead now two years, and rested her head on her hands. Her mother's life was changed in so many ways by the Hapsburgs. Liebe's beloved husband Adolph, only a young boy, had been kidnapped—surely that was the right word—into the Army. Uncle Jacob had to flee to America. A kick from a Hapsburg horse had ended Adolf's life and sent Katie across the sea. And Ephraim, Ephraim would have been a man now, in his forties, if he had stayed in Bohemia and been allowed to grow up.

Katie shook her head. Probably the only useful thing the Hapsburgs had done was give her a lovely name for her daughter. She looked at ten-year old Theresa. The child was so solemn, listening to her father. He was frightening her with his loud voice and his table-pounding. Katie would have to return her breakfast table to its usual petty battles and eliminate this talk of global war.

"What do we care about all this, BJ?" Katie said. "We're here in America. There's an ocean between us and them." She sent a reassuring smile to Tess. "This means nothing to us."

"Ach, that's what President Wilson says," stormed BJ. He was speaking German now, a sure sign that this was important. Everybody sat up straighter. "These things start small, but they grow. An obscure prince or an unknown emperor, it seems to be local and unimportant. But it becomes an excuse, a . . . a . . ." he searched for the right word and found it in English. Besides, the two youngest children couldn't understand German, and he wanted them to learn what this was all about. ". . . a justification, yes, that's it. A justification to jockey for power and prestige." He read rapidly through the article. "Saber rattling, the *Post Gazette* calls it." He looked around at his four sons. "These things always produce colorful phrases. But they hide the fact that ordinary people are going to die because of the greed and pride of a few princes."

Katie waved at the *shiksa* to clear off the table. And, with an imperceptible shake of her head and the merest drawing together of her eyebrows, she signaled to BJ to stop this kind of talk. Don't worry the children, she was saying, don't let them think they have to concern themselves with this war.

BJ caught her eye. One last bang on the table with the folded newspaper, and he stood up. "That's enough of that. Come, Tinkou, it's a beautiful summer morning. Let's walk to Jerusalem."

Theresa's face lit up. She loved these walks with her father, her hand in his. They always started along Carnegie Avenue, under the elm trees dappling the warm sidewalk with shadows. There were golden coins of sunlight under her feet. How can pointy leaves make round spots, she wondered. She opened her mouth to ask her father, then closed it again. It was better to be quiet. She didn't talk to him very often. She was her mother's little girl, unlike Helen, who was constantly in conversation with Father. Tess didn't know what to say to him, how to interest him. Better to be quiet and companionable. She tightened her hand in his and was rewarded with a quick squeeze.

Carnegie Avenue was filled with grand houses now, set back on their green perfect lawns. The sound of a mower whirred in the morning air. On the far corner was the Carnegie Library, an elegant gray stone structure looking quite the most imposing house on the block. Tess treasured the time she spent in the cool dim rooms of the library, first with Grandmother, then with Fred, and, now that she was allowed to go about by herself, alone. She often brought home four or five books, as many as she could carry at a time. She read the first sentence, and, if it caught her fancy, she added the book to her stack. She liked the importance of writing her name on the cards. Theresa

Reiter. It was a beautiful name.

Sometimes she looked into the rooms that held the books for adults. She never crossed the thresholds. The books looked the same as the books she read, all lined up on the shelves with little white numbers on their backs. What could be in those books that children shouldn't read? It made growing up seem very mysterious. What if she read books in the wrong order, didn't learn the information at the right time? This was a thought that often troubled her. She pulled again at her father's arm and again thought better of it. No silly questions. She smiled at him when he looked at her quizzically and matched her pace to his.

Now they turned left onto Versailles Avenue. It was pronounced Ver-*sails* in McKeesport, but she knew better. Versailles Avenue was a little frightening because one side of the street was a cemetery. It was surrounded by an iron fence with points at the tips like arrowheads. This was a cemetery for people who were not Jewish, and Tess wasn't sure what Gentiles did when they were dead. It was another question that she didn't want to ask her father. She always looked straight ahead when they passed the cemetery. She had never actually seen it.

They turned right at the next corner and walked down the Shaw Avenue hill, past the shul, and into the center of town. Jerusalem, to Tess, was just down the next block, two doors from the railroad track. Here was a coffee shop, The Star, quiet except for the times when a train passed by and rattled all the dishes in the place. Tess could feel the train's power in every bone in her body, but nobody else even looked up, and nothing ever broke. She and her father had their second cup of coffee of the morning, this time with *shlag*, whipped cream. And they shared a Danish. Tess tasted the word as well as the pastry, an adjective turned sweetly and stickily into a noun.

At home, Katie was helping the shiksa empty the breakfast room of the remains of the morning meal. Sydney had left early for his job in the steel mill. It was the same dangerous, dirty, hot job his father had in the early days. Two years ago, Katie and BJ had argued about Sydney's going to work in the mills. Katie wanted him to enroll at the University of Pittsburgh.

"I'm going to work in the mill," Sydney said firmly. "I don't want to go to college. I don't belong there, at least not yet. I don't know what I want to study. And besides, Fred starts college this year. He knows he wants to be an engineer. And with his stutter and shyness, who knows how long it will take him to finish. And Howard starts next year, to medical school. They both know what they want. I don't." Sydney took a breath but continued doggedly. "It's expensive to have three of us in college. Let me wait until I know what I want. Right now I know I want the money I earn. Father worked in the mills. It didn't kill him, and it won't kill me. I'm nineteen, and I think I can decide for myself what to do."

"Of course, you're big and grown up." Katie hurried into a pause. "But your father and I—we're so much older, we have experience and can tell you what's best. And this working in the mills isn't the best. Stay in school, study all sorts of things. You'll find out what you want by studying. The money isn't important. We can keep three of you in college. Your father earns a good living. *Zug* him, BJ. Tell him, tell him."

BJ shifted uncomfortably in his chair. He cleared his throat. His blue eyes met those of his son. "Sydney should do what he wants," he said. "Working in the mills won't hurt him." Then he rose, got his hat and cane, and left the house.

Katie was furious. BJ was always opposing her. Let Sydney do what he wants, indeed. How can Sydney know what he wants? He is too young. He needs guidance and a firm hand. But how could her hand guide him with BJ pulling the other way? Her lips tightened, and she shrugged.

"All right. Do what you want," she said shortly and left Sydney sitting in the living room with his shoulders bowed.

She had watched him go off to work every morning for two years in his overalls and blue shirt, carrying a lunch pail, while Fred and Howard, in tweeds or linen and laden with books, caught the street car to the University of Pittsburgh. Her pitying glance followed Sydney down the hills, down down down into the hell's furnace of the Carnegie Steel Mills. *Ach, Gott.*

She wiped her hands on her apron and sat down at the empty table. Now she had time to read the paper by herself without BJ shouting out the news and telling her what to think about it. The dispatches were worrisome, there was no doubt about it. She read every word, shaking her head, clicking her tongue. She imagined the *Boche* fighting across her Bohemian farm, bleeding into the white daisies on the lawn, defacing the little spinet she had never learned to play.

CHAPTER THIRTY-TWO
1917

THE UNITED STATES DECLARED WAR on Germany April 6, 1917. It was a Friday, and Katie was in the dining room, preparing for *shabbus*. Her cheeks were wet with tears of anger, frustration, and sadness. Why, why, why are the Hapsburgs doing this again? And why are we letting them? Where is President Wilson? He will keep us out of war! She snorted at the perfidy. She rummaged in the sideboard cupboards for candles and candlesticks. As she straightened up, two brass candlesticks dropped from her shaking fingers. She picked them up, in her distraction not bothering to inspect them for dents. She snatched up a damask napkin, forgetting to open its folds and smooth it out, putting it on as a head covering for the Sabbath prayers still folded. The children came into the room, drawn by the noise. Adolph started to giggle at the sight of their mother with a thick napkin hat. The others shushed him. The flames, reflected in the beveled mirrors in the back of the heavy sideboard, trembled in the warm breeze from the open windows. Katie glanced angrily at the six children behind her and clasped her hands under her chin. She took a deep breath to calm herself before she began the ancient prayer.

"*Baruch ata adonai,*" she began, and her voice choked. Adolph glanced uneasily at Helen.

"*Baruch ata...*" Katie couldn't go on. Helen took two napkins from the table and handed one to Tess.

"*Barach ata adonai eloheinu melech haolam.*" Helen's strong voice took over the ancient prayer. "*Asher kidshanu bemitzvotav,*" she continued and finally pronounced the word *Shabbus* to announce the arrival of the Sabbath. It was she who kissed her brothers and sister on the *kepelah*. Then she put her arms around Katie and held her sobbing mother.

Supper was soon over, and the conversation among the boys in the parlor, in spite of their mother's stern looks, was only about the war, the wonderful opportunity to go to Europe at the government's expense, a chance to see Paris, maybe even go to Chakow and Aperius where their mother had grown up.

"What's to see there?" said Katie. "It's just the Old Country. There's nothing there to see. You'll be better off staying here, getting your degrees, becoming professional men. Stop this talk of going off to war."

"But Mother, you've got to agree that it's exciting. A chance to fight for our country, a chance to get even with the Hapsburgs!" The boys glanced at each other, suppressing their laughter. Their mother did go on about her feud with the Hapsburgs. "Anyway, we have to register in June. Everybody our age does. There is no getting around it."

"Don't do it," Katie begged. "A draft is illegal. You read the papers. Eugene V. Debs says the draft is wrong in a democratic country. Wait a while and see what happens."

The boys paid no attention to their mother. But they paid a great deal of attention to each other. They spent an inordinate amount of time talking in their rooms, including Adolph in these conversations, even though he was still a schoolboy. Early in June, all four of them appeared at breakfast with serious faces.

"Mother. Father." Adolph had been chosen the spokesman because, with his cherub face, he was considered to be the one to elicit the most sympathy. "We boys have made an important decision. Since some of us may be going off to fight..." Katie gasped. "we thought we would give ourselves middle names. It sounds more dignified and... and..." He looked to the others for help.

"...and it shows solidarity," Sydney prompted.

"Yes. Solidarity. You never gave us middle names, so these are the names we have chosen to express our..." Adolph blushed in embarrassment, but went on. "...love. Yes, love. And to link our fates."

He didn't mention the fact that his brothers were worried that they would be killed in the war and wanted their names to be remembered. He shrugged off his secrets. "May I introduce..." A formal sweep of the arm. "May I introduce Sydney *Howard* Reiter." Katie's look of disapproval was replaced by one of wonder. "And Howard *Sydney* Reiter. I will from this moment on be Adolph *Fred* Reiter. And Fred..." Adolph drooped a bit in disappointment, but his voice held steady. "Fred will be Fred Martin, because Martin is the name of his favorite professor."

Adolph could not sustain sadness for very long. With a huge grin, he ordered, "Gentlemen, please stand." There was general applause around the table and looks of relief exchanged among the boys as they realized their little plan had been accepted.

On June sixth, Katie stood on the porch, her arms folded across her chest, and watched her three sons go down the hill, two blond heads, one dark, bobbing excitedly. Fred, taking time off from Carnegie Tech, Howard from the University of Pittsburgh Medical School, and Sydney, still grimy from a morning's work at the mill, were going to the Selective Service Office to register.

When they returned, hours later, Sydney was angry and stormed up to his room. Fred and Howard pummeled each other's arms and laughed uproariously at his retreating back.

"What's going on? What have you done?" Katie demanded.

"We volunteered!" Howard shouted.

"B-but Sydney just registered," Fred muttered. "You d-don't have to worry."

Katie shrieked. She rushed at them, hitting, slapping, aiming blows at their heads, their chests.

"Aw, Mama," they mumbled. "Aw, Mama... stop it...no, Mama... just a minute...." They protected themselves as best they could, raising their arms, turning, retreating. Finally Katie was exhausted.

"What have you done?" she sobbed. "What have you done." The second time, it wasn't a question.

Within the month, two letters arrived from the Selective Service office. One was an exemption for Howard because he was a medical student. The other ordered Fred to report for duty with the 112th Engineers in New Jersey.

The whole family went to the train station to see him off. Katie was quiet and tight-lipped, her sorrow completely overwhelmed by pure anger, anger at the Old Country, the Selective Service Office, and finally at Fred himself. Tess cried. Howard shuffled about, envious of the travels and adventures he would not share. Sydney was quiet, on the edge of the group, hands deep in his pockets. BJ slipped some money into Fred's hand as he embraced his son. Fred boarded the train, it started, was gone.

Katie hurried them away from the platform. "Go home now, all of you," she said. "I have some things to do. I don't want you hanging around, slowing me down. BJ, make sure they all go home." She turned away, fastening her hatpin more deeply into her heavy hair.

Outside the Selective Service office, she paused. What could she say to these men so they would not take another son from her? She mistrusted men, she mistrusted *goyim*. She looked at her reflection in the window, straightened her shoulders, and went in.

The children straggled back to the house on Carnegie Avenue. "It feels like Yom Kippur," Helen whispered to Howard. They were in their best clothes, home with nothing to do, and the main purpose of the day finished, the day itself flat, colorless, bleak as it spun slowly away.

Helen decided to change her clothes. It would pass the time. Tess followed her upstairs and watched the removal of the satin cloche, the pleated jacket with the jet buttons, the dove-colored blouse, the heavy serge skirt, and the buttoned shoes. Helen's creamy skin was slowly revealed, curved voluptuously into her corset.

Tess sighed. "You're so beautiful, Helen. I hope I look like you when I'm eighteen."

"You'll never look like this, Tinkou," Helen said. "I'm the Hungarian in the family. I'm my father's daughter, and the rest of you are mere Bohemians. But don't feel bad. *Zoftig* women are going out of style, and you're going to be just right. You're only ten years old. In eight years you'll be right in style. Stand up and let me look at you."

Tess stood and allowed herself be inspected.

"You've got nice broad shoulders and wonderful legs. Don't blush. Skirts are getting shorter. Mother's dresses hit the ground, but mine are already above the ankle. When you're eighteen, yours could be at the knee!" They both laughed at the improbable prospect. "This war is going to change a lot of things. Girls are even going to work, now that the boys are leaving for the army."

Helen drew closer to Tess. "In fact, I'm looking for a job downtown, as a bookkeeper. Don't tell anyone, because I might not be hired. I don't want to sit around the house all day waiting for a husband. I need to be doing something." Helen put on her shirtwaist.

Tess shook her head, thrilled to be in on a secret of Helen's, shocked that her sister should be considering such a thing.

"It's okay, Tinkou. When you get older you're allowed to do some things your mother doesn't approve of."

This statement reminded Tess of something. "Are you still walking out with Lou Breyer?"

"Yes I am," said Helen defiantly. She, too, had made the connection between her mother's disapproval and Lou. "Why not? He's fun, and we have a grand time together. And he's a pharmacist, for God's sake. Don't gulp like that, Nebish. That's not a bad word." But Helen was chastened. She should not have said God.

Tess's eyes widened at the profanity. This was really a *mature* conversation. She pushed on.

"And what about Fred? Is that where he was last night, saying goodbye to..." She hesitated to say the name, so disliked was this poor girl by Katie. "...Ellen Eyle?" she whispered.

"Yes he was." Helen was whispering, too, even though she knew her mother wasn't home. "Fred's twenty-two years old, for *goodness* sake. They really love each other, and they're happy together. She's a wonderful girl, really, a musician, and that's perfect for Fred. Just because she's not Jewish doesn't mean she's not good enough. And besides, she said she would convert if...." Helen realized she was talking too much to a ten-year old child.

"Don't worry about this, Tinkou. It will be all right in the end, you'll see. We should spend our worry time thinking about Sydney. Mother is determined that he won't be called up, too. She didn't get to Fred in time, but she's moving heaven and earth to keep them from getting another Reiter." Helen buttoned the last button of her blouse. "It sounds like Mother's home. Let's go help her with dinner."

Katie made sure that Fred got a letter every day. She wrote to him every morning, and the children had to write a letter once a week. "No letter, no supper," she said.

For a month, the letters went to New Jersey. Then they went to the American Expeditionary Forces in England. Fred overseas! Katie couldn't believe it. She could not contain her anxiety. *Ach, Gott,* echoed through the house. She renewed her visits to the Selective Service Office to plead for an exemption for Sydney, but she knew she had no good reason to offer.

The letter calling Sydney to the Infantry arrived in September. He sailed for England in December. *Ach, Gott,* to be on the ocean in this weather.

Sydney and Fred met once in England before they were sent to the Front. They mailed Katie the picture they had had taken together, two young men staring solemnly at the camera, their legs encased in puttees, Sam Browne belts across their chests, flat-brimmed hats on their laps. Katie put the picture on her bedside table.

Tess was now writing the required letters to two brothers in France. At first, she rebelled. "I don't have anything to say," she complained. "Nothing ever happens to me." But she was led to a chair at the dining room table and handed a pen.

"Stop muttering. Write."

To her surprise, Tess was soon eagerly putting pen to paper, enjoying the stories that she made of the events at her school and making sure there was at least one impressive new word in her letters.

"There's a new boy in my class," she wrote, glad that she could tell someone of her crushes without being subjected to teasing. "He's a peach. His name is Jere. He spells it that way even though it's pronounced Jerry. Isn't that cunning?" Cunning was this week's new word. "I wrote him a note in English class that began Dere Jere, and I signed it Jess Tess. He didn't answer, but I know he wanted to."

The next October, Adolph took a picture of Tess with his Brownie camera. She sent it to Fred. "Can you believe I'm eleven already? I miss you enormously." Enormously was the new word of the week. "Don't look at my baggy coat and the old serge skirt Helen gave me. But do admire my hat. I love hats, and I shall always wear them— great straw cartwheels and satin cloches with feathers."

And then it was 1918. And then it was November. And then it was November 11th. The morning began with the sounds of bells, far away bells from many churches.

"What's all this about?" complained Katie. The ways of the *goyim* constantly irritated her. Bells on Monday, yet.

Then the bells in the Baptist Church across the street began to toll, and loud voices were heard on quiet Carnegie Avenue.

"It's the war! The war's over!" Adolph and Howard raced to the door. "That's what they're shouting. The war's over!"

Everyone but Katie crowded onto the front porch. She leaned slowly forward, supporting her weight on hands flat on the table. Tears squeezed between her eyelids. Her heart was pounding. Was it possible that this nightmare was done?

She gathered the tablecloth into a bundle and walked blindly to the back stoop to shake it out.

"Mrs. Reiter! Mrs. Reiter!" Gradually the voice penetrated Katie's consciousness. She saw her neighbor standing on the porch next door. " Aren't you proud of your two boys NOW?" called Mrs. Benson.

"I'll be proud when I see them standing in front of me." Katie folded the tablecloth. Her heart was beating too loudly to permit a conversation. "I've got to get my children off to school. Excuse me." She shut the door gratefully behind her. She wanted this moment to be private, not a justification for the war because it had ended.

The crowd on Carnegie Avenue swelled. The four Reiter children were scattered from their house on one corner to the Library on the other. "No school! No school!" Adolph shouted, waving his arms to get his mother's attention. Katie saw BJ, his gray homburg a quiet spot on the swirl of color created by housedresses, shirtsleeves, sweaters, and bright leaves falling through the golden autumn haze. The tears burned again in her eyes. Dare she take a deep breath? Dare she loosen the tight bands around her heart? She thought not.

The doorbell rang at seven the next morning. Katie sent the *shiksa* to answer it, then called her back.

"I'll get it. Watch the pancakes."

She pushed open the swinging door into the hall. She could see the messenger boy's green uniform fragmented by the beveled glass in the door, saw his hand outlined clearly as he tried to peer in. He twirled the bell again. When she opened the door, he thrust the telegram into her hand and fled down the steps.

Katie screamed then. She screamed as she tore open the yellow envelope, screamed as she read the words... regret to inform you... your son Sydney... missing in action... sorry. Scream after scream. All morning. Through the afternoon. No doctor. Send the rabbi away. Scream after scream. No to the children. No to BJ. Screaming. Outraged. Exhausted. Asleep.

Katie was at the breakfast table the next morning. She looked levelly into each pair of eyes, ignoring their pain.

"Sydney is not dead," she said in a steady voice. "I would know it if he had been killed. I would have felt it." Her eyes sought BJ's, as if his confirmation would make it so. "He and Fred have been in my mind every minute, every second. I know Fred is alive, and I know Sydney is, too." She poured the coffee, served the oatmeal, cracked the eggs, buttered the toast, steady, steady. "What does it mean, missing in action? Just that they don't know where he is. All that confusion, no wonder. They can't find him. That's understandable."

BJ kept his eyes on his plate. The children passed the salt, spooned the sugar, stirred things.

"Did I ever tell you about my father coming home from the war?" Katie asked.

"Yes, yes!" A chorus of voices. The children were relieved by the change of subject. "But tell us again. We love that story. Especially when Liebe fainted."

Katie interrupted them impatiently. "But the important thing is that he was missing for a long time. And then he came home." A nerve started jumping around her mouth, and she put up her hand to press it. "Sydney is alive, and he'll come home."

Howard avoided Helen's eyes. Adolph looked down at his plate. Tess began to cry. "Oh, yes. I know he'll come home," she echoed.

It was Fred who came home. Three months later they were all at the railroad station to greet him. He was tall and stern as he searched the crowd, an austere young man in his immaculate uniform, hat square on his head. When he saw Katie with her arms open, he ran to her. She stood on her tiptoes to embrace him, held him tightly to her. Her eyes, just above his shoulder, searched the faces of all the stern young men as they poured from the train.

"Is Sydney with you?" she whispered.

"No, Mama. I'm alone. I came b-b-back alone." His voice broke, and he tightened his hold on his mother. But Katie had already released him, had settled her heels on the gritty cement, had turned away.

"*Ach, Gott,*" she said.

CHAPTER THIRTY-THREE
1920

"Help! I'm dying!" Tess shrieked.

Helen sprang from the other twin bed and raced across the room.

"For God's sake, what's the matter? What are you yelling about?" Helen was shrieking, also.

"I'm bleeding! There's blood all over everything! I'm dying!"

Helen caught her breath. There *was* blood all over everything! Tess's sheets, nightie, legs were all red and sticky. She took Tess by the shoulder. "Stop yelling," she hissed. "You'll wake everybody in the house."

Tess looked up at her piteously, her mouth a small O.

Helen inspected her sister. "You're not cut or anything. Your legs and arms are moving, everything seems to be working. Maybe you're just having the curse. What? You're thirteen and you never heard of that? Mother hasn't told you? No, no. It's all right. Don't start to cry." Helen tried to keep the anger out of her voice. "She didn't tell me, either. But that's all that's the matter with you. And I guess I'm the one who's going to tell you. But first I'll clean you up."

Helen got a basin of warm soapy water from the bathroom and a small roll of flannel from the bottom drawer of her bureau. Tess watched suspiciously, aware from Helen's face that the next few minutes were going to be very unpleasant. It was worse than that. She listened with growing horror as Helen delivered a detailed monologue on menstruation, most of which she had learned from Howard, now a medical resident at Montefiore Hospital.

"But you don't have hair under your arms," Tess protested.

"I shave, Nebish. If you don't, it smells."

Oh, no! Hair and smells. It was almost too much to bear. "But you don't shave down there, too, do you?" Tess wailed.

"Of course not." Helen was getting snappish. Clearly, this was not her job. "Now you've got to put this on." She had folded the flannel and pinned it neatly into Tess's underpants. "You have to change this often. Make sure you have a good supply of flannel. You can use your old nighties, but you've got to buy some flannel, too. And wash them out thoroughly, or they'll be uncomfortable."

Tess shrank back into the pillows, her eyes wide. "All right," said Helen. "I'll wash them for you at first, but then you have to take care of yourself."

"At first? What does *that* mean?"

"It happens every month. Didn't I tell you that part? And sometimes you get a stomach ache, but it goes away, and it's nothing to worry about." Helen paused and seemed to be waiting for another question. Tess searched her reeling mind for something to ask, but there was nothing else she wanted to know. In fact, she wished she were still asleep and could be forever ignorant of the things Helen had told her.

She got up slowly and buttoned her underpants, aware of the flannel bunching between her legs. She stripped the bed, vaguely ashamed, and put the linens to soak in the bathtub.

"You can tell Mama you started," said Helen. "But don't bother her with questions, and don't say you got the curse. Say you're unwell. If you want to know anything else, just ask me." Helen took Tess's dark curly head between her hands. "Don't look so glum. Everything's going to be all right. And now you'll have something to talk about to your girlfriends." Tess grimaced. She didn't have any friends.

Tess dragged her feet on the staircase, dawdled on the landing, rubbed imaginary dust from the banister. She felt definitely unwell. That was the perfect word for it. Her stomach cramped, her head felt funny, and she was sure she didn't want to go to school with that awful flannel pinned to her panties. Everybody would know what had happened just by looking at her.

She decided not to tell her mother how her morning had started. It didn't seem interesting, and, besides, Tess was worried about Katie. Nothing had been the same since Sydney had been killed. Tess was sure that he was dead, as sure as her mother was that he was still alive. Katie wrote the War Department every week, demanding news of her son. She haunted the Selective Service Office until the day it closed. They had tolerated her, then been rude to her. She cried every day, not hiding it from her family. She seemed to be getting smaller, her thin body encased in heavy black silk and wool, her graying hair pulled back into a bun, her hands forever worrying each other.

Katie's hands were swelling with the same arthritis that had so tormented Liebe. Flashes of pain contorted Katie's face as she worked around the house. And she was a virago there. Nothing was clean enough, nothing done fast enough. Shiksas came and went, almost too fast for anyone to learn their names. They couldn't clean, couldn't cook, couldn't iron well enough to please Katie. Tess had more than once felt a stinging slap across her face for reasons she couldn't fathom and was too intimidated to question. BJ, Fred, Howard, and Adolph fled every morning to the streetcar to have their breakfasts together in a restaurant in Pittsburgh, where Fred was working in an engineering firm, Howard was a medical resident, and Adolph was in his second year at Pitt Pharmacy School. Helen's beau, Lou, had convinced him that this was an interesting profession.

Tess clung to Helen as her sister moved toward the door. Helen had gotten the coveted bookkeeping job in McKeesport, and she often left with her father and brothers to have breakfast downtown before they caught their streetcar. Tess's eyes begged Helen to stay. Helen hesitated a moment, then ran down the steps to catch up with her father and brothers. Tess drooped back to the sunroom, where she now often had breakfast alone with her mother. She picked at her food. Katie was silent.

Tess was too miserable to go to school. She wouldn't go, that's what. The thought was so startling, Tess lowered her head, fearful that her mother would read the intention in her eyes. Her stomach hurt and that awful flannel seemed to be twitching the back of her skirt like a duck's tail. She was too embarrassed to be seen by anyone she knew. She would play hooky. The thought seemed less terrifying the second time around. She had never skipped school before. She had always had her lessons ready, her papers written. She was the teachers' pet. No one would ever suspect her of skipping, so she probably wouldn't even get in trouble. Tomorrow she could just say she was sick.

Of course, she could tell her mother now that she was sick. Then she could just stay home. But she didn't want to be at home for a whole day. The house on Carnegie Avenue, once so sunny and protective, now seemed cold and dark and mournful without her brothers and sisters arguing and laughing and making noise. Tess pushed her toast around the plate for a few more minutes. She was torn by an old need to be a good girl and the entirely new desire to be something else. Finally, it was time to leave the house, no matter what. She shrugged into her coat. At least she would be well covered. Tess went back to the sunroom to kiss her mother goodbye. Katie was distracted. She lifted a cold cheek.

Out on the street, Tess let pairs and trios of her schoolmates pass her. She didn't know many of them. Only thirteen, she was a junior in high school, having been passed through the second and fifth grades. She was too young to be of any interest to them, they were old enough to be fascinating to her. She dragged her feet, lonely and rejected. She walked past the school, around the corner, across the tracks, and into town.

Now what? The long day stretched ahead of her. She had no idea what to do. A quick turn through McCrory's Five&Ten. Everyone was looking at her. They knew she should be in school. She hurried out, waving at an imaginary companion beyond the door. She walked quickly to the movie theater, stepped into the shadowy recess, and spent a half-hour studying the posters. Rudolph Valentino. Velma Banky. The It Girl. Now what? The day was warm, she was perspiring in her winter coat, looking conspicuous among the sweaters and jackets. It was too late to go back to school, too early to go home. She trailed up and down back streets she had never seen before, turning corners when someone appeared on a porch to shake a mop or air a blanket. She was conscious of the heavy books on her arm, the coat flapping around her knees, an ache in her legs.

Tess rounded another corner, and a park she had passed three times already was just ahead. She sank down on one of the benches and looked at her watch. It was ten o'clock. Five more hours to go. Being good passed the time so much faster than being bad. She reached for the books she had dumped on the bench and wiped off the soot. She would do her homework for tomorrow.

Her concentration was broken by a distinct feeling of hunger. It was one o'clock already. She must have done enough algebra to take her through the next term. Then she had lost herself in *The Scarlet Letter*. What the "A" meant she could not imagine. What was adultery that poor Hester deserved such punishment? She must look up the word as soon as she got home. She felt a sudden rush of tears to her eyes. What had she herself done to be sitting alone here in the park, hot and uncomfortable, wanting something to happen that would be lovely and mysterious, wanting to be free of the feeling of sadness and responsibility. And wanting—Tess bit her lip—wanting something to eat.

She realized with a start that she should be going home from school for lunch. But she couldn't. She absolutely couldn't sit at the table and pretend she had been to school and was going back. The only other place she knew in McKeesport to get food was the bakery she and her father went to on their walks to Jerusalem. She found it in the middle of the next block. Inside, the smell was heavenly. Tess considered every succulent Danish in the open glass cases, then reached into her pocket. Of course it was empty. She never carried money to school. She always went home for lunch. Today was a school day.

She was in a state of shock. She always had lunch. It was past lunchtime. She was really very hungry. Suddenly, there was a Danish in her pocket, the very kind she always had with her father. She caught her breath as the saleslady approached.

"May I help you?" A smile, not an accusation.

"No. No, thank you. Uh... "just looking." Tess sidled to the door, frowning thoughtfully, then snapping her mysteriously sticky fingers as though she had just remembered something that needed attending to. And she was outside, around the corner, onto Market Street, and happily eating the Danish. Was it more delicious because purloined? Purloined. That was Poe. A Transcendentalist like Hawthorne.

Lost in sugary contemplation, she almost didn't see her mother walking ahead of her. Market Street was so much more crowded than other streets, pushcart vendors, gossiping women, children. Tess slowed her pace. She certainly didn't want to catch up to her mother. It was only one-thirty. Her mother, like Tess, had a furtive look about her. Where could she be going? She had lived on Market Street before Tess was born. Maybe she was going to visit a friend? Tess darted among the crowd, trying to keep the small black figure in sight. Abruptly, it was gone. Tess stopped. Her first thought was that now she could go home, because her mother obviously wouldn't be there to be surprised at her early arrival. Her second thought was for her mother. Was she all right? She walked a little farther, peeking around doorways, looking up at second-floor windows. Just where Katie had disappeared, a hand-painted sign creaked overhead. PSYCHIC. Tess had never seen the word, didn't know what it meant, connected it vaguely with physic. She knew what that meant. Was her mother sick? Relief gave way to dread. She turned her footsteps toward home. Was this to be her punishment for playing hooky, to find out that her mother had a secret illness? Perhaps she, Tess, like Hester Prynne, had committed adultery, that it meant becoming an adult—and she was well aware that she had lied, stolen, spied, and gotten the Curse.

CHAPTER THIRTY-FOUR

TESS APPROACHED THE CORNER OF CARNEGIE AVENUE by sidling from bush to bush until she could see the back yard, the sun porch, the half-curtained upstairs windows. She knew no one was home, but she had to be sure before she went in at the unheard-of hour of two o'clock on a school day. The *shiksa* was taking clothes from the line in the hanging yard behind the house, her back to the street. That meant the cellar door was open. Tess had no key. Who would give a house key to a thirteen year-old girl?

She stalked Hilda—she suddenly remembered the *shiksa's* name, Hilda—and, keeping always just behind her, reached the cellar steps as Hilda reached the end of the clothes-line. She darted down the gritty steps and into the dark cellar, heavy with the smell of wet clothes and old coal dust. From the gloom, she saw Hilda's heavy shoes and pouchy stockings on the top step. Tess knew where to hide, although the thought terrified her. Between two of the cellar's murky rooms there was a doorway, actually a short corridor, created by the four huge central beams that supported the house. The shadow here was Stygian, different from the other shadows, palpable, frightening. Howard had told her that it wasn't a shadow at all but a bottomless hole that she must always leap across lest she fall into the center of the Earth.

She believed him, then almost disbelieved him, even though she felt a pull, a vertigo, a clammy wind when she jumped. Her foot had never touched there. Now she sped silently toward the passage, squeezed shut her eyes, and slid between the beams. The floor supported her. Unable even to breathe a sigh of relief, she listened as Hilda put the clothesbasket down on the folding table and trudged back to the stairs to pull the cellar doors closed. Tess had done this often enough herself. You had to go out in the yard to fold the first door down. She counted the crunches Hilda's shoes made, decided Hilda was out in the yard, and ran as lightly as she could, burdened by her books and coat, up the inside stairs, and into the kitchen, then less carefully up the backstairs to her room.

She leaned against the closed door, her heart pounding, tears squeezing between her eyelids. What a mess she had made of the day. It had been horrible. She would never do such a bad thing ever again. Tess put the heavy books on the desk, hung up her coat and hat, and wiped her cheeks of the tears and perspiration. Then she took a scissors from the drawer and angrily cut up her best flannel nightgown. She folded a piece the way she had seen Helen do it that very morning and walked wearily into the bathroom.

Katie arrived home within the hour. Tess could hear the key in the lock, then her mother's footsteps on the stairs. *"Ach, Gott,"* Tess could hear. *"Ach, Gott. Mein Gott, mein Gott."* Tess opened the door to her room.

"Tinkou, you're home. I'm sorry I wasn't here. I'm sorry I..." Katie waved her hands vaguely.

"Mother! Are you all right?"

Katie's skin was pale, her upper lip beaded with sweat.

"Of course I'm all right. No. No! I'm not all right at all. Oh, Tess, my Tess." Katie's shoulders crumpled. She clung to Tess, clutching great folds of Tess's blouse. "I've done a terrible thing and God is punishing me. But I couldn't stand it any more. My poor Sydney. I had to know. And now I know, and it's worse!" Katie's voice was a howl.

Tess was frightened. She drew her mother into her room and sat her down on a chair, then ran to the bathroom for a glass of water. Katie waved it away. She wanted no comfort.

"I went to a psychic," Katie wailed. *Psychic.* The word on the creaking sign. Tess peered into her mother's face. "I went to a psychic." She clutched Tess's hand. "Jews shouldn't do that. Promise me you'll never do that. Promise me!" Tess nodded her head, her eyes wide.

"I took some things of Sydney's," Katie went on more calmly. "I told her. The telegram, missing in action, no body, no information, no nothing. I asked her to tell me what happened. What happened to my boy?"

Katie looked up at Tess. "Why am I telling this to you? You're just a baby, why should you listen to this horror?" But Katie was wild with grief. She couldn't stop.

"The woman, she was dirty, her room was dirty. She took

Sydney's watch in her dirty hands, and she looked at me. She looked at me for a long time. I knew I should leave, but I couldn't move. And then she said, she said, ' I see your son! He is alive but he doesn't know his name. He is sitting in a chair far away. His shoulders are bowed. And behind him, a woman is combing, combing his yellow hair.' That's all she said. I begged for more. I begged for more!"

Katie shuddered. Tess couldn't breathe.

"But she said that was all there is. No more. She gave me back the watch. She took my money. She asked me to go."

Katie looked at Tess with such hunger, such desperation, such need that Tess drew back, her hand to her throat. Katie was stung by the gesture, appalled by what she had confided. She slowly straightened her back, squared her shoulders, took a deep breath.

"I shouldn't have done this terrible thing," she said in a steady voice. "Such a *goyisha* thing to do. May God forgive me. What does this woman know in her dirty room. If she was so smart she'd have a better house. Now come, Tinkou. Your mother is a foolish woman. We won't speak of this. We'll forget it. Do your homework and then come help me with the supper." Katie put her hands on the desk and pushed herself up. "Forget about this."

Tess stared at the space where her mother had been. She put her hands up to her face. Her fingers were icy, her cheeks hot. Pictures were whirling in her mind. Sydney sitting in a room far away with his golden hair and empty eyes. A dirty room. An old witch standing behind him. The witch came out of the shadows and it was Tess. Tess hugged herself hard and bent over, groaning. Oh, she couldn't stand it. She wanted to fling herself into Helen's arms and scream out the whole story of her day. But her mother said not to speak of the psychic. Did that mean that only she and her mother would know what the psychic said? But she could never mention it again to her mother. She could not be the one to bring that stricken look to her mother's face.

Tess wobbled over to the bed and sat there, rocking back and forth, holding herself. Her mother said forget it. How could she forget it? The scene was so clear in her mind. Sydney sitting there. She could almost reach him, pull him out of that dirty room, sit him at her desk where her mother had sat.

No! No! She was scaring herself. She jumped up from the bed and patted her hair. Without looking in the mirror, she bent over the wash-basin and splashed water on her face. Now the homework.

But she had done all her homework, enough homework for a month. It hardly seemed possible she had sat in that sunny park only this morning. What a terrible day. She would never forget it. Never. She stood irresolute in the middle of the room. A deep breath. A hard tug at her skirt. Then she went down the stairs to help her mother with supper.

CHAPTER THIRTY-FIVE
1921

TESS HUMMED the Bach Prelude and Fugue as she pinned up her hair. She could feel her fingers tapping lightly on her skull as she mentally rehearsed the notes she was to play on the piano in just a few hours. Today, both Fred and Helen were getting married, a double wedding right here in the house on Carnegie Avenue, and she, Tess, was to provide the music and then stand with her sister and brother under the *chuppa,* the wedding canopy. Tess was so excited she could hardly manage the tortoise-shell hairpins. The long dark curls kept slipping through her fingers as she struggled to get the right effect. Next year she would have a haircut, a bob they called it. She would be a senior in high school and needed to look older than her fifteen years. She tucked a lock behind her ear, then tugged hard to straighten out the waves. She looked with dissatisfaction at the curly mop reflected in the mirror. It would not do at all, but there was no more time.

Helen was marrying Lou Breyer, and Fred was marrying Anna Schlesinger. Tess hadn't gotten to know Anna very well. Fred was always going to her house or taking her out. Anna was seldom invited to the Reiters'. The truth was that Katie didn't like Anna very much. The truth was that she didn't like Lou Breyer very much, either. Another Hungarian, Katie grumbled.

Tess exchanged a dark look with her mirror image. Fred had sadly given up Ellen more than a year ago. Katie had been adamant in her decision that no one could come into her house and certainly not into her family who wasn't Jewish. "No *shiksas,*" she said to her sons. And, when she reluctantly acknowledged that Helen was old enough to marry, "No *goys.* I won't have them talking about their Yiddish mother-in-law." Sometimes she got ill before Fred went out with Ellen, and Fred had to sit by her bed and stroke her hand and whisper assurances that he wouldn't marry Ellen. Then he would telephone Ellen and break their date. He was needed at home, he said. Tess stood at the top of the stairs and listened to his conversations on the phone. He never closed the door to the little room under the stairs when he talked to Ellen. The open door kept the light off, and Fred said it was easier to talk in the dark.

Fred was even more quiet than usual after he stopped seeing Ellen. Tess tried hard to make him laugh, bought him little things to amuse him, dragged him to the piano to help her with difficult passages, but nothing had taken the sad expression from his face. Then he met Anna at a dance in Pittsburgh. Slowly his smiles returned, his dark moods lightened. One night he brought Anna to supper.

"Please, call me Ann," she said. "I don't like Anna. It's so formal." She shook hands with BJ and Howard and Adolph, smiled shyly at Katie and Helen, and kissed Tess's cheek. Tess was enchanted. Ann was slender and tall, almost as tall as Fred in her high-heeled shoes. She wore a black dress with white at the neckline and cuffs. And it was short, almost to mid-calf. Tess saw Helen's eyes widen at the flash of black silk stocking as Ann bent to kiss her.

Tess was very uncomfortable at the supper table. It was not their usual evening meal with everyone talking at once. The plates were handed around by Madge, the new *shiksa*. "An Irisher," Katie had sniffed. Fred was nervous. His stutter returned. Ann often put her hand on his arm to slow him down and calm him.

But Katie couldn't object to Ann. She had, after all, dismissed Ellen only because she wasn't Jewish. Now, faced with a Jewish girl, she couldn't criticize because Ann wore short skirts, or spoke for Fred, or was possessive. Katie's tight mouth showed Tess her mother's contempt for Ann, but there was going to be a wedding, a fine affair, and Katie would make an imposing figure at the reception surrounded by her handsome family.

All four newlyweds were going to upstate New York to honeymoon at a resort on Lake Geneva. It sounded terribly romantic to Tess. Ann was lovely and sophisticated; Lou was handsome and rakish. She imagined them all on the beach in bathing costumes, having dinner in a candle-lit dining room, taking buggy rides through sun-dappled forests.

Tess sighed and plunged one more pin into her heavy hair. A last practiced expression as the demure sister of the bride and groom, and she darted down the steps into the hall where the guests were already gathering. The phone rang in the little room under the stairs, and Tess watched her mother make her apologies to Rabbi Solomon and hurry to stop the annoying bell. Tess expected her mother to reappear immediately, after her usual curt dismissal of such an interruption of family privacy, but instead she saw the door click shut and a line of light appear below it.

Tess stood bashfully among the wedding guests, trying to be attentive to the remarks addressed to her as she strained to listen to her mother's conversation. But the heavy mahogany door, carved to match the rest of the wainscoting, prevented any sound from reaching her ears. Finally she abandoned all pretense of hospitality and went to stand beside the stairs. Maybe her mother had hung up and now couldn't find the door knob. But she remembered that the little light stayed on until the door opened. Tess could think of no excuse to open the door, so she just grasped the door knob and pulled. Before the light winked out, she saw Katie's stricken face.

Tess hung up the earpiece dangling from its wire and dropped to her knees, clasping her mother's cold hands.

"What is it?" she whispered, shaking the hands hard. Katie stared into Tess's eyes.

"Get your father," she said. "Right now."

Tess threaded her way through the crowd and took BJ by the elbow. "Come quickly," she said and led him back to the hall and the little telephone room under the stairs. Then she stood just behind him, hoping not to be sent away. Katie didn't seem to notice her presence. She sat on the little chair by the telephone, BJ stood in the doorway.

"BJ, there was a phone call." Katie reached for his hand. "I just finished talking. It was the railroad stationmaster. He says a coffin with Sydney's body arrived by train last night." She spoke in a flat voice. "I can't believe it. They never told me they had found him. Never warned me." A sob escaped her lips. Tess could feel her own throat ache. "The station master says we must come this evening and take the coffin away. They won't keep it in the station over night. And we have this wedding." Katie's eyes looked wildly around the hot little room with its sloping ceiling. "It's been three years, three years . . . . " Katie's voice grew shrill. She shook herself and sat quietly for a minute.

BJ sagged against the door jamb. "We can take care of it," he finally said in a calm voice. "We'll say nothing to Helen and Fred. They must go away happily." Color began to come back into Katie's cheeks. Now that decisions were being made, she felt better. "We'll get through the wedding and send them off with smiles. Then we'll see what to do about...about this other matter. The rabbi is here. He'll tell us what to do."

Katie's face softened, and she allowed BJ to pull her to her feet. Then she saw Tess. Tess expected an angry tirade, but Katie patted her arm.

"Poor little girl," she said. "You're left with your mother and must share all this sadness. Ach, it's too terrible to have children." They put their arms around each other. Tess had never noticed how small her mother had gotten. Noise enveloped them.

"Mother! I've been looking all over for you!" Helen took Katie with one hand and Tess with the other. "Come on, we're ready to begin. Tess! Play us a joyful chord."

CHAPTER THIRTY-SIX
1921

CARNEGIE AVENUE RANG WITH LAUGHTER as the wedding party piled into cars to see the two sets of newly-weds off on the train to their honeymoon. Lou Breyer was the youngest son of a large family, and hordes of boisterous sisters and brothers and cousins shouted in Hungarian as trunks were loaded and places were found among them to sit. Everyone wanted to go to the station to see the couples off. Tess watched the crowd in amazement. Never had she seen people having so much fun. She stood on the steps, longing to join them. Maybe by just being in the midst of so much hilarity, she could laugh and joke and forget who she was.

Fred's eyes met hers, and he called to her. Her spirits soared, and she raised her arm, lifted herself onto her toes, and plunged into the melee. Then she saw her mother take Howard and Adolph aside. She saw them look at Katie quizzically as she led them to Howard's roadster, parked at the end of the row of cars. Katie's lips moved, the boys looked as though they had been struck. They both sat down heavily on the running board, heads bowed. Tess stopped, remembering what awaited them at the station.

"Goodbye! Goodbye!" Steam boiled from under the train, the wheels slipped and strained on the rails, the train jerked and heaved, gathered speed, and roared away into the twilight. Gradually, the noisy Breyers and more sedate Schlesingers drifted away, and only the rabbi and the Reiters were left huddled in the deepening gloom of the railroad station. Tess watched as the smiles slowly faded from her brothers' faces, as her mother turned to her father and laid her cheek against his coat.

They stood silently for a few moments, listening to a paper being blown across the brick floor, watching the night sky turn from deep purple to angry red as burning waste was dumped on the surrounding slag hills. The edges of the dark clouds glowed crimson.

Howard reached into his pocket for his handkerchief and blew his nose. "Let's get going," he said. Katie put her arm through BJ's, Adolph took Tess's hand, and they fell in line behind him. Blinking in the bright light, they found the stationmaster in his office. When BJ explained why they were there, the man bustled them into the baggage room, chattering about the weather, not looking at any of them.

The coffin was on a sawhorse in the middle of the big disorderly room. It was military issue, rough pine stained army brown, with military printing on the lid. Sydney Howard Reiter, November 11, 1918, machine gun casualty.

Everybody stopped. They stood for many minutes, riveted by the sight of the massive box absorbing the light and air from every corner of the room. Tess felt giddy and breathless. Her fingers tingled, her ears rang. BJ put his hand on her arm and cleared his throat.

"The hearse will be here soon to take the coffin to the funeral home," BJ said.

The stationmaster shifted from foot to foot, uncertain whether to stay or leave. "Ah. Your pastor can take care of things now," he said "I'll leave you with him." He escaped silently.

Rabbi Solomon looked anxiously at BJ and Katie. "You are having quite a day of contrasts," he said in his softly accented English. "I've made the necessary arrangements. The hearse is outside. And we'll meet at the *shul* tomorrow morning for a short service. Then we can go together to the cemetery." He looked around the group, nodding his head to elicit an agreeing nod from one of them.

"Rabbi," said Katie. Tess felt a thrill of fear. Something terrible was about to happen.

"Rabbi," repeated Katie in a stronger voice. "I must look into the coffin. I must know if it is really my son, my Sydney." She hurried on, pushing away the rabbi's warning hand. "I'll know, even if there is only a little bone, only a shred of hair. I'll know if it's Sydney. And I must know. It's been three years. How did they find him after three years? How did they know it was him? Please, please let me see inside that box."

"Now, Mrs. Reiter. Now, Katie," murmured the rabbi. "We Jews cannot open a coffin. You know that is not our way. And besides, the government says it is Sydney. It is certainly your son. The government would not be so cruel. We must get this over with as soon as possible and devote ourselves to life. You all go home, get a good night's sleep, and we will see each other tomorrow."

Katie began to cry, soft sobs beyond her control. "How will I ever know that Sydney is really dead? BJ, Howard, Adolph, help me open that lid." She started to bang on the coffin with her fists. "You can't deny me even the comfort of knowing that Sydney is dead."

Howard blinked rapidly, remembering his anatomy classes at medical school. "No, Mother. Don't do it. It would be more than you could bear to see the condition of a body after three years. The rabbi's right. The army wouldn't send us someone else's body. What would be the reason? Let's go home."

He grabbed Adolph, turned him around, and began to walk toward the door.

"It's rocks in there, just rocks. I know it," he muttered to his brother through clenched teeth.

"Yeah, I think so, too," said Adolph. "They said he died on November 11. The telegram *arrived* on November 12."

Katie sagged in defeat. Then she fixed them each in turn with her burning eyes.

"We will never speak of Sydney again," she said. "I never want to hear his name again." BJ put his arm around her waist and led her slowly from the echoing room. The coffin receded behind them, growing smaller, assuming its rightful size against the backdrop of boxes, valises, and shapeless bundles. Katie allowed herself to be put into the car's back seat, slowly leaning forward like a soft doll, until her forehead rested on her knees. Her sobs slowed. She began moaning, and this became fainter and fainter, less audible, and at last dissolved into a low hum.

CHAPTER THIRTY-SEVEN
1923

TESS WAS GRADUATED from high school in 1923, the last of the Reiters at McKeesport High School. Her graduation picture shows her solemn face gazing straight out from the frame, the mortar-board flat on her head. The devoutly wished-for *bob* had finally been achieved, but it proved as unruly as her long hair and stuck out from her head like wings. She despaired of it. She missed the touch of long hair on her shoulders, the glamour of the seductive head-toss. To remedy the matter, she tied stockings to locks of the offending frizz and languorously brushed at them as she spent long summer hours reading.

This summer was the first one she had ever spent without plans for the fall, plans to go back to school. College had not been considered for Helen, and it certainly wasn't for Tess. She had no desire to *be* anything, not a teacher or a nurse, certainly not a doctor nor a pharmacist or an engineer, although there had been females in her brothers' classes. If her parents considered sending her on for further education, they didn't discuss it with her. They had had enough trouble with Helen, who wanted to be an accountant. "Girls don't go to college," they said. And that was final.

Tess spent time with Howard, walking to the streetcar with him in the morning, meeting him in the evening to walk home, fetching his slippers as he unfurled his newspaper. Flattered at the attention, Howard was only vaguely aware that most of their conversations were about cars. Howard owned a sleek roadster that satisfied his love of speed and, he reluctantly admitted to himself, made him more attractive to girls. By the time he caught on to Tess's game, he had taught her how to shift gears.

"Now take me out on the road," Tess wheedled. "I've watched you, I know I'll surprise you with how well I can drive."

"Absolutely not! Girls don't drive cars. None of the girls you know drives a car!"

"I know," she answered smugly. "I'll be the first."

So out on the road they went, quiet country roads where only the chickens could object to the speed that Howard was encouraging in his sister. After each lesson, they stopped at a roadhouse, where Howard had a soothing beer and Tess a cup of coffee. He absently offered her a cigarette. She eagerly took it. It was so sophisticated, to relax in a seedy bar, accompanied by a handsome man—no one would ever know he was only her brother, they looked so unlike. And smoking! She coughed.

"Oh hell! Why did I do that? You're too young to smoke. Give it back!" Howard reached for the cigarette.

"No!" She snatched her hand away. "I like it. This will be our private thing. I promise not to smoke in front of Mother, but . . . " she was wheedling, " . . . it makes driving even more fun."

Howard snorted, but he agreed. Driving and smoking *was* fun.

A month later, Tess had her driver's license and the responsibility to do all her mother's errands, driving her father's car, which usually spent most of its time in the garage. The troubles this would bring she could not foresee. She knew only that she could now escape the somber house. Now she was free. She found an errand to do every day and took her own good time doing it. She drove the hills of McKeesport under their gray and sooty skies and, as summer reached its giddy peak, ventured out alone into the countryside. It was glorious! She hadn't realized that the earth bloomed in such abundance in the summer, used as she was to the drooping leaves and spindly plants valiantly trying to thrive under the rain of dirt from the Carnegie Steel Works. After a happy hour alone in the roadhouse with her coffee and cigarette, she bought fresh ears of corn and tomatoes still warm from the sun to give to her mother for dinner.

As she drew closer to McKeesport and saw the yellow clouds that forever hung above the city, Blake's "dark satanic mills" flashed through her mind—then Longfellow's lyrical description in *Evangeline* —soon she was shouting Wordsworth to the sun and flowers and green-laden trees flashing by at an intoxicating speed. In high school, she had, with her brain and soul, memorized so much poetry, and now at last she knew what the words meant, what the phrases meant, what poetry meant. She ached with the thought of it, the thought of beauty, of freedom, of loss.

"Now my life is beginning," Tess exulted. "I'm the first girl in McKeesport to drive a car, and the first girl to smoke while she's doing it."

The first pack she bought on her own slowly disappeared over the summer as Tess overcame the dizziness, the nausea, and finally the awful taste. She also discovered Sen-Sen.

She practiced before her bedroom mirror, with the windows open, of course, the gestures she had watched so often in the movies—the narrowed eyes, the smoke slowly curling from her mouth, the white tube held just so between her fingers. She really looked quite attractive in the softened reflection, mysterious, grown up. She would look good in the roadhouse.

"Yes, Mother, I'm coming." She hastily submerged the cigarette in a glass of water, then flushed it down the toilet. She popped a Sen-Sen in her mouth.

"Tinkou." Her mother was grim-faced. "Take me in the car. I need to go someplace." Katie marched out to the curb, Tess close behind asking petulantly where she wanted to go, offering to go alone.

"Just get in the car and drive where I tell you." Katie settled herself on the leather seat, slammed the door, pinned her hat more tightly into her hair.

"Turn here. Now turn there. Now up this hill and left at the top. And be quiet."

Tess made a face, did as she was told.

"Now stop! Right here!" Katie's sharp voice halted the car with a shudder. "Turn off the car."

Tess looked at her mother quizzically. What were they doing in this shabby neighborhood, parked on an unfamiliar street? She followed her mother's eyes. She saw her father, sitting in a wicker rocking chair on a strange front porch, laughing up into the eyes of an unknown woman who was lighting his cigar.

Tess sat wordless and unmoving for a moment, an hour, an eternity. She forgot to breathe, to think, certainly to feel.

"Now let's go!" said her mother. Tess turned the key, let out the clutch, slid the car backward down the street, turned around the corner, down the hill.

"I'll just say this to you," said Katie. "And then I don't want to hear any more about it. I couldn't walk here, it's too far. I had to have you drive me. Somebody called me this morning on the telephone. Ach, the telephone. It has ruined my life. Someone called me. I know who it was. I recognized that voice. She said, 'What's your husband doing on Mrs. Glizky's front porch?' She gave me the address. She hung up. Now we've seen it. And that's all. I don't want to hear any more about it."

Katie got stiffly out of the car and limped up the front walk. Tess gazed at the retreating back, now slightly rounded, the shoulders drooping. One sob escaped Tess's lips, one tear started down each cheek from her hot eyes. She felt that familiar pain in her stomach, the one she got from secrets. She knew too many secrets, all of them bad. The only fun in knowing secrets was sharing them with someone, but every time she wanted to talk about them with her mother, she was silenced with a look and sometimes with a stinging slap across the face. She couldn't go to Helen to unburden herself. Her mother could read her like a book, and she would know. Besides, Helen was having enough troubles of her own. Lou was not the perfect husband. Another secret.

And she couldn't tell her brothers. She wanted the world to be perfect to them, for them to exist only in their own perfect lives without having to worry about anything else. Fred and Ann were settled blissfully in Dayton, Ohio, with their two little boys. Howard was practicing medicine and living in Brownsville, just forty miles away. And Adolph, tired of pharmacy, had enrolled in the Wharton School of Finance. That boy will never settle down, her mother had grumbled, but Tess knew he would. He was trying everything because he was so good at everything.

It was getting late. Tess started the car again and parked it in the garage behind the house. She could smell the dinner cooking as she climbed the back stairs to the sun porch. Her father would be home soon. Home from work. She smiled grimly. How was she supposed to treat him now? What was he doing on that strange front porch? Certainly no one lit his cigars at home. Her mother never had that kind of look on her face when she did anything for him. More often then not, she brushed his gratitude aside, shook his hand from her shoulder, turned her face from a kiss. Tess did not exonerate herself from the blame. She had abandoned her walks with her father as soon as she had learned to drive.

Pots were being banged loudly in the kitchen. Katie's aproned figure moved between sink and stove. Tess reached for a potato and the peeler. Katie snatched them out of her hand.

"You peel too slow," she said. "Find something else to do."

Tess stirred the gravy. "Not that," said Katie. "It's supposed to simmer."

Tess opened the oven door. "No!" shouted Katie. "You'll ruin the temperature."

Tess grabbed a handful of silverware and backed through the swinging door into the dining room. She could see her mother's mouth open, but she didn't wait to hear what she would say.

CHAPTER THIRTY-EIGHT
1927

TESS BECAME A STUDENT at the University of Pittsburgh. She went only because Howard insisted. He had come home for a weekend visit and had actually shouted at her.

"What are you doing hanging around the house all the time?" he demanded. "You could be a college junior by this time. You're wasting your life!"

He talked to BJ and Katie, insisting that Tess continue her education. And he stayed in McKeesport until Monday and drove her into Pittsburgh. He went to the Dean's office with her, sat while she completed the application, and chose the courses she would take. Then he dumped her in front of Kaufmann's Department Store.

"Now buy yourself a Pitt uniform for the first day of school." He handed her some money. "No, no! I'm kidding!" he said at her look of amazement. "No uniform. Just buy yourself something pretty. And on September ninth you better be sitting in your seat with a pen in your hand and a notebook on your desk. I'm going to be checking on you." He drove away without a smile.

Tess wandered aimlessly through Kaufmann's. She had never been here without her mother. She tried on a few hats, turning her head this way and that before the round mirror. Not bad. She had always wanted to be the sort of girl who wore hats. She walked slowly away from a blue straw sailor, then turned back.

"I'll take it," she said. She gave the clerk some of Howard's money and then went to the dress department.

The saleslady had "the perfect dress for mademoiselle," a soft navy blue with a pleated skirt ending suspiciously quickly.

"Put these on first," said the saleslady and handed her a pair of navy silk stockings and navy blue shoes with what she described as "French heels."

Tess pulled off her middy blouse, long linen skirt, oxford shoes, and lisle stockings and slipped into the luxurious challis and silk. She slowly lifted her eyes to the three-way glass. The soft material emphasized her broad shoulders and slim hips. The skirt ended at her knees. Her legs in the blue stockings were long and shapely. The shoes showed off her high instep. She gasped. In a dream, she drew the blue hat from the box and settled it on her head.

She took a cigarette from her purse and lit it, putting the match in the chrome ashtray attached to the wall. The little metal doors clicked over it with a snap. She watched in the mirror as the smoke folded delicately under the hat brim and then floated around the light bulbs surrounding the mirror.

Well! She certainly didn't want to stay in this little dressing room looking like that. She wanted everyone to see the transformation from ugly duckling. Tess hid her purse beneath the pile of her old clothes and went out into the dress department. She wandered among the mirrored columns, admiring herself and stealing glances at passers-by. She saw two clerks nudge each other and point to her. She saw a shopper stop and look, then nod at her mirrored face. Tess didn't smile. She pretended that the outfit she had just taken off and all the dresses in her closet at home were just as expensive, just as chic, just as becoming as this one.

"Ah, mademoiselle. This dress was made for you." The saleslady was triumphant.

"Yes, I suppose so," said Tess in as bored a tone as she could muster. "I'll take it." She thought about the money Howard had given her. "And the stockings. And the shoes."

Tess hugged her boxes all the way home to McKeesport on the streetcar. Maybe going to college wouldn't be so bad. She would have the month of August to enjoy her dress hanging in the closet, and then other months enjoying the wearing of it in Pittsburgh. And there would be other new dresses, too. No more shapeless blouses and long skirts. Helen was right. She was a perfect flapper. She was perfect for the Roaring Twenties. She looked just like the girls in the ads. Maybe the Twenties would begin to roar for her.

On the ninth of September, Tess swung herself apprehensively into the streetcar and was immediately surrounded by girls she remembered from high school.

"Tess, are you going to Pitt?"

"Wizard! Come join the fun!"

"Tess, come sit by me!"

A hand reached out from the crowd and drew her to the intricately caned bench. The seat back had been switched so that two seats faced each other.

"You remember me. Yetta Rhinestein." The introductions to the other girls got lost in the shouts and laughter as more and more young people entered the car at every stop. It was a party. Tess looked around in wonder. Maybe she would have fun. She watched the animated faces, the hands waving in the air, listened to the laughter around her. Inspired, she got up, smiled shyly at Yetta, and walked through the car, holding on to the brass handles on the corners of the seat backs. She greeted girls she knew by name and was rewarded by swift hugs and friendly grins. Other boys and girls she recognized and smiled at. They waved to her. "Hi, Tess," they mouthed, silenced by the din. This was thrilling. They actually knew her name. It was too much. It was the cat's pajamas.

"This is the cat's pajamas!" said Tess to a slightly familiar face. Her mother had forbidden her to say that silly phrase.

"Yes, it is."

"I'm glad you're here."

"See you tomorrow. This is where we get off."

And the crowd swept out of the streetcar onto the sidewalk. Tess felt Yetta's hand slide under her arm.

"Well, if you're a new Pitt student, you get off here, too." They both gazed upward at the elegant shaft of Pitt piercing the blue sky. "The tallest institution of learning in the world," they said in unison and dissolved in giggles. "C'mon. I'll walk you to your first class. You'll never find the room. It's always a madhouse the first day." Yetta looked inquiringly at Tess. "I'm surprised one of your handsome brothers didn't bring you." Now Tess knew that Yetta would probably be a faithful friend.

Yetta was the perfect person for Tess to find on her first day of college, because Yetta had parties at her parents' shabby apartment. Almost every weekend. "Her mother lets her do that because she wants Yetta to find a husband," Katie sniffed as she refused Tess permission to attend. Tess begged, pleaded, wept, sulked, until finally, at the fourth invitation, Katie relented and allowed her to go.

Tess opened Yetta's apartment door and entered the smoky living room. The noise was so great that no one had heard her knock. Yetta's practice was to invite her girlfriends and to ask the men she knew to bring along their friends. Yetta's mother was a good cook, so the men always outnumbered the girls. Men were lounging on the sofa and draped over the backs of chairs. Girls, their cigarettes in long holders, were laughing delightedly at every deep-voiced comment. Silver flasks passed from hand to hand in spite of Prohibition.

Tess was lost. She stood with one group, laughing when the other girls laughed. She moved on, took her cigarettes out of her beaded bag, tapped one on her trembling fingernail.

"Let me get that," said a young man at her elbow. "I'm Ed. Ed Klee." He smiled and flicked his silver lighter. They talked. He walked her home.

Soon Tess and Ed were a steady "thing." Ed took Tess to the movies. They ate dinner in restaurants. He often picked her up in his car—a convertible!—to take her to Pitt. They attended Yetta's parties as a couple. Katie didn't seem to object to his presence in her parlour, and BJ spoke to him man to man. Tess blossomed under Ed's attention.

She was now a champion at the Charleston, patting her silken knees, waving her hands, gyrating her hips to the accompaniment of a cheering crowd. She rolled her stockings to just above her knees. She became known as "clever," having ready answers to the quick patter of the "crowd." She played the piano at Yetta's parties, pounding out intricate tunes while her liquor-filled coffee cup clattered on the lid.

It was spring, close to exam time and the end of Tess's first year at Pitt. Tess was sitting at the piano, Ed at her side. She was, by now, so used to these parties that she was relaxed, slightly mesmerized by the noise, the smoke, the sip of gin she had just had. A face suddenly appeared at the corner of the upright. Tess gasped. It was the handsomest face she had ever seen—a cocked eyebrow over snapping black eyes, white, white teeth, curly black hair barely tamed by shiny pomade.

The grin widened. "Play *Up a Lazy River*," he demanded and disappeared. She coaxed the tune out of the piano as Ed put his hand on her shoulder and started to sing. She hadn't realized until then how annoying Ed could be. In fact, she admitted to herself for the first time, he was difficult to kiss because he had bad breath. She had meant to ask Helen about that. Did all boys have bad breath? Was she supposed to pretend she liked kissing him, no matter what? Ed was the first boy she had ever kissed. And of course the only one. Except her brothers, and that was different. Besides, her brothers smelled wonderful. She craned her head around the piano, wondering when the party would end.

CHAPTER THIRTY-NINE
1927

IT DIDN'T DO TO LET ANYONE KNOW you were interested in a certain boy. In the first place, it could be bad luck. Saying it out loud or even admitting it to yourself could make the chance of a date with him disappear like a phantom in the mist. Second, it could draw attention to him and pique an interest in someone possibly more his "type" or, even more dangerous, in someone more "aggressive." And third, admitting you were "after" someone drew attention to *you*, and other girls would be watching your technique and judging your ability to vamp and maybe, just a little bit, hoping you'll fail. Tess didn't want any of those things to happen to her.

So it took five days just to find out his name. Tess had walked over to Yetta's apartment to smoke a cigarette. It was a long walk.

"That was a wonderful party last Saturday, Yetta."

"Thanks. Glad you had a good time. Your piano playing sure livens things up."

"You had lots of new fellows there last time. What was that one's name—the short boy with the sandy hair?"

"Oh, him. That's Sid Rossberg." Yetta stole a glance at Tess. "His father's Dr. Rossberg. You know. The dentist. Sid's in dental school now. He brought some of his friends with him on Saturday. But he's too short for you."

Tess laughed. "I know. That's why I want to keep out of his way." There. She had covered her tracks.

That was Tuesday.

Thursday, Tess gazed up at the art deco Pitt University building. "That's the Dental School on the sixth floor," she mused aloud. "Those guys really work hard. I guess that's why so few of them come to your parties."

"Oh, yes. Some of them come," Yetta protested, defending her hospitality. "Murray Gross was there last week. Didn't you notice him? The guy with the black curly hair?"

"Murray Gross?" Tess tasted the name. "Um, yes, I think so. Wasn't he kind of ... heavy?" She didn't bother to listen to the answer.

Tess could hardly wait until Yetta's next party. There were only a few weeks left of the semester. If she was going to "get" Murray Gross, she had to do it before summer vacation.

Murray was at Yetta's the following Sunday. Her body tingled. She knew she looked wonderful. She had finally convinced her mother that she was no longer a child, and Katie was willing to shop for expensive clothes with her and be there to admire the finished product. "A beautiful cut," she said as a peach silk settled around Tess's hips and flared at the knees. They smiled into each other's eyes in the mirror.

Tess paid special attention to Ed that night, showing him off, laughing at his jokes, encouraging him to tell stories. He became the star of the evening. Tess slipped away to the piano and tried to work out *Me and My Shadow,* which was on the music stand. Another hand reached out to turn the page. Murray Gross was sitting beside her. Breathless, she went on playing.

Later, when Murray went into the kitchen, Tess followed him. She had to say something—she hadn't yet said a word to him. She saw Yetta's little sister's jacks and ball on the table and gathered them into her hand, sinking to the floor in a graceful movement. So much for the peach silk. Yetta's mother wasn't the greatest house-keeper. Murray turned around at the sound of the jacks hitting the linoleum.

"Hey, you're pretty good," he said as he watched her deftly scoop up a jack before she caught the ball. "Let's play." He sat cross-legged on the floor, across from her. Onesies, twosies. They exchanged names, a little history, he made a pun, she topped him. Their hands touched, and Tess missed on fivesies. She bounced the ball to him. The silver jacks cascaded onto the floor from Murray's hand As the ball hit the floor, Ed came into the kitchen.

Flustered, Tess watched the little red ball disappear under the icebox as she stood up and brushed her skirt. Ed took her arm and firmly ushered her back into the living room, a confused look on his face. Tess managed what she hoped was her most ravishing smile over her shoulder.

"I promised Fanny Bernstein we'd walk home with her," Tess said to Ed, miserably aware that Murray was at the party with Fanny. Then she abandoned Ed once again, for she had only a short time to convince Fanny that the walk home together would be great fun.

The two boys laughed and joked as they made their way through the spring evening. Fanny's arm was through Murray's. She shot suspicious glances at Tess. Tess's hand was in Ed's. She was very quiet until she realized they were at Shaw and Carnegie, where she and Ed would have to turn left. She began an animated conversation with Fanny, demanding an opinion about the girls' dresses, sharing a gossipy tidbit, postponing the moment of parting from Murray.

Murray was impatient. "Why don't you two phone each other tomorrow?" he growled and pulled Fanny with him across the street and up the Shaw Avenue hill.

Tess continued giggling with Ed as they turned into Carnegie Avenue, but inside she was terribly hurt. Murray's an insensitive boor, she thought. He should have known that it was his company she was trying to prolong, not Fanny's. And besides, if he goes for girls like Fanny—she didn't know what Fanny was like and she didn't care, either—and he's rude, she didn't know what she saw in him anyway. He looks like a gangster and he acts like one, too. She leaned over and kissed Ed on the cheek. Surprised, he put his arm around her.

The next Sunday, Tess maneuvered Ed into offering to drive Murray and his date to Homestead, where they both lived, after Yetta's party. Murray was with Sue Jacobs—he's with a different girl every weekend!—and they both lived in Homestead. "That's too far to have to go on the streetcar," said Tess, aware of the illogic that it was also probably too far for Ed to have to drive there and back. Ed didn't seem to notice.

Homestead was even grimier than McKeesport, a city of endless attached three-story houses marching up and down the bare hills under a sky smoldering in the reflected slag fires. It was a company town. Everyone worked at the Homestead Steel Works. Tess had heard enough stories about Mr. Frick and his gun-toting Pinkerton men to give her a sense of foreboding in the dark streets. Her heart sank. She didn't want to see where Murray lived, and she certainly didn't want to watch him say goodnight to his date. She decided Murray could walk home from Sue's house. "Bye, you two," she waved. "Let's go!" she said to Ed, and he, startled, drove off.

"What was that all about?" he said. "You baffle me. We could have waited for the guy." Tess changed the subject.

That's that, Tess thought as she dawdled over her morning egg, watching her father read his paper and answering her mother's questions about the party in a desultory fashion. She had shown herself to be just as rude to Murray last night as he was to her last week. He'll never call. Yetta's parties were over for the summer. She would never see Murray again. She sighed, moving the egg around with the little spoon. Well, he's not so much. In fact, he's probably nothing at all. And he doesn't know I exist. He can have any girl he wants. They're all crazy about him. Well, not me! I don't care if I ever see him again.

Murray called on Monday evening.

"Who is this?" she asked sweetly, thrilled by the sound of his voice. "Of course I am." "Of course I do." "Is that right?" She laughed. She trilled. It was getting hot in the little room under the stairs. Finally he said, "Oh, by the way..." This was it. A date! "Next Sunday? The Willows?" Tess caught her breath. The Willows was the most expensive nightclub in Pittsburgh, very sophisticated. Her mother would never let her go. "I'd love to! I would! But I'll have to ask my mother. Can you call me back tomorrow, and I'll tell you definitely then?" She hung up in a daze. She hadn't expected so much.

It was going to be a difficult week, Tess thought. Today her mother would say No. Tomorrow they would argue and shout, and she would put Murray off for another day. Wednesday she would beg and plead and say Yes to Murray. Thursday her mother would say Yes. Friday she and her mother would shop for a new dress. And Sunday she would go to The Willows with the most wonderful man she had ever met.

CHAPTER FORTY

THE WEEK WAS WORSE than Tess had feared. Not only had she to convince Katie that going to a nightclub was not "fast" but also that staying overnight at the Grosses' house in Homestead was not wicked. Murray had arranged a double-date, but his friend wasn't willing to drive all the way to McKeesport to take Tess home afterward. She would have to save that news until after her mother said Yes to the Willows.

The Willows! The words sent Tess into giddy daydreams. There were many nightclubs in the Pittsburgh area, but the Willows was the best. Big bands went there, nationally famous bands, and they played jazz. Tess had never heard jazz. There was a dance floor, a big one, all the girls said, and her imagination lit it with a slowly-turning mirrored globe. She would love to dance with Murray, be in his arms. They would sit at a small table, probably with a little lamp on it—pictures from *The Saturday Evening Post* filled her mind—and look into each other's eyes. Was Murray capable of whispering sweet nothings? She doubted it. But *she* was capable of it. And she would, too, as soon as she had her bourbon with soda. She knew there was something called Prohibition, but it had never seemed to lessen the liquor she saw at parties.

Tess shook her head. She was getting ahead of herself. This date was not a *fait accompli*—her vocabulary was moving into foreign phrases. Katie was adamant that Tess not be seen in a nightclub. No nice girls went to nightclubs. They were noisy, women smoked there, men drank. Not just men! thought Tess. And there was dancing. Katie had heard about the new dances, the Charleston and the Black Bottom. Katie shuddered at the names. If a man had any respect for a girl, he wouldn't ask her to go to such a place.

Tess fingered the pack of cigarettes in her pocket. She felt a hot rush of tears because she was deceiving her mother in so many ways. Tess was the Charleston champ of McKeesport, she smoked, she drank, drank so well, in fact, that she already had a brand she asked for by name. As she turned away with a sob, Katie touched her arm.

"Ach, Nebbish, I'm sorry. Of course you want to go out and have a nice time. Why should I spoil it? You're a good girl, and you know how to act like a good girl. So go to this nightclub with your young man and enjoy yourself. Just don't forget who you are."

Pangs of guilt caused Tess to cry even harder. The easy victory was shaming. And a bigger fight was coming. She put her arms around her mother and sobbed into her shoulder, resurrecting the guilty tears into ones of gratitude.

"Oh, Mother. You've made me so happy. Thank you, thank you for letting me go." When she straightened up and arranged a smile of joy on her lips, she couldn't meet her mother's eyes.

On Friday, they found what Tess considered the perfect dress at Kaufmann's. It was black silk, soft as water in her hands, with jet beads embroidered in little curlicues all over, jet beads that swung when she walked—or danced. Katie tried to pull the neckline higher, the skirt lower.

"Are you sure that this is what everybody's wearing?" Katie asked in a small voice. Her own wool skirt came to her ankles.

"Of course, Mother. Most of them are more daring." Tess pulled the round neckline into a deep vee, hiked the knee-length skirt to mid-thigh. "This is how Yetta dresses all the time, and you know what a fashion plate she is." Katie sniffed at the mention of Yetta. She *would* be the one to let her bosom show.

The dress safely in Kaufmann's distinctive brown and black paper bag, Tess led her mother to the elevator. "Now let's go to the luggage department," she said. "I think all my stuff will fit into a train case. And I saw a cunning one advertised in the *Post Gazette*. It was even on sale." Tess grasped Katie's elbow and steered her through the metal gate and into the ornate interior, avoiding her mother's shocked look by smiling ravishingly at the elevator operator. He blushed.

"Three, please," she said sweetly over her mother's angry hiss.

"Luggage! What's all this about luggage?"

Tess motioned significantly at the uniformed back of the operator. "Mother," she said in a soft, reasonable tone. "The Willows is an hour from McKeesport. I couldn't possibly come home afterwards. Murray has invited me to stay with his family on Saturday night." There. It was out. *Invited* and *family* were reassuring touches. Nobody could possibly object to such domestic language. And besides, the occasion had acquired its own momentum. It was too late to call a halt.

Katie recognized the moment of defeat. By the time they reached Carnegie Avenue, she was exhausted with unspent anger. As Tess went upstairs to deposit her packages, Katie stood at the bottom, gazing at the hated Sir Galahad glowing on the landing. Searching for the Holy Grail, indeed. Didn't the fool know there was no happiness in this world? One sorrow piles on another. Fear multiplies, turns into constant terror. There was no keeping it at bay.

"Don't have children!" she shouted up the stairwell. "Never have children! It's not worth it! They'll kill you little by little." She clenched her teeth and went into the kitchen.

Sunday was lovely and cool, a perfect spring day. Tess climbed down from the streetcar in Homestead to be greeted by Murray. He was even more handsome than she remembered. He took her train case and steered her onto the Local. They sat close together on the cane seat, heads almost touching as they leaned toward each other to be heard above the streetcar's clatter. She was dizzy with his nearness, breathless. Every time she moved her head, the tiny bells on her tight-fitting cloche jingled. Murray was enchanted. He touched her hand. She drew shyly away, lowered her eyelashes. She was almost happy.

And yet, underneath the joy of the perfect day, the perfect man, the perfect moment, was the feeling she remembered from her other trip to Homestead, the feeling that she didn't want to see his house or meet his family. Homestead was a working class town, the people were poor. She had never met anyone from Homestead before. Everyone here worked in the Homestead Mills. Some people in McKeesport worked in the steel mills, too, but they lived in the parts of town where she never went. The Reiters lived at the top of the hill. The trees kept them from seeing the poverty and dirt. Everything was dirty in Homestead. There were no trees. Tess's smile became strained as Murray handed her down from the streetcar and guided her along the street.

It was a street of broken sidewalks, with weeds struggling through the cracks. High above was an endless row of identical double houses, reached by cement steps. The front yards were almost vertical brown banks of dirt with paper fluttering from drying clumps of grass. The weeds were bent and dusty in the spring sunshine. The sky was smudged yellow from the mills.

Tess counted thirty steps from the street to the Grosses's front porch. She grasped the sooty iron hand rail, dismayed by the thought of the rusty stripe across her white kid glove and the sweat that would appear on her forehead. Maybe her mother had been right to object to this visit. Maybe couples shouldn't know too much about each other before they get married. Maybe dinners and movies and long walks should be enough. She was panting from the long climb. "Oh Mother," she breathed as the gray house blotted out the sky above her.

Murray's brothers and sister rushed out to greet her. Her worries receded to the back of her mind as she marveled at their good looks. She pulled herself together and inspected the four of them. They had the lawless look Murray had, except they were merely hooligans, and he had the aura of a true gangster. And they were all so tall, except for Milton, small and delicate looking from the polio he had as a child. He had mischievous eyes, and he looked most like Murray, only sweeter. Tess liked him immediately. Irwin was next oldest, taller than Murray, just out of high school. Then Rhoda, already a beauty, shyly reaching out her hand and drawing it back in confusion as Tess turned to the youngest brother, Maynard.

He was unbelievably handsome—a cap of black curls, shining eyes, teeth white, white, white in a wide grin, taller than she. Tess could not hold back. "You look just like a movie star!" Twelve-year-old Maynard grinned at her. "I'm going to BE a movie star," he said.

They crowded into the house. Tess could smell onions frying. The front room was long and narrow and seemed full of furniture, something called a suite with all the pieces matching. Tess had never seen anything like it. Mrs. Gross hurried from the kitchen, wiping her hands on her apron. She was short and very heavy, her broad face flushed from cooking. She pumped Tess's hand.

"I'm very glad to meet you," she said in a warm voice. There was just a trace of an accent. Tess was listening for it, and she heard it. Mrs. Gross stood back, frankly admiring Tess's clothes. Rhoda, too, was inspecting Tess's suit as though she were memorizing its cut. Tess remembered how she had looked at Ann when Fred brought Ann home to dinner.

"Sam! Sam! Get up. Say hello to Tess Reiter." Mrs. Gross

motioned with a round arm to the man sitting motionless on the gray sofa. Tess hadn't seen him there. Ah, she thought, that's where they get their looks. He doesn't have the personality, but he's surely got the bones.

Sam Gross had a grizzled mustache and thick white hair. He was tall and thin, dressed in a gray suit with a gray knitted vest, and wearing a gray fedora. Tess was taken aback by the hat until she realized it was his American *yarmulke*. He held out a thin, strong hand to her and smiled, a sweet smile, a conspiratorial smile. He seemed about to say something, but Mrs. Gross gave him an impatient look. He sat down again and was quietly reabsorbed into the upholstery.

"*Schnapps*, Murray. Why don't you get your girl a little *schnapps?*" But Tess was too nervous to want a drink. And the delicious smell of onions was making her ravenous. It must have affected Murray, too, for he said they should go soon.

"Your room is at the top of the stairs, Tess. Rhoda took your bag up. I'll see you down here in about half an hour, okay?"

"I'll hurry as fast as I can," she said over her shoulder. The stairs were creaky and steep. The rubber treads were almost worn through. And the banister was dusty. But I don't care, thought Tess. I'm in love with Murray, and we don't have to come here very often.

She paused at the door of the first room. Rhoda was inside. She had opened Tess's suitcase, and she had Tess' black shoe in her hand, stroking its silken perfection with a dreamy look on her face.

"What are you doing with my shoe?" Tess demanded.

Rhoda whirled around, her eyes wide.

"Oh! I'm sorry. I just wanted to see..." she stammered. She fled.

Tess flung the door shut behind her but caught it before it slammed. She closed it quietly. She could hear all the sounds from the floor below and the sounds from the neighbors through the thin walls. Voices, laughter, water running. Tess unpacked quickly. Nothing was missing. Tess vowed never to speak to Rhoda again. She was seething. Her wonderful evening was spoiled. Riffling through her clothes like that. What was Rhoda looking for? Tess wished she had listened to her mother. Why had she taken this chance? Maybe Murray wasn't all that wonderful either.

Miserably, she dressed for the evening. She sat down on the creaky bed and put on her shoes.

CHAPTER FORTY-ONE

IN THE YEAR SINCE THEY HAD KNOWN EACH OTHER, Tess had never seen Murray angry, but he was surely angry now. In his effort to contain his emotion, his voice was hoarse and whispery. Tess had to lean across the table in Kline's restaurant to hear him, and he didn't meet her eyes. He stared into the recesses of the dark establishment, where the early spring crowd of lunchers kept up a steady buzz of talk and laughter. Tess tried to adjust herself to his mood. He was usually so easy-going. She felt a faint sense of unease.

"Okay, what's wrong?" she asked as she finally reached the end of all the chatter she could muster.

"Nothing, nothing." He waved her question away. But she wheedled and cajoled and finally breached his defenses. Murray hunched his shoulders, his anger returning full force.

"Those bastards!" he rasped. "Those anti-Semitic bastards! You know, there are only five Jews in my dental school class. Probably the full quota." He noticed her look of confusion and laughed. "You don't know about quotas? Oh, yeah. They accept only a certain number of Yids no matter how well we do on the entrance tests." He often said Yids for Jews. Tess suspected that Murray himself was anti-Semitic. "They're probably afraid the whole class will be made up of Yids if they give the places to the ones that get the best test scores. So they let only a certain number of us in. The bastards are always trying to mess us up, giving us the worst cases, flunking work from us that's better even than their fair-haired boys can turn out. The five of us should be at the top of the class. Instead we're barely making it."

Murray was warming to the tale. He loved to give his stories a little twist at the end, and Tess could tell that he was already editing this one so that, bad as it was, they would both end up laughing.

"So here's what happened." Murray began to grin in spite of himself. "You know, the dental school drags these guys in off the street for us to work on—bums, mental cases, you know what I mean—and this morning I find this patient in my chair. Skinny, blood-shot eyes, barely able to sit up. And old Harris says, *This gentleman needs only a cleaning Murray* and smiles at me. Everybody else gets called Doctor, but us he calls by our first names. It really makes me sore." Murray took a quick bite of lobster. Refugees from kosher homes, they always ordered lobster at Kline's.

"So I picked up the curette, that thing with the sharp curve at the end? And I started to scrape some of the tartar from around the man's teeth, and damned if his four front teeth didn't come out in my hand! Like a row of corn, they just fell out!" Murray frowned and Tess hooted.

"Oh, my gosh!" She burst out laughing. "Then what happened?"

"Well, that's the bad part. Harris was bent on humiliating another Jew-boy. He called all the men over to see what Murray had done, and then he told me I could have the rest of the day off to think about my future. He knew those teeth would fall out. He had already examined the bum. He knew the only thing holding them in was the gunk."

Tess couldn't take dental school quite as seriously as Murray. After all, it wasn't medical school, where Howard had gone and Adolph was now attending. But she comforted him as best she could. "You have only one more year to go, Murray," she said. "And besides, we got to have lunch together today. Some of the professors know you do good work. Just go back there as though nothing had happened. You and Herb and the others have to see it to the bitter end. Think how mad Harris will be when you actually graduate."

"Yeah, I guess you're right." Murray grinned and squeezed her hand. They ordered dessert and coffee, lit cigarettes, and sat smiling at each other. Tess giggled every once in awhile. The thought of the man's teeth disengaging like the little metal hooks on the newfangled zipper was a scream.

Murray paid the check, left his usual large tip on the table, and they wandered into what passed for spring sunshine in smoky Pitts-burgh. Tess took his arm. She had something to tell him, too, and she didn't know how to begin. Ed Klee was so much easier to deal with. She was still seeing him, of course. She liked to be able to say No to Murray once in awhile, and Ed didn't present any heartache. He was plain and open and unexciting, no mysterious silences, no dark gazes.

They strolled past shop windows, choosing jewelry for each other, rejecting the fox scarf for the full length mink, deciding which yacht-club emblem looked best on the blue cashmere blazer. Finally they reached Joseph Horne & Co., where the furniture displays kept them busy for a long time. Tess preferred the highly carved pieces. Children are so rough on furniture. Murray liked the new Bauhaus things. They were simple.

"When I get married..." Tess murmured into his shoulder, pointing at a Chinese red sofa.

Murray laughed. "You're going to need a rich husband and a big house to have all the furniture you want," he said.

Tess turned impatiently and pulled her hand from Murray's arm. She and Murray had been going out for more than a year. When was he going to get around to marriage? She swept ahead of him, her cheeks burning.

"Murray?" Tess slowed her steps. She had to tell him her news, and now was a good time to pay him back for his cruel remark. "My cousin Alan and my brother Howard want to take a trip in July. Alan's going to take his sister Frances, and Howard asked me to go along. We might be gone for two weeks. What do you think?"

Murray took off his hat, brushing the specks of soot off the felt. "Where are you going?"

"Lake George. In New York State."

Murray put on the hat, tipped it just right. "Well, gee. You should go. It sounds too good to pass up. You'll have a great time."

Tess gritted her teeth. Why had she put herself in such a position, practically begging him to ask her to stay? She'd show him. She would go, and she would have a great time, and she wouldn't think of him at all. In fact, when she got home, she would call Ed with her news. He would beg her not to go, and she would tell him that she had already made up her mind. She hid her disappointment in Murray's reaction. She actually did want to go, and Murray's indifference saved her from what she thought of as her worst fault, indecision. She had never been outside of Western Pennsylvania. And having Howard almost to herself for two whole weeks was nearly as good as being with Murray.

A month later, Tess put her elegant foot for the first time on the marble floor of Pennsylvania Station in New York City. Howard was beside her, so good-looking in his white linen suit, high collar, and straw boater. He led her through the vast Concourse and onto a train for Long Island, where they would spend a few days with Uncle Leo and Aunt Lena, the parents of Alan and Frances. Leo and Lena were Ritters, but Leo was BJ's brother and BJ was a Reiter. They were a family of seven brothers, and BJ had come to America with three of them. When these four boys, all younger than twenty, had gotten off the boat in New Jersey, they had insisted on filling out the immigration forms themselves, and they had spelled their own name, REITER. When Leo came later with the other two brothers, the customs agent wrote the forms and misspelled their name as RITTER. So the brothers were four Reiters and three Ritters. The Reiters had done pretty well for themselves, but the Ritters were rich, money made in the Great War from the cloak-and-suit business.

Leo had a pipe organ in his living room, and on his manicured Long Island lawn he had a topiary where he trimmed the trees himself into the shapes of lions and monkeys, exotic flowers, and caryatids. Dorothea Dix had been a paid companion to Lena when Lena had desired a trip to Europe and Leo had been unable to accompany her because of business. Tess felt like Alice *Through the Looking-Glass*.

That night at dinner, the dining room resplendent with gold service plates and a butler handing the dishes, Leo was chuckling. He put a delicate finger on the stiff front of his tuxedo shirt. The Ritters always dressed for dinner.

"When I was out trimming the trees this morning," he said, "two women in a car this big..." he stretched out his hands... "stopped and offered me twice as much as I'm getting here to be their gardener. I'm pretty good, I guess. Ah, Minnie. This is a delicious brisket," he added, smiling at the maid. "Tell Mrs. Gordon she's outdone herself again. And this wonderful food reminds me of a story that I bet you haven't heard, children." Leo loved to tell stories. He reminded Tess of Murray. At the head of the table, Lena sighed. She knew his stories tended to be long.

"You know we are seven brothers. There's Sam and Ben, that's your father, Tess. And Henry, Saul, Willie, Sam, and Nick." Tess widened her eyes at Howard. Nick was the mystery brother, the one no one spoke about. And Henry! Henry was the brother their mother was supposed to have married. She hoped the story would be about them.

"Well, this story is about Saul. Saul, you know, married a Polack, a *shiksa*. Not Jewish. But we loved Saul and didn't exclude him from the family. How could we? He was our brother, we had been through so much together." Leo looked apologetically at Lena, seeking once more the assurance that the family had done right in acknowledging Saul's shocking marriage more than three decades ago.

"One day, when Saul was still newly married, he invited us all for dinner. The six brothers and their wives. We had a lot of conversation, I can tell you, but in the end we all went. It was the right thing to do." Leo nodded, confirming his decision.

"They had a small house, but we sat down together at the table, fourteen of us. And it was a good dinner. The Polack was a good cook. We all ate well. We left empty plates. So one of the girls—was it you, Lena, or Tinnie? I don't remember. But someone asked what the meat was, it was so good. So this Polack, she didn't talk much, she piped up and said, 'Pork.' Pork! Well, you can imagine the din. Poor Saul was ready to kill her." Lena put her snowy napkin to her lips.

Leo looked around the table. Every eye was on him, every mouth—except Lena's—puckered in an O. He bet this crowd had never tasted pork. Lobster, maybe, but not pork.

"So the Polack started to sob. 'I koshered it!' she cried. 'I koshered it!' And she dragged us all into the kitchen—a kosher kitchen, Saul's kosher kitchen—where she showed us how she had taken that slab of *trafe* and laid it on the special board and salted it and drained it and—like magic, pouf! —turned it into kosher pork." Leo, shaking with laughter, wiped his streaming eyes with his handkerchief.

"Needless to say," said Leo, "we haven't been back to Saul's for dinner since. But," he added with a wink at Frances, "the meal was delicious."

The next morning, Tess regretted having to leave the handsome house of her uncle and aunt for the next leg of their journey. Uncle Leo was so much like her father, white haired, erect, impeccable and vain in his choices of suits, hats, canes. They were both men of the world, conscious of their charm and wit. But Aunt Lena, Tess thought sadly, was so different from her mother. Aunt Lena's hair was perfectly coiffed, her pink and white face unlined, her clothes expensive and stylish. Poor Mother. Tess felt the tears in her eyes as she stepped into the chauffeured Packard for the trip back into New York. Katie was now bent with arthritis, knuckles swollen and painful. Her gray hair was always pulled back into a tight bun, her clothes shapeless and old. Bearing eight children, losing three, had left her bitter and impervious to amusement. And she and BJ never shared jokes or even exasperation. There was something unpleasant between her parents, but would she ever find out how it began? Murray drifted uninvited into Tess's reverie. Did she really want to get married? Would she be an Aunt Lena, free of sorrow, gracious, or would God deal her blow after blow as He had her mother? Frances's voice startled her.

"Hey, cousin!" Frances said. "Don't drift off. There's the Statue of Liberty in the bay at the left. Look alive now. We're going to have a splendid time, unless you go all *nebbish* on us."

CHAPTER FORTY-TWO
1928

HOWARD TURNED OFF THE OVERHEAD LIGHTS in the living room of the house on Carnegie Avenue, pressing the mother-of-pearl buttons on the wall. He set the portable movie screen on its tripod, zipping up the window shade-like contraption and fastening it at the top. The boxy Bell and Howell projector was on a table at the other end of the room, its film holders looking like mouse-ears above it.

Howard had worked on the movies taken at Lake George for a month, and he was full of high spirits. Tess, worried about how she looked in the pictures, chafed under his teasing and appealed to Adolph to make him stop. Helen, curled into an armchair with her husband at her feet, her two babies asleep upstairs, looked on with matronly amusement. Katie and BJ shared the sofa. Katie was impatient. She had things to do in the kitchen, and all the clowning was getting on her nerves.

"Off with the lights!" Howard ordered, imperiously gesturing toward the fringed lamp behind Adolph. Adolph pulled the little chain.

A shaft of light hit the screen, the screen turned black, then revealed the words: CAST OF CHARACTERS. Tess giggled.

FRANCES, A RITTER... HERSELF. Frances appeared, golf club in hand, walking toward a green.

ALAN, ANOTHER RITTER... PLAYED BY HIMSELF. Alan looked at the camera, waving a golf club.

THERESA, A REITER... ALL BY HERSELF. Tess leaned forward. Her image was walking toward the camera, her dark skirt swinging, a tight cloche on her head, a smile on her face. Why, I'm almost pretty! Tess relaxed into her chair.

AND HOWARD, THE OTHER REITER... LON CHANEY, WHEW! Howard was on the screen, scratching his head, ignoring the camera. His image faded.

The four cousins appeared, walking out of the Ritters' house, dressed for travel.

ABOARD THE *FORT ORANGE,* ALBANY BOUND. Tess remembered the delight of the river steamer, sailing up the Hudson. Here were Washington Irving's Catskills, where she had heard the crash of heavenly ninepins with Rip Van Winkle, shivered at the ride of the Headless Horseman. The mixture of Dutch and Mohawk—Rhinebeck and Poughkeepsie—thrilled her with the thought of these two unlikely cultures meeting in the beautiful setting. Dinner by candlelight as history slipped past the portholes—ah, she *had* missed Murray—then to bed with the moon rising over Port Saugerties.

AT THE SARATOGA RACES! WEIGHING IN. FIND THE RITTERS AND THE REITERS. And there they were in the paddock, watching the jockeys, each with a cigarette hanging from his lip, climb onto the scales, looking so very nonchalant, as though this weren't the most exciting place in the world at this moment. Then Frances and Tess and Alan were in the grandstand, walking toward the camera, being jostled by the other sports lovers, as elegant as any true player there. On the distant track, horses were parading toward the gate. Though the pictures on the screen were black and white, accompanied only by the whirr of the projector and the muttering of the audience, Tess relived the vivid colors, the expectant roar of the crowd as the horses reached the starting gate.

FIRST RACE. OUR *TWINK* LEADS! WE WIN! Twink, the horse chosen because his name sounded like Tinkou! Tess felt she had run the race, hair flying in the wind, to arrive triumphant at the finish, to receive the cheers of the crowd, the victorious look on Howard's face. And there he is, below in the infield, bareheaded in a sea of straw boaters, all turned toward the track except Howard, who is looking at her. He slowly lifts his hand and waves.

This scene, supplied by Tess with color and sound, was so melting that she felt tears rising in her eyes. Howard's bright hair caught the sun, his handsome face was upturned and joyous, his hand above the crowd seemed a valedictory. It was not, of course, a goodbye—it was the beginning of what was possibly the best two weeks in her life, so far. But she was touched to the soul by the sight of her brother, alone in that crowd, raising his hand to her. She gulped and snuffled, missing the scene where all the cousins except Howard struggled to hit a golf ball off a tee. She had such a wonderful time on this trip, free from the sadness of her mother, free from the secrets that abounded in her house, free from the feeling of responsibility for everything. What on earth was she crying about? Howard had treated her like an adult, not in any condescending way nor to amuse Alan and Frances, but with an easy camaraderie that eliminated her self-consciousness and allowed her to enjoy herself. In the dark of the living room, she surrendered to silent weeping.

Tess raised her head just in time to see her screen self being kissed by her cousin Alan. His kiss had troubled her. She and Alan and Frances had been on the porch of their Saratoga hotel, horsing around for Howard's camera. They were laughing in the morning sunlight, full of high spirits, pushing each other a little, roughing each other's hair. Alan pretended to capture Frances, who escaped his grasp, and he then turned to Tess, pinned her arms, and kissed her on her mouth. She was taken aback by the boldness of it. Kissing was a serious business, and now almost her whole family had seen her in the arms of a man, even if it was just her cousin. She held her breath. What would they say? Would they laugh? Or think her a fallen woman!

"Oh," said Katie. "That Alan seems to be having such a good time. Doesn't he look like his father, BJ?" BJ's nod was lost in the darkness, but Tess smiled into her handkerchief as she wiped her eyes. She vowed to stop turning molehills into mountains.

After Saratoga, the Ritters and the Reiters had taken the train to Lake George, just an hour away. The resort where they stayed had all the sports Howard loved—swimming, golf, tennis, and horseback riding. Tess was grateful that her brothers had seen to it that she did all these things. At least she wouldn't make a fool of herself. The golfing was fun, especially since she was dressed so well in a drop-waisted blue dress with a matching cloche and two-tone golf shoes, cleated and tongued. Her swing was average but better than Frances'. Frances ducked her head. Tess could see it in the film.

And now Howard was in his glory. RANKING TENNIS STAR...AND HOW RANK! But Howard was not rank. He was excellent. Tess watched the small figure on the screen returning every shot, backhand, forehand, all graceful. The grayness behind the courts was Lake George. Tess could see it in all its blueness in her mind's eye, the white trellis rimming the courts catching the sparkles through the lattices.

INTRODUCING TWO EDERLES, A SEA LION AND A PORPOISE. Alan, Tess, and Howard were strolling from the cabins toward the camera. Alan wore daring modern bathing trunks, and Howard had on swim pants with a singlet top. Tess was between them, in her black wool bathing suit with a white belt. They were teasing her, and she was laughing. Tess leaned forward in her chair. Maybe Helen was right. She did look pretty good. Her legs were long and shapely, her stomach flat, her hair, the bob all grown out, was in a bun at the back of her neck. She looked happy. But she had tried a little flirtation with the tennis pro, and he hadn't paid any attention. He treated her the same way he treated Frances. Tess sighed. Alan and Howard, on the screen, were slapping each other on the back, and *she* remembered it was at something clever she had said. And now she was in the lake and swimming—swimming well, her stroke long and smooth. What a miracle to be able to see herself as others might see her. Maybe she actually was pretty, maybe she looked good in her clothes, maybe she didn't have to think about it anymore. What a relief that would be.

The flickering sign on the screen said THE RITTERS EVEN WENT HYDROPLANING ON LAKE GEORGE. Katie gasped.

"What? What? Hydroplaning? What is that? Is it an airplane? Up in an airplane? How could they do that dangerous thing?" All conversation in the darkened room stopped. "Look at that Frances in her beret, getting into that contraption. Doesn't she remember she has parents? And Alan! Alan is older! He has to take care of Frances. How could they? And together! I can't bear to watch." Katie covered her face with her hands.

"Now, Mother," Howard said, apprehensive about the scene after this one. "You know it turned out all right. Alan and Frances are home safe and sound." He paused nervously. "And Tess and I are, too."

Tess remembered, guiltily, the discussion before the airplane ride. They decided to go two by two—Tess and Alan, Fran and Howard— just in case anything happened. *Just in case* seemed merely a figure of speech at the time. The brightly colored plane was bobbing prettily on the water, the seats were upholstered, the pilot was dashing—it all seemed quite tame. Then, somehow, they had gone as brothers and sisters. Fran and Alan were on the plane, taking off into the blue, blue sky, the motor between the wings making a deafening racket, the plane wobbling off the lake into the air, fading to a speck. Howard was filming as the Ritters came back smiling, exhilarated.

AH! AND SO DO THE REITERS! So she and Howard had climbed aboard. She hadn't noticed whether Alan had filmed her flight. But he had. There it was. She was laughing, but she was wildly frightened. The Tess on the screen put on a leather helmet, pulled goggles down over her eyes, waved, became a dot in the firmament. The unimaginable noise precluded any talk, so she had looked down on the choppy waters of the lake and the treetops of the far shore, wondering if she would ever see her mother again. So frightened was she, she realized later, she never thought that she might not see Murray again, either. The plane banked and the world tilted, her stomach tilting with it. She clutched the straps around her shoulders. Landing was the answer to her fervent prayer.

"I don't believe you did that," Katie said, as she stood up and tightened her apron. She cast a black shadow on the screen.

"Wait, Mother, there's more," Tess said desperately. "Look now. We all went horseback riding. There are the jodhpurs you bought me, and that pretty pink shirt. And now look. I'm kissing my horse. That's how they do it in the movies." Katie sniffed. She had never been to a movie. She started toward the kitchen.

"I'm glad you had a good time on your vacation," she said over her shoulder.

CHAPTER FORTY-THREE
1929

TESS, DESPAIRING, REMEMBERED watching her mother retreat to the kitchen that disappointing night almost a year ago. Katie's shoulders were bowed, a listless hand pushing open the swinging door to the kitchen. Tess knew that more and more she was a disappointment to her mother. Katie depended upon her to be a good girl, to be sensible, to do the right thing, but their definitions of those terms were so different. Tess was the last child at home, living under the microscope of her parent's attention that had previously been focused on seven different children. Tess thought her mother would be proud of her daughter's pluck in braving the skies in an airplane. Instead, her mother was appalled that Tess would take such a chance with a life which was so important to her mother. *Two* lives, actually, because Katie probably thought that Tess should have prevented Howard from going up in that airplane. Tess saw herself as forever squirming and scheming to lead her own life, while at the same time needing her mother's approval more and more. It was a terrible trap.

Now the date was June Sixth, 1929, and Tess was sitting on her bed listening to the rattle of a cold rain against her window as she reread her diary. Murray had given her the diary four years ago, when she was just eighteen. She could hardly believe she had known Murray since she was seventeen. It was hard to imagine that so much time had passed. The diary was a five-year diary, with that many years on one calendar page, five lines to each year. It didn't allow much room for soul-searching, but looking back over the five years certainly allowed Tess to search her soul now.

Murray had pasted a thumb-nail sized picture of himself inside the front cover—he was so handsome—and on the fly-leaf had written: *If at any time you are out of sorts and would like to know if I still love you—in case I'm not around to answer your questions—just unlock this token and you will find an answer which should cheer you—I love you truly —*

Well, she was "out of sorts" and needed cheer. Could she get it from her diary? She had begun writing in it when there were only a few days of her seventeenth year left. It seemed so long ago. The first month was full of work at Kaufmann's Department Store, Pitt, lunch dates, and calls—calls from Phil and Ernie and Murray and Ed Klee and Harold and Dave. Who was Harold? She didn't remember him. She read "So Big" and saw two plays, *Peter Pan* and *Wildflower*. She took care of her nieces, Louise and Ruthie. She did and said and helped and went, but never seemed to think.

The diary was now open to August 25. That was the day of her first fight with Murray: *He reprimanded me for going with all those fellows—said I was "absolutely losing myself": shocked!* Tess remembered that day. She had ranted and raved at him, arms akimbo, eyes blazing. How dare he criticize her? She watched him grow pale. At last he stood up, croaked a "So long," and left—actually slunk—out of her living room and into the night.

The next morning she wrote in the diary: *Lost quite a bit of sleep last night. But that's all right, because I'll have plenty of time to make it up. I'm through with men! One's worse than the other, if possible.* But then she had done an odd thing. Odd, but typical. I'm always of two minds, she thought, always burning a bridge behind me but with not quite hot enough a fire.

She remembered putting down her signature green-inked pen and taking up a dull pencil on her desk, but she didn't remember why. She turned to the next page. There, on the four lines dedicated to September First, 1929, four years into the future, she had written: *On August Twenty-Seventh, 1925, I decided that I shall be married on this day—to whom, why, wherefore, and how are minor questions.* Through with men, indeed.

She had been touched to the core by his strangled goodbye, by his hunched shoulders, his sheer vulnerability. A desire to protect him rose strongly in her. She would hold his hand, she would make him a success, she would show everyone what she could do. She felt suddenly powerful and in control.

Now she leafed through pages of Leos and Bills and Sams and Harolds and Daves. But always there was Murray, and her best adjectives were spent describing the times with him. Then mostly blank pages. For almost two years.

Two years when her happiness in love was changing to bitter ashes. Some time in 1927, it must have been the summer, because Tess remembered the dining room fresh with flowers and an evening breeze coming through open windows; she had invited Murray to dinner. She had looked forward to it with joy, because Howard and Adolph liked Murray and there was laughter and ease when they were together.

They were waiting for the current *shiksa* to bring in the coffee, when BJ asked Murray how he had happened to choose dentistry for his profession. Profession was a big word in the Reiter family. All of BJ's sons were professional men—Howard and Adolph, changing his future once again, were physicians, Fred a civil engineer, and BJ, in his gray suits and silk ties, considered himself a professional as a member of the Metropolitan Insurance Company Million Dollar Club. He wore proudly on his lapel the Metropolitan pin with three diamonds, signifying his three years as a member of that exclusive organization.

Tess trembled. She knew the story of Murray's dental school decision, and she hoped it would sound serious enough in her parents' estimation.

"Well," said Murray. He loved to tell stories, and he had polished this one to perfection. "You remember that to get into Pitt, you had to take a test to be admitted into their various majors. I was going to be an engineer, because I was good at mathematics. I had a teacher in high school, Mr. Knox, who loved numbers and made math exciting. He taught us to add columns of four numbers across and four numbers down in our heads. He gave us mathematical mysteries and then showed us how to unravel them. I was the best student in the class, and he advised me to go into engineering. He said I was a natural.

"So the morning of the engineering school test, I got up raring to go. It was snowing hard, but I thought I could make it to the streetcar from Homestead into Pittsburgh. But when I got to the bottom of the hill, the blizzard was so bad the streetcars had stopped running." He looked around the table to make sure they knew the severity of the storm.

"I made it back home. My mother was in the kitchen." Tess knew that Mrs. Gross was always standing by the stove, stirring something.

"She asked me why I was home so soon, and I told her about the streetcars. 'Go get the Pitt catalog,' she said. 'What tests are given tomorrow?' I read out the list to her." Murray cocked an eyebrow.

Here comes the punch line, Tess thought. "So my mother said, 'Dentistry. That sounds good. Go tomorrow and be a dentist.' I did, and that's why I'm a dentist."

Murray smiled at the story with a twist, but Tess thought of her brother Adolph who was now a doctor after so many false starts. He probably didn't want to be a doctor any more than Murray wanted to be a dentist. Men had a hard time. They had to find a way to make money so they could support a wife and family. Girls were taken care of by their fathers until they got married, and then their husbands took care of them. Her own job at Kaufmann's on Saturdays was just a way to pass the time and to meet Murray in Pittsburgh for a Saturday night date. All she really did was sign the register in the morning and then wander about the store trying on clothes or meeting other sales-girls in a dressing room to gossip and smoke. Then she signed out at night and collected her pay envelope. She was glad she was a girl. Tess couldn't look at her father. The story was funny to her the first time she heard it—she knew it wasn't the whole truth. Murray always left out the serious parts to make a story better. And Howard and Adolph were laughing. But not her father and mother. Her heart sank.

That night, Tess awaited the knock on her bedroom door, and it came just as she was getting into bed. Her mother kissed her and plumped the pillows. "Don't think of marrying this boy, my Tinkou," she said. "He's handsome and he's clever, but he will never earn a living for you. You must think of this. When poverty comes in the door, love flies out the window. You go on seeing your other young men, and you'll find one just as handsome but with better prospects." Another plump of the pillow and she was gone.

CHAPTER FORTY-FOUR
1929

TESS LEAFED THROUGH THE DIARY, the gold-edged pages crackling in her hands. Almost a year of blank lines. She had done what her mother had said, had gone out with all those boys. Ed Klee was constant, and the Jakes and Lous and Carls and Als had come and gone. She wrote about Yetta and Marge and Phyllis, and of course Helen and her children. But the fun had gone out of it, and she was her old happy self only with Murray, and even that had changed as she wondered in the silent moments if she really could guide their destinies. She *did* like pretty things, she *did* like parties, she *did* like restaurants and plays and vacations. Cars, too, and flowers on the table. Would she be able to give them up?

Tess wasn't accustomed to examining her sad thoughts. She had enough of them when she was young. Everything changed when she got to be sixteen and went to college and had dates and met Murray. I hate being sad and not getting what I want, she whispered to herself fiercely. She turned the page and found a lonely entry, scribbled across ten calendar days, before the long drought of unhappiness.

I, almost twenty years old at the time when my feet should be firmly set on a road to somewhere—wavering, faltering, no training behind me, no goal in front of me. Is it a matter of beating ineffectual wings against the wall of Inevitability? Tess paused and smiled. She really wrote well. Too bad she didn't write more about her feelings when she was happy. The other pages were full of doings, not thinkings. But maybe she wasn't thinking a lot when she was happy. Maybe happiness doesn't need to be examined. It just...happens. Isn't that what Tolstoy said? Anna Karenina was happy until she fell in love. Is it love—that most wonderful of things—that dashes one's hopes? Don't think that. Read on.

But enough of that! No wonder that people grab at their chance of happiness, lest they lose or miss it, giving all, taking all, draining the cup to the end, emptying Life's bag of tricks—and complete happiness is never attained. Every cup of joy has its bitter dregs, every bite of sugar its bitter after taste, every rose its thorn, every silver lining its cloud. Tess winced. She deeply felt the emotion that inspired that sentence, but she also regretted the staleness of the phrases, the use of four examples rather than the classical three. Surely she could have done better than that.

And then there's such a grim finality about life. It can't be undone and started over again. Days, action, words even are so irretrievable. Only one certainty of bliss. If one could stay on the heights and have them remain the heights. Oh, what can one do—what can one do? Life's purpose is so awfully immersed in darkness. You can't recognize the happiness of one person's complete understanding—feel the saving grasp of one—man's, I guess—hand, be surrendered to one man's enduring passion. If life were only a long moment filled with carefree youth! Here I am again—deep in the sea of despondency. I think my life will always…Always…what? What? Tess shook the diary. No words fell out. What was she going to say that day a year and a half ago?

Tess stood up stretched. It was the middle of the night. She should be in bed. But she wanted to relive the experiences that had brought her to today. She reached again for the diary.

A month of blank days until January Twentieth, just before her birthday last year: *After long months of bitter neglect, the prodigal daughter returns. Moved by the sad events and the proximity of her birthday, she once again renews acquaintance with the book of her miserable memories.*

She was now writing across the days in her hurry to get to the awful news that January 1928, had for her: *Fate is often cruel, or seemingly cruel—and the stream which meanders so serenely on its way to happiness is often broken in the middle by rapids and currents—its placidity shattered by winds of adversity and waterfalls of unforeseen misfortunes.*

The love of Murray and myself and the lovely future we had planned for ourselves seems threatened by the fact that he is not succeeding, that he needs money badly, that he is moving to New York. Where once was the steady light of my complacency, the rosy gleam of our dreams, the golden knowledge that the future was ours, that Life was made for us, there remains the fitful flickerings of doubt, uncer-

tainty, and the ashes of Hope.

Irony of ironies, Murray was leaving for New York to seek his fortune on the very day after her birthday. He had despaired of starting his practice in the Pittsburgh area. He had visited a dozen dental offices, but nobody was hiring a new untried dentist to share a practice. He had thought of opening his own office, but that was an expense he could not even contemplate. And now his New York cousins had suggested that he come to New York, stay with them, and try his luck in a bigger city. They knew many dentists, they said. They could help him get a job.

These cousins, Mike and Manny Granich, older by ten years, were the children of Murray's aunt, his mother's sister, Brenda Firestone. Murray had spent many idyllic high-school summers with them on the Lower East Side. He and his cousins spent Sundays tramping the streets looking at the wonders and the mundane of the city in the 1920's. They explored Hester Street and Little Italy and Wall Street. The brothers had a heightened sense of beauty and organized their trips around special things, like fanlights and doorknobs and wrought iron.

On the days Mike and Manny worked, they gave Murray lunch in a bag and ten cents. Five cents was to travel the subway wherever he wanted to go, and the other nickel was to get back home by six o'clock. That meant he could surface at Coney Island or Central Park or Queens or Brooklyn, all magical names to Murray.

He remembered these excursions with delight—the noise, the energy, the endless variety of people. The days usually ended too soon for him, but he gleefully faced the challenge of rush hour home, amidst the felt hats and worn briefcases, ready for the rich promise of his cousins' company when he got back to their crowded apartment. He never could figure out what his Uncle Pincus did. Pincus was home writing in the back room most of the day, or else sitting in a coffee shop with friends. Murray's mother said with a sneer that Pincus was a revolutionary, which meant to her that he didn't work and her poor sister had to go out every day and earn a living for the family. But Mrs. Gross still allowed Murray to go there every summer, happy to have at least one child out of her house for a while.

The day before Tess became twenty-one, she met Murray for dinner and they: *talked and talked. He seems very sad at leaving. He feels that he is leaving his whole life behind, but he didn't suggest my waiting for him or keeping on loving him.* She spent her birthday *so miserable, cried all morning.*

Tess turned the page. Here she was back again with her happy green pen and once again filling a week of January days: *He is coming back in June for me. Our love is too strong to die. We are going to be married! He loves me so intensely. We are going to live happily and fully. He is going to lay the foundation for our happiness in June or before, we are going to build strongly and firmly. He kissed me and kissed me, picked me up and whirled me. My Playmate! I am going to be his and he mine. I'm engaged!*

And so Murray had gone off to New York. The parting at the station was not the sad ending she had feared, but the beginning of their life together. He had agreed to say his goodbyes to his family at home, and Tess took him to the railroad station alone. They had hugged and kissed and murmured, and she had watched through tear-filled eyes as the train grew smaller. Bitter-sweet, she thought.

She wrote in her diary: *Starting our life together in a new world, each with our interests, separately, collectively, and our love, our youth. Why shouldn't we be happy. Material comfort is not the only thing. We will have that anyway and better—a spiritual happiness that two people whose personalities, loves, and perspectives are so attuned to each other can make for themselves. Our future is going to be free-dom, congeniality, sympathy—not a humdrum affair of bickering and fighting. Our cup will be flowing over.*

The old house creaked and moaned as the night grew cooler. Tess pulled the quilt up over her knees as she remembered that within a week after leaving for New York, Murray had a job. Elated, she had tucked his letter in her purse and driven to Brownsville to share the news with Howard.

They met at a restaurant—not a good one, Brownsville had no good restaurants—and started off with drinks and cigarettes. Tess maintained her allegiance to Canadian Club and soda. She burbled on about how wonderfully Murray was doing, how proud she was of him, how bright his future looked. No one knew yet that she was engaged to Murray, but there was no doubting her feeling for him. Howard listened, amused and silent and, at dessert, changed the subject.

Tess was incensed. "Don't you have something to say about this?

I drove all this way so that I could get you to admit that you were wrong about Murray. You must know that I did. I don't usually show up on your doorstep unannounced. Can't you at least tell me that you might change your mind about him?"

Howard reached across the table and covered his sister's tense fist with his hand. "Tess, you know how much I like Murray. He's good company and fun to be with. I just don't want you to get too involved with him. I am skeptical. Yes, that's the word. I'm skeptical about his ability for success. I just don't think he's serious enough to earn a living." Howard smiled at her, as though to say the subject was exhausted. She didn't smile back. When he began to tell her of plans to move closer to downtown Brownsville, she let her thoughts wander—she, who hung on every word her three brothers chose to lavish on her. The dinner ended, she merely offered her cheek, and was on her way home, despondent and angry.

That was the beginning of another downhill swoop of the roller-coaster. The next day, she got a letter from her brother Fred, in which he wrote: *lovely dreams fade when pitted against grim reality.* They must spend all their time talking about her—poor Tinkou. And the next day, a letter from Murray. It seems that in order to practice dentistry in New York, one must have two years of New York professional schooling!

Tess remembered raging around her room. Why didn't he find that out before he left? How can he be so impulsive? Why didn't he plan better? Maybe everyone is right. Maybe Murray will never amount to anything! Break this engagement? No! I love him too much. We will find our footing soon and prove to everyone that we can make a life together.

Tess met him at the railroad station a month after he left. She remembered that she was ready to comfort him, hold him, assure him that her faith in him was not shaken. He must be devastated, poor lamb. But Murray's hat was tipped just so, his eyebrow cocked, his clothes fresh and neat. He didn't look defeated at all, Tess had thought. She now remembered her — what was it — disappointment? Her disappointment that he wasn't taking this setback more seriously? Disappointment that he didn't need her care and comfort? But in the joy of kissing and hugging and both talking at the same time, she had forgotten her confusion.

She flipped through the pages to the end of 1928. Blank pages in the leather diary, except for New Year's Eve: *sick as a dog. Went to bed and stayed there. Murray came over. I wasn't too sick to beat him at pinochle.*

CHAPTER FORTY-FIVE
1929

TESS, ABSORBED IN HER DIARY, was startled to hear the soft sound of the clock on the living room mantle strike two. Two in the morning! But she wasn't tired, and it was too fascinating to read about the story of the last five years of her life. It had a bit of Jane Austen—but her family thought that Murray wasn't good enough for her, not *too* good, like Mr. Darcy. It had a definite beginning, middle, and end. Not a morbid end, but an end that was really a beginning in itself. She stretched her arms and leaned back on the pillows again.

She had gotten to the part in the diary when Murray had returned from New York. The first thing they had to do was to find Murray an office. Tess remembered reading the want ads, traveling to possibilities, and working hard to keep Murray's spirits up. Her own, too, she admitted. But once Murray had an office, once there were people who actually called him Dr. Gross, their lives would be so much smoother. Her father would have more respect for Murray, her mother would realize Murray's potential, and her brothers would stop giving her advice about her future.

By the end of January, the roller coaster on which she imagined herself was once more on an uphill climb. After the dreadful spiral of Murray declaring defeat in Pittsburgh, his hopeful move to New York, the shattering blow of the need for more schooling to enable him to practice there, a seeming miracle happened.

Lou Breyer told them that in the very next building to his pharmacy in Charleroi, a town only a few miles from Pittsburgh, a dentist was trying to rent his fully equipped office for a year while he took refresher courses at Ohio State. Tess was ecstatic, and by the middle of February, Murray was a practicing dentist in Charleroi, Pennsylvania.

Tess continued working at Kaufmann's Department Store on Saturdays, and she and Murray met as often as possible in Pittsburgh before they took their respective street cars, she to McKeesport, he to Homestead. Tess decided she would be his bookkeeper—recording his income in her diary. By the first week in February, he had taken in one-hundred and seven dollars. They were dazzled by the sum. By the end of the month he had sixty-two dollars more, and the first week in March he showed her one-hundred and eight in cash. The next week eighty dollars, the next one-hundred and twenty-nine, the next sixty-nine, and at the end of March eighty-five more. Tess visualized the money growing in Murray's bank account, a huge pile of gold waiting to shower them with happiness.

The first week in April, the roller coaster started downhill again. Helen and Lou were having a terrible time. Helen was pregnant again, but Lou spent most of his time carousing with his many brothers and sisters—those Hungarians!

Murray's family were Hungarians, too, more fond of eating and play-acting than getting down to the business of life. Tess's diary read: *Life has again resumed the figure of a puzzle and a problem. With Lou and Helen before me as a "horrible example," I am again questioned about Murray's qualifications as a husband. Howard was here. He said there was something funny about our not setting a wedding day. Why did we wish-wash around if we were so mad about each other? Which, of course is a very sensible question. And he said that, while I felt that I couldn't get along, couldn't live without him, I should be very careful.*

Because Murray doesn't have the past, and judging from every indication, hasn't the future of a successful man. And I grant the truth of that! Has the fact that I allow everyone to sway me its basis in the fact that I don't love him enough? Am I waiting for him to be a success? If so, I'll wait all my life. I must either love him immensely as he is or give him up. I must either resign myself to living under conditions hard and bitter and unconducive to love, or resign myself to living without him.

Two-hundred and forty-five dollars in April. Oh, it was so slow! One-hundred sixty-six dollars in May.

"Let's elope, Murray. Please, let's run away and get married. Everything will be better once we're married. We'll call Dr. Solomon at the *shul* in McKeesport. He's known me since I was a baby. He'll do this for us. Let's call him and make an appointment to get married on June Sixth, that's this Thursday. Five days from now. We'll just show up, and he can marry us in his study. We'll make it for five o'clock, and then we'll go out for dinner, and then—" she screwed up her face— "we'll each go home and tell our parents."

Murray jingled the change in his pocket as he spoke to the rabbi on the telephone in Lou Breyer's pharmacy. "Yes, Rabbi, yes." A wink and a cocked eyebrow at Tess. "That will be fine. —How many people?" Tess shook her head violently. "Not many at all. Very few, in fact. Everybody will be working...Yes...Thank you. See you at five o'clock...Yes. Thank you. Um...Thank you." He put the earpiece back on its hook.

Lou Breyer was leaning on the counter when they came out of his back room "Yeah, I heard. But, believe me, I'll keep your secret. I think you're doing the right thing, kids." Lou spoke like the Dead End Kids in the new talkies. "I'll never tell, you can count on me. But you know that old battleaxe—sorry, Tess, but your mother doesn't like me, and I'm not overly fond of her—doesn't want any of her children to leave and get married. How Fred got out I don't know. And look at Adolph and Howard. They've had plenty of chances, but once they bring them home to mother, that's the end." Lou looked embarrassed but defiant, too. Tess had a sudden insight. Could her mother have caused some of Helen's unhappiness? No, it was too disloyal a thought. She thrust it from her.

"So," Lou continued after a throat-clearing, "it's best you do it your way and when you want. But I'll tell you what. I'll go home early on Thursday. And I'll be waiting in front of the *shul*. I'll take you out to dinner. How's that for a celebration?"

Lou's faith in their decision made them both feel better, more like a couple, more like adults making mature decisions.

At a quarter to five on Thursday, Tess and Murray knocked on Rabbi Solomon's study door. He opened it with a smile, beaming at each of them in turn, then looked beyond them at the empty corridor.

"Why, where's your mother, Tess? You're early. Are your parents coming by themselves?" He ushered them into the comfortable office, lit by the late afternoon sun.

Tess suppressed a giggle as she stood nervously in the middle of the room.

"Rabbi," she said in a voice she didn't quite recognize. "We're eloping. Nobody knows we're doing this. It's going to be a surprise—

a wonderful surprise—for everyone." She looked imploringly at Murray. He put his hand on her shoulder.

Dr. Solomon crossed behind his desk and sat down, arranging his hands in a little tent in front of him. How rabbi-like, thought Tess. He's going to try to talk us out of this. She steeled herself.

"Now, children," the rabbi said. He looked at them each in turn. "This is a surprise to me, too. And a difficult one. You said nothing about elopement on the telephone. I've known your family for a very long time, Theresa, and I'm not sure I can do this to your mother. She would take it very badly if she were to be deprived of sharing the happiest day in your lives. Tell me why your marriage should be such a secret."

Tess began in a rush—the strength of their love, their need to be together, the *slight* disapproval of her family, their own confidence in their future. Murray nodded from time to time, leaning forward, his elbows on his knees, his eyes on the floor. Finally, the rabbi raised his hand.

"I am reassured this is not a hasty decision. You've known each other five years. You're both of an age to make this decision. I'm going to call your mother, Theresa," —Tess gasped— "and explain to her how I feel that this is your decision to make and urge her to come and share this important ceremony." He raised his hand again to stop her tearful disagreement. "I promise I will persuade her to come and participate, not prevent. What is your telephone number?" Tess gave him the number. Her mother hated the telephone.

Tess heard the rabbi's quiet voice only as background to the noise of her pounding heart and the ringing in her ears. She gazed about the study, trying to focus on the serenity to quiet her anxiety. The neat shelves of books were starred by her tears, the dark wood, the heavy Turkish rug, the draped windows swimming.

"She will be here soon," the rabbi said in his soft accent. "Now, sit here and talk of your future while I prepare for mine. I have to write down what I will say to you as I join you in holy matrimony." He smiled at his Protestant joke. "And I have a sermon to prepare for tomorrow's services." He picked up his pen and began to write. Tess lifted a watery smile to Murray, and they retreated to the chairs in the corner of the room.

When Katie arrived, she opened her arms to Tess. *"Ach, Liebchen,"* she said. No blame, no recriminations. Just her usual sad smile, a kiss on Murray's *kepelah*, and the rabbi married Tess to Murray.

They emerged from the shul into the gathering twilight, and there at the curb, as promised, was Lou Breyer, flowers in hand—and Helen. Oh, Helen. Tess shouted with delight as she hugged her sister. How awful it would have been not to share this joyous moment with her sister, her only sister, her best friend. Tess cried again in Helen's arms.

Lou handed them ceremoniously into his car: "a little crowded, but who cares on this wonderful evening" and they were off to Kline's in Pittsburgh, where Lou had made reservations for a wedding supper. Katie, over her vegetable soup and scrambled eggs, was shocked at the food her children ordered, but she held her tongue. Lobster! And liquor, too. She had never even imagined it. It was awkward enough allowing Lou Breyer to buy her dinner, and now they were all looking at her to set the tone.

She raised her water glass to toast her new son-in-law and her beloved youngest child. Tess was unbearably grateful to her mother for her acceptance of what must have seemed to her a very rash act on Tess's part. She would never be able to repay Katie. Tess was so happy. She put her hand on Murray's knee. He put his arm across the back of her chair. Everyone relaxed.

There was a tap on Tess's shoulder. She turned to meet the fond gaze of Ed Klee. Unprepared, speechless, her eyes wide, she turned to Katie.

Once again, her mother showed her quick grasp of a difficult situation. "Ed," Katie said. "How wonderful to see you. We are having a celebration of Tess's marriage to Murray." She smiled at her new son-in-law. "Will you please have something to drink with us, a little schnapps, perhaps. Sit down and join the festivities."

Ed paled. He looked at Tess with a face of sheer hopelessness. He removed his hand from her shoulder as though suddenly burned, and backed away. He mumbled something, began to say something to Murray, and fled the restaurant.

Tess was appalled. Had she led him on so much? Had she hurt him so much? Her objections to Ed were so myriad, surely he never thought she would marry him! Apparently he did think so, and so did her mother, who rested a stern glance on her. A small cloud of guilt sailed across her rosy landscape that she did not try to banish. She *should* feel guilty. Poor Ed. Why did he have to show up?

Yet another clumsy moment as they left Kline's, all but Katie slightly tipsy with happiness and alcohol. How would they sort themselves out for going home? Where was *home*? The last street car for Homestead was coming around the corner, its bell clanging for a quick decision.

Murray moved toward the street. "I guess I'll go home and announce the news," he said. He grasped Tess for a quick kiss, put his lips gently to Katie's forehead, shook hands with Lou and Helen, and was gone.

So here was Tess, sitting alone in her bedroom on Carnegie Avenue at three in the morning. Can it be so late? she marveled. She had read her diary right to today's page. Where is my green pen? Too tired to look for it, she found a blue crayon on her desk. A crayon? It must belong to her nieces.

She wrote on the lines for June 6, 1929: *Married*. And fell into bed.

CHAPTER FORTY-SIX
1929

TESS WOKE UP LATE the next morning. The sun was streaming in the window, warming her narrow bed, glinting off the silver brushes on her bureau, embroidering with gold the flowers on the upholstered armchair. Married more than twelve hours, she thought. It's no different from not being married. Why do people make such a fuss? She laughed aloud as she put on her slippers and went downstairs.

"Thank goodness I don't have to be at Kaufmann's until noon," she said to her mother. "I've been late so many times, I don't think they would forgive me if I did it again. Even with such a good excuse."

Helen was visiting with her two little ones, Louise and Ruthie, and trying to hide her advanced pregnancy under a large sweater too warm for the June morning.

"What?" she said. "You can't go to work anymore! You're a married woman now. Married women don't work." Helen was adamant, ignoring the fact that *she herself* worked except for when she was pregnant. *Pregnant and working* married women was too much even for her to contemplate. "Sit down and enjoy your breakfast while Mother tells you about your nice surprise."

Katie cupped Tess's chin in her hand and kissed her on the forehead. "Ach, Tinkou," she said. "You look like a radiant new bride. Let me tell you what I did. I telegraphed all your father's brothers and told them that you had been married. And your Uncle Willie wired back this morning that he wants to give you and Murray..." she stumbled over the name, but her smile was genuine, "...you and Murray a present of a week in New York." She waved the yellow telegram in the air, then put it down in front of Tess.

Helen could not be quiet. "And he's reserved you a room at the Manger Hotel and booked a drawing room on the train. Imagine! A drawing room! You'll leave tomorrow morning. Isn't that exciting?"

Tess was overwhelmed. A whole week with Murray in New York.

It was too amazing to be believed. She looked from face to face. They were awaiting her reaction as avidly as she was checking theirs. It must be true. She let out a whoop.

"So," her mother continued, relieved. "Get in touch with Murray. You can ask him to dinner and to spend the night." A look of apprehension crossed Katie's face. Helen smirked. Katie gave her a withering look and went on. "Then your father and I can take you to the station. Or Helen. One of us."

Dinner was a raucous affair, with Helen's two little girls in attendance. Helen loved to dress them up. Louise, her straight blonde hair chopped off below her ears, usually appeared at special occasions in a Little Lord Fauntleroy suit, blue velvet and white collared. Ruthie, a pixie with dark curls, was always beruffled. Lou was there, also. Katie, in the presence of *two* sons-in-law whom she found distasteful, struggled to make sure that everything went off smoothly. At eleven o'clock, Helen, Lou, and their children went home. BJ said goodnight and went up the stairs. Katie watched Tess and Murray follow him.

Murray had never been upstairs in the Reiter house. Tess led him into her bedroom. She had pulled the big old armchair close to the window, which she opened to the soft summer air. She drew Murray to the chair and bent to take off his shoes. She tossed hers into the darkness behind them and settled on his lap. There were fireflies sparkling in the garden below, and a full moon rode the sky above. They both sighed and, punctuating the stillness with murmurings and promises, watched the morning sun finally rise.

It was Helen and Lou and their two little girls who drove Tess and Murray to the station in Pittsburgh and saw them into the Pullman car. Everyone wanted to inspect the drawing room and were visibly disappointed by its size, although Louise and Ruthie had to be physically pulled from the triangular sink in the corner when the conductor cried "All aboard!" Tess and Murray waved as Pittsburgh slid away.

The newly-minted Dr. and Mrs. Gross had the second dinner seating. Their names were actually on a card clasped in a little silver paper clip. Tess had never seen her new name written by anyone but her. She had doodled it for years on notebooks and paper napkins. But here it was on their very own table in a restaurant rushing east through the twilight to New York. The candlelight gleamed on the thin pewter vase with its single carnation and on the snowy napkin firmly buttoned to Murray's shirtfront. Tess felt smug.

The porter was pulling down the berth in their little cubicle when they returned after dinner. Murray looked nervous, but Tess wasn't. Not a bit. She had been looking forward to this night for at least three years, and she was going to enjoy it, savor it, and participate in it fully. She couldn't wait.

They awoke next morning tangled in each other's arms. There had been much cracking of elbows and knees against the drawing room's metal walls, eliciting giggles and shushing, but altogether things had gone quite well. Murray had been as untutored and frightened as Tess, but their silly sides trumped their ignorance. They declared themselves truly and happily married.

When Murray got out of bed, they became aware of the blood-soaked sheet. "Oh my God!" Tess shrieked, euphoria fleeing. Murray took her in his arms once again. "That's something that happens the first time. It's stopped by now, I'm sure. We're almost in New York. Let me get dressed first, and I'll go into the corridor. You can clean up then." He gave her a reassuring smile, wrapped her in the blanket, and hurried himself into his clothes.

When he had gone, Tess tried to wash the sheet in the tiny sink, but it was just too small. She rolled it up into a ball and pushed it under the berth. "I'll worry about that later," she thought. "I'm just too happy now. What a night! Thank God it was Murray!"

By mid-morning they were in their room at the Manger Hotel. They flung themselves once more into bed, a larger one this time, eventually to sleep until sundown.

It was a week of adventure in New York City in 1929:

Visiting: Tess's Uncle Willie and Aunt Tillie; Alan and Frances — remember the trip to Lake George?; Murray's cousins Manny and Mike; Tess's Uncle Leo, who gave them a check for two-hundred and fifty dollars — a fortune, and enabling them to buy orchestra seats at the theaters at the exorbitant price of seven dollars and fifty cents; Tess's Aunt Fanny and Celia and Tina Seldon and cousin Ruth.

Eating out: Park Central Hotel, Horn & Hardart's, Ceylon, Feltman's.

Getting culture: Paramount Theater; Blackbirds *at the Ettinger Theater; the Flea Circus; Grant's Tomb; Museum of Natural History;* Strange Interlude *at the Golden Theater; Billie Dove in* Careers *at the*

Strand Theater; Coney Island; Street Scene *at the Playhouse Theater;*
Four Devils *at the Roxy movie theater.*
   Shopping: Sarnoff's on Fifth Avenue, Dunhill.
   Sinning: Julius's & Lee's, two speakeasies in Greenwich Village.
   Tess cried in the train on the way home to Pittsburgh. *Oh! I hate
to leave New York and my honeymoon!* she wrote in her diary.
   Katie and Helen met them at the station in Pittsburgh, Katie with
a perfunctory kiss on Tess's cheek, Helen with an enquiring look and
a hug. Tess chattered happily about their New York adventures,
vaguely aware that if she did not do so, there would be a stony silence
in the car.
   Finally, Katie interrupted her. "You should save your stories until
your father can hear them at dinner," she said. "We have made some
plans. We think Murray should bring his things to us and live here
until you two get settled into something of your own. Living apart
won't be a good thing. How does that sound?"
   Tess was dumbfounded. She hadn't thought of anything beyond
the honeymoon! Of course! She and Murray must live together. Why
had they accepted so easily that he would live in Homestead and she
in McKeesport? Everything happened so fast. And, of course, they
didn't have enough money for their own house or apartment. But
Murray sleeping in her bedroom? Murray having dinner every night
with her mother and father? She shrank from the thought. But it had
to be done. They both took their suitcases up to her room.
   Tess went downstairs to help her mother with dinner, but Katie,
unsmiling, waved her off. Helen, too, was cool and distant, not at all
inclined to whisper with Tess about their newly similar experiences.
Tess was disappointed. The elation of the past week was wearing off
too fast. What was troubling her mother and Helen?
   The next morning, a Sunday, Tess and Murray went to Helen's
house for breakfast. While Lou and Murray played with the little girls,
Tess cornered Helen in her kitchen.
   "Okay, Helen," she said in a tough Joan Crawford voice. "Let's
have it. Why are you and mother treating me like a stranger? What
have I done wrong?" She ended unintentionally on a plaintive note.
Not Joan Crawford at all. More Mary Pickford. She became apprehensive when Helen turned a chair around and motioned to Tess to
sit.

"Tinkou, I promised Mother I would say nothing about this to you. But it's not fair that you should have noticed something wrong and not be told what it is." She closed the swinging door to the kitchen. Tess trembled.

"Well, here it is. I mean, you've got to know what we know. That is, I shouldn't be the one to tell you, but I always am." Helen? At a loss for words? Tess braced herself.

"Okay." Helen looked as though she were about to dive into an icy stream. "You remember that you and Murray spent Friday night on Carnegie Avenue, the night before you left for New York?" Tess nodded, bewildered.

"Well, Mother went upstairs after you left to clean up your room and...uh...well...change your sheets..." Tess remembered with a guilty start the bloody sheet she had left behind on the Pullman. "And there it was, your pristine bed, all made up, and no...no...bloody sheet. We know that you and Murray had...did...were...well, you know, before you were married. We never thought you would do that. Mother is very disappointed in you. And she is angry at Murray. She blames him."

By now, Helen was dabbing her eyes with a linen napkin from the table, Helen who never cried. Tess was speechless.

"But I'm not mad at you," she went on. " I don't blame you a bit. I wish—maybe if I —anyway, you've been a good girl all your life. And that wasn't a bad thing to do. And even if it was, being bad just once—or twice —doesn't seem all that important." By now Helen was rambling, afraid of the imminent silence.

"How awful! Doesn't anybody know me? Can you honestly think that Murray and I—that we—I can't believe it! It's too terrible of you and mother," she sputtered. "And to inspect my bed sheets! It sounds feudal! It sounds Victorian! Murray and I sat up all that night. We watched the moon go down and the sun come up." She began to sob.

"We were so happy, and now Mother has to spoil it. How could she? Why didn't you...?" Tess took a deep breath.

"You must tell Mother what really happened, Helen. I'm counting on you to do that. I can't bear even to think about this. And Murray and I have to find our own place as soon as possible." Tess dried her eyes on another of Helen's linen napkins. "Now. Make the coffee strong, please. Let's eat."

That night Tess wrote in her diary: *How transient everything is. We've waited five years together. I lived twenty-two years for this occasion—now my honeymoon is over and life becomes once more planning for something vague.*

And the next night: *Monday. Murray took up his work again this morning and I was on hand to speed him on his way. Murray came back to McKeesport for me at 6:00 and we drove to his mother's to have dinner and pick up his things. Stained my green dress. I weigh 123 pounds.*

She closed the leather cover, snapped the lock, and flushed the key down the toilet.

CHAPTER FORTY-SEVEN
1930

FOR THE NEXT THREE MONTHS, Tess was on hand to speed Murray on his way to work. The rest of every day was very like all the days preceding her marriage, except that she did not go to her job at Kaufman's Department Store ever again. She helped her mother in the kitchen, she did some of the shopping, she met her friends for lunch, she tried to maintain a discrete silence in her bedroom. After a while, she and Murray did not even talk about moving into a place of their own. Frankly, there just wasn't enough money to support such a place.

One sunny Wednesday afternoon, Tess had just said goodbye to Yetta after lunch in Pittsburgh. Tess enjoyed her lunches with Yetta. Yetta wasn't married, and Tess enthralled her with tales of married life, feeling confidence at last after being the youngest and most innocent of Yetta's party circle. Also, Tess had met Murray at Yetta's apartment, so Yetta felt a proprietary interest in everything that happened to them. She listened, attention unflagging, as Tess repeated domestic conversations, domestic disagreements, domestic bliss.

Yetta had complained bitterly that she had not been invited to the wedding, but that was forgotten now that Tess was a settled married woman of three months. Tess was always euphoric after a lunch with Yetta and not in the least anxious to go home and be a dutiful daughter. It was a lovely day, and Tess was loathe to have it end on Carnegie Avenue. I'll just drive over to Charleroi and surprise Murray, she said to herself. I'll whisk him away after his last patient, and we'll have dinner at one of the roadhouses between there and McKeesport.

The top was down on her little roadster, and she sped over the country roads, humming the latest rag tune. She pulled up in front of Lou Breyer's pharmacy and parked, giving the car's hood a strong thump as she finished the song. Tess shaded her eyes and looked up at the second floor windows. The original dentist's name was still on them in sober Roman letters, but soon Murray would have windows of his own and his own name in strong Gothic script.

She opened the door at street level and climbed the stairs to the second floor. There was a door at each end of the hall. The closest one was Murray's. She hadn't been here in over a month. Why had she stayed away so long? The drive from Pittsburgh to Charleroi was actually short, so why did she avoid it? She should be checking to see if the office was clean and that the magazines weren't too old. No more, she vowed. Once a week. She would pick him up, and they would have an evening out. She smiled, anticipating his pleased surprise. She would just sit down with his patients in the waiting room, and he would find her there.

Her gloved hand reached for the doorknob. She turned it this way and that. It was locked. Tess checked the little watch on her wrist. Three-thirty. The dental day surely wasn't over. She shook the knob, rattling the door against the jamb. There was no light coming through the frosted glass. Obviously, the lights inside were not on, the door was certainly locked. She began to be frightened.

Tess reassured herself that she had seen Murray off to work that morning. There was a phone at the Carnegie Avenue house and a phone in the pharmacy. If anything had happened, surely Lou would have called. Murray probably said hello to Lou every morning. If Murray didn't get off the trolley, Lou would eventually have called. So it would be Lou who would know where Murray was.

Tess could feel the perspiration gathering on her forehead. In the dim light, she checked herself in the mirror in her compact and did some repair with the powder puff.

The door to the pharmacy jingled shut behind her. No one was at the counter. Tess took a deep breath and, as the panicky noise in her ears subsided, heard voices coming from the back of the store. Someone's here, she thought, and closed the door harder this time, but the bell didn't get any louder.

All right. I'm *mishpocheh*, I'm a relative, she said to herself. Surely a relative is allowed to go behind the counter. She went behind the counter, turned at the prescription shelves, and found herself in Lou Breyer's back room. Everything was amazingly clear— the men's ties, stripes for Murray, birds for Lou; colorful bottles of pills and elixirs on shelves; black and white tiles on the floor; the perfect Os on the mouths of Lou and Murray; the cards on the table. Murray and Lou were playing cards! Pinochle, to be exact.

"What are you doing here, Murray?" she asked, in a perfectly reasonable tone. But then she realized *what* he was doing there, and her voice rose. "Why aren't you in your office?" And then her voice became quite strident. "It's three forty-five. Why aren't you in your office?"

The noise from a scraping chair. "I better go, Lou. Thanks for the … lunch. Come on, Tess. We'll talk in the car." He took her shoulders and turned her around.

Tess drove. "Listen, Tess. Things aren't going well at the office. Hardly any patients. Most of them decided to wait until my landlord got back. And there aren't any new ones coming to me. I couldn't tell your mother that I wasn't doing business. It's what she expected, I guess. So I come to the office every day, and Lou and I, well, we filled in the time. I didn't know how to tell you. Things will get better. I know they will. We still have nine months on the lease. Things are bound to change. I know they will." He trailed off.

Tess compressed her lips, "Things *won't* change," she thought, "not unless I change them. We've got to get away from here. Go live by ourselves, be responsible for ourselves. I don't want to be embarrassed for Murray. I don't want to make excuses for him any more."

"Isn't there some kind of magazine where dentists advertise for help? Some sort of professional thing where you can learn about dentists and job possibilities? I know Howard and Adolph get a medical journal. Is there a dental journal?"

Her voice was dangerous, and Murray's was hoarse, a sure sign that he was miserable. "*The Dental Journal.* I get it every month." He didn't sound interested in what her ideas might be, damn him.

"I want the last two issues, and soon. And the next one, too. As soon as it comes." She huffed off into the house, and Murray followed abjectly.

"Ah, Tess," sighed BJ when he found her poring over the journals and had heard the story, told to him in angry burst. "Why didn't Murray come to me? I would have helped him. Happily. Let me help now. Your mother and I don't want you to move away. Let's see what we can do together."

"No, Father," Tess said firmly. "We have to be on our own. And look what I've found here." She had marked a page in *The Dental*

Journal. "This sounds like something that would be right for us. 'DENTAL OFFICE SEEKING ASSOCIATE,'" she read from the place she had marked. "And it's in Johnstown. That's less than a hundred miles from here. I'm going to call this number right now."

Soon she had Dr. Louis Finklestein on the phone and had made an appointment for Murray to be interviewed.

When Murray returned from Johnstown, he was elated. "He hired me!" he exulted. "We talked awhile, he let me work at the chair for an hour, and he hired me! I start in September! That's two weeks from now! Let's drive to Johnstown together and find a place to live. Some of my classmates are there—Kaplan, Brody, Bloomberg—they'll help us look."

Tess waited impatiently for Murray to thank her for her brilliant idea, to shower her with praise for opening this new door for them. Her face was expectant, but the gratitude didn't come. Disappointed, she turned away. Maybe when they got settled in Johnstown he'll realize how much she had done for him.

The next week, they were in Johnstown, and Lillian Kaplan, Jane Brody, and Sally Bloomberg helped them find an apartment. "We better start small," Tess insisted. "Don't forget, there is a six-month trial period." Tess remembered that two of Murray's trial periods had ended badly.

They found a studio apartment that was a good price. "It's small," conceded Jane. "But as long as it's big enough for a bridge table, it's perfect!" They all laughed.

That night, Tess and Murray were invited to dinner at the Finklesteins. Tess dressed carefully, wanting to impress Murray's new employer with their sophistication and reliability. How to combine those attributes in a dress, a pair of shoes, and a hat she did not know. And besides, Murray was so charming; they probably wouldn't even notice her. She seethed a bit. After all, she was the author of this adventure. When would she get the attention? Never mind. They were here, this was now, and their future together was beginning at last.

Dr. and Mrs. Finkelstein—Call us Lou and Faye, please—looked like brother and sister. Both were in their forties, very short, round and soft, pink and white. They could have been the couple atop a middle-aged wedding cake. Lou was balding, Faye's beautifully marcelled bob was turning silvery-gray. They were both elegantly dressed in tailored suits, his tan, hers lilac.

Their house was a direct reflection of their impeccable taste—white stucco, two storied, separated from the street by a faultless lawn. Inside, there were no sharp corners, everything was curved and pillowy, all was cream and pastel. Tess had never seen anything like the low upholstered divan, the picklewood coffee table, the polished aluminum lamps. Tess pictured her parents' Victorian living room, dark and crowded with somber furniture. The setting sun diffused the room with a golden light as Faye handed round the Manhattans, mixed by Lou in a flashing shaker.

CHAPTER FORTY-EIGHT
1932

SHEER UTTER HEAVEN! That is how Tess described her life in Johnstown, Pennsylvania. Ready-made friends in Murray's Pitt classmates: the Bloomburgs, Kaplans, and Brodys—bridge playing, poker loving, ready for a good time. They knew all the speakeasies, all the good restaurants, all the places to dance and have fun. A kind employer, Dr. Finkelstein often invited Tess and Murray to dinner. Murray's mischievous eyebrow once more signaled his jokes. Tess was able to take a deep breath without murmuring Oh my God. Things were good.

By 1931, things were *so* good that Tess and Murray moved into a larger apartment—big living room, passable kitchen, nice bedroom. The bridge table was up permanently. Poker and bridge were now accompanied by dinner. Tess's mother bought a little spinet piano for Tess and had it delivered as a surprise. Tess felt she had everything she wanted, everything she hoped for, everything she worked for. Murray didn't say so, but she thought he felt the same way.

One day after the turn of the year, Murray came home cold, wet, and troubled. Tess's heart sank as she helped him off with his snow-bedecked overcoat and put his gloves and scarf on the radiator.

"Is something the matter, Murray?" she asked hesitantly, already flinching at the expected bad news.

"No. No. Well, yes," Murray admitted. "It's a moral problem, nothing earth-shaking." Tess's face cleared. She thought she could handle a moral problem, only that she didn't want to.

"Do you remember meeting Ethel, Dr. Finkelstein's office girl?" Tess would have called her a receptionist, but never mind. "Of course you do. She's right there at the front of the office. Anyway, I think she's been stealing money."

"Oh, no," Tess groaned. This was bigger than she had feared. "How do you know? And why doesn't Dr. F. know? He should take care of it. Not you."

"Well, I always walk my patients to the waiting room door. Ethel doesn't see me most of the time, but I hear her tell the patients what the charge is. She usually says a dollar or two more than we actually charge, and I think she puts the extra money in her pocket. She probably makes twenty dollars a day, and that's a hundred a month and more than a thousand a year!"

Tess was shocked. She had never actually known someone dishonest. Except herself, of course. Her face reddened as she remembered the Danish she had lifted. But that was a necessity, not stealing. And she had done it only once. But Ethel! Middle-aged, overweight, efficient Ethel! "Are you sure, Murray? I can hardly believe it! And why doesn't Dr F. know? And she's really stealing from his patients, not him. It's complicated."

Murray's voice was getting hoarse, a sure sign that he was upset. "That would bother Dr. F. even more. And I've worked there for five months. Ethel has been with Dr. F. for thirteen years. I know I ought to tell him, but will he take my word over hers? Could I lose my job?" Tess winced. "Ethel might lose hers—*will* lose hers. Do I want that? I don't know what to do."

Tess put dinner on the table, and they chewed over the problem with the meatloaf and through coffee and cigarettes. An anonymous letter, an anonymous phone call? Tess could be an irate patient calling to complain that she was charged more this time than last time? No, that wouldn't work. The files were there with names on them, and Ethel wrote the correct amounts in the files. Who would Tess say she was, anyway? Dr F. knows all his patients. Confront Ethel? Murray wouldn't do that very well. So the question was, tell Dr. F. or not tell Dr. F.?

They went to bed, tossing and turning. At about two A.M., Tess said, "You've got to tell him." Murray said, "I know."

Murray went to work the next morning haggard, his voice grating with tension. Tess spent the day working out difficult Rachmaninoff chords and pacing the living room, four steps each way, and muttering *Oh God*.

Murray arrived home, late but jaunty, driven by Dr. F. himself in his midnight-blue Cadillac.

"I did it! Dr. F. was shocked, but he believed me. That's the thing. He believed me. We talked for an hour—about the office, about how much he valued my work—and about how difficult he knew the decision to tell him must have been."

Tess blew out her mouth in a sigh of relief. It could have turned out so differently. "So—what's he going to do? How is he going to prove to Ethel that he knows she's been stealing from his patients?"

"All we could think of is to call this week's patients and tell them something—maybe that we forgot to write the charges in the file, and ask them how much they paid. Then compare it with what Ethel wrote in the file. I just hope that this isn't the week she decides to give up her life of crime." Murray grinned, Tess laughed in relief. That couldn't happen, could it?

By the middle of February Ethel was gone, by the beginning of March Evelyn was at the front desk, and by the end of June Tess was pregnant.

She was young and healthy, no morning sickness, bridge games until the early morning hours, drinking and smoking as much as usual. She loved thinking about the baby, and everyone made a wonderful fuss—holding her chair, taking her arm, making sure she was warm enough. The attention was bliss. Even her mother, with five grandchildren already, was solicitous rather than interfering. Howard and Adolph visited Johnstown, Helen came with her three children, the newest, Regina, almost a year old. Katie and BJ spent a weekend, staying in a hotel and enjoying a dinner that Lou and Faye held in their honor.

This is all too good to be true, breathed Tess. And of course it was. Unnoticed by the Bloombergs, Kaplans, Brodys, and Grosses, there had been a stock market crash in 1929. Lou Finkelstein had noticed. By 1931, he was hard-pressed. He and Murray spent many afternoons in the office without seeing a patient. Medical visits were usually the first thing to go when budgets got tight. Murray was pleased to sit in Dr. F.'s private office and talk. It didn't occur to him to wonder how they got all the free time.

At the beginning of December, Dr. F. asked Murray to stay late.

"Murray," he said. "Have you realized that our business is falling off—rapidly, I might add, rapidly?" He didn't wait for an answer. "I won't beat about the bush. I can't afford to keep you on. There's not enough work for two of us here, and who knows how long this is going to last? I've got to let you go. You've been a good colleague, I've been proud to have you here, but I can't afford you any more. I may not be able to afford my wife any more." He paused for a rueful smile.

"But don't think I'm just going to turn you out on the street." Now Murray smiled. "I've met with my accountants, and we've come up with a workable plan, I think." Accountants? Plural? Murray wasn't quite taking it all in.

"There's a town—Punxsutawney, about sixty miles from here—that they say the depression hasn't hit." *Depression.* Murray hadn't heard that word before. "It's coal mines and farms and a coke industry. People seem to be passing the money around their little area. No bankruptcies, no bread lines. We think you could make a living there, and I am willing to set you up in an office."

All this Murray repeated to Tess when he got home. She watched him coming down the street, no jaunty step this time as he approached the front door, no smile with a perfunctory kiss.

"Dr. F. said we could stay until April, so you can have the baby here in Johnstown the way we planned. He and I will go to Punxsutawney and find office space and a house for us." Murray finished his coffee and lit a cigarette. "Of course, he will share in the profits for awhile, until he's got his investment back. But he'll be fair to me, I know. I think it will be okay. He wouldn't set me up in an office if he didn't think I could make money. You know what a good businessman he is. He's even got accountants working for him."

"But why is he willing to set you up in an office? Isn't that a big expense? Why is buying you an office in a strange town cheaper than keeping you here? I don't get it." There's more to this than Murray is telling me, Tess thought. He's not looking at me while he's talking. Something else is happening. I know it. He's talking with that hoarse voice. It's a dead giveaway. "And all our friends! Oh, Murray, we can't leave all this fun, this beautiful apartment, this good life we've made here." She felt the tears come. "And where the hell is Punxsutawney, anyway?" she hiccupped. "I can't even spell it! I don't want to go!" She wailed and clutched her belly. Murray turned up his hands.

Sadness was dealt with the cards at the bridge games. Murray smoked his way through pinochle and poker. Early in March, he and Dr. Finkelstein returned from Punxsutawney with a lease on an office and an apartment, both to be occupied in May. The deal was done. Maybe it will be another adventure, Tess thought. And besides, she had more on her mind than the move to Punxsutawney. Her baby was due in a few weeks.

"Oh, I know it will be a boy," she exulted. "Mother had three boys before she had a girl. And Fred has two boys. Of course, Helen has three girls. But that was probably Lou's fault. He's such a Hungarian. Oops!" Tess's hand flew to her mouth She had forgotten that Murray's family, too, was Hungarian. But he wasn't listening. He was sitting, hands between his knees, gazing at the carpet.

He's probably thinking about the baby, she thought. *What shall we name him? Another Sydney, after her dear brother, killed in the war? Probably not. Too confusing, with Fred's Sydney. Maybe get paid by someone to remember a beloved child? The money would come in handy.* The first baby belonged to the mother to name, she remembered her own mother saying. Probably her mother would have something to say about the name. She missed her mother. She couldn't wait for Katie to arrive and find her with a baby boy in her arms.

Tess remembered being in McKeesport, at the dinner table, just before Helen's third baby had arrived. They were going through names, and Helen couldn't decide. She had received several offers from friends of Katie's who longed for a baby to be named after someone who had recently died in their families. The discussion had been quite boisterous, especially with Howard and Adolph at home. There were puns and jokes about the various proposed names, and all but BJ were exhausted from the laughter. There was a lull.

BJ pushed back his chair. "My mother's name was Pearl," he said in his soft accent and left the room.

But Helen's baby came, and it was a girl, and she was named Regina. Tess never knew if money had changed hands. But it didn't matter. She wouldn't do that anyway.

On a Thursday night Murray, terrified, drove Tess, terrified, to the Johnstown hospital. She was whisked away, and he was left alone to pace the floor and smoke, just like in the cartoons.

At nine minutes after two on Friday, March 31, Tess and Murray become the parents of a baby girl. There was a moment of crushing disappointment, then Tess ran her finger over the baby's soft cheek. Girls are good, too, she decided, not as good as boys, but the only alternative. Maybe the next one will be a boy.

Murray came every day Tess was in the hospital and accepted

with grace the decision of his wife and mother-in-law that the baby would be named Liebe Sydney after her great-grandmother and her war-lost uncle. Katie and Tess, after testing the name and finding it melodious, after shedding a few tears over their losses, had suddenly realized that Katie's mother, Liebe Friedman, had married Herr Gross after the death of Adolph. Her name had become Liebe Gross! This baby was Liebe Gross. They digested this coincidence in amazement.

Tess was determined to enjoy her two weeks in the maternity ward, entertaining guests, feeding the baby from a bottle every four hours, and napping every chance she got. She sensed it would be the only two weeks of regular sleep she might have in the next year. She was quite annoyed therefore, when Murray came, toward the end of her stay, with a troubled look and his foreboding hoarse voice.

He gripped her hand. "Punxsutawney is a really pretty town," he began. "You'll like it. It's in a valley, so some parts of it are hilly and some flat. There's a river running right through the middle of town, although they call it a creek. Actually, they call it a crick." He grinned. His eyebrow cocked. But he was looking at her closely. Was this supposed to be a sales talk? Tess didn't think so. She didn't have to be sold on moving to Punxsutawney, it was a done deal. She braced herself.

"And there are two movie theaters in town, the Alpine and the Jefferson." Tess looked at Murray in mock amazement. Imagine! Two! When she didn't care if there were any.

But finally Murray reached the point, the crux, the gist, the nub, the heart of the matter he was keeping from Tess all these weeks.

"Here's what is going to happen in Punxsutawney," he said, his hand clutching hers on the white coverlet. "Dr F. is willing to subsidize me only if I become an advertising dentist." Tess gasped. For a professional man, that was a denigration of all he had learned, turning one's back on all that professionalism had come to mean—integrity, respect, reticence, responsibility. Even Painless Parker, the butt of jokes, had changed his first name legally so as to be able to describe his dentistry without advertising.

Tess swallowed hard. "Keep going," she said. "What else?"

"It could be worse," Murray said. "Dr F. has rented me an office and a space outside on the building wall. But it will be *his* name on the advertisement, not mine. But it will be my address, my office," he finished lamely.

Tess's face crumpled. To be the wife of an advertising dentist. She remembered discussing advertising with Howard and Adolph. Business was slow for them in the beginning, and Katie, in all innocence, had suggested they put an ad in the paper. They were shocked. Even BJ had taken her to task. "Professional men don't advertise," he had said sternly. "That's part of what makes medicine a profession. It would fly in the face of everything medicine stands for—the long years of study, the ability to alleviate suffering, the respect of colleagues. That would never do! They will have to earn their patients, just like every other doctor."

And Murray! He's so proud. This will be a terrible thing for him. How will he hold his head up, even in a backwater like Punxsutawney? The joy of motherhood fled.

Tess and Murray took Liebe home to their bright Johnstown apartment. Tess put the baby in her new crib and walked through the rooms that she hadn't seen in two weeks. She touched the sunny wallpaper, scuffed up a spot on the dark oak floor, opened the silverware drawer. How can I leave here? Tess thought in despair. This is where our life is supposed to be, not humiliated in some strange town.

CHAPTER FORTY-NINE
1933

TESS COULD FEEL THE THRUM OF MUSIC beneath her feet as she paced the living room of her apartment in Punxsutawney. It's probably Roy Rogers or Gene Autrey, she thought. Or maybe Flash Gordon. For the last four months, Tess and Murray had lived above the Alpine Movie Theater. Tess's feet and legs were abuzz with the movie music from seven to eleven every night and during matinees on Saturday and Sunday. The adventure movie music was interchangeable, although the singing cowboys had some quieter times when they serenaded girl-friends. Dale Evans, Tess remembered from the poster. Tess had gotten used to the hum quickly, actually grateful that it might drown out Liebe's crying.

She clenched her fists as another wave of sobbing came from the bedroom. So far it had been fifteen minutes. She was watching the clock on the wall. Only ten more minutes and she could go in, change the baby's diapers, and give her a bottle. Tess knew she could last ten more minutes. She had listened to the crying and screaming for a whole hour once, and she had almost lost her courage. By the time Tess had picked her up, Liebe was hiccupping and exhausted. Tess had been exhausted, too.

There was a knock at the door. Tess jumped, assailed suddenly by two conflicting emotions—joy that something might happen that would get her quickly through the next ten minutes and dismay that someone would find her in such a state, a distraught woman pacing the floor as her baby screams in the next room.

She opened the door and found her landlady, breathing hard from the two-flight climb.

"Mrs. Gillespie! Please come in." Tess opened the door wide. "May I get you something to drink—tea, coffee?" Tess glanced again at the clock on the kitchen wall. Five more minutes. "I've got your rent money right here."

"No hurry, dear," Mrs. Gillespie said. "You just get the baby. I can wait."

Tess kneaded her hands together. Mrs. Gillespie was a great deal older than she and probably not up on the latest child-rearing methods. Tess had two brothers who were doctors, Howard and Adolph. This surely entitled her to feel part of the medical community herself. It was their best friend who had delivered Liebe, and he had warned Tess not to let the baby take charge of their lives.

She expounded this carefully to Mrs. Gillespie as Liebe cried and the crib rattled in the next room. "Every four hours, the doctor said," Tess explained. "Babies don't need to be fed more often than that. Crying does a baby good." Tess ignored the doubtful looks. "It strengthens their lungs. I can't let her rule the roost." She recognized the cliché as the doctor's and immediately regretted it. She soldiered on. "The doctor says not to give in." She looked at the clock. Two more minutes. "The bottle is warming now. One more minute and she'll be ready."

"If it's all right with you, dear, I'll wait and meet the baby. I haven't seen her yet ... " The timer bell rang, and Tess shot into the bedroom, shouting over her shoulder to Mrs. Gillespie that she should make herself comfortable.

Tess picked Liebe up and held her close, the baby's heart thumping against her own, her hair in tight wet curls, her face red and streaming.

"Hush, hush, baby," Tess crooned as she changed the wet diaper and dropped it into the pail. She carried Liebe, still hiccupping, into the dingy kitchen, snatched the bottle from the warming pan, and tested the milk on her wrist. Just right, I hope. She sat down in the chair opposite Mrs. Gillespie. The baby drank and gasped, drank and gasped, the bottle soon empty. With a ragged sigh, she fell asleep in Tess's arms.

Mrs. Gillespie watched all this with some concern. "Well, things certainly have changed. When my four were little, I was jiggling them all the time. I nursed them, too, but I guess that's considered old fashioned now. That was years ago. They're all grown up, with kids of their own. Do you think I could hold her?"

Tess checked the wall clock again. The doctor said fifteen minutes of holding after the bottle, then into the playpen or her crib. "You can hold her for ten minutes, it you like." Tess handed Liebe over. She marveled at seeing her baby in another woman's arms. Liebe had so filled her life for the past five months that Tess imagined her as being much larger, huge in fact, like a vast balloon obscuring her horizons. She was amazed that the baby was so small, so adorable. She sat back, staring.

Mrs. Gillespie looked down at the sleeping baby. The red blotches had disappeared with the milk, and the little face was rosy and composed under golden ringlets. Liebe opened her blue eyes once to check Mrs. Gillespie out, then closed them again in perfect baby sleep. Mrs. Gillespie looked at Tess—black hair, brown eyes, olive skin.

"What a beautiful child," she said, and lowered her voice to a whisper. "Is she a-d-o-p-t-e-d?"

Tess smiled. She heard this same question every time she went shopping for groceries with Liebe in the buggy. She had perfected her answer. "My father and brother are blond. Recessive genes. You know how that works." They usually didn't, but it shut them up.

Mrs. Gillespie was a soft, motherly woman, with an air of capability about her. She watched the sleeping baby for a while, captured by the freshness, the deepness of the sleep. Then she looked at Tess with compassion.

"You've been here five months, now, Mrs. Gross," She said. "Have you been able to go out? Have you met any people? Made friends? Maybe you've been going to church? That's a good place to meet people."

Tess drew in her breath, made a quick decision. "I don't go to church, Mrs. Gillespie. My husband and I are Jewish." She waited.

Mrs. Gillespie didn't miss a beat. Tess relaxed. "There aren't many Jewish people in Punxsutawney, are there?" Mrs. Gillespie asked. "But there are some." She changed the subject. "This little one feels quite relaxed," she said. "Maybe I should tuck her back in her crib." They went into the small bedroom, dark and neat, and settled Liebe on her stomach.

Tess made tea, grateful for someone to talk to. They chatted amiably—whether Costanza's was the better grocery store or the A&P, had Tess tasted the ham sandwiches at Isaly's. Tess shot a quick look at Mrs. Gillespie—did she know about Jews and ham? But apparently she didn't because the conversation continued smoothly.

How was Dr. Gross's practice coming along? Wonderfully, thank goodness. His appointment book was full, drop-in patients all the time. Punxsutawney must have needed another dentist —especially one as good as Murray, Tess added quickly. She saw Mrs. Gillespie reluctantly to the door. So nice of you to stay. I don't get much company. And then Goodbye.

Tess was much surprised, a week later, to hear footsteps coming to her door again. She opened it to three ladies, hatted, gloved, panting. And maybe Jewish! They looked Jewish. Could it be? Three Jewish women at her door!

"Mrs. Gross?" said the flowered toque. "We just learned you had moved to town and decided to call. Since you don't have a telephone, we thought we would just stop by. I hope we won't inconvenience you." Gloved hands shot out. Tess drew them inside, mentally going over her supply of cream, sugar, cookies. Enough cups, thank God.

"I'm Flora Brody," said the large, heavy woman in figured black silk. "This is Lillian Jacobson and this, Ruth Pete." Ruth was tiny, up only to Tess's shoulder, and sweet-faced, with a little nose that looked like it had been transplanted from a fledgling budgie. "Molly Abelman wanted to come, but her brother is visiting her from California. He's a movie star, so he doesn't get to come here very often." Flora was very proud to show off this cosmopolitan aspect of Punxsutawney.

They arranged themselves on the sofa and two chairs in the living room. The furniture from Johnstown fit well into the apartment, and its freshness somewhat overcame the gloom. Tess sat on the edge of her chair, trying to remember names, trying to be hospitable as she listened with her third ear for Liebe, who was unaccustomed to the sound of so many voices.

She was able to make coffee and present it in her pretty tea service before she heard the baby wake up. She made a quick decision to get Liebe before she cried—just this once—and show her off to company. She emerged from the bedroom with the perfect angel, powdered and sweet, to the oohs and aahs of the ladies.

Lillian was the mother of two little boys. "What a darling," she said. "Those blue, blue eyes and those blonde curls. You are a darling," and she held out her arms. Liebe clutched Tess's hair.

Ruth stood up. Her voice was low. "Come to *me*, dear child." Her arms, too, were outstretched. Liebe leaned into them. Ah, Tess thought, my best new friend.

Flora Brody was older than the others, unmarried, like Ruth. "She *is* a darling," Flora said. "Those blue eyes, that blonde hair." She looked at Tess and lowered her voice. "Is she a-d-o-p-t-e-d?"

Tess murmured about father, brother, and recessive genes. Liebe was content to be with Ruth, transfixed by her large pearls and interesting nose, which she tried to tweak. Ruth laughed delightedly and sat the baby in her lap. She took off her necklace and made a game, while Tess talked to the others. Mutual friends in Johnstown, the problems of being new in a community like Punxsutawney. Punxs'y, they said, we always say Punxs'y. It's shorter.

When it was feeding time, Tess sat happily in their midst with Liebe, who held the bottle in her own chubby hands, so unlike the baby who grasped and gasped after being left to cry for the allotted time.

"You're busy with the baby and all," said Lillian into a conversational pause. "But we wondered if you play bridge. We have a weekly afternoon game—with Molly, too, of course—but usually one or two of us can't make it. With six possibles, it would work out. And if we all show up, we can have sit-outs. We take turns. The three of us live on Church Street and Molly on Mahoning. It's an easy walk."

Tess mentally removed her bridge table from the closet and set it up in the living room. It would fit. And she would make the Velveeta cheese roll-ups that Faye Finkelstein always served. A bridge game. A gift from heaven. She could even put Liebe in her high-chair when it was her turn, with toys and a full tummy she would be quite happy. Tess accepted gratefully, holding back tears.

"Murray—my husband—would be willing to take messages at his office, I'm sure. His telephone number is eight-four, easy to remember. And if I can't come, I'll have him call you. Otherwise, I'll be there, for sure. And you must come here, of course, when it's my turn."

There was much chatter about times, addresses, arrangements, that Liebe followed with her eyes. Then it was time for the ladies to leave. Tess, the happy baby in her arms, closed the door behind them, smiling, it seemed, for the first time since she had arrived in Punxsutawney. Punxs'y. How had these wonderful women—these Three Fates—arrived at her door in the nick of time?

Mrs. Gillespie, she realized. An angel of mercy.

CHAPTER FIFTY
1934

TESS AND MURRAY DIDN'T LIVE ABOVE the Alpine Theatre any more. Murray, in spite of the Depression, was doing well in his dental practice. They were enough money ahead to start paying off Dr. Finkelstein for his financial backing of Murray's office. Tess could hardly wait to get Dr. F.'s name off the building and try to overcome the stigma of being an advertising dentist. They had moved to a house at five-thirty-two West Mahoning Street.

This house was west of downtown, a less desirable part of town as judged by whatever passed for high society in Punxsutawney. It was a perfectly normal kind of house, red brick, two stories with an attic and basement, except for one fascinating feature—it was a double house. Everything on one side of the house was reproduced in reverse on the other side of the dividing wall. Tess was aware that each time her foot touched a stair-step, there was an answering creak at the Alexises. Each time Edith Alexis emptied the bathtub, Tess's water pipes gurgled. Tess was now in her element, keeping a real house at last. Her Johnstown apartment furniture fit well into the Punxsutawney living room, the little spinet finally having a proper wall to show it off. She had a bedroom with a working fireplace in it, luxury of luxuries, and in it her bedroom furniture looked quite elegant.

She bought—in Pittsburgh, of course, at Sloan's—a dining room set, very Rococo, so that bumps from future tricycles would not make a difference, a chair for her bedroom with a lamp to sit beside the fireplace. The baby's crib and rocking chair and chest fit just right in the middle bedroom.

Tess had achieved her dream—a husband, a house, a baby. And a dog. Rather, Murray had bought a dog. A dog had not figured in Tess's plans. It was hard enough to take care of a baby. She didn't want the extra responsibility. But Nicky stayed and grew up with Liebe.

After three years in apartments—small apartments—Tess would

have to learn how to keep house. She never thought about it at home, where there was always a *shiksa*. She quickly became aware of a domestic rhythm in the neighborhood, and her wash was soon fluttering with all the others on Mondays.

Her wash was never the first out: Mrs. Alexis usually won that contest; her husband was an engineer on the B&O Railroad; they got up early. But she was never the last, either, and got some satisfaction from that.

She wrote penny post-cards to her mother, proud of her ironing day, her shopping day, her scrubbing floors day, and the fact that she still had the time and patience to attend to an active two-year old. Her mother read these cards as complaints of an over-worked mother.

"You're working too hard, Tinkou," her mother wrote. "Please get yourself a maid." Every letter—and they wrote to each other once a week—contained this entreaty. Finally Katie wrote, "Get yourself a maid. I will pay for her." The next correspondence was an actual letter in an envelope in which was enclosed a dollar bill "for the *shiksa*." Tess was mortified. Did her mother think they couldn't afford hired help? Did she think Murray was not doing well?

The ad she put in the paper, *The Punxsutawney Spirit,* read: WANTED. A YOUNG WOMAN TO ASSIST IN THE HOUSEKEEPING. LIVE-IN. $5.00 PER WEEK, ROOM AND BOARD. ENQUIRE 532 WEST MAHONING STREET ON WEDNESDAY OF THIS WEEK.

I hope that's the end of it, thought Tess. Who reads this little paper, anyway? She could at least tell her mother that she had tried.

She was wakened early Wednesday morning by the murmur of voices. She dressed quickly and went downstairs. Looking out the front window, she saw a mob of girls sitting on her porch and standing on the sidewalk in front of the house. At least twenty, maybe thirty. Oh, my. What would Mrs. Alexis think? Tess was not prepared for the response to her ad, nor was she prepared to be an employer. The first thing was to open the front door, she guessed, and she did. The murmur grew louder. She opened the screen door, and the group fell back a little.

"Thank you so much for coming," she faltered. "I didn't expect so many of you. How shall we do this? Um . . . who was here first?" Tess knew she should be establishing some sort of authority from the very first, so a *shiksa* would respect her, no matter which girl she hired. "I guess I should see you in some sort of order." Alphabetical? Height? What to do?

A young woman from the middle of the pack raised her hand. "Missus, Missus," she called. She wriggled her way to the front. "I was here first! And I wanted you to see me first." She ignored the jeers. "So I took the name of every one who come. In order." Looks of belated comprehension from the others. She walked up the porch steps to face Tess. "Here's the list. Everyone's on it. But I hope you'll talk to me first." Her smile charmed Tess, who breathed a sigh of relief and invited her inside.

"My name's Ginny—Virginia." The girl put out her hand nervously, not quite as comfortable as she had been outside.

"Please sit down, Ginny," Tess motioned to the chair and went into the dining room, opening and closing drawers in the breakfront until she found her own pencil and paper. "Let's see the list." It was written neatly, with addresses beside each name. The girls were mostly from the small towns around Punxsutawney—Walston, Rossiter, Elk Run —from the farming and mining families.

Tess poised her pencil over the tablet. "Now... "She was at a loss. "What... can you iron?"

Ginny smiled. "Of course, Missus. I got three brothers and their wives. They all live with us. Their kids, too. They all work out—outside the house, that is. I iron for all of them. And cook, too. I can cook most anything. Spaghetti, macaroni and cheese, chicken. And I'm eighteen years old." She went on with her qualifications, eager to shine.

Tess was full of admiration. She was learning from Ginny's conversation what she should ask the other girls. But this was a good one. Tess couldn't imagine that she would find anyone better than Ginny.

But she must see them all. That sounded like the fair thing to do. She asked Ginny to sit with her while she interviewed the others. They came in one by one, shy, diffident, anxious. They were mostly Polish or German girls, second-generation, from hard-working and hard-up families, dressed in what were called wash-dresses, some flowered material made up at home into a loose-fitting dress with a belt of the same material around the waist and tied in a bow behind. They all could cook, iron, clean. They all loved children. They were all happy with Sunday off. They all wanted the five dollars.

It was past lunchtime when, Liebe on her hip, Tess was finished with the interviews. The girls were still on the sidewalk awaiting her verdict. Tess asked Ginny what she thought about them. Ginny said she was most taken by Margaret Morris, a pudding-faced young woman in her twenties. Margaret seemed serious and capable, they agreed. But Tess had made up her mind early and wanted Ginny. Ginny had a personality, a sense of humor—they had tittered together between interviews—Liebe was happy on Ginny's lap. Ginny was already almost a member of the family. Tess was impressed with the list Ginny had made and felt she was a person who could improvise, who could rise to a challenge, who could face an emergency.

"You come work for me, Ginny," Tess said. "I want *you*."

Ginny suddenly became nervous. She squeezed a very surprised look out of Liebe, who was sitting on her lap. "Missus," she said. "I really want to work for you. I think we hit it off, and I like your house, what I seen of it, and I would be pleased to take care of it and your baby just like you would want me to. But I got something to tell you. It wouldn't be fair to you if I didn't. What I've got to say is that I... that I..." she flushed and lowered her head. "Missus, I've got to tell you that I've got a baby of my own." She smoothed Liebe's blonde curls. "A baby." She looked in the little girl's face. "A baby. Just like you."

Tess was thunderstruck. She hadn't imagined that any girl would leave her husband and baby to work as a live-in.

"But where's your husband? Is he going to like your being away for six days a week?"

"That's just it," Ginny said, lifting her head and looking Tess straight in the eye. "I haven't got a husband. I got myself into trouble. But my folks was good to me and let me stay and have the baby. My Ma takes care of her. One more baby in the house is hardly noticeable. But I hafta go out to work to earn my share of the money. You know how hard times is now."

Tess could hardly breathe. What she thought was a nice girl had really been a fallen woman! Pregnant and not married! How could anyone end up like that? She couldn't allow immorality into her house, could she? She had Liebe to think of. But Ginny had seemed so perfect, and nothing had changed except that Tess knew one more fact about her. What should she do? Ginny was obviously intelligent, obviously honest—she didn't really need to tell Tess about her baby. Tess would never have found out on her own. What should she do? She felt sweat on the back of her neck.

She absently took Liebe out of Ginny's arms and walked back and forth. Ginny looked up at her expectantly, not dropping her eyes, not looking ashamed. Tess felt that the next few minutes would define what kind of a person she, Tess, was, what kind of character she had. But she could hardly think. The time to make up her mind was *now*. If she let Ginny go, would that mean that she herself was moral or cowardly? If she hired her, would that mean she was compassionate or unprincipled? How could she have let her mother put her in such a position? Why wasn't her mother here now to tell her what to do?

With these thoughts rumbling like thunder through her head, Tess found herself at her front door, her hand on the knob. She opened the door and, looking at the floor, motioned for Ginny to leave. She heard the girl gasp but saw only her neat black oxfords as she passed through the door.

Margaret Morris became the new live-in maid of the young Dr. Grosses. Tess never forgot Ginny.

CHAPTER FIFTY-ONE
1934

TESS AND LIEBE WERE EATING LUNCH in the dining room. Tess finished with hers and was smoking a cigarette with her coffee. Liebe was tearing the toasted cheese sandwich into bits and drowning them in her tomato soup. "Don't do that, Liebe," Tess said. "Eat your lunch like a good girl."

"I'm done," Liebe announced and slid off her chair. The soup bowl fell with a thud onto the crimson and black Turkish carpet, the thick orange liquid seeping through the fringe onto the dark wooden floor. Liebe looked at her mother in consternation, but Tess took the familiar spill with equanimity. Now she had a maid.

"Margaret! Please bring a wet towel and some newspapers." Margaret appeared and Liebe ran shrieking to her mother. Margaret wearily patted the carpet and floor with the wet rag and laid newspapers over the dampened wood.

"Thank you, Margaret," Tess said.

Liebe was now more than two years old and becoming aware of the world. She was able to climb the stairs, slowly and with deep concentration. And she often tumbled down them when, in her haste to find out what was going on downstairs, she caught her toes in her opposite pajama leg and went head over heels. After the first hysterical descent, she quite enjoyed the falls and was able to curl up in a ball and land laughing at the bottom against the front door.

She had discovered likes and dislikes. She disliked eating, and she very much liked the fuss her mother made when she didn't clean her plate. She liked rides in the car. Her father had a black Chevrolet coupe with a rumble seat. She always sat on her mother's lap and gazed happily at the passing scenery. Sometimes she was allowed to help her father push the ivory-topped stick between them. She disliked long rides to McKeesport and sometimes to Johnstown. Once the car left Punxsutawney, she got carsick. On these long rides, her mother usually wore her pajamas and a washable house coat, carrying her clothes in an overnight case. Liebe threw up and not always with warning.

Liebe liked being pretty and wearing nice clothes. She thought when the ladies bending over her stroller and touching her curls said Oh, is she a-d-o-p-t-e-d? —that they were finding her too adorable for words she could understand. She was careful about being neat and not getting her dress dirty. She liked watching herself in her mother's triple-mirrored vanity when her mother tamed her wild tendrils into Shirley Temple curls. But getting the snarls out was painful and, as she twisted and turned to get away from her mother's strong hairbrush, her mother would always say, "Sit still! You can do this to your little girl when you've grown up." Liebe *didn't* like that!

And Liebe loathed Margaret. When her mother was home, Liebe ran screaming to her side when Margaret came into the room. She couldn't discern what Margaret was doing in her house and especially what she was doing there at night. Most visitors were long gone by bedtime.

She usually did what Margaret told her to do, but she grasped the concept more quickly if it was accompanied by a stern look from her mother. She understood that she must be with Margaret in the kitchen when the bridge ladies came and took over the living room, but she stood by the kitchen door listening to the laughter. When Tess and Murray went out for the evening, she made sure they knew how unhappy she was going to be. She howled and hollered, clinging to them until they firmly shut the door on her anguished blue eyes and trembling mouth. Then she dried her eyes and climbed resignedly into Margaret's lap for an hour of reading and milk and cookies before bed. She immediately forgot her misery, and she absolutely could not remember why she didn't like Margaret.

One night when she was home alone with Margaret, Liebe grew impatient with the slowness of the unfolding plot of Cinderella, a story she knew so well she could follow every word on the page. "Read faster, Margaret," she said. "We won't get finished before it's time to go to bed."

Margaret couldn't hurry. Ill-educated and incurious, she had to look at each word carefully before she could pronounce it. And she was tired, too, and anxious for her own cookie and cup of coffee.

"I can't go any faster," she said irritably. "Read it yourself, if you're in such a hurry." She dumped Liebe off her lap, threw the book on the floor, and flounced into the kitchen.

Liebe was dumbfounded. No one had spoken to her like that before. She climbed back onto the sofa and fidgeted a bit, her eyes on the swinging door to the kitchen. But Margaret didn't come back. Liebe could hear pots banging. She sat for a while, turning the pages of the book, but still Margaret didn't appear.

After a few eye-rubbings, she decided she was sleepy. Would Margaret put her to bed? A few moments wait, and she climbed down from her perch. Still no Margaret. She tried a few sobs, but she was too tired to really wail, and the heavy door to the kitchen was closed. It was bedtime, so she trudged up the steps herself, turned left in the hall and went into her room. She was too little to reach the light switch, but the room was dappled with summer moonlight, and she wasn't afraid. Her pajamas were hanging on a hook high on the closet door, too high for her to reach so she climbed into her crib, still dressed, and closed her eyes.

Some time later, she heard Margaret's heavy tread on the stairs. Without thinking, she drew the summer quilt to her chin and lay quite still. Margaret turned on the hall light and came in to look at her. Liebe, pretending to be asleep, actually fell asleep, but she was wakened by the familiar crunch of the Chevrolet's tires in the alley next to their house and then the sound of the garage door opening.

Liebe stood up in her crib and looked out the window. Tess and Murray were walking across the moonlit yard. She thought of the hateful Margaret and how her presence enabled her parents to go away and leave her. She was uncomfortable. Her socks were damp in her shoes. Her dress was twisted and tight. Her hair was sweaty. And Margaret was happily asleep in her own room.

She waited until the key clicked in the lock and then began to howl. She rocked the crib. She jumped until the springs sang.

Margaret, disheveled from sleep, rushed into the room. And that was how Tess and Murray found them—an inconsolable little girl still in her clothes and shoes, the *shiksa* obviously just out of bed. Liebe stopped crying as soon as Tess picked her up. She watched Margaret's face as Tess berated her for neglecting her child, for sleeping while her baby was awake and needy, for betraying her trust. She felt uneasy, watching Margaret's face crumble and her chin wobble. Liebe felt that she had done something naughty but could not remember what it was. And as she tried to remember, she fell asleep on her mother's shoulder.

The next morning, Liebe was awake with the birds, her eyes clear blue, her skin pink and dewy, her bare feet pattering about the kitchen. She smiled up at Margaret and pulled at her skirt. "Pretty color," she said. She sat at the kitchen table and allowed Margaret to open her soft-boiled egg. "Ummm. You make good eggs." She took Margaret's chin and turned her face to her own. "You cook good." She was ready to play or to help or just to giggle with her dear friend Margaret, but Margaret didn't smile back. What was wrong with Margaret?

CHAPTER FIFTY-TWO
1935

MURRAY'S DOG NICKY wasn't allowed in the living room. Murray had trained him well, and Nicky stopped at the edge of the dining-room rug, wriggling and squirming on his belly but unwilling to go any farther no matter how much he was coaxed by visitors. He was a small terrier, a mutt really, and Liebe loved him and played with him and especially liked walking him in the evening with one hand in her father's and the other holding the red leash.

Murray had trained Nicky by the time-honored method of giving him a treat if he did well and promising a treat if he did better. The best treat he could think of was a tiny square of Murray's own favorite treat, Hebrew National Kosher Salami. Nicky had one tiny square, Murray had two tiny squares, and by the time Liebe was old enough to observe this process, she got three tiny squares. On Liebe's tongue, kosher salami was the ambrosia, the manna, the amrite of human sustenance.

Two conspirators of equal culinary appreciation, Liebe and Murray quickly progressed from little pieces to whole slices to—wonder-of-wonders—salami sandwiches with tomato and mustard. The pinnacle of taste thrills was a salami sandwich on *challah*, the braided bread with which the Jews welcomed the Sabbath on Friday nights. Liebe called salami "Nicky meat."

Tess, Murray, and Liebe went fairly often for a weekend in McKeesport and Homestead, about a hundred miles away—a three-hour trip plus the time it took to stop and allow Liebe to throw up on the side of the road. They spent the nights with Katie and BJ, Tess's parents, on Carnegie Avenue and drove to Homestead to see Murray's parents on their way home Sunday afternoon.

After tasting salami, Liebe no longer objected wildly to these trips because, after leaving Homestead, they drove to Pittsburgh and the Jewish section—Squirrel Hill —where they bought enough salami to last until the next visit. Liebe was enchanted by the name of the street and even more by the fact that here were the kosher stores where every succulent thing she loved to eat was bought. She could hardly contain her enthusiasm for the food as she pressed her nose against the slanted glass.

Inside glowed the orange of the barbecued cod and the tangerine of the lox, so oily that it could not be contained in mere wax paper. In delectable profusion were pastramis and corned beefs and pickled tongues and knishes and kishkas and rye breads, black breads, challahs, the *flayshig* separated by impermeable glass from the *milchig* sour creams, farmers cheeses, rich butters.

She tore herself away from this abundance only to run to the front windows, where there was the possibility that she might see the Squirrel Hill squirrels. She did not want to miss the regiments, battalions, armies of squirrels doing amazing antics in her imagination. She was ever convinced that they appeared the moment she turned her head. But the possibility of a squirrel parade was secondary to the fact that Squirrel Hill was the place where Nicky meat was bought. She felt she had to stay very close to her mother to make sure salami was somewhere in the many bags carried out to their car and stowed in the rumble seat.

The year Liebe was three, Tess wanted to be with her family in McKeesport for the Passover *seder*. Tess did not keep a kosher home, but her mother did—and Murray's mother, also. And Tess thought it important to observe the holidays and celebrate the stories that made her family Jewish.

Also to share in the work, because Passover meant that every dish and spoon and pot, *flayshig* and *milchig*, had to be removed from Katie's kitchen and replaced with the Passover plates, spoons, and pots, *flayshig* and *milchig*, which were kept the rest of the year in a little shed in the backyard. As Tess, Katie, and the current *shiksa* carried heavy loads, Liebe was entrusted with the cups. She took one at a time, conscious of the responsibility, placing it carefully on the shelf in the shed and bringing a *Pesach* cup back to the kitchen.

"Look, Grandma! I did it all by myself."

The Seder the next night was a bit much for a just-three little girl. She was sent off to look for the *affikomen*, having no idea what it was but still disappointed to the core when her cousin Jeannie—Regina—

found it. This started the evening with tears, which then elevated into hysterics and became a torrent calmed only by Liebe's being tucked into bed by her Uncle Adolph just after the soup but before the chicken.

So it was that, the next morning, a very hungry little girl wandered the upstairs hall and finally into her grandparents' bedroom. Katie had long been downstairs supervising breakfast for at least ten people, but BJ was sitting in bed, fluffy pillows behind him and a tray across his lap, having coffee and reading the paper.

"Climb in," he motioned and flipped back the quilt so she could join him.

"Wait, Grandpa. I want to get on at the bottom and see all the animals." She dragged the steps to the foot of the bed and climbed up.

She had first seen this quilt when she was brought to the Carnegie Avenue house after having her tonsils out. She had arrived drugged and crying in pain to find a bed and this magical quilt ready for her in her grandparent's living room. She had forgotten the pain and remembered only the flashing colors, the fantastic animals, the magic of this creation of her grandmother and the great-grandmother she had never known but had been named for.

"Oh, Grandpa! I remember all these dogs! And look at the elephants! What are these? Yes! Pineapples! And the Tree of Knowledge! That's very important!" She inched her way up the quilt her grandmother and great-grandmother had made, revisiting her favorite things, unfaded even after all these years.

Finally next to her grandfather, she leaned against her own pile of pillows and allowed the *shiksa* to place a tray across her own knees. She peered interestedly at her grandfather's tray. On it were his coffee mug, matzos, cream and sugar, a cup of butter, and a saltcellar. On hers was a lonely cup, but it caught her interest.

"Grandpa! Am I going to have coffee?"

"Now watch this, Liebchen," BJ said. "This is how to enjoy breakfast in bed." He broke a matzoh in half and buttered and salted it. Then he poured himself a cup of coffee, put in cream and sugar, and broke the matzoh into it.

Liebe watched intently. "But, Grandpa," she said. "There already is something in your cup. What is that?"

"This is my moustache cup, Liebchen. You don't want me to get my moustache full of coffee, do you?" Liebe shook her head, making her curls dance. "I'll get a special cup for you as soon as you grow a moustache." Liebe giggled and rubbed her lips. "Now are *you* ready for your *Pesach* breakfast?" BJ poured an inch of coffee into Liebe's cup, added a great deal of cream and sugar, then broke the buttered and salted matzoh into it.

Liebe wriggled her toes under the quilt. She surveyed the expanse of the bed, snuggled into the warmth of her little nest, and took a taste of her Passover breakfast. "Delicious," she pronounced to BJ's amused blue eyes. "More."

BJ read her various items from the newspaper and listened gravely to her comments. "Let me see that picture, Grandpa." BJ showed her the grainy photograph of Franklin Roosevelt, FDR in the paper. "Um," she said. "Efdy looks like a nice man. But let's get up now."

BJ rang the bell by the bed and soon the *shiksa*—Rosie, Peggy, BJ never could remember—appeared to take the trays. "Get dressed, little one, and we'll take a walk to Jerusalem."

Liebe loved these walks with her grandfather, he so handsome in his gray fedora, his chesterfield coat, a shiny cane in one hand and her little fist in the other. They walked by the cemetery, where she usually clutched him a little harder, down the hill past the *shul*, and into the sugar-and-spice smelling coffee shop where he fed her cupcakes or Danish.

"No cupcakes today, though. Remember it's *pesach*," he said. Her face fell. "But maybe a surprise at Woolworth's." She skipped to her room to change out of her pajamas. She had the best grandpa in the world.

Late that afternoon she was still wearing the dress she had begged and pleaded and cajoled her mother into letting her wear for the walk to Jerusalem. This dress had a perfect circle of a skirt, and Liebe loved to twirl until she was dizzy, the skirt rising and falling around her like the waves in the ocean. Of course, she had never seen an ocean, but it must be almost as pretty as her skirt. Her father took many pictures of her in this dress, posed against the living-room wall at home, the skirt held in a perfect half-moon, the lights aimed so that her shadow loomed behind her.

She was in the sunroom where Katie and Tess were talking. Katie was crocheting one of the endless complicated designs with which she edged her pillowslips, and Tess was smoking a cigarette.

The murmur of their voices was the background for the tea Liebe was serving her dolls in the little tea set her grandfather had bought for her at Woolworth's. Jebby —Jebby, her favorite, but no clothes, poor thing—was asking for sugar. Liebe twirled toward the kitchen, her skirt undulating around her, and collided with the sideboard. The tray holding her grandmother's cordial glasses teetered on the edge and fell to the brick floor with a crash.

Tess stood up with a scream. Katie gasped, her crochet hook in mid-air. Tess looked at her mother. What should she do? It was an accident, but maybe some sort of discipline was called for. She had never spanked Liebe, but maybe her mother thought she should. Katie had often spanked Tess. But maybe her mother would rather she console Liebe and merely sweep up the shards. Or maybe the look on her mother's face meant that she should take a very strong line here. But maybe her mother thought that accidents do happen. Or maybe her mother thought that she should exercise some authority over a willful child. Maybe. Maybe. These thoughts flashed through her head with the speed of light. She had to *do* something.

Liebe's hairbrush was on the table. Tess had read about spanking with a hairbrush. She grabbed it with one hand, Liebe's arm with the other, and before she knew what she was doing Tess had Liebe across her lap, her skirt pulled up, her panties pulled down.

Which side of the brush? Katie was looking at her—in approval or aghast? Tess couldn't tell. Her arm came down and the bristles hit Liebe's bottom. The little girl's screams slowed Tess down. Two more should do it! She watched the little drops of blood rise to the surface of the glowing skin, set Liebe on her feet, and fled to her room. She couldn't believe what she had just done.

Katie folded Liebe in her arms. They were both breathless, Katie with shock, Liebe with pain and astonishment. Her sobs gradually subsided.

"Grandma! I'm sorry! I'm sorry!"

"That's all right, Liebchen. I know you didn't mean to." She paused, at a loss to explain to the little girl what had happened. She decided she would never be able to explain it. "Let's take care of you." Liebe's trembling hand in her arthritic one, they climbed the back stairs to the bathroom, with a stop in the kitchen for a tub of sour

cream. Liebe showed Katie a watery smile. Sour cream made everything all right.

And it wasn't that Katie spooned sour cream into Liebe's mouth.
Katie, for years, had been soothing the scratches and abrasions of her
children and grandchildren with a soft coating of sour cream and the
application of a special leaf she remembered from her childhood in
Bohemia and found as a weed in the backyard at Carnegie Avenue.
The sour cream was cooling, and to the leaf were ascribed special
properties that very quickly stopped the pain of the scraped knee or
bloody elbow.

Perched on the mahogany toilet seat, Katie turned Liebe over on
her lap and gazed in dismay at the polka dots of blood. The pink skin
was quivering, little dimples appearing as Liebe clenched her bottom
in pain. "Just sour cream for now, " Katie said. "There is no way to
put on my special leaf or to bandage you up. But you'll feel better in
a few minutes, I promise."

Back on her feet, Liebe could feel her whole body relax. She
looked pitifully up at her grandmother. "Thank you, Grandma," she
quavered. "I feel better now."

Liebe's hand again in hers, Katie went slowly down the steps, the
front ones this time, where Sir Galahad still guarded the landing and
shed stained glass colors across the hall below. Liebe always had a
question about the austere figure. By this time, she knew he was a
knight—an identification that necessitated a lesson on homophones—
and that he wore very heavy clothes. Today, he merited merely a
glance. Katie had planned a surprise for Liebe, her youngest grandchild, and this seemed the perfect time to reveal it.

"Come with me, little one," she said. "I have something to show
you in the cellar." Liebe shuddered. Was this more of her punishment?
She hated the Carnegie Avenue cellar because it was vast and dark and
scary. Her cousin Jeannie delighted in pointing out abysses and caskets
and huge spider webs that she would never be able to avoid without
Jeannie's help. She hung back, and Katie mistook her reticence for
physical pain.

"I know it hurts," she said. "But when you see what I have for
you, you will forget all about your poor little bottom."

Liebe crept down the steps behind Katie, her hand clutching
Katie's skirt. They went around the gigantic furnace, past the coal

room, through the laundry room with its deep tubs and built-in scrub boards, and finally were in the farthest corner, lit by half-windows high up on the wall. Katie reached up and pulled a string, turning on the naked light bulb that swung back and forth over a card table, covered with a pretty cloth and displaying a serrated knife, a breadboard, a *challah*, and a salami. A salami! Liebe looked at her grandmother in amazement.

"I can be naughty sometimes, too." Katie said to her granddaughter. "No bread during *pesach*, right? But I thought you could not stay away from Nicky meat for such a long time, so I made this little spot just for us down here. It's our secret." Liebe was thrilled. "I think this is the perfect time for a salami sandwich, don't you?" Liebe nodded. "And I think I will sit down for our little feast." She cupped Liebe's face in her hand. "Do you feel well enough to sit down, too?" Liebe's eyes filled with tears. "No. I thought not. But just you wait. God will understand that a combination of sour cream on your little *toushie* and salami in your sweet mouth, although not kosher, or a little bread at *pesach*" ...she emphasized this with a gentle shake of the little chin... "are just the thing for pain and suffering."

CHAPTER FIFTY-THREE
1935

LIEBE LOVED TO GO GROCERY SHOPPING with her mother every Tuesday. It was an all morning affair, starting with Liebe getting dressed up after breakfast. Tess laid Liebe's clean clothes out in her bedroom and stayed with her while she peeled off her pajamas and put on her shopping clothes.

"I want to do it myself," Liebe said, so it took about an hour, with her mother there to help with the buttons and snaps. First were the white socks with a little embroidery around the tops. They had to fit just so. Then, the shiny Mary Janes with the difficult buckles at the sides, always starting off on the wrong feet. And last, the party dress—Liebe was invited to few if any parties, and shopping was the most festive thing imaginable—that Tess had starched and ironed the night before.

Tess did laundry on Mondays and hung the clothes on three lines at the back of the yard, near the swing attached to the big elm. Tess trusted only herself to do this job. Margaret was upstairs doing the dusting and vacuuming. The wash was done in the cellar, in a big Maytag. Liebe was fascinated by the wringer, into which Tess fed the dripping clothes, which came out the other side all flat. Tess's arm was forever out, keeping Liebe away from the relentless rubber rollers.

"Stay back!" she repeated over and over. Liebe couldn't imagine where the danger lay. It looked too much like fun.

Then up the cellar steps, with the doors folded back above them, and across the yard with the heavy basket.

Tess lifted Liebe onto the swing and gave it a big push. Liebe swayed there dreamily, watching her mother hang the clothes on the line, inching the bag of clothespins ahead of her. Mrs. Alexis always left the pins attached to her lines, but Tess told Liebe it was not tidy to leave the pins, her only criticism of their orderly neighbors.

At least once a morning, the B&O freight train rumbled by on the other side of the fence, its whistle howling as it approached the crossing a few blocks away. Liebe jumped from the swing to put her hands over her ears. But in truth, she relished the mournful sound and the trembling she felt under her feet.

Tess sat Liebe on the swing again, gave her another push, and went into the garage, bringing out three long wooden poles with notches at the tops. She hooked the sagging clothesline into a notch and lifted the pole high in the air, planting the other end firmly in the ground. The sheets billowed and crackled like sails as they took the wind. Liebe was enchanted.

Monday nights were ironing nights. Tess did her own ironing, too, because she listened to her favorite radio programs as she ironed.

"But can't I help with the sprinkling?" Liebe asked. "That's not dangerous. I won't get flattened or burned. Please let me help." Tess thought of the fifteen-minute job that would now take an hour, but she nodded her head and pulled a kitchen chair up to the drain board by the sink. She provided herself and Liebe with small pots into which she poured water. Then she showed Liebe how to dip her hand in the water and shower it all over the clean clothes. Tess rolled the sprinkled clothes into tight bundles and tucked them into the clothesbasket.

After dinner, the ironing board went up and the radio went on. By this time, Liebe was in her pajamas, but she sat at the kitchen table with her milk and cookies and tried to make sense of *One Man's Family*, a half-hour radio story about a big family in Sea Cliff, part of San Francisco.

"What are they talking about so much?" She whispered as loudly as she could.

"Quiet! I'll tell you about it in the morning. Go to bed now, Liebe. Up you go." Liebe hated being old enough to put herself to bed. "I'll be up in a minute to kiss you goodnight. Go! Now!"

Liebe dragged herself slowly up the stairs, listening hard for the next program. She had many questions about the next program that had never been answered to her satisfaction. Here it came. She recognized the music. "What's a cattle cave?" she yelled from the fourth step.

"Cavalcade! Cavalcade! It's *The Cavalcade of America*", Tess answered automatically. Cavalcade was as mysterious as cattle cave, but Liebe's father was giving her the eye, so she continued the trek to her room. Tomorrow was shopping day. That cheered her a little.

Tuesday morning Liebe was lying on her mother's bed, carefully so as not to wrinkle her dress, and watching Tess in the triple mirror as she prepared for their journey uptown to shop for groceries. Liebe thought her mother quite beautiful and couldn't wait until she, too, would lean into a mirror and powder her face with a fat, pink powder puff and shape a pretty mouth with a bright lipstick. Tess pulled on a slip, and it went over her head, sleeking and glossing as it reflected light from the windows. Sitting down on the vanity stool, Tess drew on silk stockings, smoothing them up over her legs and, standing, checking the seams in the mirror. Little contraptions on elastic magically appeared, three at each leg, and Tess fastened the stockings to these, bending and turning, graceful as a dancer. Liebe sighed happily. Her mother stepped into high heels, buttoned the cream and lime-green dress up the front, and pirouetted for approval.

At the bottom of the steps, Tess gathered her hat, purse and grocery list. Liebe stood on the seat of the green stroller, trying to wriggle into it without disturbing her dress.

"Why, Liebe," said her mother. "I think you're getting too big for the stroller." Tess lifted her out. "I think you're a big enough girl to shop on your own two feet. Let's go!"

Hand in hand, they walked five blocks up Mahoning Street to town. They passed the Abelmans' house, but no one was on the porch, then the Heckendorns' where there were five red-headed brothers. Liebe could hear them yelling. She gripped Tess's hand more tightly. A man on crutches passed them. Probably wounded in the war, Tess reflected. She felt the familiar tug on her heart when she thought of her brother Sydney. Liebe smiled up at the old man, then noticed he had only one leg.

"What's..." But Tess shook her arm roughly.

"Keep walking. I'll tell you later." Out of earshot, Tess turned Liebe toward her and looked down into her eyes. "That man got hurt because he didn't hold his mother's hand when he crossed the street. You must always hold my hand when we cross the street." Liebe nodded vigorously.

Past Sears, past Harl's Shoes.

"Good morning, Mr. Harl." Tess made sure she greeted her husband's landlord politely, although all she ever got in return was a surly nod.

"That's Daddy's office," Liebe said to him, pointing to the second floor, but he had gone into his store. Tess could not imagine how he could resist her charming daughter, but there it was.

Past the Smart Shop and Rosenthal's, and then across the street to the A&P. Liebe held on to her mother's hand for dear life. She didn't want to lose her legs.

Inside, Mr. Walkup, the butcher, greeted Tess with a smile. "Hello, Mrs. Gross. How's the Doc? What can I get you?" Tess ordered steaks and chops and hamburger and calves' liver, enough for the next week, now that they had a refrigerator. She walked through the store with the grocery clerk, reading him her list as he gathered bags and boxes, some on shelves so high he had to use his mechanical stick with the claw at the end. Corn flakes, Bon Ami, Wonder Bread, Clabber Girl, those two tomatoes—no, three—that head of lettuce, beans, cucumbers, maybe one of those calavos Murray had introduced them to, Heinz vinegar, Crisco, six ears of corn, and much more. Two large paper bags awaited Tess at the front counter.

"That's a lot to carry, Mrs. Gross," the clerk said as Tess tucked the change into her purse.

"We'll manage, won't we, Liebe?" Tess said. Liebe drooped by her side.

"Mommy, I'm tired." Tess had a bag in each arm and Liebe holding on to the strap of her purse.

"We'll walk slow, darling. It's only a few blocks, and you're such a good big girl."

One block. "Mommy, I'm tired."

Two blocks. Liebe sat down on the flower box in front of Abelman's store. "Mommy. I'm tired!"

Tess could feel the perspiration gathering on her forehead. She shifted the bags. There was no way she could carry them and Liebe, too.

"I know what we'll do. We'll cross the street and go back just one block to Sears and buy you a tricycle. You've always wanted a tricycle. Then you can ride home, and I'll be able to carry the groceries." Liebe looked doubtful.

Tess managed to fit Liebe's hand between hers and the paper bag.

"Let's go!" She dragged the terrified little girl across the street and into the cool interior of Sears. Liebe pinched her legs surreptitiously. They were still there.

"What a darling child," the sales girl said, stooping down to look into Liebe's face. She looked up again at Tess. "Is she a-d-o-p-t-e-d?" Tess was too tired to explain about the genes.

"We need a tricycle," she said.

Out on the street, the noon sun was beating down. Tess put the grocery bags on the sidewalk and lifted Liebe onto the tricycle seat.

"This is going to be such fun," she said grimly. "Put your hands here, and your feet there, and just push the pedals around. You can do it." Liebe couldn't. Finally the tricycle went backwards a few inches. Liebe could not make it go forward. Tears rose in Liebe's eyes. A scream rose in Tess's throat.

Ten minutes later, they emerged from Sears again, with a red Radio Flyer. Liebe was hunched in the front of the little wagon, her legs crossed, the groceries were behind her, the tricycle on top of the groceries. Tess heard eggs crack when she piled the tricycle on the bags.

They arrived home to the sound of the telephone ringing. Tess dragged the wagon inside.

"Hello!" she answered angrily. "Howard? What do you want? I'm busy." She removed her hat and pushed the damp hair off her forehead. "Oh... oh... How? Yes. Yes..." She put the earpiece on the hook and sat down. She started to cry.

"Mommy! What's wrong?" Liebe scrambled out of the wagon and crawled into Tess's lap. "What's wrong."

"It's Grandpa! Grandpa died!"

Liebe blew a little bubble of relief. "That's all right then. Don't cry. He'll be better soon."

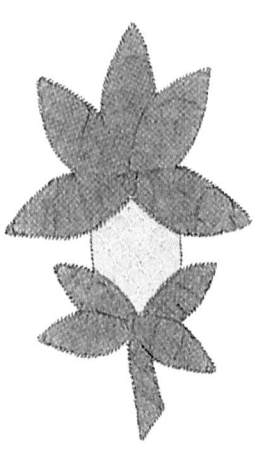

CHAPTER FIFTY-FOUR
1936

LIEBE WAS STARING OUT AT THE RAIN, her elbows on the windowsill, her fingers drawing lazy pictures in the steam from her breath. She was bored, bored, bored. The rain had started three days ago, melting the early March snow, not only around her house but also on the hills surrounding Punxsutawney, turning the Mahoning Creek into a tumbling river. The day she and her mother had gone shopping—was it only yesterday?—they had gone in the car, it was raining *that* hard. Murray had taken out the rumble-seat so that more groceries could fit in, but even then Liebe had a bag on her lap and two under her feet. She had never seen so many groceries.

On the way home, they stopped on the Mahoning Street Bridge to look at the water. It was so close under the bridge that some splashes got on Liebe's yellow galoshes and Tess's stylish boots. Tess took Liebe's hand and hurried her back to the car. Oddly, they took the groceries, not into the kitchen, but upstairs, piling the cans and bottles and boxes against the wall in Margaret's back bedroom. For some reason, Margaret had been sent home.

"When it's raining like this, it's best for Margaret to be home," Tess said vaguely, and Liebe was glad to be rid of Margaret for whatever reason.

She sighed herself into the kitchen, and Tess allowed her to put on her heavy coat and stand with Nicky on the back porch. The first day of the rain, Liebe and the little dog stamped through the backyard puddles, but now there was just one puddle covering the whole yard.

Watching the rain was amusing for a while, but now the while was over and Liebe went disconsolately back in the house. "What can I do?" she whined.

"Play with your dolls, draw pictures, torment the dog! I don't know. I'm busy." Tess had been cross lately, very tired and peevish. She was also getting fat and wearing funny clothes. Liebe tried to stay out of her way, but staying in the house for four days was making Liebe a bit quarrelsome, also.

"I don't like my dolls," she said. And it was true. She had several dolls, all nameless, but she had seldom lifted them down from the shelves. The only doll she truly liked was a non-descript rubber baby with painted-on hair and a belly button. She had owned this doll for some time, nameless, until the day she and her doll were sitting in Murray's lap. Murray was reading a history of the Civil War, and Liebe was playing with the buttons on his vest. He turned a page, and there was a picture of a handsome soldier wearing a large-brimmed hat with a flowing feather. Sword, boots, semaphore moustache, piercing eyes.

"Why, that looks like the man on Grandma's quilt," Liebe said. "What's he doing in your book?"

Murray cocked his eyebrow at her. "It's not the same man, but I'm amazed you remembered," he said. "They do look alike, don't they? But that man was a hussar, and this man is a Civil War general. His name is J.E.B. Stuart." He read to her some of the chapter. She listened attentively to the very end.

"Jeb," she said. "That's a nice name. That's what I'll call my doll." She held the hapless baby up by the neck. "Jebby. Jebby. That just fits."

The next day it rained, and the next, and the next.

"The water is over the bridge, Tess," Murray said when he came home from work. "We better start moving upstairs."

"I should do a wash," said Tess. "It may be the last chance." Her voice trembled.

She and Liebe went down to the basement. Water was leaking under the windows. The cement walls were darker, damp and covered with streamlets. While the Maytag was doing its work, they piled the boxes of soap and bleach and bluing into a carton.

Then, with the basket of wet clothes under one arm, Tess held Liebe's hand and led her up to the attic. The attic door was in the master bedroom, and Liebe hated to look at it. Who knew what was up there and might come down in the night? And here she was, going up the dark stairs once again at the end of her mother's arm.

But at the top of the stairs, she drew a sigh of relief. It was just the same as before—clean, empty, and bright as it could be on a dark rainy day. The attic stretched across the whole double house, the Alexis half and the Gross half. On the other side of the wall where the Grosses steps came up, the Alexises steps went down. Liebe felt strange walking on top of the Alexises. She tiptoed.

Tess strung the clothesline through the grommets on the wall, pulled it taut and tied the end to a big hook. Liebe handed her the wooden clothespins, Tess snapped the clothes smartly and hung them up.

That night the Alexises—it was Mr. and Mrs. Alexis, even after three years of being neighbors—came to visit. Liebe couldn't remember ever seeing them before, and she was very interested in what was going on. But, after milk and cookies, she was marched up to bed. She fell asleep to the sound of soft talk downstairs and hard rain on her window.

The next day was anything but boring. Mr. Alexis and Murray, for reasons unclear to Liebe, were carrying furniture from downstairs to upstairs. Mrs. Alexis was helping Tess pack everything from the kitchen into cardboard cartons, the two of them with their heads together and no place for a little girl. The dining room chairs went into Margaret's room, the living room sofa and armchairs were put along the length of the upstairs hall. Liebe, ignored, tried a few forbidden jumps on the sofa. Nobody paid any attention. Soon she was leaping from her parents' room to the bathroom without touching the floor.

Downstairs, both men looked at the dining room table and sideboard and shook their heads. Too heavy. Tess and Mrs. Alexis emptied the sideboard into boxes. At times, they all went to the windows and looked out. The water was lapping at the porch stairs.

"What's that noise?"

Mr. Alexis mopped his forehead with a red bandana. "That's the water coming into the cellar through the windows, I guess."

"My Maytag," moaned Tess. Mrs. Alexis looked sad.

"Here's what you can do, little one," Tess said, finally realizing that Liebe was having far too much fun in the upheaval. "On the back porch is firewood." Liebe nodded, bouncing her curls. "I want you to get a piece at a time and carry it up to my room and make a neat pile by the fireplace."

Liebe, aware of the formidable responsibility, transferred each stick upstairs, dodging around the adults and carrying her burdens much more precisely than she had ever carried a doll. Her pile was very neat, and she finished at the same time that every moveable piece of furniture had been stowed upstairs.

"Now we're going to help Mr. and Mrs. Alexis," said Tess.

The water had already started seeping up between the boards on the porch. Murray lifted Liebe over the banister, and the four adults swung themselves around it and onto the Alexiseses's porch.

Mrs. Alexis made a little nest for Liebe in the corner of the living room and gave her two monkey dolls that she had made out of Mr. Alexis's long white socks with red stripes around the top. Liebe was enchanted. Murray and Mr. Alexis started moving furniture upstairs, Tess and Mrs. Alexis packed boxes. When they looked out the windows, water had covered the porch.

"We better hurry," said Mr. Alexis.

The Grosses had never been inside the Alexises half of their double house. Although it was a mirror image, it looked very different. The wallpaper depicted sheaves of wheat on an ecru background. Instead of sofas and armchairs, Mrs. Alexis favored rocking chairs. Instead of a Chinese red rug, on her floor Mrs. Alexis had hooked rugs, rugs she made herself out of material from her husband's worn railroad uniforms.

Liebe ran her fingers over a rug. She had seen Mrs. Alexis on the back porch, a large wooden hooked needle in her hand, producing the long braid that she then sewed into various sized rugs. Liebe wished her mother could do that.

As the last box was stored upstairs, Liebe screamed. Water was coming in under the front door.

"Upstairs, kiddo," said Murray.

"Be sure you have matches and candles," said Mr. Alexis. "We can share with each other through the attic. I'm sure we've forgotten lots of things we should have, but maybe not the same things." The men shook hands. Tess and Mrs. Alexis hugged. Liebe waited impatiently on the bottom attic step. She wanted to get back to her parents' bedroom and start playing house.

Checking the water would become an occupation during the next four days. Enduring Liebe's crawling under end tables and over footstools in the upstairs hall, they made their way through the hall. Murray turned on the light. The water was over the first stair, shining darkly, menacing.

"Oh, God," sighed Tess.

"Let's have dinner. You're both hungry and so am I." Murray swung Liebe under his arm, went back into the bedroom, and closed the door.

Murray thrived on gadgets. He spent time in hardware stores, he visited the kitchen section of Kaufmann's when they were in Pittsburgh, he was thrilled that his sister Rhoda was dating Ralph Grinberg, third generation of the Grinberg Housewares Emporium in Homestead—there he got a discount. Now he was perfectly prepared to make a grand dinner for three in his bedroom.

"We've first got to eat the things that will spoil the quickest ," said Tess, fluttering her hands and wandering aimlessly around the crowded room. "Maybe we should... "

Murray took her elbow and guided her to the bed. "You stretch out and direct. I'll do the cooking. The two of you... " he patted her stomach "...have done enough for today."

He quickly built a fire in the fireplace and tucked into it three potatoes that he found in the waste paper basket, wrapped up in their special shells (Kaufmann's, 98 cents). He located the picnic cooler in which he had stored the steaks and other meat, kept cool by the ice cube trays especially made for it (Grinberg's Housewares $2.50). He set up the grill (Punxsutawney Hardware, $3.50) and loaded it with some of the burning logs from the fire. On top of this he put a T-shaped contraption that held the steaks and enabled him to turn them over when the time came (Grinberg's $1.50). While the steaks sizzled, he found the Primus Stove (Kaufmann's $6.95) under the bed and pumped it until it gave a satisfactory hiss. On this he put the saucepan full of green beans from the can he opened. He whistled while he worked and did a short, graceful two-step for Liebe. She smiled contentedly. What could be better than a picnic on a rug?

The bed lamps flickered and went out. "Oh, God," said Tess. The firelight bathed the room in gold. In their little cave, they ate a good meal.

Two days passed. The water was up to the fifth step. But on the third day, the sun rose into a cloudless sky, and the water never reached the sixth step. The bedroom was strewn with coloring books and crayons, and the walls hung with lines of girls and boys cut all together from folded newspapers. As the dusk fell around them, Tess, Murray, and Liebe finished a dinner of canned spinach, canned peas, canned asparagus and Oreos. Tess lit a candle. Suddenly Liebe shrieked and plastered herself to her father's chest. Nicky burrowed a hole in a pillow, and even Murray was shaken. There was a face at the window.

With Liebe clinging to him like a limpet, Murray went to the window and opened it. A fireman! Two firemen! Three firemen! Standing on the sloping porch roof! And behind them was a rowboat.

"Hi, Doc. Remember me? Al Gresock? I'm a patient of yours." He opened his mouth and pointed to an empty space at the back.

"Of course. Al." Murray, emitting a sigh of relief, thrust his hand out the window, and it was grasped by a heavy glove.

"Mrs. Gibson..." Al jerked his head toward a woman sitting in the boat. "Mrs. Gibson told us your wife is pregnant." He blushed under the big red hat. "The hospital is high and dry on top of Jenks Hill. We'd be glad to take her up there. She'll be fine. They've got electricity and hot water and a kitchen. What do you say?"

A shower! Tess started to gather up clothes. "But—but—can you take Murray and Liebe, too?"

Al Gresock shook his head. "It won't be more than two days before the water goes down," he said. "I can come back with more food, but I can only take people in real need. Like your wife, here. What do you say?"

"Go, Tess," said Murray. "We'll see you in two days. And we've got a good routine here. You know we'll be all right. You should go." Liebe rocked back and forth on her heels. The only thing better than having the full attention of her mother and father was having her father all to herself.

"Yes, you should go, Mommy. We'll see you in two days."

Tess crawled slowly through the window and was immediately swept up into Al Gresock's arms so she wouldn't slide down the steep roof. He deposited her carefully in the boat, held steady by the other firemen, then clomped back to the window.

"Well, Doc," he said. "I guess I got to carry your baby before you did. Heh, heh, heh." He threw a kiss to Liebe, climbed into the boat, and rowed away.

Breakfast the next morning was not the hated Quaker Oats but hot dogs impaled on sticks and held over the open fire. Tucked into warm buns, they were smothered in mustard and ketchup and relish. Liebe ate on her father's lap, sticky and satisfied. It was the best breakfast she had ever had.

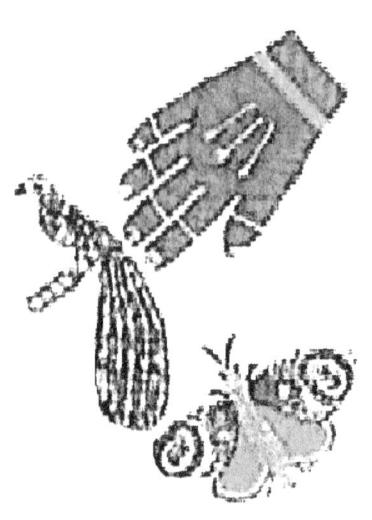

CHAPTER FIFTY-FIVE
1936

SPRING ARRIVED, swelling pale greens in the trees, trailing pink across the sky. The waters receded. Five-thirty-two West Mahoning Street slowly resumed its original form, living room and kitchen downstairs, separate bedrooms upstairs. Liebe was a naturally neat child—well, not naturally neat. But she had been told so often how neat and tidy she was that she worked really hard to uphold that reputation. Her favorite job was helping her mother put the kitchen to rights. And, after the flood, this particular talent of hers was in great demand.

The main reason Liebe liked kitchen chores best was that in the kitchen was a secret staircase. Next to the drying board of the sink was a door, and inside that door were steps that led nowhere. They stopped at the ceiling, not being needed any longer for access to the second floor. Inside it was forever twilight, and on these steps Tess kept dishes and glassware. And on these steps, Liebe was learning her numbers.

Tess handed her a dish, Liebe dried it with a linen towel, Tess said, "Step three." And Liebe would count her way up the steps. She could get to the fifth step without bumping her head and to the eighth and last step by making herself smaller and smaller. By this time, and Liebe was just four, she was working on adding and getting an idea of subtraction.

Tess said, "This goes on one step plus two steps," and Liebe found the magic of three steps. "Now," Tess said, "Come *minus* two steps," and Liebe found herself miraculously back on step one. The kitchen was soon in order.

Margaret had returned, and with her came another job that Liebe found enchanting, cleaning the wallpaper. Wallpaper cleaner came in big cans. Inside was a heavy chewing-gum-like pink material. A treat for Liebe on shopping days was a large pink wax thumb that Tess bought in the candy store on their way to town. This thumb fit over

Liebe's own little thumb. It had a smooth texture, a candy aroma, and, when its potential could no longer be resisted, made a delicious wad in the mouth. The flavor was quickly sucked out and a gray disappointing mass was discarded.

When Tess opened the cans of wallpaper cleaner, Liebe could not believe her eyes. Enough thumbs to last a year! Tess barely caught the little hand before Liebe had the poisonous stuff in her mouth.

"No! Liebe! Looks like—ain't is!" Tess heard herself repeat her sister Helen's admonition that had so mystified her own early years. "This is *not* that thumby stuff. This is for cleaning wallpaper. I'll show you how, and you can help Margaret."

Tess looked sadly at her once-beautiful wallpaper, stained to a height past her shoulder. She gathered a fistful of the pink material, rolled it into a ball in her hand, and made a swath across the paper. It left a clean path. When the outside of the ball was covered with dirt, Tess kneaded it so that the dirty stuff was inside and pink again on the outer surface.

"And when the whole thing is dirty, we throw it away and start a new ball."

Liebe worked near the baseboard, Tess slightly higher, and Margaret on a ladder. With Liebe's help, the two-day job became a three-day job, but Tess had nothing but time as she waited for the new baby.

When June came, Liebe was officially informed that a new baby was coming—just like Jebby, but able to cry and eat and, eventually, walk and talk and play—and they were on their way to Grandma's house. Tess had decided she wanted to have this baby in McKeesport to be near her mother. They were traveling in their new Chevrolet— no more rumble seat—with a back seat where Liebe could sit by herself and throw up, if she were so inclined, into a paper bag.

Which she did, but it did not dampen her excitement to be visiting Carnegie Avenue and seeing her three cousins. She hadn't been aware that she had these cousins, but Tess explained that she had seen them every time she had been in McKeesport.

"Remember? One is Louise, she's twelve and has yellow hair cut short?" Tess reminded her. Louise's hair was cut like Buster Brown's, a little boy with a bowl haircut who, with his dog Tige, was the emblem for Buster Brown children's shoes. "And Ruthie? She's got dark curly hair? And Jeannie, who is just a little older than you and will play with you." Liebe vaguely remembered such girls, but, no matter who they were, she was looking forward to someone to play with.

When Liebe arrived at her Grandma's house, she always went first to her grandmother's bedroom to renew acquaintance with the magic quilt. She crawled on its surface, tracing the hands and peacocks and Tree of Life and the dark hussar.

"Where's Grandpa?" she asked but was immediately shushed.

The upstairs bedrooms were full. Howard and Adolph were home to see Tess, and Murray was staying for the weekend, so Katie had made a special room in the basement for Liebe and Jeannie, who was invited to stay to keep Liebe company. Because it was summer, the coal room was empty, and Katie had the *shiksa*—Liebe knew her name, Hannah—scrub it down. In it, she put a mattress, fluffy pillows, a table, and a lamp with a pink silk shade. Liebe had fond memories of the cellar, where Katie had fed her clandestine salami sandwiches during Passover. It was different being there with Jeannie.

"Don't step there, Liebe!" cried Jeannie as they came to a column casting a deep shadow on the cement floor. "That's a horrible hole that goes down to the bowels of the Earth! Jump over it! Quick!" Liebe trembled and jumped as far as she could. She slipped her sweaty hand into Jeannie's.

Tess and Helen came to tuck them in, then left with a strict admonition to turn out the light in five minutes. Neither Liebe nor Jeannie had any idea how long five minutes was, but it didn't matter. They were alone in a basement corner, and all the adults were upstairs.

"Look what I've got," said Jeannie and drew from under the pillows a flashlight. "Turn out the light, and I'll show you something."

Liebe crept out of bed to switch off the little lamp. The basement room was still lit by the lurid flames from the steel mills, almost two miles away. Liebe didn't like the flickering and flashing. She hurried under the covers.

"You hold the flashlight—like this—now watch," said Jeannie, and with her hands she made shadow rabbits and birds and dogs dance on the spotlighted plaster wall. Liebe couldn't manage any animals, but she happily held the flashlight for Jeannie. Jeannie was a star, Liebe a grateful audience. When Jeannie had exhausted her repertoire many times over, the little girls cuddled in bed.

"Guess what song this is." Jeannie tapped out a song on Liebe's leg. Liebe thought and thought. All of Jeannie's games were new to her, and she dreaded not being clever enough to catch on. This was the advantage of having older sisters. Liebe wished her mother would bring her an older sister instead of a baby. "*It's Mary Had a Little Lamb.*"

Liebe finally realized what was expected of her and tapped out *Frere Jacque* on her cousin's back. Then Jeanne fooled her two times with songs Liebe had never heard of. As Liebe was searching her mind and finally hit on *The Good Ship Lollipop*, she fell asleep.

The next day, Liebe followed Jeannie the same way Nicky followed her, a faithful dog to Jeannie's masterful ways. Across the street from Grandma's house was a Baptist Church, surrounded by low cement posts connected by heavy, rusty iron chains. These were perfect for two little girls to swing on. And the sloping lawn, green and bedewed, was an invitation for a dizzying roll.

When they got home, Katie inspected them. "Jeannie, I don't know how you can get so dirty and Liebe stay so clean. Go call your mother and ask her to bring you a clean dress for dinner." Jeannie slouched off with a scathing look at Liebe, her lower lip thrust out.

Dinner was boisterous. Murray, Adolph, and Howard were punsters, Helen a great teller of jokes. Liebe sat on her grandmother's lap, her Uncle Howard at the other end of the table. Where *was* Grandpa? But she had been shushed, so she kept her question to herself.

The next morning, Murray left for Punxsutawney. "I have to get back to Nicky, you know. Be a good girl, and I'll see you soon." Hugs and kisses and a little pout, but Liebe still had Jeannie.

Three days later, Liebe woke to find her mother and grandmother and Jeannie gone and her own little suitcase by the front door.

"Jeannie had to go to school today," her Uncle Adolph said. "And your mother's gone to the hospital to get your new baby, and Uncle Howard's gone to help her. Grandma's there, too, to keep her company. And you..." Uncle Adolph picked her up and tossed her, screaming with delight, into the air. "You're going to visit your other grandmother." Liebe had to think a minute.

She seldom remembered she had two grandmothers.

In Homestead, Liebe and Adolph climbed the cracked and weedy cement stairs that had so dismayed Tess seven years earlier. Liebe vaguely recalled the long line of attached houses, one of which contained her father's family. Her hand clutching her uncle's, she looked up at the gray houses brooding against the sky. She hoped it would be a short visit.

Inside she found Grandpa Gross—now she remembered him!—sitting in a corner of the sofa, dressed in a dark suit and with a fedora on his head, his sad brown eyes brightening at the sight of her. She leaned against his knee and listened to Adolph talk to Grandma Gross. That's who she was! Grandma Gross, her father's mother!

"Well, little one..." Uncle Adolph grabbed Liebe around the waist and turned her completely over in the air. He said into her laughing face, "...I'm leaving you now."

Leaving! No! "I don't want to stay here," she cried. "Take me home! I want my mother!"

Adolph's hand was on the doorknob. "I'll call you every day. You be good." And he was gone.

Liebe turned around, unable to catch her breathe. She was surrounded by four very tall people, her uncles Irwin, Milton, and Maynard, and her Aunt Rhoda. She felt like a small flower in a forest of great trees. Rhoda knelt down next to her, her face close, too close. Liebe sobbed and sobbed. Here's a new stuffed animal for you. No! Grandma bought you a new dress. No! A piece of candy? Tempting. But NO!

Tired and damp, Liebe crawled up on the sofa next to her grandfather, tucked her curly head under his arm, and cried and cried.

She was soon worn out and permitted herself to be led to the dinner table. The smells were irresistible. Grandma Gross was a good and generous cook, her mashed potatoes laced with melted chicken fat and onions, the thin kosher steaks salty and juicy. And wonder of wonders, cream soda on the table. Pop, soda, soft drinks, none of these substances had ever touched Liebe's lips in the house of her dentist father. Now here was her glass filled with the sugary liquid and a big bottle in the middle of the table to provide more any time she wanted. She allowed her face to be washed, her hair smoothed, her meat cut, her glass filled and filled. By the time dessert arrived, she was drooping over her plate. Taken upstairs by Aunt Rhoda, she was undressed and tucked in, to sleep a deep sleep punctuated by small sobs.

She awoke with a shriek in the strange room, but Aunt Rhoda was right there, to dress her in her favorite overalls, and help her brush her teeth and tame her hair. All morning her uncles amused her, playing games, taking walks, reading aloud. Then in the afternoon—"I'm too old to take a nap! I'm FOUR now!"—Grandma Gross looked at her children in a panic.

"Two weeks!" Grandma Gross said. "Tess will be in the hospital for two weeks! How will we keep her happy that long?"

Uncle Maynard stood up. "Maybe she'd like to see the attic." He held out his hand.

Liebe shivered. Another attic! She didn't want to go, but she put her hand in his. Her father had told her to be a good girl, and she didn't want to disappoint him. She and her uncles, Milton, Irwin, and Maynard trooped up to the third floor.

The attic was dim, lit by two windows and a bare bulb hanging from the ceiling. Liebe fastened herself to Maynard's leg.

"What's that?" she quavered.

"A dressmaker's dummy," said Irwin, drawing the figure into the light. "Your grandmother used to make all her own clothes, and she fitted them on this contraption. But she was a lot thinner then." Laughter all around. "But look at this!" He flung open a large wooden trunk and pulled out treasures, piling them on the floor. A feather boa he hung around Liebe's neck. A diamond tiara he put on her head. A scepter went into her eager fingers. And a velvet cape settled on her shoulders.

"Oh! My!" Liebe could not believe the riches spread out on the dusty floor. Soon, Milton had a glued-on mustache and metal helmet, Irwin a sword and shield, and Maynard a tall red hat with bells. Liebe was enchanted. She could be happy here forever.

"And look at this!" In the corner, taller than Liebe, were an African mask and a spear. And in a second trunk, a clown costume with an accompanying big red nose. This was immediately affixed to Liebe's little one. She gazed at herself in a tall spotted mirror.

"Oh, my," she breathed again. "Where does it all come from?"

"Didn't your daddy tell you? We're all—him, too,—hopeless actors. We all wanted to be actors before we became dentists and engineers and hairdressers, but we've lost our hopes. Why, your daddy used to play hooky from school all the time to go to the Davis Theater. He learned more from the vaudeville acts there than he ever did from the teachers." This was a new side of Daddy. Maybe that's where he learned to take quarters out of her ears and make spoons leap into water glasses.

"These are all the costumes we've worn in plays, and some of the stuff people just gave us. Anyway, it's great, isn't it? You can put on as many plays as you like. We'll help." Deep-voiced agreement.

The two weeks sped by. There was dress-up every day, games and walks, teasing and tickling. Liebe dimly realized that she was the first grandchild here and was happy to be adorable and perfect. Her uncles, grandparents, and aunt hung on every word she said. She displayed her mathematical knowledge, as much as she had acquired on the eight secret steps.

"And I know my letters, too," she announced to her audience. "Listen. A-D-O-P-T-E-D," she sang. Astonished silence. They looked at the little creature with her pink cheeks, rosy lips, golden ringlets, and blue eyes, and exchanged ironic smiles.

"Yes," they agreed. "You are a fairy princess, come to grace our table." The tiara was brought down from the attic to make her last dinner with them a royal occasion.

CHAPTER FIFTY-SIX
1936

THE NEXT MORNING LIEBE WRIGGLED on the front seat of Uncle Milton's car. "Mommy will be there, won't she?" Liebe asked, every few minutes.

"Yes, and your new baby, too. His name is Benjamin Joseph, after your grandfather. Will you remember?"

Liebe knew she wasn't supposed to talk about her grandfather. "Drive faster," she ordered.

Soon they were driving up the Shaw Avenue hill and turning into Carnegie Avenue. And there they all were. Her daddy was there with his camera set up on the sidewalk. He met her at Milton's car and squeezed her hard. As he took her hand to cross the street, she noticed the bent fender and hanging headlight of their new Chevrolet.

"What happened!" she gasped and gripped his hand more tightly.

Murray laughed as he exchanged a glance with Milton over her head. Milton looked concerned. "I was in such a hurry to get here to see you and the new baby I ran into a deer on the road." Liebe's forehead wrinkled.

"What happened to the deer?"

"Oh, he just got up and shook himself off. He also gave me a dirty look. He probably had children of his own he wanted to see again, too." He shook his head at Milton and turned down his mouth.

Liebe suddenly remembered her mother! Her mother standing alone on the porch with a baby in her arms. She shook off her father's hand and dashed across the street, ignoring his shouts and all thoughts of legless men.

"Mommy! Mommy!" She was home at last. Home was where her mother was, and here she was. Liebe tugged on the baby's blanket. "Mommy!"

"Hush! Get away!" Tess shook off the little hands. "I'm getting my picture taken with my little boy." She gestured to Murray to get on with it.

Liebe backed away, stunned. She crossed the porch and opened the screen door, the oohs! and aahs! of the gathered Reiters swelling behind her.

Inside, the house was dim and hushed, dark and cool in the summer afternoon. She grasped the banister and started up the stairs, trudging past the white horse and rider flashing color onto the landing. She reached her grandfather's bedroom and stumbled to the steps leading to the high bed. She was about to throw herself onto the beloved quilt when she realized it wasn't there! The bed was all white, smooth and pallid under a sheet. Where was the quilt? She rubbed her knuckles in her eyes. More tears spilled out and down her hot cheeks. She sat on the bottom step and gave way to her anguish.

Katie found her there. "Liebchen! What is the matter?" She painfully pulled the stricken child on to her lap. "Hush, now. What are you going on about?" She lifted the damp curls from Liebe's forehead.

"Grandma! Grandma! Where is the quilt? Where did it go?" The words came out in fits and starts.

"Oh. Is that all? I took it apart to make a cover for your new brother's crib. Here. Come in the next room." Katie stood up with a groan and allowed herself to be dragged by the hand down the hall and through the next door. "There! You see. It's on little Benjy's bed."

There, behind the crib bars, Liebe saw a fragment of the quilt, the Tree of Life, the jeweled hands, a little bead-eyed dog or two, an ostrich, surrounded by the complicated edging, but nothing else. A *sample* of the quilt, an *intimation* of the quilt, but not the quilt.

"And here! Here's the rest of it." Katie went to the closet and pulled out a soft bundle wrapped in a creamy sheet. "Here's the rest." She opened the bundle, spilling out the long edging of twined ivies and blossoms and the remnants of the mutilated quilt.

Liebe was stricken beyond tears. She had loved the game of Boo! when faces had disappeared behind hands and appeared again. And Which Hand, where candy had disappeared behind backs and then appeared again. And Hide and Seek, when people had hidden themselves and then appeared again. But her Grandfather never came back!

And the Magic Quilt! She knew she would never see it again. She slid her back down the wall until she was sitting on the floor. She gazed at her shoes. She didn't hear anything her grandmother said.

THE END

COLOPHON

This book uses *Sabon* for body type, created by Jan Tschichold who was born in Leipzig, Germany in 1902 and who died in Switzerland in 1974. He created *Sabon* in the early 1960s, naming it after a Lyonnaise punchcutter who originally brought the *Garamond* typeface to Frankfurt.

Jan Tschichold was the world's foremost typographer and book designer of his time, advocating a "new typography" in Germany before the Second World War. He was known to have created as many as 20 modern typefaces which have since been lost when Hitler came to power. Forced to flee to Switzerland, Mr. Tschichold further developed the sans-serif and modern typestyles, and wrote on "asymmetric typography," which focused on having the type fit the function of a book. As Penguin's paperback designer, Jan Tschichold developed the clean, fresh and modern style much revered by booklovers everywhere.

Founded by printer/poet Kate Hitt in Santa Cruz in 1993 to address social, economic, environmental, civil rights and women's issues, Many Names Press continues to produce and publish award-winning trade and fine press literary books.